THEREIN LIES THE PROBLEM

Steve Dupont

Skull & Bones Publishing

Birmingham • Glasgow • Los Angeles

Skull & Bones Publishing
A Division of *TOA MediaCorp LLC*
SkullandBonesPublishing.com

Copyright © 2007 by Steve Dupont
Cover illustrations by Steve Dupont
Published by arrangement with the author
ISBN: 978-0-6151-3947-0

First Printing: January 2007
The "Skull/Shield/212" logo is a trademark of *Skull & Bones Publishing*.
Printed in the United States of America.

DEDICATED TO

People who can read.

THEREIN LIES THE PROBLEM

Chapter 1

If there is a God, Lester imagines Him wanting to drop from the heavens and slide down the edge of The Pyramid, robes flapping, His Holy Mouth agape with sheer exhilaration. WHEEEEE! All the way to the ground where, needless to say, He'd stick the landing.

"My depth perception is all bollocksed up," Tim says, looking up at this geometric monstrosity. He is only 17, and thus any number of things could be bollocksed up at any given time.

Lester cracks his neck from side to side and it makes a sickening noise like a rhino walking across a carpet of live beetles. He signals the crane operator with a wave of his hand. "You'll hurt your neck that way, son."

Lester and Tim both speak in English accents, as in, from England.

At 5,330 feet, this crane is one of a dozen such feats-of-engineering that share the title of World's Largest. The steel cage clatters to the ground behind them and Lester throws the heavy steel bolt on the door.

"All set, my boy?" Lester grins idiotically, raising his eyebrows like a toothpaste spokesman.

"All set," Tim says with resolute excitement, as if preparing himself for a skydive.

After securing the door, Lester picks up the phone. It is coated in yellow rubber for a safety reason he can't figure out but nonetheless appreciates. "The monkeys are in the cage."

They lift off slowly, then continue to accelerate. 9.8 meters per second, per second, to be exact. Just like an object falling in the earth's atmosphere, except in the opposite direction. Aside from its speed, the distinct advantage of this elevator system is the 360-degree view it affords – although it takes some getting used to, even by those not otherwise susceptible to acrophobia.

Looking straight down, Tim feels as though the earth is falling away into space. Now he looks straight ahead at The Pyramid. Again the illusion of movement, but this time his internal gyroscope says the cage is swinging, as opposed to The Pyramid sloping away. Wrong again of course, and the irony is lost on him (that he would think the earth moveable and The Pyramid immovable). "It's fucking brilliant!" he exclaims.

"Watch your mouth! You're welcome to curse and grunt like a heathen on your own time," Lester says. He soaks in the view for a moment before breaking down. "But it is fucking brilliant, isn't it!"

"I told you."

"Yes, indeed, it's coming along very nicely … That whole skeleton there is plastic with a core of ceramic, son. Space-age polymers as they say. Twice as strong as steel and ten times lighter."

"I know."

"How do you know?"

"Because you told me. Like a hundred bloody times."

"Well, make it a hundred and one, then!" Lester says.

"So we're going all the way to the top?" Tim says – this being his first ride.

"Better yet, all the way to the Apex!"

"Can we go down to The Casino after that?"

"What do you think?"

"Yes?"

"No!"

"Why not? You said yourself it's open for business."

"Not your business! You're never to set foot in there, understand me?"

"Why?"

"For the same reason you don't set foot inside your mother's womb after you're born."

"Mum's dead."

"Not *your* mother. *One's* mother."

"That doesn't make any bloody sense."

"Because I said so then!"

* * *

A few meters below the level of the apex point itself, a temporary catwalk extends around all four sides of The Pyramid. A tall, chain-link fence ensures safety, but Lester has an unfounded premonition of danger as the cage settles into its berth. He grabs the bars on the door and braces himself, as if the bolt might snap like a pretzel at any moment.

"Relax, dad. See, we're touching down."

"Yes, of course we are," Lester recovers. He unbolts the door and steps out of the cage, followed by Tim. The inside of the observation deck also has a protective steel fence to inhibit one from falling into the center of The Pyramid. Lester and Tim lean against this fence and peer down into the yawning expanse of beams. Through gaps in the latticework they can see miniscule specks of green artificial turf on the Arena floor, nearly three quarters of a mile away.

Tim looks like a man having his first orgasm. "Holy ..."

"Breathtaking, isn't it?" Lester turns around to survey the vast conurbation of humanity that is PyraVegas.

Tim follows suit. "Who lives out there?" he asks.

"We live out there. But hopefully not much longer."

"Who else?"

"People," Lester says. "Just like us, but nothing like us."

"Yeah, but what do they *do*?"

"What do you think they do? They work like dogs at something or other. Very diligent, you have to give them that. First rate people, nothing like dogs a'tall actually."

"I heard Seth Jipt has some thugs beat you up if you don't get to work on time."

"And where the bloody hell did you sponge that up from?"

"Nowhere."

"Out with it! I want the names!" Lester says with mock urgency.

"Fine. I overheard Chutney talking to Doctor Schnitzelweiner."

"I'm sure they were speculating. Wildly, I might add."

"Whatever."

"Not that I would rule out the possibility of that big oaf doing it, mind you. The lesson I'm trying to impart here concerns the matter of truth, not ethical behavior."

"Okay."

"Okay, you get it?"

"Okay, I get it," Tim says, snickering to himself behind his father's back, but not unnoticed.

"So, boy, what do you say we kick the football round a bit?"

* * *

Tim kicks off to Lester, who waits at his own goal line. They are both decked out in full pads, Tim in white, Lester in blood-red, and Tim runs straight toward Lester at full speed. Lester fields the ball on the run at the seven yard line and runs straight ahead between the hash marks, also at top speed. They negate each other's kinetic energy at the 21 yard line, a violent collision that sends them both reeling backwards. Tim hits the turf, but Lester places a hand down and remains upright. He spins around, pauses for a second, disoriented, then takes off again, flattening Tim as he tries to get up.

Lester dashes for the end zone, but Tim has scrambled to his feet and is gaining ground fast. Around the 50 he grabs hold of Lester's jersey from behind and swings him around several times in giant circles, but Lester does not go down. Then he jumps on Lester's back and Lester carries him, stumbling and staggering, until he collapses with the nose of the ball stretched over the goal line.

They both roll over onto their backs in opposite directions and they just lie there, panting heavily, gaping at the sheer massiveness of The Pyramid from a reverse angle. Lester speaks first.

"I reckon all that tennis has softened you up."

"Bugger off," Tim says, although he knows it's true.

Chapter 2

Five years later …

Lester reaches up and grabs hold of the microphone stand. He pulls himself up one hand at a time, as if climbing a rope out of quicksand, and the noise level raises yet another notch. Lester rips the microphone off the stand now, tosses the hood back from his face and leads The Arena in a final chorus:

"So listen here my friends,
Your search for peace is done.
And you're not the only one,
Who wants to make amends."

"This is the zero hour!
You've got to seize the power!"

The Visionaries Band takes it home with a crescendo of guitars, horns and drums, which receives a deafening ovation from the inhabitants.

* * *

A lone spotlight pierces the darkness and reveals Lester at center stage. He has changed out of the cloak, now wearing a black tuxedo and a gold bow tie. Before him stands a plain wooden podium. His sandy blonde hair is cropped short all around and neatly combed to one side, his sideburns trimmed just above the earlobes. His eyes glow stronger than ever with youthful passion – a natural radiation that seems to bend the space-time continuum itself. After some discontinuous cheering, The Arena eventually falls silent. Lester leans forward ever-so-slightly into the microphone.

"Welcome to your new home," he says, extending his arms as though inviting a warm embrace. This draws a mighty roar of approval. "Indeed … indeed …" He waits for the noise to subside again before continuing. "I will now delve immediately into our business here tonight, starting with some guidelines for this most joyous of ceremonies. I know you are all very excited, and understandably so, but I would appreciate you refraining from outbursts of applause, as well as cheering, whistling, clapping, stomping, hooting, hollering and so forth – unless I prompt you in the following manner."

Lester lifts his hand, palm up, in a manner not unlike a waiter hoisting a giant serving platter above his head. He holds there a moment before turning his palm over and lowering it to his side.

"You have to trust that it will be better for everyone this way. Now then, let's try it once for proper effect."

He repeats the gesture, only this time the crowd responds with a boisterous display. And when he lowers his hand, they become hushed all at once like a switch has been thrown. "Excellent. You see, this requires discipline, but the result is not altogether unpleasant, is it? … A rhetorical question."

Pockets of applause flair up in various places around The Arena, but mostly in the upper tier. "Thank you," Lester says.

He reaches into the podium, producing an orange and a glimmering silver dagger with a bronze handle. He sets the orange down on top of the podium and turns the dagger over in his hand, as if examining each side for imperfections. Then he begins cutting the orange into wedges, with every little sound being funneled into the arena by the ultra-sensitive microphone. When he reaches eight wedges, he takes a pause and holds the dagger out at arm's length to call attention to it.

"That's double edged. For convenience. Now, be assured, this society is indeed one that will require discipline from all of us. But the intention is that we need *not* be conscious of this fact. I think you understand what I mean. Nevertheless, I'll be telling you again soon, you can rest assured of that … Ah!" Lester pleasantly snaps up one of the orange wedges as if noticing it for the first time. He inserts it in his jaws and closes his lips around the peel. Leaning closer to the microphone, he sucks and slurps every drop of orange juice in the wedge before discreetly removing it from his mouth and tucking it inside the podium somewhere. "Mmm. Very refreshing. A great deal will be asked of each of you, but I think you will find that fulfilling your responsibilities here will be effortless and natural. Like swallowing."

Lester consumes another wedge in a similar manner as before. "Delicious. You see, for the majority of us, this type of indulgence, this privilege …" he says, waving a hand over what's left of the orange. "This was once taken for granted. But times have changed, have they not? Well, this is precisely why we are here. To find such things as everyday luxuries again. To feel like a part of something again, to feel comfortable and safe again. And to truly *live* once again, in harmony with our fellow man!"

Lester raises his hand and the crowd shows its approval with raucous cheering and applause. He lowers it – silence. He produces a green bottle of beer and a glass, and then pours the beer into the glass. He takes a long draw, gulping loudly. Or so it seems, by virtue of amplification.

"Aaah. And to think, there are also those among us who have never experienced these simple wonders. To you, I say this: Do not expect sympathy or exoneration, only fulfillment. Trust that these gifts will exist in abundance here, and anything else you desire must only be asked for. Not always provided, understand. But if not, only for your own good. And more importantly, the collective good of this society ... this civilization ... that will raise us all to heights never before reached by mankind!"

Lester solicits the crowd noise again, this time by raising both palms, and he allows the bedlam to carry on for some time.

"All I ask in return is your willingness, your trust and your loyalty ... All I ask in return is whatever it takes."

Chapter 3

Going back in time now ...

Lester has lied plenty of times, but never in front of a television camera. As far as the fledgling reporter and the rest of her donut-eating news crew are concerned, this posh midtown-Manhattan office indeed belongs to him, Lester Ginn, self-made millionaire and commercial real estate tycoon. If Tina weren't a hack who only got the network job because of daddy's connections, perhaps she'd be more concerned about the glaring inconsistencies afoot. Like the diploma on the wall, issued to one Gregory S. Pembroke (self-made millionaire and commercial real estate tycoon). Or the fact that Lester's wearing a tie both striped and polka-dotted, as well as an egregiously undersized corduroy sport coat.

The point, however, is that Tina didn't do her homework. So thanks to a corporate team-building seminar and a favor owed to Lester by one of the building's security guards, his plan is coming together quite nicely. Perhaps the difference-maker is his long, athletic frame and his boyish good looks – with his sandy hair combed to one side – or his sugary English accent. But more likely it's a combination thereof that makes him so endearing and winsome, even in a striped, polka-dotted tie and an egregiously undersized corduroy sport coat.

It's his eyes too, though. He has a way of engaging you with those bright green eyes, a way of locking you in with some sort of metaphysical tractor-beam. You might call it charm, charisma, intensity or even effervescent virility, but there's something else. A spark, a flash of brilliance, a true vision in the existential sense – as though he's not seeing you in the present moment at all but in some parallel reality, at the zenith of your human potential.

"You'll have to excuse my rather gauche appearance," Lester says, with a smile bright enough to cut through London fog. "You see, I'm volunteering at a soup kitchen this afternoon. Ladling up a bit of gruel, you know, for the disadvantaged up in Harlem. So a designer suit didn't seem quite … suitable, I thought."

"I respect that, Mr. Ginn," Tina says, trying much too hard to impress him.

With downright presidential bearing, Lester tightens the knot on his tie and smoothes the front of his threadbare sport coat as he scrutinizes the camera angle Tina has chosen. "Are those diplomas in the shot? Because I worked hard for those you know."

"Yes, they sure are, Mr. Ginn," Tina says, checking the viewfinder again just to be sure. She goes over to the desk, where a white sheet is draped over a pyramid-shaped object. Lester follows her and lightly slaps her hand when she tries to steal a look underneath.

"Ah-ah. No peeking, Marcy."

"Actually, it's Tina."

"Right, right, forgive me. Nevertheless, no peeking."

Tina gestures to the pyramid. "Is this the …"

"Yes, naturally …"

"Well, should we get started then?"

His eyes glassy all of a sudden, Lester stares over Tina's shoulder for a moment before regaining focus. "Very well then, let's get started, shall we?"

"Bob!" Tina shouts into the hallway. Then again, even louder, "Bob! We're ready!" And a moment later the portly cameraman shuffles in, chagrined at having cut short his masturbatory session in the women's restroom. With the vigor of a shackled inmate he takes his position behind the tri-pod.

"Right here, Mr. Ginn, next to the … thing," Tina says.

"We're rolling," Bob says.

"And three, two, one … It's been over ten years since the nuclear disaster at—"

"Excuse me," Lester says, "I'm sorry to interrupt. But since this isn't live, did you say nuc-uler?"

"No, I'm pretty sure I said nuclear," Tina replies, lacking confidence.

"I think you said nuc-uler," Bob says spitefully.

"I'm sorry if I did. Nuclear. Nuclear. Okay, let's go again. Three, two, one … It's been over ten years since the nuclear disaster at Yucca Mountain leveled the city of Las Vegas and turned a large part of the state of Nevada into what we now call The Glass Desert. Many experts have said rebuilding would be impossible. But now, one man says he plans to do just that – and in fact erect the largest man-made structure in history. His name is Lester Ginn, and he's been kind enough to invite me to his midtown office today for a sneak peek at what he hopes will turn the once-dubbed Sin City into Ginn City."

Lester grins at the camera, his eyes now shimmering with childlike enthusiasm. He's thinking, *I don't know about Ginn City, Marcy! I mean Tina! That sounds a bit self-important but regardless … It's going to happen! By hook, by crook or by divine bloody intervention it's going to happen! How, you say? Because an idea this good cannot wither and die on the bloody cross! The bloody cross of what, anyway? Reason? Chance? Ill circumstance? Hey, that rhymes. Shut up! We mustn't make any reference to crosses or anything bloody for that matter. Just the nuts and bolts. Oh, the glorious nuts and bolts!*

He's not aware of it, but his mouth has fallen slightly agape and he's panting happily, like a golden retriever set for another run after the stick. Not very tycoon-like at all, in fact.

Chapter 4

E very day, Seth Jipt's 89-year-old mother prepares his favorite lunch of bologna and pimento cheese sandwiches on pumpernickel bread, with the crusts cut off. At age 55, and not suffering from any disabilities aside from a pessimistic worldview, Jipt is more than capable of making his own lunch – or hiring a world-class chef for that matter – but his mother seems to enjoy the routine so he figures, hey, who is he to stand in the way of her fleeting happiness?

The elder Mrs. Jipt moved up from Midland, Texas a year ago when her husband passed away and, despite her complaints about Atlantic City, she has no trouble passing the time in her son's 15,000-square-foot mansion. She spends most of her days and nights holed up in the basement, on the computer, bidding in various gimcrack auctions and playing the sort of interactive video games called *Operation Bloodbath* or *Terror Force*, in which she orders missile strikes or slits the virtual throat of some third-world dictator being portrayed by a 12-year-old boy in Wichita. This takes the burden off Jipt and his wife, Lynette, although they've had live-in help for years and, besides, their relationship is not exactly a house afire in terms of sexual passion anymore.

Born and raised in Midland himself, Jipt is a bona fide southern gentleman, steeped in football, oil and cattle ranching, his voice worn smooth as a cowboy's saddle horn from years of scotch and cigars. His father was a cattle rancher and an oil man both, and he raised his only son to follow in his footsteps. But it wasn't to be.

When Seth finished high school his wanderlust drew him to Las Vegas, where he was beguiled by the ever-seductive allure of lady luck. He worked hard and kissed the right asses, ascending from janitor to change-maker to dealer to pit crew to pit boss to VP of Security to VP of Operations in less than ten years. He was living the fantasy, rubbing elbows with entertainers and movie stars, dating showgirls (often two or three at a time) and making gobs upon gobs of money. He then went out on his own, fetching top dollar for his consulting expertise. And before too long, if you didn't have Seth Jipt design your casino you were either his sworn enemy, a communist or a damned fool.

Due to Jipt's wild success, few were either dumb enough or audacious enough to declare themselves his enemy. Instead, his penchant for extracting the most money from the most people the quickest made a lot of businessmen rich beyond their wildest dreams.

The point is that Seth Jipt was *somebody*, and thanks to a well-timed vacation to Acapulco, he remained somebody after Vegas was zapped off the face of the earth by the infamous Disaster at Yucca Mountain.

For the reader's sake, we will not plunge into the technicalities of what went wrong and why. Suffice it to say that the U.S. Government packed weapons-grade uranium into this mountain for the better part of two decades, and said material evidently decided it didn't want to be cooped up in there anymore. I.e., *KABLOOM!* Gross miscalculations were made and the responsible parties were ruthlessly sacked for all the public to see. And, had it not been for the events just described, Seth Jipt would not be where he is today. That place being god-forbidden Atlantic City, New Jersey, in a preposterously large house, eating bologna and pimento cheese sandwiches and watching some madman on the news at noon.

On the 56-inch plasma screen television, Lester Ginn looks remarkably lifelike indeed. "You're quite welcome!" he says. "It's lovely to have you here today, Marcy."

"Tina."

"Right, right! Well let's see what all the excitement is about, shall we?"

Showman-like, Lester dramatically rips the sheet away, revealing a highly detailed, cross-sectioned architect's model of what will henceforth be referred to as The Pyramid. It contains a number of distinct levels, yet they are virtually indistinguishable to Jipt in spite of his set's 3.3 gigapixels of digital image quality.

Lester takes a half-step back and looks upon it with wide-eyed wonder, like a child having just unwrapped his first bicycle on Christmas morning.

"And there it is! Cleverly called … The Pyramid!" he says.

"And inside is a hotel-casino, a sports arena and an entire city where people live, is that correct?"

"There's a whole lot more actually – but not inside here. This is only a model, you see … The Pyramid itself will stand exactly one mile high!"

Chunks of bologna and pimento cheese splatter across the television screen, ejected violently from Jipt's mouth as he barks out, "What!?"

"And, indeed, it will be an entire civilization unto itself! It's quite extraordinary! You see, this grid here, with the little cubes? Well, the cubes are actually flats where the inhabitants will live. And some will also be used as shops, restaurants and so forth. The possibilities are virtually endless."

"What!?" Jipt says again, like a 250-pound parakeet. He rakes a stout-fingered hand through his thick gray hair, front to back, as if trying to plug holes in his skull and keep his brains inside.

"But that's not the most cunning part!" Lester continues, gesturing for the camera to come in tighter (it does not). "Look here! These cubes, you see, actually move round in the grid! In three-dimensional space, mind you!"

Lester demonstrates mime-like in the air before him, as if his hands were two of the cubes. He moves them at right angles in various directions, all the while continuing to pierce the camera lens with a look of rapt excitement. "It's quite extraordinary!" he says, further punctuating the obvious.

"So if I lived there, for example, I could just drive my cube – my apartment – right up to a restaurant?" Tina says.

"One better! You would simply tell your computerized butler what time you'd like to dine and the restaurant would meet you automatically. No driving a'tall!"

"My computerized butler?" Tina says.

"What!? Where the hell's the money coming from?!"

"Seth?! I can't hear you!" Jipt's mother calls weakly from the kitchen.

"I'm not talking to you!" Jipt snaps back, like a surly teenager.

"Well, shut off that TV then! Lunch is almost ready!"

"Ma! I'm eating lunch right—" Jipt is interrupted by the phone ringing. It's his right-hand man, Tommy Hawkins. "Hello? … Hey Tommy, yeah, I'm watching it … I have no goddamned idea. I don't know how we never heard about this thing … Yeah, do me a favor and find out everything you can about this guy, will you? All right, good. See you first thing tomorrow."

Jipt slams the phone down, and by this time Tina has thrown it back to her chuckling cohorts in the studio, a couple of rubbery anchors named Mike and Sherry.

"Thanks, Tina," Mike says. "One mile high … boy Sherry, I wouldn't want to be at the top! Ha ha!"

"Ha ha. You've got that right, Mike," Sherry says. "I'm a little scared of heights myself."

Not sure what to think of all this, Jipt mashes down the OFF button on the remote and stares blankly at the screen, like a goldfish pondering the inscrutable world outside his bowl.

Chapter 5

L ester owned a car at one time, a vehicle of marginal structural integrity that was confiscated by impatient creditors. While this was unfortunate, the real tragedy would have been losing the ten-speed bicycle stowed in the trunk – *would have been*, if not for a strongly worded letter issued under the signature of Quimby Miles, Esq., Lester's fictitious attorney, which prompted the expedient return of the bike in full working order. This epitomized a real success story in Lester's mind, a cost savings of at least $200 according to his best estimate. That is, $100 for a new bike and another $100 for the investment of time and rigmarole that would have been necessary in obtaining it.

Lester does this as a course of habit – estimates the cost savings of everything from a discounted box of cereal to feats of home maintenance, such as unclogging the toilet or garbage disposal without professional assistance. He began keeping a running log in a notebook when he was 18, and now at age 33 he still carries it on his person at all times (when he's wearing clothes). The total cost savings to date is $99,028.15, a number he's quite proud of. That averages out to approximately $20.87 a day. What Lester cannot figure out, however, is what happened to all that money.

Back to the bicycle though, and Lester's activity at the moment, which entails riding it through Queens, New York, at full throttle, dressed in complete American football regalia. Helmet, shoulder pads, the whole nine yards as they say. This is not for safety purposes, as one might guess, but actually because Lester is on his way to a football match. In spite of his English roots, he prefers the pad crunching, helmet bashing violence of American football to international football (soccer), in which more dexterity and raw skill is generally required. His team is called The Pirates and their uniforms are blood-red with gold stripes, which is meant to be indicative of the two things Pirates relish most (aside from wenches): gold and blood.

Careening down the sidewalk, Lester rounds a corner at breakneck speed and plows through a peddler's flimsy card table, sending imitation designer sunglasses and watches flying everywhere. The man curses him in some guttural foreign language and Lester apologizes telepathically, as he's too fearful to stop. Not to mention a half-hour late for the match against his friend Pedro's squad, the Tough Hombres. He veers into the street, causing several cars to honk and screech to a stop, jumps the curb on the other side and pedals off through the grass of a small park, cutting straight through windrows of shrubbery and beds of delicate spring flowers.

Once through the park, he crosses the street on the other side in similar fashion, paying little heed to traffic, and launches himself into a row of metal garbage cans on the opposite sidewalk. This serves two purposes. One, to introduce the taste of pain to his lips and the flow of adrenaline to his veins (these are lumped together for administrative reasons), and two, to ensconce his uniform with the foul smell of rotten garbage, which is utterly revolting to his opponents, often causing them to choke and gag at the mere thought of tackling him. Indeed, at only 175 pounds, what Lester lacks in size he must compensate for with sheer wit and cunning.

* * *

The Pirates defeated their arch rivals (and only rivals), The Tough Hombres, 83-77, in a stunning, no-holds-barred, sudden-death finish, during which time Lester both received and doled-out fierce, almost sadistic, punishment.

Now, drunk with new hypotheses and still dizzy from the repeated blows to the head, Lester pedals haphazardly through the streets of Queens yet again. He sideswipes a newsstand or lamppost here and there, but otherwise rides with competence and resolve. When he finally reaches his destination, the Golden Horseshoe Bar, he finds the Visionaries already settled in, watching a soap opera on the bar's black and white television. They are: Dr. Madeline Chutney (a Brit), Dr. Patricia Katz (a German), Dr. Helmut Schnitzelhaus (also a German), Dr. Chili Brown (a proud African-New Yorker) and Dr. Wong "Spoon" Ping (a Chinaman).

The story of how Lester and these five individuals came to meet and become known as the Visionaries is really quite simple and straightforward, so it will be told as a quick aside.

To be accurate, these are the second generation of Visionaries, the offspring of another group of friends who called themselves by the same name. Prior to entering the Royal Navy, Lester's father, George Humphrey Ginn, met Chutney's father, John Chutney, when they were both scrawny undergraduates at Oxford. Both lovers of football (soccer), pint-drinking and grandiose ideas, they hit it off right away. Over time their friendship became quite robust and, in subsequent years, George met Vernon Brown, an expatriate American scholar, and Lee Ping, a Chinese businessman in the steel trade – while John brought Herbert Schnitzelhaus and Hans Katz to the table, both of whom he met while on holiday in Düsseldorf. A highly successful cross-pollination of friendships then ensued, and eventually they all settled in Portsmouth, a port city and site of Britain's principal naval base, about 100 miles southwest of London on the English Channel. There they raised families, their children played and went to school together, and everyone got along rather swimmingly.

The second generation of Visionaries did not all end up in New York City by pure coincidence. Each transgression was unique and circumstantial in its own regard, but the telling of these stories is meant for another time and place altogether. So with that, back to the matters at hand we shall go ...

The Golden Horseshoe is a quintessential dive bar, popular among social outcasts and mainstream reprobates alike – in addition to the Visionaries, of course, who merely choose it for its low profile and the motherly charm of Yolanda, the bartender and chief proprietor of the establishment.

"Well, well, well, look what the cat drug in!" Yolanda says, sliding a tumbler of whiskey across the bar to Lester.

Absorbed in the drama of daytime television, the others merely raise their glasses to say hello. They are hardly surprised by Lester's tardiness, his haggardness or even his downright putrid odor. Chutney is the only one who even bothers to get up for a proper greeting, and as she starts to give him a hug she thinks better of it.

"My goodness," she says, drawing back and flipping her mane of chestnut hair from one shoulder to the other. "Did the cat urinate on you as well?"

"Smells more like vomit," Schnitzelhaus says.

"I thought you looked quite handsome on the television earlier," Katz says smiling, although her Germanic features make her look more cordial than friendly.

"Why, thank you, Patricia. It's nice to see that some of us have a morsel of civility remaining ... All right, mates, enough of the pleasantries, then ..." Lester says, removing his helmet before chugging back the whiskey. "Aah! Wooo!" He coughs a few times.

"Damn that's smooth! Well, let's call this meeting to order shall we? Dreadfully sorry I'm late but ... very well then!" Lester says. "Could I have everyone's attention in the bar, please? That's right, I think you know the routine by now. Kindly move along then. Don't forget your personal belongings. The nearest exit may be behind you."

Some random patrons file out, but a feeble old man and a teenaged punk remain behind. Lester approaches the old man, who is engaged in the arduous process of shelling a peanut.

"Mr. McDuggins? You can bring that with you, how about that? There we are," Lester says, helping him to his feet. He gets him on his way toward the door and wheels on the punk, who's smoking a cigarette defiantly in the corner.

"That means beat it, man!" Lester says. There's a brief moment of silence in which they stare each other down, and then Lester really explodes with a banshee-like shriek. "Now! You stupid wanker!"

The punk is obviously frightened but does a decent job of hiding it as he swaggers briskly out the door. Chili and Schnitzelhaus push some tables together and Ping wheels a chalkboard out from the back room. Lester struggles out of his shoulder pads and jersey, and Chutney pulls him aside, fixing her lovely, compassionate brown eyes on him.

"You need to call Svetlana. She phoned here again – said she's been trying to reach you for days. The poor girl is worried sick about you, Lester."

"Svetlana? Damn, I got a bit sidetracked. Caught up in things, you know, stuff and whatnot ... Worried about me? My god, is everything all right?"

"Fine. She just wanted to remind you to pick up Tim and Anna after school today."

"Damn!" Lester says in a self-deprecating manner, followed by a long pause. He grimaces and screws his face around in various gestures of disappointment and anger. "Damn it! How could I let this happen, Chutney? My own son for God's sake."

"There there."

Lester rests his head on her shoulder and she turns away, gasping for fresh air.

"It's okay, Lester. You've still got a few hours before school lets out."

"I forgot though, that's the bloody point!"

"Perhaps you would have remembered," she says, pulling back. "Lester? There's something else. About The Pyramid ... Your bit on the news was, well ... I thought we agreed this was all just amongst us."

"All I wanted was to stir up some interest, you know, test the waters as they say. After all, who knows, maybe—"

"Lester ... it's all good fun to make believe but you've got to draw that line, you know what I mean? It's just a fanciful sort of hobby Lester, and you have to accept that it won't be anything more."

"But—"

"Please. Listen to me, dear. Right now, I think you need to focus on what's real, okay? Your son. Svetlana. She loves you, Lester. Very much. And you're breaking her heart with all this nonsense. I mean, how long have you been together, five years?"

"Mm," Lester utters. "Almost six now, I reckon."

"Well, don't you think it's about time you got married? You know, settled down?"

Lester stares at Chutney for a moment, his expression some mix of anguish and fear. In fact, it looks as if he may begin to cry. But he turns away, changing tone altogether. "All right, then! Dr. Ping, why don't we start with you. I believe you have an update for us on the status of your operations? Oh wait, the chalkboard." Lester flips the large, schoolhouse-style chalkboard around and draws a giant triangle. "I beg your pardon, Doctor Ping, you have the floor."

"Yes, thank you," Ping says, adjusting his thick bifocals, which are constantly sliding down the bridge of his nose. What makes matters worse is that the lenses are arranged in upside-down fashion, requiring him to crook his head back to see anything at a distance. He clasps his hands together as if to implore and begins his report, making more frequent eye contact with the black Formica tabletop and the ceiling than with his colleagues. He is shy and exceedingly intelligent — in fact, he appears to make pained efforts to check his mental advances to allow for his brain and mouth to generate coherent speech.

"As you know I have been working for quite some time to develop a viable way for the cubes to travel in the grid."

Lester sketches the grid in the middle of the triangle with criss-crossed lines.

"Well I may have the answer!" Ping says, jittery with excitement. "Instead of tiny wheels or ball bearings as we discussed before, we can use the mag-lev technology!"

"Like on those bullet trains?" Chili says.

"With electromagnets?" Lester says, eagerly.

"Yes, the same," Ping says.

"I knew it! Excellent work Ping!"

Yolanda serves up sangria from a wooden pitcher teeming with chunks of fresh fruit.

"Mmm, brilliant," Lester says, sitting down at the table. He attacks his beverage with ambitious gulps. "Aah! I trust this can be worked into your plan from a materials standpoint, Dr. Schnitzelhaus?"

"Yes, of course. In fact, the beams I had in mind are made not of steel or wood, you see, but of highly advanced polymers, reinforced with carbon nanotubes, which are light, which are strong, and which are natural insulators of heat and electricity. So this will be very efficient."

"Smashing!" Lester says, offering up his glass, and everyone joins in a merry toast.

"Chili," Lester says, once the din of laughter and merriment has subsided, "Does this sound cost-feasible to you?"

"Seeing as though we've got an imaginary budget? I would say so."

"In your professional opinion, though, assuming real monetary resources could be drawn upon."

"Sure, why not. I mean, it's not like we're encrusting the place with diamonds or something. We're not, are we?"

"No."

"Good. Well, it ain't gonna be cheap, but it sounds doable with those modular building techniques the boys have talked about. Hey Ping, what's the top speed on one of those cubes anyway?"

"About ten miles per hour. Going up will be a little slower."

"I've written a program to control the speed and the various changes in direction," Katz says. "The computer will also choose the most desired path from point A to B and, of course, avoid any other cubes along the way."

"Except when you want to dock up with another one," Chutney says, sweeping her mane of sandy hair over a shoulder.

"I'd dock up with you any day, sweetheart," Lester says.

"Lester, please."

Katz continues. "Right. With the user interface, one can choose to have his cube take him straight to a particular destination or arrive there at a prescribed time in the future."

"Excellent then! Chutney, I do hope this sounds like an inhabitable place from a sociological perspective."

"Yes, of course. If we're careful."

"In other words, if we're careful to pick the right fools to live in this thing," Chili says.

"In a manner of speaking, yes," Chutney says. "If we are to maintain a balanced system, in which individuals are required to contribute very little or no work in exchange for material goods — and since our plan is to eliminate the need for work, and for currency altogether – well, outside of The Casino, that is — Chili and I have worked through this — it is important that the inhabitants are inclined to take on responsibilities, even if they're only imagined. And furthermore, it is important that the inhabitants are undyingly grateful for the opportunity to live in this society. In essence, they must worship The Pyramid in the way that many farming cultures worship their land."

"Well said, love! I only understood a small part of it, due to my state of disorientation, but well said indeed! I say we drink to it!" Lester says, and he toasts Chutney's glass first. She blushes at the attention, smiles and takes a drink of the refreshing sangria.

"I think everyone would agree that we have many obstacles to overcome in the sociological arena," Lester says. "And I for one think Chutney has done a marvelous job thus far."

This meets with yeses and here-heres from around the table, and after a short time Lester continues. "We've got many obstacles yet to overcome, so we must always be mindful of this. Yet, on the other hand, we have many extraordinary breakthroughs to celebrate. And I believe you have another one for us, don't you Dr. Schnitzelhaus?"

"Yes, this is true," Schnitzelhaus says, stroking his bushy mustache. "The addition of a new level!"

"A new level?" Katz says. "You mean you've had a new level up your sleeve all this time? Out with it now!"

"You sneaky bastard!" Ping says, laughing.

"Well, it's an old idea actually, but if you'll remember we didn't think we could have a Recreational Level with extensive amounts of vegetation, earth and so on. Because of the weight. Well, I've solved it."

Ping, who's quite beside himself with gaiety and drunkenness, says, "You've invented a special type of dirt!"

"No no, I've developed a structural plan to compensate for the massive weight. I think perhaps we can even have a pond!" Schnitzelhaus says.

"With paths?" Chutney asks. "For walking and riding bicycles?"

"I think this can be arranged."

"Lovely," Lester says. "Now, on the other end of the spectrum. Let's talk about The Casino for a moment."

"The Casino is where people will pay money to lose at games," Katz says, mocking the culture of gambling.

"More or less," Chutney says. "Really, they're paying for the excitement of almost winning."

"The slimmer the chances, the more exciting it is when they actually do win," Chili adds. "Say what you want about it, but The Casino makes it all happen. Without The Casino we have no influx of cash and no means to support the inhabitants' consumption of goods."

"Like beer," Lester says.

"Yes, like beer. And cupcakes. And whatever else we're planning to give them."

"Where's cupcakes?!" Ping blurts out, and this meets with a few chuckles around the table.

"Then we'd better make sure there's no shortage of people who enjoy losing at games," Katz says jokingly.

"Oh, there are plenty of those to go around," Lester says. "You know what they say, a sucker born every hour."

"Every minute," Chutney corrects him.

"Even better! Why doesn't everyone consume a bit more of this delicious sangria!"

Feeling the need to stretch his legs, Lester rises, distributes some more sangria and walks over to the chalkboard. "And they will flock to The Casino, not only because it will be the largest and most grandiose, if you will, known to exist on earth, but because it will be part of this," he says, outlining the entire Pyramid in yellow chalk, for effect. "It's quite extraordinary! And oh-by-the-way! I shouldn't have to remind you that it will harness the power of the sun! And provide shelter from the sun at the same time! And the rain, and the cruel elements! And the cruelties of common everyday life! A refuge … yes. A spectacle … yes, yes, yes. A utopia? Hmm … Someday we may be lucky enough to find out …"

At that, Lester becomes exceedingly lightheaded. He raises his glass, leaning against the chalkboard for support, and the Visionaries raise their own glasses in a silent, pensive toast – as if in honor of a dear old friend who has passed on before his time.

Chapter 6

S andeep walks around the concourse with the help of a brand new prosthetic leg. The leg does not articulate at the knee, so his gait is somewhat hitched, but it sure beats hopping. People flood out of The Arena and branch off in different directions, all becoming absorbed by the crowd. And for the first time Sandeep realizes that a disproportionate number of them also appear disabled in some way, some with canes or crutches, others with eye patches or hook-hands (none with both, however).

Finding the exit he was instructed to use, he turns and passes through a set of automatic doors on the outside wall of the concourse, labeled N-21, and then queues up in a hallway to wait his turn. Despite having been thoroughly instructed on what to do, Sandeep cannot remember if he's supposed to check in with the man at the front of the line or not. He admires the man's gold officer's cap and matching epaulets.

"Hi there, hon," says the woman in front of him. She has no apparent handicap, just a chunky physique and a thick Minnesota accent. "You don't have to check in or nothing, just get in line."

"Thank you," Sandeep says, and he can't help but remember how Lester had called these "golden words" during several classroom lectures on politeness.

"You're welcome, hon. I don't know about you, but I can't wait to get to my cube. It's just so darned exciting."

"I also feel great excitement and eagerness," Sandeep replies, taking some of his newly learned English for a little test drive.

"You know? I mean, they showed us them pictures or drawings or whatever, but it'll still be neat to see the real deal is what I'm saying."

"Yes, I agree," Sandeep says, thinking this a good, polite response without egging her on much further. She turns to a man in his mid-twenties who has a long white scar on the front of his neck, and Sandeep tunes out their conversation. He studies the man in the gold cap again as he works his way down the line, asking for names. Now Sandeep recollects the process, and he knows he won't have long to wait.

* * *

Sandeep reaches the front of the line and the elevator doors open. He is ushered inside the roomy compartment, along with a dozen other inhabitants, and less than a minute later the doors open again. They exit, joining several hundred other people in one of The Grid's four main elevator stations, which consists of a wide, square-shaped walkway around a bank of 36 elevators. On the outside of the walkway, each of the four sides has three portals, labeled A-C, D-F and so on, corresponding to the inhabitants' surnames. Each square portal marks the beginning of a corridor, and each corridor is lined with more elevator doors on either side. Behind these elevator doors, the inhabitants' cubes are docked and waiting, as indicated by the names displayed above them on digital readouts. Timing is critical in this process, otherwise it could take several hours for everyone to reach their cubes, and another man with a gold cap stands in the hallway, answering questions and otherwise helping those in need.

Sandeep does not need help, however. The process is coming back to him now, and he easily finds the readout that says, GANESH, SANDEEP. He presses a button and the doors open directly into his cube, the moment he's been waiting for, and he enters with a flutter of excitement in his belly. He can see that the HoloVision is turned on and projecting the image of his computerized butler on a round platform in the center of the room. The figment of the elderly Indian man, who has a red turban and a white beard, beckons Sandeep to enter. So he does, and the doors whoosh closed behind him.

"Welcome, Mr. Ganesh," the man says with an accent similar to Sandeep's. Please, have a seat and relax."

Sandeep marvels at the realism of the hologram for a moment, having seen his butler on a computer screen during the creation process (near the end of orientation), but never before in three dimensions. He chooses the armchair over the couch, both of which are red on a background of white – as the floor, walls and ceiling are composed of a frosted translucent plastic. It's white for now, anyway, because Sandeep has not yet requested to pixelate it. And he thinks perhaps he'll go with an exposed brick motif on the walls, with windows looking out over the skyline of New York. Hardwood floors, with Persian area-rugs and—

"Mr. Ganesh, I invite you to pick up the device sitting there on the table."

Sandeep had not noticed the rectangular silver object, which is roughly the size of a deck of playing cards. He knows what it is, but his Butler politely reminds him anyway.

"As you surely recall, that is your computerized Butler, which gives you access to me, as well as other systems within The Pyramid, including the HoloVision."

The holographic image of Sandeep's Butler disappears and a video image appears on the sleek little device. "Of course, you also have the option of viewing me in this way." Another video image pops up on the wall. "Or this way, if a video wall is available, of course."

The video image disappears now and is replaced by the following text scrolling across the screen: OR, THE OPTION OF NOT VIEWING OR HEARING ME AT ALL.

The hologram returns and his Butler says, "The choice is yours. Before I leave you to your personal business, are there any destinations you'd like to set at this time?"

"No, thank you," Sandeep says.

"Well, if you need anything, please don't hesitate to ask."

"Thank you," Sandeep says, and like a genie the Butler vanishes again.

* * *

As his first order of personal business, Sandeep has chosen to spruce up the (virtual) decorating a bit, and it's turned out just as he envisioned, with the exposed brick and the skyline views and everything. The room is divided into three main areas: the living room, the kitchen and the dining area. There are no partitions or interior walls, and each of the four main walls has an identical set of elevator doors in the center, labeled by the four points of the compass (N, S, E and W). At each corner of the room is a symmetrical inset, two of which are closets, one a half-bathroom and the other an elevator.

Sandeep steps into the elevator and then steps off a few moments later, onto the second level, which upholds the Manhattan-loft motif. A queen-size bed rests against one wall, beneath another simulated picture window. Black dressers on either side of the bed double as nightstands. Opposite the bed, the other half of the room is split between a sitting area and a bathroom, which includes a shower stall, toilet and vanity. A curtain attached to a track on the ceiling can be drawn around this area for privacy, but it's open at the moment.

Sandeep opens one of the closets and finds his clothes stacked neatly inside. In the other, fresh towels and linens in his favorite colors: red, yellow and green.

"Minesh?" Sandeep calls to his Butler, by the name he's chosen for him, and the old man appears in the center of the room an instant later, just as he had done on the lower level.

"Yes, Mr. Ganesh?"

"I'd like some music, please. Something with sitar."

Minesh obliges him with a traditional selection, but it's not quite what Sandeep has in mind. "More modern, please, Minesh."

"More up-tempo, then? Perhaps something with elements of pop music intermixed?

"Yes, exactly," Sandeep says, astounded at the computer's ability to anticipate his needs. "Thank you."

"You're quite welcome, Mr. Ganesh. Anything else?"

"I was just going to clean up and go to bed," Sandeep says, unaccustomed to the constant attention but nonetheless comfortable with it. Enthralled by it, in fact. "Is there perhaps some cricket I could watch?"

"Yes. Two live matches are currently available, as well as the archives, of course."

"Is India playing in either of the live matches?"

"No, I'm afraid not, Mr. Ganesh. England versus Sri Lanka, and Korea versus The Philippines."

"Hmm … how about the famous match between India and Pakistan? I can't remember the year, but it was for the World Championship at least 10 years ago …"

"More than 20 years ago?" Minesh queries for parameters.

"I don't think so."

"Give me just a moment, if you would please, Mr. Ganesh."

"Okay, I think I'll brush my teeth," Sandeep says. He feels silly for a moment, for having shared this detail – again – with a computer. But Minesh just seems so real, so personable.

He opens the mirrored medicine cabinet and finds a full assortment of personal care products stocked inside. Not all the brands he is familiar with, but all the types of products he prefers on a regular basis: bar soap, shaving cream, razors, baby powder, moisturizing lotion and, of course, toothpaste and a toothbrush.

Sandeep has always taken a keen enjoyment in christening a new toothbrush and in squeezing the first portion of toothpaste out of a new tube. And, as he thinks about it, he cannot recall having ever experienced both in a single occurrence before. He watches himself in the mirror without realizing that his technique is atrocious (if Jipt were here, he'd have a fit). However, he does realize is that his teeth have become rather yellowed over his 40 years, although he's proud of still having them all intact, despite his troubles.

He looks around himself in the mirror and sees that Minesh's image has given way to the cricket match in question, which is only just beginning.

"Better fast forward some, Minesh," Sandeep says, rinsing off his toothbrush and returning it neatly to the cabinet. "This match goes on for days."

Chapter 7

Wake up and dance – that's the routine Lester and Svetlana have followed since their honeymoon, and today is no different. This morning's music selection, chosen randomly from a prescribed set list, comes compliments of Lester's favorite classic British rock band, The Swarthies. It might also be described as a fusion of blues and punk, with a twist of classical thrown in for good measure. Svetlana dances in the center of the bedroom, on the HoloVision platform spinning and twisting with her arms raised above her head. The HoloVision swirls bright tropical fish all around and on top of her body, which is about half-covered by a petite silk nightgown. Meanwhile, Lester orbits her like a planet spinning round the sun, but the irony is lost on him. He lifts his knees and pumps his arms in synch with the rhythm, despite his ankles and wrists being strapped with heavy magnets. His ankles both carry a positive charge, his wrists negative, but he still manages to get himself stuck, ankle on wrist. As a result, he tumbles to the hard floor, which is polished black, like onyx. Seeing that he's okay, Svetlana giggles and leaps on top of him like a cat.

It's the first day of Pyramid living for the inhabitants, but not for Lester and Svetlana, Tim, Anna and the Visionaries, who have been here for the past month. During this time all the vital systems were tested and modified as necessary – the "debugging period" as it was called. It was a success in all regards, the perfect culmination of a near-perfect construction process. The most important, and also the most remarkable, statistic of note here is that not a single man or woman perished on the job. Several died of natural and otherwise unmanageable causes, but not a single fatal accident occurred. As Lester touted all along, safety was indeed paramount.

Over the course of these 30-some-odd days since moving into their new home, Lester and Svetlana have expanded their routine beyond the waking up and the dancing, as one might imagine. After all, productivity is not an estranged motivation in Lester's mind. Its definition is simply tweaked a bit. Breakfast comes next, often featuring some of Jean-Sebastian's latest scone, crumpet and muffin innovations. Jean-Sebastian is the resident chef, who came very highly recommended by Squeakins and who was, in fact, lured away from one of Squeakins' prior employers in France. Jams and various preserves are also commonly had, along with tea. Today's locale of choice is The Lanai, or the (retractable) balcony off the Master's Quarters that also includes a pair of hammocks, a shuffleboard court and a driving range. At an altitude of approximately 6,710 feet above sea level, The Lanai is often buffeted by high winds, but today is crystal clear with just a light breeze. Absolutely delightful, as long as one isn't afraid of heights.

"You know," Lester says, chewing a mouthful of buttered crumpet. "It's a shame those Egyptian kings never got to enjoy the fruits of their pyramidal vision. I mean, it wouldn't have been quite so dramatic as this, but ..."

"My family is coming next week. All of them," Svetlana replies after a sizeable pause.

"If you're trying to dampen my spirits then you'll just have to try harder. The weather is just too delightful this morning. Not too hot, not too cold. Although this tea is a bit cold, isn't it?"

"Yes."

"I thought so. Boy! Boy!" Lester shouts, and Squeakins appears a few moments later, tuxedo-clad and ready to take orders. "Boy, please have them reheat this tea. It's gone rather tepid."

"I'll just have them send a fresh one up, sir."

"Well, I'd rather just reheat this one. I mean, it's a smashing brew and there's no reason to waste it."

"Very well, sir," Squeakins says, taking the pot away.

Lester turns back to Svetlana. "All of them?"

"Yes. I'm sorry, but they're very excited about it. They'll stay out of our way, I promise."

"No, don't be sorry about anything. They're your family, after all. I'll have Squeakins set up some accommodations downstairs."

"I thought maybe we could just get some hotel rooms, because they will probably spend most of their time in The Casino, anyway."

"The Casino!? Absolutely not, I wouldn't think of it. We've got plenty of room for them up here. What do they plan to do in The Casino, anyway?"

"I don't know. Gamble, I suppose."

"That's preposterous, I really don't see the attraction to gambling. Especially when we're giving them the money to gamble with for heaven's sake!"

"Well, sweetheart, look at it this way. We won't have to give them any more money if they win it in The Casino."

"What makes you think they're going to win? Look, it's not the money that's at issue, here," Lester says, being firm and sincere, not argumentative. "Come to think of it, I'd gladly pay them to avoid The Casino altogether."

"Everyone has their tastes, Lester. They think it's fun, and it's not like they're the only ones. Just look at those trains," Svetlana says, as two simultaneously dart into and out of The Pyramid far below.

"They run non-stop, twenty-four hours a day," Lester says, with a combination of awe and disparagement. "Full of people. Their pockets full of money. Burning holes, as they say."

"Different people have different ideas of fun."

"Dumb ideas."

"Now you're describing my family," Svetlana says in a lighthearted warning.

"Right. Sorry about that. Well, I shouldn't knock it, should I? The gambling. No, I shouldn't. After all, it's what affords us our preferred pleasures, isn't it?"

"Exactly."

"And there's our tea now! Piping hot, I can tell by the steam."

Chapter 8

After a night of undisturbed slumber, the likes of which he has never experienced before, Sandeep awakens and rubs his eyes. A figure stands before him that doesn't appear to be Minesh. All he can tell is that he's taller, and white … until his vision finally clears up. It's Lester. Or rather, his holographic doppelganger, standing motionless in the center of the room, appearing to gaze out at the digital skyline above Sandeep's head.

"Good morning," Lester says, chipper and smiling. He snaps his fingers and, like in the Arena the night before, the sound is amplified throughout the room. "You had a delightful night's sleep and are ready for a productive day as a member of society. You feel energetic, optimistic and unabashedly joyful. You will be courteous and kind to anyone you meet today, and derive great pleasure from helping them. You will consider your fellow inhabitants as you would your beloved family, placing their needs above yours – and trusting they will do the same for you. You are truly grateful to be here, and the last thing you want is to squander this opportunity. Am I right?"

"Yes," Sandeep says, almost too readily, having fallen under Lester's hypnotic spell.

"Brilliant. As a result, you will do your best to be conscientious and careful, and to follow the guidelines set forth in the name of safety. After all, safety is paramount. You will not harm anyone, and you will not be harmed. Now get out there and have a wonderful day!"

Like a magician, Lester snaps his fingers again and disappears. By the time Minesh appears an instant later, Sandeep has already forgotten about the little pep talk, yet the message remains with him. He is so excited about the day that he can barely stand it.

Chapter 9

Sylvia's kitchen is typical of a middle-class suburban home. Only this one happens to be in PyraVegas, as evidenced by The Pyramid looming in the distance like a freakishly symmetrical mountain made of pure gold. The younger of her two boys, six-year-old Michael, sits at the kitchen table eating his cereal and toast. And opposite him, Anthony, who's nine, stares out the window at The Pyramid, his food as yet untouched. Dressed in a tuxedo with a triangular name plate, Sylvia rushes around in an effort to keep everyone on schedule.

"Anthony. Earth to Anthony."

"What?"

"Are you going to eat your breakfast?"

"Yeah, mom."

"Well, let's see some hustle then," Sylvia says, taking Michael's dishes. "We're running late. Bus comes in fifteen minutes."

As a single mom, Sylvia feels like she's fighting a constant uphill battle to get the boys to school, and herself to work, on time every day. She, too, has heard the rumors about Seth Jipt's team of enforcers. But she's also heard first-hand accounts saying there's little to worry about except a reprimand and a docked paycheck. Although, as far as she's concerned at the moment, that might be worse than an actual slap in the face.

As she rinses the dishes and puts them in the dishwasher, Sylvia wonders what Rodney is doing. Shortly after being rejected as a potential Pyramid inhabitant, she got back together with him, against her better judgment of course. And they next thing she knew, they had two kids. On her worst days, she curses herself for having brought them into the world by an abusive father. But nevertheless, she loves them more than anything. She glances at The Pyramid and consciously spins her thoughts positive again. *Remember what you had before*, is what she tells herself on these occasions. *Remember, and then forget. With any luck, maybe he's dead.*

Sylvia nudges Michael and Anthony out the door just as the school bus is pulling up to the house. She hugs and kisses them goodbye and they hurry on board. The bus pulls away in a cloud of black smoke and she wonders – as she does every day at this moment – why they can't have electric buses (answer: because of Jipt's ties to the oil industry). About five minutes later, The Pyramid Casino employee bus pulls up, and she climbs in.

The bus takes her to the nearest of the four major train hubs, PyraVegas Station North, where it dumps her into a veritable beehive of activity. Throngs of people move every which way on the eight train platforms, some coming and some going. They include casino workers like her, dressed in tuxedos and elaborate period costumes, as well as tourists representing every color of the rainbow.

Sylvia navigates through the bustling mass to her designated train, the number seven, and boards it. She sits in a seat marked RESERVED FOR EMPLOYEES and allows herself to feel a twinge of satisfaction. After all, it was her suggestion to The Union leaders that started the process. The remainder of the train fills up around her until those standing are shoulder-to-shoulder. *Bing!* "Doors closing," the pleasant female voice says, and the train accelerates out of the station.

Sylvia is lucky enough to have gotten a window seat this morning. As the train shoots past the innermost echelon of PyraVegas, she stares across the shimmering Glass Desert floor at The

Pyramid, its apex obscured by the roof of the train. She wonders what the inhabitants are doing, what she might be doing if she were among them, and finally, what Lester Ginn is doing. But these are frustrating lines of thought, because she has no idea where to begin her assumptions. And she has no idea what to assume because she has no first-hand knowledge of The Pyramid outside of The Casino. She knows about the City Level, the Recreation Level and The Grid in broad terms, as they've been described in the media, but she's never seen so much as an artist's rendering of them.

About three minutes later, the train slows to a stop in The Pyramid's North Station. The doors open and more than half the riders empty out onto the platform, the tourists snapping pictures and looking all around like aliens stepping off their spacecraft onto uncharted soil. She remains on board, and less than a minute later, the train stops in Central Station, where it trades transferring passengers. Another minute after that, the train pulls into South Station, where Sylvia disembarks.

She follows a group of people dressed like her, heading for the Classic Vegas section of The Casino as they shuffle under an archway labeled EMPLOYEES ONLY. She passes through a security checkpoint, where she's subjected to x-ray and other scanning procedures, including a biometric thumbprint scan, before stepping onto one of a dozen massive escalators.

The escalator takes her to the Employee Terminal, where numbered gates are arranged around a cavernous hallway, very similar to an airport terminal. Sylvia works in Classic Vegas, sector 31, so she walks to Gate 31, as logic dictates. Once there, she takes a seat and waits for her name to be called. She picks up the money section of The PyraVegas Enquirer, which features yet another article shamelessly hyping The Casino and heralding it as the backbone of PyraVegas society. *More like a wishbone*, Sylvia thinks, imagining herself whipping an arena full of Union members into a frenzy. *And we're getting the smaller piece! No, what about, And we're the third player in the game! No, too obscure …*

"Sylvia King," the woman at the desk announces, and Sylvia wonders how much more or less she's getting paid for that job, which is so much easier than hers, although monotonous.

Sylvia walks past her, swipes her card over another scanner, and walks through a thick metal door into the "decompression chamber" that separates The Casino from the Employee Terminal. Entering The Casino itself, Sylvia does not even fight the initial sense of depression. It's short-lived and, therefore, tolerable. She arrives at her station, a blackjack table, and scans her ID yet again. The current dealer cashes out and then swipes out, leaving Sylvia with five patrons. They include two Japanese businessmen, a Midwestern couple in their Sunday best and a young woman with purple lipstick and a latex dress. Sylvia suspects this woman is a prostitute, because she's seen her before – hanging around other Japanese businessmen, in fact.

As Sylvia made a conscious effort earlier to turn her thoughts positive, she now makes a similar effort to turn them off altogether. This is the only way she can perform her duties with the required degree of efficiency. She takes some hard-earned cash from the Midwestern man, a chickenfeed distributor, and using the Lucite money paddle, she slams it into the padlocked hopper.

Chapter 10

When the appointed time comes on the daily checklist, Jipt does not think, for example, *I am going to brush my teeth now*. Instead he thinks something that, when translated, might be closer to, *Time for the Brushing of the Teeth*. It's as if he were referring to an interpretive dance. And one could certainly attempt some sort of metaphorical sorcery here, arguing that, in essence, it's just that. An interpretive dance, the most cogent themes of which are vanity and paranoia.

At the moment, the dance has turned grotesque, compliments of The Emptying of the Bowels. Becoming woozy from the pungent stink, Jipt reaches back and flushes the toilet. The proverbial mercy flush. Then he takes a bowl of potpourri from the gigantic oak wall unit behind him and lights some of the bark and flower petals with a match, being careful to blow them out quickly afterward. The good news is that this helps dissipate the foul, gassy odor. The bad news is that he's not yet taken his final bow to the audience – in this case, nature itself.

Ever since switching to a largely vegetarian diet, including tofu and various other soybean-based delicacies, his gastrointestinal system has been appallingly out of kilter. However, it has afforded him idle time to work against other items on his daily personal hygiene checklist. The Clipping of the Nails, the Plucking of the Eyebrows, the Trimming of the Ear-Hair and so on. And he's needed all the extra time he can get, due to the inevitable cracks, crevices, wrinkles and folds that have developed with age – on his face and neck alone.

However, at the moment, he's merely staring blankly out the window at The Pyramid. And unlike the views enjoyed by most PyraVegas residents, his is unobstructed thanks to his mansion being perched on a hill of excavated earth from The Pyramid's foundation.

"Seth?" Lynette calls from the other side of the door. "It's been over an hour. What are you doing in there? Tell me your not … doing the deed again."

"I'm taking a squat. So I'd appreciate some—"

"I'm coming in then." Lynette barges in, all dressed up in heels and pearls for one of her First Lady's Luncheons – basically glorified sewing circles for well-to-do housewives. At 58, her natural beauty still shows, although the hair dye and liposuction help, too.

"Christ Lynette, we've got five other bathrooms …"

"There he is, the mayor, sitting on his throne. I don't get you, Seth. You're back in the big time again, what you've been wanting for the past 20 years, and now you're shitting it away … literally."

Jipt gets up in a huff and buckles his trousers. "But it's not on my terms, Lynette. I mean, goddamn it, I'm out here dealing with political bullshit all day long and—"

"Not all day long," Lynette retorts with a puckered brow, fanning the air in front of her.

Jipt ignores her, pointing at The Pyramid and continuing, "And that son of a bitch is living high on the hog up there, siphoning off half of the daily take for his little philanthropy project. It's official now. The *inhabitants* moved in yesterday." He makes quotes in the air around *inhabitants*, which is uncharacteristic, and comes as a surprise to him.

Lynette, on the other hand, cakes on another layer of mascara at the brightly lit, double-sink vanity, listening with an air of insouciance. "Bitch, bitch, bitch. Listen to you. I tell you what Seth, I think this opportunity came along ten years too late. You've lost your edge."

"What the hell do you know?"

"Well, I know you control the purse strings. The airport and the train station, for starters. And I know that your constituents are the ones who schlep to that casino every day to work. For god's sake, if it weren't for you, that thing never would've been built in the first place."

"I'm sure he would have found another way. For chrissakes, with as many gizmos as he's prolly got up there, it's a wonder he ain't making water out of air!"

"Now you're babbling. Just think about it, Seth. You've got this guy's nuts in a vice and you don't even know it."

"Oh, yeah, you've really got it all figgered out. What am I supposed to do, blackmail the guy?"

Lynette continues applying makeup for a moment or two before shrugging her shoulders.

"Are you kiddin' me? It'd be a goddamned public relations—"

"There you go again, babbling. Maybe you've been breathing too much of your own poison gas."

"It's from your goddamned diet!" Jipt yells.

"I won't even dignify that with a response because you know I know what's best for you. Now listen. Why do I always have to spell everything out lately? You're not snorting coke, are you?"

"For chrissakes, no."

"All right," Lynette says, raising the pitch in her voice as if she only half-believes him. "Maybe you just need some vitamins or something."

"Yeah, next thing you know you'll be feeding me tree bark and acorns and crap."

"The Union, Seth. The answer is The Union."

"Huh?"

"You don't blackmail Ginn, you get The Union to do it for you, dummy."

"The Union? That's your big idea? Their left hand doesn't know what the right's doing. Useless."

"Speaking of hands," Lynette says, tipping her bulbous hairdo in the general direction of the other sink, while finishing her lipstick.

"I'm washing them, I just—"

"Like to use *this* sink."

"Yeah," Jipt roars, covering his anal retentiveness with unjustified anger.

"Well, by all means then," Lynette says, sliding down to the next sink and washing her own hands. "Like I said, you're losing it."

"Hell, The Union can't even organize around a piddling issue like reserved seats on the train for crying out loud."

"Wrong again, toilet boy. They've had those for over a month now."

"What difference does it make? That's what I'm saying. They can't get together on any big issues."

"They've got crummy leadership."

"Exactly," Jipt says, naïvely thinking they might end the argument on common ground.

"So fix it," Lynette says. "Start grooming somebody for the job. Like this woman who pushed the seat issue through. Sylvia King I think her name is. She's black you know."

"Great, so she can really rile up the crowds, is that what you're saying?"

"Well, most of The Union is minority, isn't it?"

"And why would I want to strengthen The Union, anyway? So I can cause headaches for myself down the road? So they can demand goddamned silk pillows to sit on?"

"See, you're missing the big picture again. That's not what they really want."

"They've already got the highest wages and benefits in the world. Well, adjusted to cost of living."

"That's not it either. It's staring you right in the face."

"The Pyramid. They want to live in The Pyramid," Jipt says, trying to seem like he's known all along.

"Thank God, at least you have one brain cell left."

"But again, I don't see how that helps me."

"Helps us," Lynette is quick to correct him. "You said yourself, all Ginn really cares about is his philanthropy project, right?"

"Right."

"Well then, that's what you threaten to take away from him."

Chapter 11

The final bell rings at New Bristol Preparatory School as students in grades six through twelve pour into the hallway. They are dressed in the traditional English prep style – white Oxfords and navy blazers for the boys, navy skirts for the girls.

Anna Shcherbakov, a tenth grader, is among them. Anna is mature for her age, both physically and cognitively, and her golden blond hair serves as a beacon for the opposite sex, a breed she considers altogether heathen and loathsome at this stage in life. As usual, a few of these genetic deviants are waiting to assail her with their revolting displays of chest-puffery. She opens her locker and loads books into her satchel, paying no mind to the hovering jock and his sidekick.

The girls who occupy the neighboring lockers then arrive, a flamboyant redhead and a brunette with glasses, and they make some flirtatious gestures toward the boys, tossing their hair about and so on. Unlike Anna, they have hiked their skirts up past the knee in an effort to make themselves more beguiling.

"Hey ladies. Anna," the jock says. "I was wondering if you could tutor me in *French* this afternoon … at my place. Ha!" He makes the word French sound dirty as he looks to his sidekick for approval.

"Okay, here's your first lesson. *Si vous ne partez pas, je vous introduirai l'estomac*," Anna says, in a perfect French accent.

The jock looks puzzled and turns to his sidekick, who, by virtue of being a sidekick, is smarter but not as good-looking as his buddy. "What'd she say?"

"That if you don't get lost she's gonna—"

Anna punches him in the gut. Hard. The sidekick laughs, as sidekicks are wont to do. "Punch you in the stomach. Ha!"

"Bitch."

"Drop dead."

The jock smirks, as if this exchange has somehow furthered his cause, and leads his sidekick off down the hallway in search of weaklings to persecute.

"What's your problem?" the redhead says, "Todd is like the hottest guy in school."

"Yeah," the brunette adds, "I heard he, like, dated a girl from NYU last summer."

"Whatever. He's an asshole."

"Oh, I forgot, you already have a boyfriend – little Tim Ginn!"

The girls have a laugh at Anna's expense.

"Don't be stupid. I look after him, that's all," Anna says, defensively.

"I heard he, like, plays with himself in class – he can do it without using his hands!"

"I heard his dad is, like, a magician or something."

"Yeah, and he has big orgies and stuff."

Anna slams her locker shut. "Where'd you hear that, from your mom?" She turns and walks briskly away from the girls, who roll their eyes and exchange *whatever* expressions.

* * *

In front of the school, a sixth-grade boy sits on the sidewalk, clearly isolated from the other students, with his back against the wall of the building. This is Tim Ginn. He is small for his age, his hair is tousled and his clothes look roughed-up. He is oblivious to the laughing and shouting around him, as he draws intently in a spiral-bound notebook.

Anna emerges from the school, disregarding the calls of yet another group of boys. She sees Tim and lightly kicks his foot as she passes by.

"Come on," she says, and Tim scrambles after her, his untied shoelaces lashing against the pavement.

* * *

Svetlana Shcherbakov stoops over her kitchen table, ironing one of Anna's shirts with the phone pinned awkwardly to her ear. She is tired and stressed but nonetheless looks beautiful in the crimson silk robe, her blond hair still wet from the shower. She speaks with a Russian accent.

"Yes, I know. I know." Her voice is naturally strong but sounds weak now, her words trailing off.

The apartment is unsuitable for dinner parties, the rooms too small and too sparsely decorated. There are no replica Faberge eggs, no ornate chandeliers, cute hand-painted *matryoshkas* or richly colored tapestries. But at least it's clean and relatively safe, which are Svetlana's chief concerns. Her pride might allow her to invite some friends round for tea, but she can't afford good tea and, besides, has no good friends apart from Lester and Chutney anyway.

"I know. Please. My paycheck is next week. Just give me one more week."

She hears the deadbolt turn and the door open in the living room, which is adjacent to the kitchen, and then the sound of Anna and Tim giggling and roughhousing.

"Next week, okay? No. I have to go."

Anna playfully pokes and tickles Tim as they enter the kitchen.

"Hey mom. Who you talking to?"

"Just a friend. Here, hang this up."

"I didn't know you had any friends."

Svetlana gives Anna a severe look, then turns to Tim.

"Hello Tim. My goodness, look at you! Have you been picked on again?"

Like his father, Tim has an English accent. "No mam."

"Liar," Anna says.

"Tim. You were, weren't you?"

"Yes, mam."

"Tell her why," Anna says. "Go on ..."

Tim shakes his head.

"They had to stand up in his class today and tell what they want to be when they grow up. Tell her what you said Tim."

"I'd rather not."

"Tell her!" Anna says again, pinching his arm.

"A pirate, mam."

"A pirate?" Svetlana says, being careful not to sound too critical. "What a silly idea. I can't imagine where you got such a silly idea as that."

Chapter 12

The prior occupant of Lester's apartment in Queens was an eccentric Mexican dwarf named Jimmy Changa, who made some notable modifications to suit his stature and his ever-changing whimsy. And since the place is a setting for scenes to follow, we will now undertake a virtual walkthrough.

Upon turning the knee-high doorknob and entering from the building's interior hallway, one finds himself in a room spacious enough to fit a couch and a chair on the narrow side and two couches end-to-end on the long side. Lester has but one couch, however, and one chair, arranged in an L-shape around a pinewood coffee table shaped like a coffin, which comes in handy for the storage of reading materials, foodstuffs and so on. This nook serves as the living room area, and is lent further charm and ambiance by a rather unique chandelier, skillfully fashioned from driftwood, sea glass and copper wire. Like the doorknob, this was installed by order of Jimmy, who evidently lacked the motivation, or the ladder, necessary to remove it.

The wall behind the couch is adorned with a colorful and exquisitely detailed seascape mural portraying a man of small stature (assumedly Jimmy himself) in knight's armor, riding a sea horse and jousting against a colossal swordfish. The wall is also peppered with yellow sticky notes, although Lester has taken some care not to obscure key elements of the fresco.

The wall opposite is stacked floor-to-ceiling with shoeboxes of different shapes and sizes, each labeled with a yellow sticky note. These labels, however, fail to disclose the contents in explicit terms such as SOCKS or LIGHT BULBS, but instead take the form of clues like FOOT PUPPETS or HOLD ABOVE HEAD TO SIMULATE A BRILLIANT IDEA. By Lester's way of thinking, this is not only jolly good fun but also a security measure, the rationale being that a burglar's eye might be caught by a box labeled WATCHES, whereas WRIST-MOUNTED SUNDIAL DESCENDANTS might be easily overlooked.

To round out the decoration in the living area, Lester has a dry-erase board mounted next to the door. The board is full of writing scrawled in various directions, but the marquee billing goes to Lester's To Do list, which reads as follows:

TO DO:
1.   BUY CRUMPET INGREDIENTS
2.   MAKE CRUMPETS
3.   EAT CRUMPETS
4.   DO NOT DIE

If one were to walk to the other end of the room, he'd find the pea-green shag carpet eventually giving way to a cheap and ill-maintained linoleum tile floor. This was once the kitchen, and still is, although the appliances have been removed in lieu of miniature counterparts that sit atop a loft in the corner. The loft is triangle-shaped to fit snugly in the corner of the room, is accessible by a bamboo ladder, and contains a miniature oven/range, refrigerator and set of cabinets and drawers. Above the lofted mini-kitchen, a mirror is positioned on an angle such that a person in the living area might take note of certain culinary techniques or simply monitor a pot of boiling water.

The sheltered area below the loft is used primarily for storage and preparation, such as the chopping of fruits or vegetables. It is cordoned off by black velvet drapes and is thus called The Velvet Cave. In an effort to underscore the appropriateness of the name even further, Lester has upholstered the cabinets with black velvet and, as a result, it is quite dark indeed, even when lit by the one 40-watt red light bulb. This creates the intended effect of an actual cave or perhaps the deep hold of a submarine, both of which please Lester very much.

There are two doors off the kitchen area, one to the side that leads to the apartment's only bathroom and one in parallel with the front door that opens into the bedroom. The bedroom is large by New York City standards but small by your average suburban standards, even for a dwarf. It contains a bunk bed amateurishly constructed out of scrap woods, with a double mattress underneath and a single one on top. The bed was intended to resemble a ship, however, it looks more like a hillbilly's backwoods shanty topped with a skull and bones flag and a large, bus-style steering wheel.

Opposite the bed is a study area with a desk – or rather, a card table – with two metal folding chairs and a miniature bookcase on top. Like the living room, the walls are pasted with numerous yellow sticky notes containing reminders like BRUSH YOUR TEETH THREE TIMES DAILY! and DON'T STARE AT THE SUN! as well as miscellaneous slogans like TWO WRONGS MINUS TWO RIGHTS EQUALS FOUR WRONGS A.K.A. BIG TROUBLE! These examples are typical, as most contain exclamation marks (in some cases, two or more). The walls are also decorated with posters of various American football stars like Paul "Mayhem" McArdle and Randy "Smokescreen" Patton – some being Tim's favorite players, and some Lester's.

The bedroom also has the apartment's only window, which leads to a fire escape and a view of the greater Rothchild Street area four stories below.

* * *

The living room resounds with the *tic-tic-tic* of fencing epees handled by two skilled swordsmen.

"Arrgh!" Lester exclaims, shuffling backward, on the defensive, pretending to be stretched to his absolute physical limit by his son. "Yes! Excellent! Parry and riposte! Good! Oh! Double attack! Take that! And that! Oh, you're too fast! Too nimble!" Lester backs up to the couch and intentionally falls onto the cushions. Then, in blocking an attack, he releases his sword as if Tim has knocked it loose with sheer power. "Oh no!"

Tim springs up on the couch and steps on his father's chest, pinning his sword to Lester's neck. "I've got you now, you scoundrel!"

"No, please! Spare me!"

"Never!" Tim says. "You're finished! Ha ha ha!"

"But remember ... I know where the treasure is."

"Where?"

Lester looks around, as if for eavesdroppers, and then says, "Come here, I'll whisper it."

Complicit in the game, Tim removes his sword from Lester's throat and, as he starts to lean closer, allows himself to be dragged down. Lester tickles him all over and they both laugh and shriek with delight.

When things settle down again, Lester says, "Never spare your foe when he's down, son. Never ... All right, I think it's somebody's bedtime."

"Story time?"

"Oh, hungry for a yarn are you? Perhaps about pirates?"

"On the high seas!"

64

Lester and Tim retire to the bedroom, and once changed into nightclothes, Lester goes to the miniature bookcase, which is no larger than a box of tissues. It contains upwards of 50 miniature volumes of Pirates! On the High Seas!, an epic micro-novel by Curtis Rhubarb McChuckumchuckum, and with his thumb and index finger Lester gingerly removes volume 18.

He climbs to the top bunk, where Tim is nestled in, and adjusts a magnifying glass that is attached to the bed frame by a spring-loaded arm. He holds the tiny book below the lens, opens it and removes the tiny bookmark. He clears his throat.

"Heh hem! Now then, let's see where we left off. Tim? You awake?"

It seems that all the swordplay has worn Tim out, as he is fast asleep with a teddy bear under his arm, smiling contentedly like no true pirate would ever do.

Chapter 13

Three weeks following Svetlana's unceremonious termination from Kriechev Laboratories – and after repeated late-night sessions marked by hush-toned, lachrymose arguments and love making – Lester and Svetlana find themselves at JFK International Airport, on the verge of parting ways for an indefinite period of time.

Their eyes are red and puffy, but now Svetlana's look is a mixture of exhaustion and placid resolution against the feelings she has taken such pains to bury deep inside her heart, where her mind cannot easily access them. Lester, in contrast, is a veritable basket case. He's the equivalent of a television band that's being tuned recklessly from station to station, except that instead of news, movies and sitcoms, each station offers a glimpse of a different emotion – agitation, frustration, hopefulness, sincerity, remorse, sadness, fear … and so on, and so on.

"Svety, please, please don't go. Please, please, please."

"It's too late. I don't want a scene in front of the children."

"I know things seem bad here, love, but it's going to blow over – just a streak of rotten luck …"

On the floor behind them, Tim and Anna play a solemn game of backgammon. Tim is too naïve to cry, Anna too proud.

"Do they have football in Russia?" Tim says.

"No," Anna says.

"That stinks."

"They have hockey and basketball and soccer though."

"You should teach them football."

"Teach it to all of Russia?"

"Maybe just to some important people, and they could teach everybody else."

"I don't know any important people. I don't know anyone except my relatives, and I haven't seen them since I was little."

"How little?"

"This big," Anna says, leaving no more than a centimeter between her thumb and index finger.

"No!"

"No, but smaller than you."

"I'm not that small anymore you know. I'm growing."

"Just make sure you grow more this way than this way," Anna says, indicating height versus girth.

The voice of the gate attendant interrupts them. "This is the final boarding call for Flight 1591 to Moscow."

Svetlana says, "My mother is picking us up at the airport. Do you want me to call you when we get there?"

Lester stares blankly at the passengers queued up at the gate.

"Come Anna. Time to say goodbye."

"Wait!" Lester says.

"Yes?"

"If you stay I'll turn myself around – I'll quit all the silliness – I promise! We'll get a nice little place and I'm sure Chutney or Ping or somebody could get us some real good paying jobs."

"Perhaps someday. Goodbye Lester."

"Wait! One more thing ... I love you, Svety."

"I love you, too," Svetlana says, unable to hold the tears back any longer.

At the same time, Anna and Tim release each other from a somewhat awkward embrace, and Anna says, "You take care of your dad, now. Keep him out of trouble. And don't let those boys bully you. Steer clear of them. And if that doesn't work, bite them."

"Okay."

"Bye kiddo."

"You're coming back soon, right?"

"Yeah, pretty soon," Anna says, misty-eyed, trying to stay strong for Tim's benefit more than her own.

"Okay, bye," Tim says sheepishly.

Svetlana turns and ushers Anna away after placing a tender kiss on Tim's forehead.

Lester wants to rush after them. He wants to grab them and hold them tight and prevent them from going. He can't, however, and not because he knows it's the wrong thing to do and that it would further upset Svetlana but because his legs won't move and his vision is helplessly blurred by the tears. All he can see is two spots of blond hair, glowing like haloes and then fading into the darkness of the tunnel.

Chapter 14

In spite of his conscious effort to forestall it, Sandeep's behavior has availed itself of a daily routine. Granted, no two days are exactly the same, filled with new encounters, new discoveries and new insights, but like everyone he has his preferences. After breakfast he typically returns to his cube, where he goes to the bathroom, brushes his teeth and lies in bed surfing the HoloVision, while Minesh sets a meandering course for the bottom of The Grid. The choice entertainment often includes cricket, game shows or historical documentaries.

Then he visits the City Level, where he likes to drive around in one of the little bumper cars, stopping every-so-often for miscellaneous errands – picking up his laundry or a can of shaving cream, for example. He delights in the fact that no one is in a hurry. No one begs for change on the sidewalk. No one insults another for minor trespasses. It's as if all the negatives of city life have been filtered out – the pollution, the filth, the car horns – while all the positives have been retained, even enhanced. The buildings are freshly painted. The windows are unbroken. The faces of passersby with nary a frown, nary a scowl or a leer, only smiles.

While hanging a right on the corner of Affability Avenue and Perspicacity Street, Southeast, Sandeep remembers the point Lester himself once made, while leading a class called The Importance of Proper Posture, Mental and Otherwise, about the trend in street names. They're all qualities, all virtues, one should emulate and strive to exemplify on a daily basis. Temperance Boulevard, Munificence

Lane, Jovial Junction. Sandeep does not know what perspicacity means, so he intends to ask Minesh.

"Minesh," Sandeep calls, but there is no response. He reaches behind him to where the electronic butler device is wedged in the plush leathery fault created at the junction of his seat. Sliding it around his belt to his right hip, Sandeep calls again, "Minesh," just as he rams the car into a woman crossing the street. The rubber bumper knocks her feet out from under her, and she rolls off the short hood, just inches from Sandeep, and onto the hard plastic street. A bag of fruit falls from her hand, a few oranges rolling to the curb.

"Oh no!" Sandeep cries, but before he can even get out of the car, the woman is surrounded by other inhabitants, who determine she's okay and help her up. "I'm so sorry, Miss. Are you okay?"

"Yes, I'm fine," the woman says.

"Is everything all right?" Minesh calls out from Sandeep's belt. "Was there some sort of an accident?"

"Yes, but it's okay," Sandeep says, remaining in the car.

"I can dispatch medical assistance if required."

"I'm okay," the woman says convincingly, brushing some invisible dust off her slacks. "It just surprised me, that's all."

"Perhaps you should see a doctor anyway," one of the bystanders says, a young man with long hair and tattoos, who looks like a musician.

"I'm a doctor," says another woman from outside the circle, whose car was heading the opposite direction as Sandeep's before the accident.

"No, really, I'm fine," the victim reasserts, taking the bag of fruit and smiling at the man who collected it for her. "Thank you."

This man is 40-ish, Vietnamese, and he smiles back at her before turning to Sandeep with lips pursed and eyebrows raised, like the cool babysitter about to dole out some rare admonishment. "You really should be more careful."

"I know, I'm sorry," Sandeep says. "I'm not used to the driving yet, because I never owned a car."

"You'll get the hang of it," the Vietnamese man says, his expression warming. "Just remember to look where you're going, okay?"

"Okay," Sandeep says, relieved that an official accident report would not be necessary. He does not want to have a record of slipshod behavior. There is no Slipshod Street and never will be, for good reason.

* * *

After finishing his business and pleasure on the City Level, Sandeep typically goes up to the Rec Level. If he could ride a bicycle, he would, but instead he drives again. He is still shaken from the accident, and focuses intently on the path ahead, steering with the utmost vigilance. And in spite of his fear of hitting another pedestrian, Sandeep enjoys himself by recalling another one of Lester's maxims – that fear should not be resisted, only ignored once its lessons are taken to heart. By this way of thinking, Sandeep knows he's being more careful. In fact, he's being as careful as can be, without sacrificing his freedom to relish the moment. He knows it's a delicate balance that must be struck, and he's getting better every day at striking it.

After yielding to oncoming traffic, Sandeep bears left at a fork in the path and rides over a bridge spanning a creek. Then the path turns right and follows the meandering water, past tennis courts and horseshoe pits, through groves of trees and even a small Japanese pagoda. Eventually he reaches one of four small ponds, where a regatta of miniature sailboats is taking place. The boats move along at a good clip, in proportion to their scale, aided by a steady cross-breeze.

Sandeep pulls off onto the grass, deciding to stop and watch for a while. He hauls himself out of the car and walks over to one of the contestants sitting on the shore. It is a man with a long, wavy beard, dressed as a Rabbi, who holds a remote control device with two levers and an antenna.

Sandeep has always subconsciously judged one's personality by the time it takes to skip over common pleasantries and get to meaningful discussion, and for this reason he has always been drawn to religious men. He's always found them as good conversationalists, fervent listeners and willing givers of advice. Not that he seeks advice at the moment, just pleasant conversation.

"Hello," Sandeep says.

"Hey there," the man says in a slight Yiddish accent. "Take a load off why don't you."

Sandeep sits on the lush grass next to the man, at an appropriate distance. "My name is Sandeep."

"Nice to meet you, Sandeep. I'm Herschel."

"Which boat is yours?"

Herschel points to a boat near the middle of the pack, rounding one of the tiny red buoys. "Number thirteen, my lucky number."

"That's strange," Sandeep says.

"Superstition, I know. But why believe it's unlucky when you have no proof? Or in my case, when you have proof to the contrary? You see, my son was once in a coma for twelve days. And on the thirteenth he woke up."

"Ah," Sandeep said. "That's great. Is he also here in The Pyramid?"

"No, I'm afraid he passed away. Later that same day, in fact."

"Oh, I'm sorry," Sandeep says awkwardly, embarrassed at his lack of sensitivity.

"Don't be," Herschel says forgivingly. "I don't regret that day because my son died, I am grateful for it because he came out of the coma. Because I got to talk to him one last time, and help him … come to terms, you know."

"It must not be easy to think that way."

"Not at first. You're right, Sandeep. But in situations like that, I've learned you just need to rationalize your choice of feelings. Stack them up like you would choices of house paint or snow tires, you know what I mean? Then and only then can you select the feeling, and the rationalization for that feeling, that's best for you in the long run. No different than choosing a religion, as a matter of fact."

"Do you still …"

"Preach the word of God? No, mostly just the word of Herschel these days, as you can tell from my rambling. I still look the part, though, I know. I don't like shopping for clothes. And besides, I couldn't imagine myself dressed any other way. It's just part of my identity, I suppose, whether I like it or not."

"But you choose to like it, yes?"

"Right. After all, it saves me time in the morning."

"You don't miss your religion though?"

"No. I mean, it's not like a watch or a pen that I misplaced. I still have my faith, I just don't teach it to others anymore," Herschel says, steering his sloop around the opposite buoy on the figure-eight racecourse. "Coming about!"

"What's that?" Sandeep says, unfamiliar with the nautical terminology.

"Coming about. That's what you say on a boat when you're turning around. So everyone knows to duck for the boom. The boom? It's the horizontal bar, there, that holds the bottom of the sail."

"Oh."

"See it swing around?"

"Yes," Sandeep says.

"Well, on a real yacht it is much faster, and heavier. It can knock you overboard like you're a bowling pin."

"Which boat is winning, anyway?"

"I think it's number five, that's Mrs. Reynolds across the way there. But we don't really keep track," Herschel says with a shrug.

"Then why does everyone go around in the same direction?"

"I don't know, to avoid collisions? That's a good question."

"Maybe because it's more relaxing that way," Sandeep conjectures. "Because you don't have to always be deciding which way to turn next."

"Mmm hmm, and you don't have to guess what others will do, either. I think you may have a point there," the Rabbi says. "Sounds like a parable of some kind, except I'm not sure what the moral would be."

"Maybe that routines are good for you," Sandeep says.

"Speaking of which, I usually eat lunch around now. There's a great little deli over in the northwest corner there. You want to join me for a bite?"

"Deli? Sure," Sandeep says, fondly recalling his job of 20 years, slicing meat and mopping the floor. So fondly, in fact, that he suffers an ephemeral pang of regret, and this surprises him. Especially because the experience was often mundane and even dismal on occasion. And what also surprises and frightens him to a certain extent is how easily The Pyramid made him forget all about it in the first place, for good or bad.

"If you'd prefer some other kind of food …"

"No, it's fine. It's just … I used to work in one, when I lived in New Jersey."

"Good memories or bad memories?" the Rabbi asks.

"Both," Sandeep admits. "And sometimes it's hard to tell them apart …"

Chapter 15

After waking up, dancing, having sex, playing tennis and eating breakfast, Svetlana and Lester typically go for a swim and a steam in the Roman-style baths. They do this to refresh and invigorate themselves, but also just to defy the old adage about eating and swimming afterwards. Next, they shower (which often entails another round of sex). Then it's off to "work," Lester to rehearsal in the Ship Room and Svetlana to The Habitat, where the chimpanzees reside.

The Ship Room is a wide-open room about the size of a large high school gymnasium or small college field house. However, there are no bleachers or basketball courts. As one might guess, the centerpiece is indeed a ship – a fetching galleon called *The Heinousmeistress*. She's a storybook pirate ship outfitted with three towering masts, a raised quarter deck at the stern and dozens of cannons lining the gunwales – as well as her namesake, a hauntingly gorgeous banshee-woman flying under the bowsprit. *The Heinousmeistress* is mounted on a series of hydraulics, and the room's floor around her is painted a deep blue with patches of white, like the sea. Curtains swirled with various shades of gray and black hang from three of the walls, an impressionist's stormy sky. The fourth wall is solid windows from floor to ceiling, but the moment Lester enters, similar curtains begin to draw over it, too. As a result, the sunlight is squeezed down to a tiny sliver, which appears to cut the ship lengthwise like a laser beam.

The ship is surrounded by four two-story-high scaffolds, as well as four giant fans capable of rotating 180 degrees. Lester is about

10 minutes late, due to a particularly enjoyable shower with Svetlana, so everyone has already assembled for rehearsal. Everyone except Tim, that is. Ping, Schnitzelhaus, Chili and Katz are positioned on different scaffolds, where they are able to control the hydraulics and the fans, as well as lights and various sound effects.

Lester parts the drapes and walks briskly around the ship from stern to bow, not bothering to inspect her hull as he normally does. But normally he's on time, as is Tim.

"Morning everyone! Sorry I'm running behind today, I really don't have any good excuse. Not one that could be shared in good taste anyway," Lester says with a devious smile.

"I thought I noticed you walking a little bowlegged this morning," Chili says with a laugh, picking up on the clues.

Squeakins emerges from behind the curtains on the windows-side, temporarily splashing a wave of light over the ships bow. "Will you be changing into wardrobe today, sir?"

"Yes, I think I will. What do you think, mates, a dressed rehearsal today?"

"Yes, good," Schnitzelhaus says, speaking for the group in his directorial capacity. "Although we're still missing our young swashbuckler."

"Any idea of Tim's whereabouts, boy?"

"He's on his way, sir. Yardley just woke him about ten minutes ago," Squeakins says, referring to Tim's computerized butler.

"He needs to stop carousing at the pub until all hours," Lester says. However, the tone of his voice betrays his disinclination to confront his son on the issue.

Squeakins does not respond, as he believes it's never a butler's place to offer opinions on personal matters, even if solicited.

"You have that costume ready?"

"Yes," Squeakins says, leading him through the curtains into the sunlight. There are racks of clothes and shelves with other assorted props, and Squeakins removes a hanger containing some pirate garb while Lester removes his shirt and pants.

"He probably went back to sleep, that slothful—"

"Hey," Tim says, bursting through the curtains behind them. "Sorry I'm late."

"Ah, there you are," Lester says. "I was about to sick the dogs on you."

"I woke up, but then I fell back asleep again."

"Mental discipline, son. Getting out of bed in the morning is all about mental discipline, especially when that three-ring circus is going inside your head, eh? There are two kinds of people in this world, son. Those who get out of bed because they have to, and those who do it because they want to. I beg you to remain in the latter category."

"What about the invalids and the shut-ins and whatnot who never get out bed at all?" Tim says.

"Don't get smart with me. You'll be punctual from now on, do you understand? You're wasting my colleagues' time, not just my time, get it?" Lester says with a hollow sense of authority.

"Yes, father," Tim says, half-hearted in his own right.

"Very well," Lester says, closing the final button on his ruffled blouse. "Let's get going now. Dressed rehearsal today!"

* * *

Lester and Tim stand aboard *The Heinousmeistress*, Lester on the quarter deck, at the helm, and Tim on the main deck, where he struggles with the heavy rigging of the mainsail.

"Now then," Lester says. "Where were we?"

"Act two, scene five," Schnitzelhaus calls from his scaffold, which is about 20 yards off the portside of the ship. "Ready?"

"Let's have it."

Like an orchestra conductor, Schnitzelhaus signals to the others and they cue the various elements of the storm. The fans begin to blow, and water pumped in front of them is dispersed into droplets like slanting rain – accompanied by a barrage of thunder and lightning. With two joysticks Chili maneuvers the ship itself via the hydraulics. Her bow rises and falls, trailed by the stern as if rolling over massive waves, and she sways about 10 degrees from side to side. Squinting into the gale, Lester grips the wheel.

"And ... action!" Schnitzelhaus says.

"Right!" Lester says. "Forgot my bloody line!"

"Weather's turning!" Katz reminds him, following along in her copy of the script.

"Weather's turning mates! We've got to stay ahead of the storm! Give me full sail, Archibald!"

"Are you bloody mad, captain?! You'll capsize her!" Tim warns.

"I'm captain of this ship, you fool! So you'll obey my orders and mind your tongue, unless you want it removed by my sword!"

Tim draws his sword, a bladeless fencing epee. "You'll have to kill me first!"

"As you wish!" Lester draws his own epee and leaps down from the quarter deck. An animated duel ensues, the momentum changing hands several times as the evenly matched swordsmen drive each other to and fro across the deck. The ship continues to roll and pitch like a giant mechanical bull and finally Tim corners Lester at the bow.

Lester attempts to climb up onto the bowsprit to gain an advantage, but he slips. Dropping his sword, he grabs hold of the arm of *The Heinousmeistress* herself, at the last second, narrowly averting a fall overboard. Tim's character is frozen, unsure of whether to let the captain perish or to save him – so he'll have the satisfaction of killing him personally.

"Leave me, Archibald! Save yourself before it's too late!"

"No, Captain! I won't!" Tim says, dropping his sword. "Here! Take my hand!"

Lester's face contorts with mock-pain as he reaches out, and Tim pretends for a moment that he's too far away. Then, finally, he grabs hold of Lester's hand and pulls him up onto the deck. Lester executes a dramatic collapse and Tim kneels beside him, still clutching his hand.

"Captain Goodfellow!"

In a quick reversal, Lester is suddenly on top of Tim, holding a dagger to his throat. "You should have killed me while you had the chance, Archibald. You bloody fool. Mutiny is not forgiven by acts of mercy aboard *The Heinousmeistress*, and thus you will have to pay the price … the ultimate price."

Just then, the ship rocks violently and Tim seizes the chance to push Lester off of him. Lester goes tumbling backward across the slick, simulated wood deck and crashes into the gunwale on the starboard side. The dagger pops loose from his hand and Tim stumbles toward it, his sword having slid even farther away. They both lunge for the dagger like it's a football lying in the end zone – and reach it at the same time. They struggle, rolling across the deck, and slam into the main mast. With a sickening thump, Lester's head actually hits first, and he pretends to slump unconscious, the rain beating against his lifeless face. Tim wrenches the dagger out of his hands and raises it high in the air. But before he can plunge it into Lester's heart, there's a flash of light – much more intense than the other lightning – followed immediately by a deafening crash of thunder.

"Aaaah!" Tim bellows, his body seizing from the make-believe jolt of electricity. The dagger falls from his hand, clattering harmlessly to the deck, and Tim collapses on top of Lester.

"Cut!" Schnitzelhaus yells. The storm ceases all at once, and the ship comes to rest in its original position.

"Ouch," Lester says, rubbing his head. "I hope you got all that."

"What do you mean?" Schnitzelhaus says. "It was fantastic, but ..."

"We don't actually have any cameras, do we?"

"No. It's a play, not a film."

"Right, too bloody bad." Lester says, letting his head fall back to the deck with a *thud*.

Chapter 16

Technically speaking, The Habitat is a 1.1-acre scientific complex located just above the line of demarcation (separating The Grid from the Upper Echelon). It was built especially for Svetlana and five chimpanzees, who include Gabby, one of Svetlana's old friends, now a 36-year-old female acquired via special arrangement from the Moscow zoo; Dominique, a 13-year-old female and former institutionalized lab chimp, donated by the French Government as some sort of twisted diplomatic olive branch; and three male chimps who have been together since birth – Banga (meaning Sword) Escobar, 29; Njanu (Young Bull) Gonzales, 25; and Yera (Warrior) Diaz, 21 – who share a rather deplorable past. Their life in captivity began when they were plucked from the Ugandan rain forest by an intra-African coalition of thieves and smugglers (thus, their African first names). These rogues sold the chimps on the black market to the highest bidder or, as it turned out, the two highest bidders. Banga and Njanu went to a wealthy drug kingpin in Mexico, while Yera drew a terrorist group in Egypt with an affirmed hatred of western civilization as a whole. There, he was treated humanely but trained for a suicide mission – to kill thousands of foreign tourists around the Great Pyramid at Giza. But before the plan could be executed, he escaped.

Yera was captured by the Egyptian government and allocated to a defunct state program run by a corrupt technocrat, who then reinserted the 15-year-old chimp into the black market. Within days he sold to the same Mexican drug kingpin who bought his childhood mates, and who was indeed a savvy patron of the black market. In spite of his day job, he was not a wholly impious man either, just naïve, as he tried to care for the chimps as ordinary house pets. However, their wild behavior and his wild temperament ensured this arrangement would be short-lived. They were essentially prisoners. In fact, Banga and Njadu, now called Escobar and Gonzales, had been relegated to cages for 20-plus hours a day – long before Yera (renamed Diaz) even arrived. In protest of their detention in the cramped, dirty jail cells, the chimps made a tremendous racket at all hours, and the kingpin tortured them for it, causing them to make more noise. And thus, the vicious cycle of abuse began.

But luckily for the three chimps, the cycle ended when an anti-government guerrilla group (oddly enough) captured the kingpin, executed him and stole all his drugs and money, along with the chimps. They were brought to a remote camp situated in a jungle that was not terribly unlike their Ugandan home. Unfortunately, their heavy shackles and chains prevented them from enjoying the fruits, so to speak, of this environment. That is, until Diaz hatched yet another escape plan – this time taking Escobar and Gonzales with him.

Having heard stories about these ill-fated chimps – and assuming it wouldn't be long before they fell into the wrong hands again – a dedicated and well-intentioned American animal rights group found the chimps. However, not having the funds or expertise to care for the chimps themselves, they transferred them to the Bronx Zoo. It seemed like a judicious decision at the time, but the traumatized chimps stirred up trouble from day one. They ganged up on the other chimps, fighting viciously, and also showed aggressive behavior with the zookeepers – the last straw coming when Diaz literally bit the hand that fed him.

So then it became a matter of what to do with them, of who would take them. Other zoos weren't interested, nor was the entertainment industry, and the zoo refused to sell them into laboratory research or to private owners – which basically left Svetlana, who was somewhere in between the two. And considering she had the means to build a customized home for them – and offer a half-million-dollar grant to zoo on top of that – the negotiation process amounted to little more than a handshake and a toast of champagne.

* * *

Of The Habitat's vegetation, approximately half is real, the other half quite realistic, but fake. And the real trees, shrubs and mosses of course need light to sustain themselves, so The Habitat has been built long and narrow to afford maximum window exposure. However, in order to maintain even a half-real, simulated rain forest environment, the vast majority of the light must come from above. This way, the fruit trees get the high quantity they need, and the layers below – the shrubberies and mosses and such – get the smaller quantities they need. So in order to make this happen, The Habitat has been designed in a very specific and ingenious manner.

Imagine The Habitat as a cross-section – a right triangle, only a few units from isosceles (39 degrees at the base), about 50 meters tall at it's highest point. Now, starting about half way up that vertical wall, draw a horizontal line. When it reaches the hypotenuse (the windows), drop it to the base, so you have an inscribed rectangle bordered by two equivalent triangles. That rectangle constitutes the habitat area itself, where the chimps and the vegetation live. The triangle directly above the habitat has mirrors on its vertical wall, which rotate with the sun to deflect the maximum amount of radiation down through the canopy. And the other triangle offers a convenient, well-lit observation area to aid Svetlana in her studies. This area is called The Laboratory. However, in this case the term carries no burden of clinical, or otherwise malicious, connotations. It is more of an observatory, but the term Laboratory merely implies that data is not only being collected but processed and theorized-upon as well. With any luck, conclusions may even be drawn.

Svetlana makes use of an aerial lift, similar to those used in industrial settings, so that she can get as close as possible to the chimps when they're high in the trees. The machine consists of a wheeled chassis that supports a platform, and this platform can be raised up to 20 meters in the air using a hydraulically driven, scissor-style arm that expands like an accordion.

Svetlana has the platform extended to its maximum height, and from her vantage point she can see Gabby and Dominique perched high in a date tree, grooming each other. She sits atop the platform, at a desk, in front of a laptop computer, typing various measurements and observations into a spreadsheet. Thanks to streaming digital video, she knows that "the boys" are roughhousing and eating down below, about 100 meters away.

This is only the second day that the chain-link curtain has been open, which had previously divided The Habitat in two – and segregated the boys and girls. No altercations have occurred between the groups, thus far, to Svetlana's great relief. But she has fitted all five chimps with unobtrusive ankle bracelets that, when activated, can deliver a non-lethal dose of electricity. In fact, Svetlana tested one of the bracelets herself, which was part exercise in safety and part lesson in responsibility. In other words, she knows it won't kill them but that it hurts like hell, the theory being that she'll refrain from pressing the button unless truly dire circumstances arise – if one chimp were on the verge of killing another, for example, which is not at all uncommon in the wild.

In spite of their surprisingly rapid acclimation to The Habitat, Svetlana remains quite wary of the boys. Yet, at the same time, she understands that mistrust is the principal root of their pent-up hostility. Her goal is to build trust one step at a time, one day at a time, until she feels comfortable approaching them in their own territory. She is in the process of acting out this scenario in her mind – how she will remain calm and offer gifts of fruit – when Chutney surprises her from below.

"Hello up there! Svetlana!" Chutney says.

"Hello, I didn't hear you come in," Svetlana replies, throwing a lever that starts the platform on a gradual decent.

"Sorry to bother you again, but I wondered if I might loiter a bit, you know, watch the chimps for a while."

"Of course, Chutney, be my guest," Svetlana says. "They are fascinating, aren't they?"

"Utterly. It strikes me as odd, that I've spent most of my career studying human behavior and the dynamics of human society, without even thinking of our origins. I mean, that's rather an oversight, isn't it?"

"Maybe we should write a book together," Svetlana says, hopping off the platform as it comes to rest. "I'm amazed at how much of myself I see in them. Especially Gabby, with her protective ways. She seems to have adopted Dominique as a daughter or a niece."

"That's them up there?" Chutney points.

"Yes, they're so adorable …"

"How about you?" Chutney shifts her tone. "It's awful I haven't been able to see you much, I've been so busy. First getting ready for the inhabitants, and then, you know … I can't believe we've been here almost three months already. So how have you been getting on?"

"Great," Svetlana says without a trace of unease. "Just great. This place is so incredible, you know? Like some sort of fairytale kingdom."

"With it's fairytale king," Chutney says, unable to resist the lighthearted jab at Lester.

"Yes ... but he doesn't like to think of himself that way, thank goodness."

"Oh, I know, I was just—"

"I don't want to be a queen, Chutney. Just a scientist, a wife and a mother."

"Well, I'd say you're doing a smash-up job at all three."

"That's good, right? Smash-up?"

"Yes, of course."

"Thank you. After so many years with Lester, I still forget some of the English expressions ... Well, what do you say we try and find the boys?"

* * *

"Can they see us?" Chutney asks, approaching the glass.

"No, it's a mirror on the inside."

"Who's who?"

"That's Gonzales grooming Escobar. And that's Diaz over there by himself."

"Escobar is the alpha male, right?"

"Yes, he's the largest and the oldest. As you can see, he has the loyalty of Gonzales. But Diaz is a little more rebellious."

"They don't like each other?"

"I don't know how much personality has to do with it. It's more of a power issue, I think. They fight sometimes, but all for show so far. Kind of a mind game, you know?"

"Kind of like when boxers feel each other out in the early rounds, perhaps."

"I don't know much about boxing, but that sounds possible."

"I don't know much about boxing either, come to think of it. He looks rather menacing," Chutney observes, as Diaz scampers part way up a tree, swings on a branch to an adjacent tree and then leaps back to the ground.

"Watch," Svetlana says. "I think he may charge."

Diaz indeed appears agitated, bearing his teeth and beating the ground, while looking in the direction of Escobar and Gonzales. But he doesn't charge. Instead, he runs up the tree again, making a loop similar to before.

"Well, maybe not," Svetlana says, making some notes on a small pad, to be incorporated in her spreadsheets later. "I'm glad, actually. He's been picking on Gonzales a lot lately, trying to impose his own authority. The next step may be to challenge Escobar directly for the alpha position."

"Are you afraid they'll hurt each other?"

"A little, yes," Svetlana says, looking up from her notes to make solid eye contact with Chutney. "The alpha male will not usually step aside for a rival."

"So the only way to unseat him ..."

"Is by violent force," Svetlana finishes, pursing her lips and not wanting to utter more forbidding words like *maim* or *kill*, for reasons of superstition.

Chapter 17

Tim writhes in ecstasy on his back as Anna's pigtails bounce, swing and flip above him, like rope ladders dropped from a gyrating rescue helicopter. She is doing all the work, eyes closed, head tilted back, and this suits him just fine because he loves to watch her. He reaches out and cups his hands under her breasts like a corset, pushing them up and together. During the construction period he had sex with a few random PyraVegas girls, but it was nothing like this. Right now he couldn't spell his own name, much less hers.

"Ah! Ah! Aaaaah!" she squeals, finally collapsing on top of him. Her skin is hot and covered with gleaming rivulets of sweat. Her eyes are still closed, and she's panting lightly on Tim's neck. He runs his fingertips down her spine and she shivers.

"I love you," he whispers.

"No you don't," Anna replies matter-of-factly, also whispering.

"Yes I do."

"No, you don't," Anna says with more emphasis, rolling off of him.

"Whoa!" Tim cries, unable to bear the post-coital sensitivity. "Hey, what'd you do that for?"

"I should say the same to you," Anna says, wrapping herself in a white terrycloth robe.

"What do you mean?"

Anna paces across the bedroom to the wall of windows and stares out at the sun-drenched cityscape of PyraVegas. "You know what I mean. I thought we had an understanding."

"I don't remember agreeing to anything."

"Not an agreement, an understanding. Unspoken. Apparently not, though."

"But I do love you."

"See? There you go again. Do you want to ruin everything? Is that what you want? To impose a whole new set of protocols on our relationship?"

"Protocols? Uh … no."

"Well, that's what you're doing."

"Anna, come on. You love me, too, so what's the big deal?"

"The big deal is … I don't know, this just doesn't feel right anymore."

"It felt right a couple minutes ago," Tim says sardonically.

Anna turns to face him, her arms crossed in a gesture of stubbornness. "Tim. We can't just forget who we are, you know?"

Tim slips on a pair of boxer shorts decorated with cartoon monkeys and approaches Anna with open arms. "Sure we can. Come here."

She shies away at first, as if unwilling to gloss everything over so easily, then she submits to a long embrace. "It's complicated."

"So? What's the difference if we love each other?"

"It's just that … there are different kinds of love, Tim."

"And …"

"And I'm worried that we're mixing them up. I mean, brothers and sisters don't—"

"Hey, hey, hey," Tim says, taking a step back. "Let's not go there. Technically we're not."

"We might as well be," Anna says, pulling back even further and turning her back again.

"So you don't love me in a romantic, man and woman sense, is that what you're saying?"

"No. Well, yes … maybe. I don't know, I just don't know!" Anna says in frustration, running and flopping onto the bed. She buries her face in a pillow.

Tim has never seen her in this state before, and is unsure of his next move. Indeed, things have become more complicated. He cannot help but compare the situation to a chess match, except one that he's trying to lose without being obvious about it. Luckily, he has some expertise in this area, having eclipsed his father's superiority some years ago and, thus, having his victory soured one too many times by Lester's tantrums. However, unlike chess, he has no prior experience in this particular game, and cannot even conceive of all the possible moves.

He sits down on the bed next to Anna and tickles her ear with the end of a pigtail. She swats it away like a fly.

"Anna?" he says. No response. "Anna, it seems like you're thinking about this too much, you know? That's why you're mixed up. I mean, it's like … it's like that movie we saw about the two blokes and the dolphin? What was it called?"

"Porpoise," Anna says into the pillow.

"Porpoise, right, not a dolphin. What was it called?"

"Porpoise!" Anna repeats. Tim can never remember the titles of books or movies and it drives her crazy.

"Right, right. I don't see why they always have to have those simplistic titles. Anyway, you know how the scientist bloke was always having those dreams that he was a baby porpoise? And the porpoise was having dreams of being a baby human? But the fisherman guy—"

"They weren't dreams, they were flashbacks."

"Huh?"

Anna turns over. Her face is red, but she's no longer crying. "They were flashbacks to their previous lives. The man was a porpoise and the porpoise was a man."

"Bollocks!"

"Tim, don't you remember? The fisherman died trying to save the porpoise caught in his net."

"So?"

"That was the scientist."

"What? I thought the fisherman was the scientist's father."

"Never mind. What's your point, anyway?" Anna says.

"My point is that it's bloody confusing! You could look at it as a nice buddy story about a guy and a porpoise, but then when you overanalyze it—"

"I'm not overanalyzing it. I just understand what it was about."

"Fine. But I think you're overanalyzing your feelings," Tim says.

"They're feelings. They are what they are, Tim."

"Right, but I don't see why you can't just ignore the complicated ones. I don't see why we can't just go on the way we've been going."

"We just can't."

"We can't?"

"Not right now. Not until we sort everything out."

"I just don't see what there is to sort out."

"Well …"

"You care about me, right?" Tim says, his eyes widening expectantly. "Like, if I was tied up on the train tracks and a train was bearing down on me, you'd be scared, right?"

"Yes, of course."

"And you like being with me, right? Doing stuff together?"

"Yes, of course, Tim."

"We have fun."

"Yes."

"And this bedroom stuff …"

"Yes, it's also fun."

"So what's the problem?"

"Tim … how can I put this? Okay. Remember the time we found that big box full of light bulbs and dropped them off the fire escape?"

"Yeah, that was fun."

"It was, I agree. But it wasn't fun anymore when we got in trouble."

"No."

"You remember why we got in trouble?"

"Because they weren't our light bulbs and that lady's dog hurt his paw on the broken glass. I don't see how this is relevant."

"We didn't think about the consequences. We need to think about the possible consequences of what we're doing."

"But we've already done it. What are you saying, that we should buy new light bulbs and sweep up all the broken glass?"

"I'm not sure that analogy makes sense anymore. All I'm saying is that we take a step back and think everything out before it's too late."

"What do you mean, too late?"

Anna props herself up on an elbow and takes one of Tim's hands in hers. "Think about it, Tim. Boyfriends and girlfriends break up, right?"

"Yeah, but—"

"No buts. It happens all the time. Marriages end in divorce all the time. Couples turn against each other. I don't know how it happens, but it does, and to good people. Look at my mom, look at Chutney, look at Chili, the list goes on and on."

"But we're different."

"Are we? How?"

"I don't know, we just are," Tim says, looking blankly past Anna, out the window.

"It's a risk, Tim. I'm just saying we need to think long and hard about it, whether it's worth risking everything we have together."

Tim looks at her again, this time with spite in his eyes. "Fine. You just let me know when you've thought about it," he says, pulling his hand free and storming out of the bedroom.

Anna does not call after him or succumb to any outbursts of emotion, yet her expression betrays a forlorn lover and also a concerned older sister. She lets her head fall back onto the pillow and closes her eyes, imagining a school of porpoises arching over the water, without a care in the world aside from being eaten alive.

Chapter 18

To say everything in the Upper Echelon is strictly off-limits to the inhabitants would not be entirely true (which is why that has not been said). By docking at a special station at the top of The Grid, one can take a special elevator to the Complaint Confessional, an amalgamated replica of the "sin bins" made both famous and infamous by the Catholic Church. However, as the name implies, one does not confess sins in the Complaint Confessional. He or she confesses complaints, gripes, protests, criticisms and suggestions. In other words, it's just a fancy, ritualistic and grossly inefficient customer service line. Lester himself presides over the Confessional, holding office hours for at least one hour per day, on average.

He doles out all sorts of advice through that mesh screen. More advice than forgiveness or apology, without question, as he has yet to concede a Pyramid-wide solution to any individual problems, even when they recur often. Today's confessors include a single, black, middle-aged man who argues there's a shortage of eligible women in the inhabitant population. It's a relatively common complaint. The demographics had been intentionally weighted toward couples with no children, or those with qualifying children who were fully grown. And the single inhabitants were screened for their attitudes toward love and marriage. Many of those chosen were the solitary types – the individualists, the scholars and the asexuals to name a few – who desire to go through life unfettered by the intimate needs of other human beings. Perhaps some of their attitudes have changed. Either that or they lied on their questionnaires.

"Did you answer the questionnaire truthfully?"

"Yes, but—"

"That's quite all right, as long as you were truthful. Often, in life, the attainment of certain things makes us wish to attain other things, wouldn't you agree?"

"Yes," the man says, sounding gracious for his empathy. Apparently Lester's reputation for impatience has preceded him.

"Of course you would. It's only natural. Would you consider yourself a handsome man?"

"Well ... no. I got acne pretty bad."

"Still? At your age? How old are you?"

"Forty-one."

"Poor bastard," Lester mutters.

"I beg your pardon?"

"Huh? Right. Well, I'll see what I can do about making some acne treatment available. In the meantime, I suggest you masturbate more often. Do you masturbate currently?"

"Maybe once a week."

"That's inadequate. I'd strongly recommend you intensify your regimen to once a day, perhaps first thing in the morning and before you go to sleep at night."

"Wouldn't that be twice a day?"

"Yes, now that you mention it, twice a day would be better."

"Only problem is, sometimes it's hard for me to ..."

"Hmm, I see. Well, there's some spectacular adult programming available on the HoloVision. I'm not a big fan of it myself, but it does seem to have wide appeal."

"They've got porno movies?"

"Yes, of course, anything you can think of. Just ask your butler about it. No need to be bashful, he's just a computer, programmed not to pass judgment."

"Okay, I'll give it a try. Thank you, Lester."

"You're welcome. By the way, I couldn't help but notice you used the phrase, I beg your pardon, earlier."

"Yeah, I guess I did. I'm sorry if—"

"No no, don't be sorry. I'm sure you meant it colloquially. But all the same, please do not make a practice of begging. No pardons will be granted, because that would be tantamount to quitting, wouldn't it?"

"I don't know, I guess."

"Well, you'll just have to trust me. You're not a quitter, are you?"

"No, Lester, I didn't mean—"

"I know you didn't," Lester says, resuming the clerical tone. I'm simply making a point. Now get out of here. Go have some fun."

Then there's the woman who complains about being deprived of her favorite brand name products, such as "Fizz-o-licious" Diet Fizzo Cola and Grandma Unice's Homemade Ice Cream. Lester has noted a spike in such complaints lately, most coming from The Pyramid's older inhabitants. And not just about food. They find fault with the mattress, the sofa and the kitchen sink. Nitpicking little details, for which Lester has precious little tolerance. The woman continues naming products, evidently reading from a list, and Lester interrupts her.

"Excuse me," he says. "Please, that's enough. I am not without such preferences myself. For example, I used to fancy a sort of biscuit called Whittaker's. My goodness did I love those Whittaker's. In fact, I would often catch myself saying, 'I need some Whittaker's!' We say such things all the time but it's an appallingly bad habit, isn't it? It's really quite preposterous, isn't it? I mean, you cannot possibly tell me that your health and well-being depends upon the consumption of a name brand soft drink, can you? Nor is your identity tied to it, despite what the advertisements may tell you. So I suggest the following. First, substitution. If you want a Fizzo Cola, don't have a soft drink a'tall. Instead, bake a cake, go for a walk, masturbate. Something else that makes you feel good, understand?"

"Yes, Lester, I do," she says, with the obedience of a shylock under the gun of an angry mobster.

"You appreciate the opportunity you're being given, don't you?"

"Yes, of course, Lester, I—"

"And you don't want to jeopardize that, do you? After all you've done to get here?"

"No, of course not, Lester."

"Good."

Next up is a paranoia case, a man who fears his cube will become stuck in the grid, fatally trapping him inside. Lester has been seeing about one or two of these types per week since the opening ceremonies, but this young man is particularly neurotic.

"What if I can't make it to a Replenishing Station in time?" he says in a Boston accent.

"Your cube is programmed to automatically find the nearest station, with plenty of time to spare."

"But what if something happens and the batteries run down or I run out of water or something?"

"In the case of emergency, you can draw power directly from the grid, or a Mobile Replenishing Station can be dispatched to you."

"Really?"

"Yes, there's nothing a'tall to worry about."

"What if I run out of air?"

"Well, you don't have a tank of air, or anything like that, remember? Air passes through vents on the exterior of the grid and then on your cube itself. Unless the earth's atmosphere ceiling becomes lower than a mile – well, about half a mile for you – then there shouldn't be a problem."

"The earth's atmosphere is getting lower?"

"My heavens, no, I was just making an example, perhaps a sloppy one. Everything's just fine. However, you may want to visit the apocethary and ask for something to cheer you up a bit. Either that, or try masturbating more often."

Chapter 19

Seth Jipt's office high atop the Fortuna Hotel and Casino in Atlantic City, New Jersey, looks as if it were posthumously co-decorated by a French king and an American frontiersman. The place is chockablock with marble statues, crystal chandeliers, burled walnut furniture and dead animals, from elk to walleyed pike.

At the moment, Jipt stands in front of the gold-framed mirror in his private bathroom. Although he has several dozen tubes in reserve, he is determined to tap every last dollop of toothpaste from this particular tube, so he lays it flat on the vanity and works it over with the titanium handle of his cordless electric toothbrush, squeezing out another acceptable portion. He returns the tube to its drawer, confident that it's good for another two or three applications, and then brushes his teeth with the meticulousness of a savant, a process that takes about five minutes.

Indeed, he is afflicted with a compulsive nature with regard to the teeth brushing, and to personal hygiene in general, as he spends a solid three or four hours a day in the bathroom. By his way of thinking, it's a battle with many fronts, requiring almost round-the-clock attention – brushing, flossing and whitening of the teeth, shaving of the face, brushing of the hair, trimming of the fingernails and toenails (he secretly obtains manicures and pedicures on a regular basis), and washing of the hands, not to mention eyebrow and nose hair and knuckle hair maintenance.

Someone is knocking on the door of his main office, so he quickly rinses out his mouth, wipes away the remnants of toothpaste with a delicately embroidered hand towel and returns to his desk. He figures it's probably just Hawkins, but if not, he wants to create the illusion that he's hard at work.

"Hey Seth! You in there?" Hawkins says through the thick oak door.

"Come on in."

Tommy Hawkins is Jipt's right-hand man. At 40, he's very similar to the person Jipt was fifteen years earlier, except that he benefits more from his intellect and easy-going charm than from raw political acumen and a cutthroat desire to succeed.

At six-two, Hawkins is also taller than Jipt ever was – and more handsome, his hair brown where Jipt's is gray, his complexion tan where Jipt's is ruddy.

"Hey there Seth, how you doing?" he says, pulling up a chair. He sits, placing a thick leather dossier between them, on the edge of the desk.

"Aw, could be better, Tommy … couple of goddamned Puerto Ricans took us for fifty grand this afternoon. Want a drink?"

"No, no thanks. Maybe later on. Blackjack?"

"Poker. And it's not the money – hell, that's chump change – it's the principle, damn it. We got 'em on surveillance though. If those wetbacks ever show in here again I'll personally—"

The intercom chimes on Jipt's desk. He presses the button.

"Yeah."

"Um, Mr. Jipt, Mr., um, Hawkins is here to see you," says Vicki, Jipt's secretary. She has a serious um-problem and it drives him crazy.

Jipt gives Hawkins a look, combined with a slight shaking of his head, as if to say, *Dumb bitch.*

"Well, I'm busy, Sharon."

"Vicki," Hawkins whispers.

"Vicki. Tell him to come back tomorrow."

"Yes, sir," Vicki says.

Jipt releases the button and says to Hawkins, "New girl – not too bright, that one. Nice tits though, eh?"

"Mmm," Hawkins utters with a quick nod, as to avoid egging him on.

"I mean, why do you think I hired her? Ha ha!" Jipt says for his own benefit, laughing heartily, while Hawkins forces out a chuckle to maintain airs. Then something catches his eye in the window – the lack of something, actually – and his face drops as he spins around. "Where in the hell is the goddamn ..."

"Yeah, I was going to mention that, Seth. The city said we had to take it down," Hawkins says, referring to the enormous balloon that had been tethered to the top of The Casino for the past few days, advertising their new game, Diamond Ball.

The game is Jipt's latest brainchild – basically roulette using a round, five-carat diamond in lieu of the traditional ball, which can be won by playing a nearly impossible combination of bets. The balloon was also his idea, a 100-meter-high monstrosity painted to look like a diamond, with the words DIAMOND BALL emblazoned on either side in massive silver letters.

"When?"

"This morning."

"Shit, I didn't even notice before ... The city? Why?" Jipt says, grimacing as he spins back around.

Upon breaking bad news, Hawkins always monitors Jipt closely, as he's been known to throw things. "They said it blocked out the sun."

"Well, of course it blocked out the goddamn sun! Clouds block out the sun all the time, but you don't see the city banning them!"

"You're right, Seth, it's partisan bullshit. It's pretty obvious Jerry's still pissed off about the whole campaign finance deal."

"So I gave his opponent a little more. What the hell does he expect?"

"I don't know."

"Goddamned democrats. Well, it'll be on the news tonight. More free publicity."

"Maybe you should run against him next time around," Hawkins says, half-jokingly.

Jipt rubs his chin for a moment, staring at the wall behind Hawkins, which indicates he's giving an idea serious consideration. "So, you learn anything about this Ginn character?"

"Sure did," Hawkins says, patting the dossier. He opens it and hands a stack of eight by ten photos to Jipt, who proceeds to flip through them.

Photo 1: Lester in a park amid some kind of mock courtroom setting with various other people, most homeless-looking, acting as judge, jury, etc.

Photo 2: Lester haggling with another man in front of a bus, which is painted like Air Force One – but the detail on the side says AIR HORSE ONE.

Photo 3: Lester walking down the street, making a mess of himself trying to eat a foot-long sub sandwich while carrying a briefcase.

Photo 4: Lester walking out of a porn shop with a neon sign advertising PEEP SHOWS.

Photo 5: Lester on his fire escape, squirting a water gun into his mouth.

Photo 6: Lester in a park, playing chess with a man who appears to be unconscious.

"He's Lester Eliot Ginn," Hawkins says, referring to a hand-written page. "Thirty-three, lives in Queens with his son, Timothy Finnaeus Ginn, twelve, appears to be self-employed far as I can tell. Runs some kind of seminars or something. Does some freelance editing work too – amateur plays, novels and so forth."

"What kind of seminars?"

"Self-help type stuff it sounds like. I don't know, some new age bull crap. Oh, get this. He's also a hypnotist. Graduated from Rumplestiltskin Junior College with a degree in hypnotism! Ha!"

"Hmm, sounds like a damned loon to me ... well how much is the son of a bitch worth?"

"That's the kicker," Hawkins says, shuffling to some photocopied bank statements. "He's got nothing far as I can tell ... less than a thousand bucks here and no offshore accounts that showed up on the report."

"How about family?"

"None that I could track down. His father was a pretty renowned officer in the Royal English Navy, but he's been dead over fifteen years."

"Hmm. Associates?"

"Well, he's got a girlfriend – at least a gal I'm assuming is his girlfriend, but she's even more broke than Ginn. Her name's Svetlana Shcher-bak-ov or something or other. Russian. Works for Kriechev Laboratories as some sort of a lab tech. Got a daughter of her own who goes to school with Ginn's boy. She's not the mother of Ginn's boy, though – mother's name was Richards, died in childbirth."

"What about her family, the Richards girl?"

"Nothing. They're over in England. Just regular blue collar Brits. Anyway, then there's this group of folks he meets up with pretty often. There's five of 'em, and these folks are pretty interesting."

Hawkins leans over and prompts Jipt to shuffle forward to a photo of the Visionaries in front of the Golden Horseshoe Bar.

"There they are. Go ahead and flip forward, I got some close-ups."

Jipt flips to a photo of Ping. "How about you, Tommy! Quite the shutterbug."

"Thank you. I shot for the school paper back at AU. That's Wong Ping, doctor of mechanical engineering, astrophysics and several other fields of engineering and mathematics. A real brainiac. Worked for NASA until recently – now he's a free agent. Go ahead."

Jipt flips to a photo of Katz.

"Patricia Katz, doctor of computer science. Runs a consulting firm based in Germany but she's got some big clients here. Not sure how active she is in the day-to-day business though."

Jipt flips to a photo of Chili.

"Chili Brown, doctor of economics and music theory. Also has a law degree. Professor at Columbia. Used to be quite the basketball star for G-town."

Jipt flips to a photo of Schnitzelhaus.

"Helmut Schnitzelhaus—"

"Let me guess, a goddamned doctor."

"Of architecture and materials science. Designed that new museum in Seattle, you heard of it? The one that looks like a spaceship? Anyway, he's pretty well-respected in those circles evidently – been on the lecture junket for a couple years far as I can tell."

Jipt flips to a photo of Chutney and whistles as if to say, *Wow, she's good looking.*

"Tell me about it," Hawkins says. "Madeline Chutney, British ex-pat, doctor of sociology and author of numerous books – most about Socialism."

"She's a goddamned commie?"

"Socialist."

"What's the difference?"

"Not sure."

"Well, I don't care if he's got a doctor of spitting in the air and catching it! Where's the money coming from?! Tell me that!"

"Well, as brilliant as all these folks appear, none seems to have been able to amass any great wealth. Maybe he's got silent partners out there somewhere."

"Hmm," Jipt muses, picking at one of his cuticles. "Well, only one way to run this thing to ground."

He presses the intercom button.

"Vicki?"

"Um, yes, Mr. Jipt?"

"We need to get a man named Lester Ginn in here ASAP. Mr. Hawkins will give you all the info on his way out."

"But I thought—"

Jipt releases the button, cutting her off before the inevitable "um."

"Is it even possible to build a pyramid one mile high?" Jipt says.

"I don't know Seth," Hawkins says, closing the dossier. "But I won't lie to you, I sure am curious to find out. Assuming we have a piece of the action of course."

"Mmm hmm," Jipt says. "I reckon we might need more than a little piece though ..."

Chapter 20

Lester is quite pleased with his first attendee, who has followed his instructions by displaying her nametag at breast level. It reads: HELLO, MY NAME IS MS. BO PEEP. Lester greets her in character of the portentous, ultra-charming English game show host, who just-so-happens to be wearing an Italian suit purchased in Vietnam — or rather, bartered-for in Vietnam with illegally imported dried halibut snacks (quite salty).

"Well hello … Ms. Bo Peep! Fantastic to see you and your lovely nametag darling, come on in. First paying guest of the night! Day! You are paying, are you not Ms. Bo Peep?"

"Oh yes," she says. "Here's my fifty dollars in cash just as you said." By her accent and appearance, she is likely Swedish or Norwegian. She can't be a breath older than 21 and has a shapely bosom nestled beneath her midriff-baring sweater.

"Well that's just ducky Ms. Bo Peep. Just ducky. Feeling limber this afternoon Ms. Bo Peep?" Lester says. He likes to start right in on the psychological fabric of his clients, regardless of age, sex or gender. Needless to say, though, sex is always appreciated.

"Why yes," she says. "I stretched thoroughly beforehand just as you said."

"Yes, indeed! Ms. Bo Peep, let's come inside now, there we are, now you just get yourself comfortable and situated over in the waiting room here and we have a delightful selection of publications for your enjoyment. I must say, that is a ravishing skirt, just short enough, and the white socks – the hair so neatly braided – I'm extraordinarily ravished right now. Let's keep the inner dialogue true to its namesake please! Thank you. Now Ms. Bo Peep, recline, relax, make yourself at home. A delightful selection of publications for your edification and enjoyment."

"Thank you."

"How about something to refresh you? Some libation perhaps, yes? A cocktail as they say? I've got just the thing for you! Liquid Velvet Number … Five!"

"Why yes, that sounds wonderful, thank you."

As Lester prances off to the Velvet Cave Ms. Bo Peep takes up an issue of Robotic Butler Magazine, which features a tuxedo-clad robot on the cover serving caviar and champagne from a silver platter. A few moments later, Lester parts the drapes with a flourish and appears wearing some elaborate and very bizarre headgear consisting of a tape recorder and two speakers duct-taped to an old leather football helmet. The cassette player is on top and the speakers affixed to either side like big square elephant ears. He reaches up and presses a button, which cues up some very lively bluegrass music interwoven with fiddles, banjos and slide guitars, and he dances a few steps puckishly before handing the green, frothy cocktail to Ms. Bo Peep.

"*Wah-lah*, as the Chinese say."

"Thank you, mister …"

"Ginn! So sorry! Ginn, yes," Lester says, returning with haste to the kitchen.

"Like gin and tonic?"

"Oh! Ever so close, Ms. Bo Peep. I've got an extra n though, you see. It stands for something. Can you guess? No, of course not. It stands for nothing! Ha ha! Take that as a lesson, Ms, Bo Peep. You should always stand for something, even if it's nothing."

She smiles and sips her drink.

"It's good, isn't it? Family recipe, top secret. Now then! Let's get that curry started, get the show started, eh?"

Lester turns up the music, which is really jumping now, and climbs the bamboo ladder to the kitchen, where he shuffles around on his knees and juts his head in and out like a pigeon as he attends to the business at hand. Sizzling in a wok, the garlic is dark brown and crisp so he removes it with a spatula, satisfied that its flavor has been infused into the oil.

"This is extra-virgin olive oil Ms. Bo Peep. I prefer it to the virgin. Not that there's anything wrong with virgins! And the oil, you see, has been infused with the flavor, the very essence, of the garlic and the curry. We too can become infused with things, can we not Ms. Bo Peep? Prejudices and ambitions, Mmm? Although it's better to be in-fused than con-fused, eh? Eh?!"

Lester shuffles about the kitchen with precision and grace in his mind's eye, assembling most of the remaining ingredients with a fervor only found in an individual who is undyingly indebted to something, one who is driven by a higher power or one who is just stark raving bloody mad.

"Why not electromagnets Ms. Bo Peep? For heaven's sake, the advancements these days are astounding. Scientists are working round-the-clock on identifying a solution. Not creating it, see! Identifying it. The difference is important … all these elements you see are quintessential to the underlying plan! And you, Miss Bo Peep, are equally quintessential! And perhaps soon underlying! He he! Look at this view ladies and gentlemen!"

Lester rocks back on his knees to view Ms. Bo Peep in the mirror. Ms. Bo Peep giggles because she finds Lester quite amusing despite his perplexing manner of speech, and Lester giggles also – at the sight of her fulsome breasts gyrating beneath her sweater.

"Okay now, the curry you see is so very critical in this process as well as the cooperation of the police, and hopefully the police won't just decide to knock on my door for some reason because that music is so bloody loud coming from my head, and a fiddle at that, and you're so bloody … nubile! And youthful! And they will most certainly be alerted to your erratic behavior if not mine!"

Lester has just added onions and spinach to the infused oil and is busy stirring the mixture with a wooden spoon when there's another knock at the door, this one more assertive.

"Man alive! They're fast! Could you be a peach and get that, Ms. Bo Peep? I must focus on my work. Because the work, Ms. Bo Peep, the work is what this is really all about."

"Oh yes of course!" she says with virgin-like enthusiasm. Ms. Bo Peep is downright beside herself with happiness at the opportunity to answer the door, police or no police. Hers is the brand of enthusiasm rarely seen, except in one who is either too young to know any better, a total stranger to emotional distress or cranked up on super-potent narcotics.

In this case, Lester can only hope for a combination of all three. He disappears into the Velvet Cave again and begins his sound check. He stops the tape and adjusts a football coach-style microphone in front of his mouth. His voice is now amplified at top volume through the helmet-mounted speakers. "Sin-fin-gin, grabble-doo, scriggity-rumple, stedmunjommit!" His babbling is so incoherent that some might even mistake it for a rare, even dead, language.

"Hello there," says Ms. Bo Peep after opening the door.

"Hi!" says a man in his mid-thirties, dressed casually, neatly groomed, perhaps of South American descent, no nametag. He looks Ms. Bo Peep up and down rather indiscreetly. And, as he's rather handsome himself, Ms. Bo Peep looks him up and down as well.

"Hi, come on in."

In the meantime, Lester has started the music again and becomes temporarily entwined in its flamboyant weave of sound, twisting furiously and poking at the air with his index fingers. He feels the onset of the song's finale and with one concerted effort he bursts forth, parting the velvet wildly, taking one giant stride just as this impressive crescendo occurs, fiddles and other stringed instruments all stopping in unison. He stretches his arms to either side and says, "Ladies and gentlemen! I'm so bloody happy to be playing with these men!" Then he angrily bends the flexible mouthpiece away from his face. "That's it! We're going to need more concentration out of everyone from this point forward! Is that clear? Ms. Bo Peep? Okay then." He returns the microphone to its rightful position before continuing. "It's conceivable you know that, given the right circumstances, I would be successful in — we would all be successful perhaps in … how are you today, sir?"

"Great, thank you," the man says. He is calm but visibly apprehensive. He has likely heard about Lester in the process of being referred to "The Seminar," but one can be prepared for Lester only to the extent that he might prepare to ride an angry bull without pants.

"Well then, that's great. So what do we call you sir?"

"You can call me Arturo."

"Can I call you Fantasmo?"

"I'd prefer Arturo."

"Very well then, suit yourself. Artuche, you can call her Ms. Bo Peep and me Captain Ginn," Lester says.

"Arturo."

"What did you call her?! You just shut your filthy mouth, you depraved bastard! This is a nice, innocent girl here. Are you alright, Ms. Bo Peep?" he says, caressing her shoulder.

"Yes, fine, thanks."

"Very well. Now, please make yourself comfortable Artuche, take a nametag and have a seat right over there with Ms. Bo Peep and do not grope her until I say the word. I will bring you your allotted refreshment. Liquid Velvet Number ... Two?"

"Yes, thank you Captain Ginn. And, eh, my name is Arturo?"

"Hell if I know. Oh, I see! Not Artuche, then? I rather like Artuche but if you insist. Ms. Bo Peep, would you see to it please that Horatio is made comfortable and then tied up. Tightly, but not too tightly. There is some sisal rope under the sofa cushions I believe. Very strong rope. Oh yes, and his fee of one hundred U.S. dollars. I trust you will collect that as well Ms. Bo Peep."

Lester disappears into the folds of the Velvet Cave again. He changes the tape and starts the new one playing, which is comprised of heavy blues guitar, bass, drums and harmonica. He twists his long, sinewy body all around, dancing and moving, arms whipping around like uncontrolled fire hoses. Every range of emotion in the conceivable spectrum is manifested on his face.

Lester is a human being, you see, who is exceedingly fragile of mind. In fact, the filter that contains the various frequencies of emotion bouncing around within him is tremendously thin — like the thinnest gold leaf – one atom thick. When a particularly volatile wave punches through the surface, punches out even one single atom, the result can be disastrous, like a space capsule losing pressurization and *Bam!* The whole thing implodes, then explodes as all these emotions are blasted out. The end result, as it so happens, is a state that makes him highly vulnerable to gravity.

He reels to the floor and lies motionless for some time upon the manuscript he is being paid at this very time to read. Then he wrenches it from in under himself and looks at it with a blank amazement, as if having just unearthed a holy relic. He springs to his feet, adjusting the helmet and microphone and opening the curtain again like a true showman, sharp yet graceful. He reads the manuscript silently at arms length, then looks up with a profound grimace. He rips out a handful of pages.

"This is crap! Absolute crap!" he says, waving the pages madly in the air with his larger-than-average hands. He rifles the manuscript at Arturo, missing badly. "The bloke cannot afford to grind up cornmeal by hand with real bits of corn, all the while the villains are bearing down on them! That's mad. It's preposterous! I do wish we had some, though, don't you? Mmm, cornbread. And this woman, she is not useful a'tall, just sitting idle while the evil villains bear down on them. And the costumes. No mention of the costumes. We will require tailor-made costumes made with outlandish amounts of feathers and silk. Silk and feathers I say! It's not written in the script. We have no key details here! This is all bollocks anyway!" he says, moving towards Arturo then veering off to fetch up the manuscript.

A new tune has begun and the music begins to reel Lester back in as he knew it would, almost dragging him to the floor again in the process. It does. He crawls to the television as Arturo looks on in horror, Ms. Bo Peep with delight.

"The duck!" Lester says, reaching for the life-sized duck perched atop the television. He pulls it down to the floor as if saving it from the line of enemy fire. Leering and paranoid, he clutches the duck to his chest. Then there's another knock on the door and he snaps back into a more lucid state, as the deep-throated, self-assured verbiage of the showman prevails once again.

"Does anyone know what this is?"

"It's a duck," Miss Bo Peep says.

"Very good. Yes, indeed, it is a duck. Does anyone know what it's made of?"

"It's made of—"

Lester interrupts Arturo. "Ms. Bo Peep, I'll give you first opportunity since you answered the first part so nicely."

"Wood?"

"No, sorry."

"No?" Arturo says.

"No indeed. It's poly-mer-ized."

"Polymerized what?"

"Never mind that! This duck is worth more than it's weight in gold you fool!"

"Sorry Captain."

"That's perfectly alright, common mistake," Lester says, continuing to broadcast as he starts back up the ladder. "By Jove that smells good. The electric coils! They're too bloody hot! I must attend to that — oh thank heavens it's not incinerated, better get that broth going, chicken cubes, chicken cubes, chicken cubes, where would I be if I were a chicken cube?"

"Excuse me, Captain?" Ms. Bo Peep says. "Would you like me to get the door again?"

"I don't know. Do I?"

"Yes, I think so."

"Okay then, yes. I'll defer to your expertise, Ms. Bo Peep, as you performed this duty so ... dutifully the first time."

She opens the door but nobody is there. She looks left and right down the hallway.

"No one's there," she says.

"Perhaps we didn't hear the door a'tall," Lester says. "Ever think of that? Or it could have been pranksters. There has been word of pranksters and hooligans round here lately. Ms. Bo Peep?"

"Yes?"

"I vaguely recall issuing a series of commands not too long ago. Have we any progress as yet?"

"Yes, I've got his fee right here and—"

"Tie the fool up please!"

"Yes, okay."

"Now. Let's see if we have a winner ..."

Lester jerks the drawer clear out of its slot and across the room entirely. It smashes into the far wall by the door.

"Incorrect!" Lester says, opening and closing the other drawers. "I don't believe we — blast it — I don't believe we have any chicken bouillon cubes. Never mind that, we shall divert our attention to the making of cornbread. Eggs, and butter, and ... oh, and curry. Where in god's name is the curry how could I have lost the curry? I will find it, by god."

The oven explodes into flames at this point, likely due to the fact that it's been on broil for three days. Lester cracks the oven door and thick smoke billows out. "Eeek!"

The pinwheel nature of the music becomes mentally debilitating now until he remembers the bucket of dirt on the fire escape and also that he heard an "expert" tell him of its outstanding smothering properties. He is particularly alarmed because of the impending delay in his arrangements.

"I need some more bloody wine. Boy! Where's my wine? And bring me some cashews while you're at it. Fine, peanuts then. Are you suggesting that I embody a condition known as crabbiness? Hmmm. Still the fire? Blast! The blasted dirt!"

He imagines redoubling his efforts at this point in time as he clambers down again, walks briskly to the fire escape without even banging his head on the windowsill, fetches said dirt and returns only to see that the fire has gone out of its own accord.

He is relieved and his thoughts suddenly wander back to the fire escape, and to the watering can he often uses to douse the old man who lives in the flat below. The man is usually quite exhausted from having struggled out of his wheelchair and through his window onto the fire escape and often falls asleep there, enduring the wrath of the storm undisturbed.

Chapter 21

"Thanks for meeting me, Chutney. I've never been here at night before," Anna says, looking around The Gardens, which are adjacent to The Habitat and similarly abound with vegetation. They sit on a bench, on the side of a walking path, and nearby a waterfall cascades into a small pool containing large, bug-eyed goldfish.

"It's so tranquil, isn't it?"

"Yes," Anna says, distantly.

"It's been a while since just the two of us talked. What's on your mind these days?"

"Nothing much, just the daily routine, you know. My tennis game is getting a lot better."

"Oh, good," Chutney says, her subtle mannerisms also adding, *But that's not what you want to talk about, is it?*

"Tim and I have been spending a lot of time together."

"So I hear. He's become quite a handsome young man."

"Yes ..." Anna says, blushing without complement of a smile. "It's funny you say that actually because ... well ..."

"You've been romantically involved."

"Yes. How long have you known?"

"I haven't. It was an educated guess you could say. After all, I assumed you didn't want to talk about tennis."

"No ... do you think my mom and Lester know?"

"Again, this is an educated guess, but I'd say not."

"But what if they do?"

"Well, then they do. You can't reverse it."

Anna looks worried.

"I'm sorry, that wasn't very helpful," Chutney continues. "Knowing Lester, if he knew and didn't approve, you'd probably know about it. At least Tim would. Not that you need Lester's approval."

"Right," Anna says facetiously. "Good one."

"In theory is what I mean. Granted, it would surely make your life more difficult if he opposed. But I think your mom would say something either way."

"She could be in denial."

"Possible. But I don't think she'd have a problem as long as you're happy."

"Yeah ..."

"Well, are you, Anna?"

"Happy?" Anna says, stalling.

"Yes."

"I don't know, Chutney."

"That's a problem, then, isn't it?"

"I was happy at first. I mean, I thought I was at least, when I was all caught up in the excitement of it. It's like ... how do you know the difference between happiness and excitement?"

"Excitement might be considered a form of happiness, don't you think?"

"Yeah, but it's not the real thing, you know? It's like when you look forward to your birthday and then it's just like any other day except you get a bunch of stupid presents and get sick and fat eating so much cake."

"You'd better watch out," Chutney says wryly. "Imagine how cynical you'll be when you're my age."

"You know what I mean."

"You're afraid your relationship with Tim will end in disappointment."

"Or worse," Anna says.

"Right. Or worse. Heartbreak, agony, malice …"

"Yeah."

"Been there, done that," Chutney says, taking a jar of peanut butter and a plastic spoon from her purse. "Want some?"

"Extra crunchy?" Anna says.

"Of course. I won't touch that creamy rubbish, except maybe in a serious pinch, you know. I've only got one spoon."

Anna takes the jar and spoon and wastes no time digging in. "Mmm, that's good."

"It's even better with banana," Chutney says, pulling one from the depths of her purse like a magician.

Anna laughs. "My god, Chutney! What else have you got in there, a white rabbit?"

"Yes, I believe … oh, he must have escaped. But I do have a rather ghastly collection of hairbrushes, if you're interested."

"I'm good with the peanut butter, thanks," Anna struggles to say. "Hey, what's it called when you're afraid of getting peanut butter stuck to the roof of your mouth?"

"Arachibutyrophobia."

"Wow, that's a mouthful, huh?" Anna says, laughing at the pun, and Chutney laughs along with her. "How do you know that, anyway?"

"I know a lot of stupid stuff," Chutney says. "Especially about peanut butter."

"Like what else?"

"It takes over five hundred peanuts to make twelve ounces of peanut butter."

"Wow."

"But you don't really care, do you?"

"What? Sure I do."

"No, I think you're just trying to avoid discussing your little situation."

"Yeah, you got me. I love peanut butter though. Here, take this away before I finish it."

"Don't worry, there's more where that came from," Chutney says, taking a spoonful herself and working it around in her mouth. "It sounds like you love him."

"I do love him. I just don't know …"

"If you're in love with him."

"Exactly. I'm torn, you know?"

"You don't want to lose what you already had … that friendship and mutual respect."

"Exactly."

"It's an age-old riddle, Anna. And I hate to say it, but in many ways love is like gambling. You might lose everything, you might hit it big or you might just break even."

"That's the cynicism you're talking about, huh?" Anna says, smiling nervously.

"Yes, I suppose it is. But it's also different from gambling in a number of ways," Chutney says. "For starters, you can beat the odds depending on how much you're willing to invest. Love doesn't take any skill, but it does take effort. Don't let anyone tell you otherwise."

"I know. I just don't know what I want. It used to be, I'd picture myself in the future, married, with kids, living in New York, or London, or Paris maybe, and now …"

Chutney is about to say something when her electronic butler calls to her from the bottom of her purse. Its persona is that of a blithe young Aussie called Nick. He is programmed to flirt, yet to maintain professionalism and appropriateness at all times. "Miss Chutney?" he says. "Sorry to pester you, but Lester's calling a meeting upstairs."

Like a schoolgirl being called to the principal's office, Chutney rolls her eyes at Anna. "What's it regarding, Nick?"

"I don't know, Miss Chutney. Afraid he didn't say. I could speculate but I'm not—"

"Programmed to, I know, Nick. That's okay. I'll be up there in a minute."

"I'll send the word along."

Chutney sighs and pats Anna on the knee. "Well, duty calls, Anna, I'm sorry. I'm afraid I just muddied the waters for you here. But maybe we can get together again soon."

"Yeah. You did help though, really. I just need to think about it."

"Well, don't think too hard."

Anna's round eyes narrow and the corner of her mouth indicates a smirk. "That's exactly what Tim said."

Chapter 22

Jipt got a full manicure in anticipation of the ribbon-cutting ceremony, because he would be shaking hands with a lot of people. However, he purposely omitted all three varieties of hand cream from his morning hygiene docket, an antibacterial lotion, one enriched with vitamin E and another with effervescent aloe. Could he obtain one product with all three features? Yes, of course. But he doesn't believe it's as effective as his triple-moisturizing approach. Besides, his hands are so large that he would go through a bottle a week. At least this way, he only has to replace all three bottles once every three weeks from his massive inventory in the basement.

He is generally pleased with the condition of his hands this morning. They are smooth and soft overall yet have a gentle coarseness like high-grit sandpaper. Perfect for that impression of a hard-working guy who knows the meaning of physical labor – and who just-so-happens to be one of the most powerful businessmen in America. Or, rather, one of the most powerful American businessmen (remember, technically speaking PyraVegas and The Pyramid are each freestanding nations).

Jipt grasps the one handle of the giant plastic scissors and, along with the president and CEO of JumboSave Incorporated, pretends to cut the pre-severed ribbon in front of the store. Flashbulbs pop and Jipt smiles half-convincingly. But when he releases his grip on the flimsy scissors and shakes the CEO's hand, his expression changes to one very closely resembling true pleasure. It's the classic "grip and grin" pose – the only part of these ceremonies from which

Jipt derives even the most infinitesimal thrill. There's something about that moment, the split second when the deal is symbolically captured on film, which makes all the rigmarole tolerable. He's not even sure why – perhaps because it proves he went through all the rigmarole in the first place, not only for his own benefit but for someone else's. Maybe not the community at large, as he often portends, but just the man at the other end of the handshake – in this case, Marty Simmons, the CEO of JumboSave Incorporated.

Jipt works the large but uninspired crowd gathered in the mega-store's parking lot, shaking hands and even signing an occasional autograph, but that's not the worst part. It's the inevitable questions from the press that are totally unrelated to the current proceedings. Jipt sees these situations as a nuisance and potential for error, but thus far he has taken Hawkins' advice to humor the reporters, keeping his answers upbeat and, most importantly, keeping them short.

"Mayor Jipt!" one of these pressmen calls, extending a bulky, antiquated tape recorder. "Do you endorse Sylvia King in her candidacy for Union president?"

"Ms. King has made tremendous contributions to The Union, and I've been delighted to see the resulting benefits for The Casino workers," Jipt says, winking almost unnoticeably at Hawkins, who's hanging back behind him, ready to step in with an "urgent phone call" when he gets the signal.

"Mayor Jipt!" an older female reporter says. "How do you respond to claims that your dual-role as mayor and casino CEO constitutes a conflict of interest?"

"Wow, that's a real tongue-twister, Alice. How many times did you practice that in the mirror this morning?" Jipt teases her, and most everyone in the press corps forces an obligatory chuckle. "Seriously though, the answer is no, I don't. Think about it, if you're a farmer, you take care of your fields, right? But that doesn't mean you neglect your wife, does it?"

"So, is The Casino your wife? Or is it the fields, meant to reap a bountiful harvest?"

Jipt scratches the back of his head like a dog with fleas. This is the sign, but Hawkins is distracted by the JumboSave guy, who's trying to schedule a one-on-one meeting.

"I'm sorry, I didn't catch that last question Alice," Jipt stalls, glancing over his shoulder and still scratching away. Perhaps it's his icy look that causes Hawkins to notice him finally. Taking the phone from his pocket, he politely excuses himself from the conversation and pretends to answer it.

"Yes," the reporter says. "You compared your situation to a farmer and—"

"Excuse me, I'm sorry," Hawkins interjects, tapping Jipt on the shoulder and extending the phone. "It's urgent."

"I beg your pardon, ladies and gentlemen," Jipt says without any trace of a smirk. "Thank you." He takes the phone and immediately turns away, toward the black limousine, and starts walking with purposeful strides. "Seth Jipt, here! Yes, yes of course! Whatever we need to do to make them happy!" he says loudly, so everyone will overhear him.

Hawkins opens the door and follows him inside the car. As soon as the door closes the smile disappears from Jipt's face and it grows even redder than before. "Goddammit, Tommy! Were you just going to let me roast up there, like a pig on a goddamned spit for chrissakes?"

"I'm really sorry, Seth, but Marty was really bending my ear. Looks like you handled it okay, though."

"Of course I did, but that's not the goddamned – never mind, forget about it. Look, I apologize, Tommy. I think it's this diet that's making me irritable." He cups a hand to his forehead. "I feel a little warm."

"Probably just the sun," Hawkins says, hoping to mollify him.

"Mm," Jipt utters, and he can't help but wonder how much more of this he can stand, as he stares out the window at The Pyramid, imagining how much better things must look from way up there in the sky.

Chapter 23

With his arms tucked behind him like a ski jumper, Lester leans his forehead against the south windows of the Apex Conference Room. His eyes are closed. Behind him, the Visionaries sit around the dark slab of a table, awaiting his answer to the question of what to do with all the mail piling up, most of which is assumed to be either fan mail or hate mail.

"You see," Lester begins, clearly addressing another topic altogether. "Darkness is something which is not absolute, as light is not. Yes? We all know from our reading that light is transmitted in variable frequency waves, and that these waves are bouncing all round us most of the time, right? Agreed then. But darkness, on the other hand, is something ... an entity perhaps, which is largely devoid of waves, isn't it? And what about sound? Sound also takes the form of waves, waves of air particles moving other air particles ever-so-slightly. If we make no sound there are few waves. If we shutter the windows and turn the switch off, there are few waves. *Or are there?!* Are there, perhaps teeny, tiny little waves, still bouncing about like little bloody laser beams, at such subdued frequencies that our inferior human mechanisms cannot process them? It's an extraordinary principle really, along with the one that says darkness is defined by an infinite sliding scale, you see? This scale may slide until reaching infinity in an infinite amount of time. Time! Oh yes, we've really botched it up now, haven't we girls?" He pauses and chuckles to himself, the sound of which he imagines is drowned out by the raucous laughter and jubilation of the schoolgirls in his classroom ...

"Lester? Woo-hoo! Hello!" Chili says. It's his week to chair the staff meeting, therefore it's his unspoken responsibility to steer Lester back on topic.

"Huh? Yes? What is it?" Lester says, looking disoriented as he wheels around.

"The mail? What should we do with all the mail?"

"Right, right, the mail ..."

"Perhaps we could ask for inhabitant volunteers to read it, and report anything significant," Schnitzelhaus proposes.

"Like what? Pictures of naked ladies? Ha ha!" Ping says, cracking himself up, as usual.

"Like death threats or something."

"I'll read it myself," Lester says defiantly.

"Lester," Chutney says. "We're talking about thousands of letters. Tens of thousands."

"Well, we can't have inhabitants reading this stuff, that's for sure. Lord knows what unspeakable profanity lay within those envelopes. Not to mention egregious grammatical style."

"Lies," Katz corrects him.

"And lies! Excellent point, Patricia."

"No," she says, giggling slightly along with the others. "I mean—"

"Ah, yes! You got me!" Lester says, catching on. "That's exactly what I'm talking about. Egregious grammatical style! I did that on purpose to illustrate my point. No, I didn't. I confess. Well, anyway, I suggest we have Ms. Tiddybar allocate some of her administrative staff to opening and sorting the mail into main categories. Anything written in crayon, for example, obviously from a young child or an imbecile, should go into one pile. Certainly anything from the U.S. government, or any foreign government for that matter, should go in a separate pile."

"Pictures of naked ladies?" Ping says again.

"By all means, a separate pile."

"Death threats?" Schnitzelhaus says, following Ping's lead.

"Burn those without delay," Lester says. "That's the last thing I want to see, apart from the letters of immodest flattery and supplication. Burn those as well. Is someone writing this down? Who's the scribe this week?"

"I got it," Ping says, scribbling furiously on a yellow legal pad.

"Oh, good heavens. It will take the forensic experts at least a month to decipher those chicken scratchings. Very well, then. Is that all?"

"No," Chili says. "We've got a few more items to cover."

"These were determined to be the least important, though, right?" Lester asks. "We covered the most important topics first, did we not?"

"The first item was whether we should switch from double-ply to single-ply toilet paper."

"Hmm ... wishful thinking on my part, then. What did we decide anyway, I can't even remember."

"No. We decided that would send the wrong message."

"Yes, indeed. If we were using our heads, we would have started with the single ply."

"Anyway," Chili says, trying to keep things moving. "The next item is a visitation request by Richard Thurston, he's the president of the world communist party."

"Dick Thurston?" Lester says snidely, taking up his pipe from where he set it down earlier, on the fireplace mantel next to the prismatic pyramid. Lester pokes at the vanilla-flavored tobacco with his thumb and discovers that it's still smoldering. "Ouch! Son of a bloody ... ouch." He sucks on his thumb like an infant to quell the pain.

"Yes, apparently so," Chili says. "At least he's not called Dick Cummings or something."

"Pinko bastard ... denied! What do you think, Chutney?"

"I think you're Mr. Bossy Britches today. No, I don't see what good could come from it," she says, avoiding direct reference to the allegations that Lester, himself, is redder than Santa Claus' overcoat.

"Anyone else disagree? Very well, then. Is that all?"

"No. There's one last item," Chili says, reluctant to continue. "Leave requests."

"As in, requests to leave The Pyramid?"

"Yes."

"My heavens, for good?"

"Yes."

"In writing?"

"Yes, but it's—" Chili begins to explain.

"We need damage control!" Lester says, jerking his head back and forth as if watching a game of table tennis.

"Lester," Chutney intervenes. "It's only a hundred people, and most are—"

"A hundred people!" Lester squawks. "In the past week?"

"No ... since the very first request, which occurred in week two. You said to shelve the debate until the number reached a hundred, remember?"

"No ..."

"Barring any medical emergencies," Chili adds. "But there haven't been any so far."

"Well, of course not!" Lester says, pacing briskly, puffing his pipe and gesturing with his hands. "They've got some of the best doctors in the world at their disposal. They've got all the comfort and entertainment imaginable at their disposal. And they want to dispose of it all! Why would they want to make the biggest mistake of their lives? Well, I won't let it happen. It's my duty not to let it happen – the very duty they entrusted in me, by agreeing to live here in the first place. All requests are denied! Denied! Bloody denied!"

"Don't you want to hear some of the reasons?" Chutney asks.

"No! Well, yes, actually, do tell. Give me the best ones."

"Well, they fall into a few broad categories, okay? Homesickness, maladjustment, loneliness and paranoia."

"Ah-ha!" Lester exclaims. "The homesick are either sick with nostalgia or delusional about the comfort and security of their prior living arrangements, eh? They need a shot glass bearing the name of their hometown and plenty of liquor to drink from it. The maladjusted are clearly malnourished of ideas. They need companionship and mentoring, as well as more time to gain strength. Which brings us to the lonely, doesn't it? They need companionship too, and some might even make good mentors. Let's figure out a way to introduce the lonely to the maladjusted."

"We could have a party!" Ping blurts out. "With liquor!"

"And disco dancing," Chili says.

"And bobbing for apples," Katz says.

"And rooster juggling!" Schnitzelhaus says.

"Rooster juggling? Where on earth are we going to find a rooster juggler on short notice?" Lester replies.

"I just wanted to see what you'd say."

"No rooster juggling. Otherwise I think the idea is a gem," Lester says, puffing proudly.

"What about the paranoids?" Chutney says.

"Ah, yes … the paranoids. What kinds of paranoid are we talking about? Like that a snake might be lurking in the toilet bowl, that kind of thing?"

"No, more like paranoid that the U.S. government will invade The Pyramid. Or worse, drop a great big bomb on it."

"Egads. How many of those?"

"A handful. Four particularly bad ones."

"Well, we can't very well have these paranoids spouting off their paranoia to the general populous now, can we? On the other hand, expelling them would be a validation on our part, wouldn't it? At least symbolically, of their fears."

"I don't think anyone would miss them," Schnitzelhaus says.

"Perhaps not, but it's the principle of the thing ..."

"We do have a long waiting list of qualified candidates," Chutney reminds him. "Any one of whom would jump at the chance ... and most live in PyraVegas, anyway."

Again, Chili backs Chutney up. "Some people want out and some people want in. Sounds like a quick fix to me, Lester."

Lester continues to pace, mutter and make hand gestures as if making a point to himself. It's not clear whether he's comprehended anything Chutney or Chili have just said. "Look, there are two kinds of people ..." he finally says, and The Visionaries let out a collective groan, having heard this many times before. "Fine, fine. What we've got here is a symbiotic relationship, have we not? I'm thinking on a macro scale now. Take lichen for example. Lichen, after all, are really two things, does anyone know what?"

"Algae?" Ping says.

"Algae is one! Very good, Dr. Ping!"

"Fungus," Katz says.

"Yes! Excellent. Now, the fungus provides the structure – the body – that houses both organisms. You follow? The algae, what it does is produce sugars that feed them both. See? Each can live without the other – but together! Together they are stronger and more ..." Lester is at the window again, gazing over the unsightly sprawl of

PyraVegas. "But this! This has become a parasite! Squeezing, tightening, choking us off … there are two kinds of people! Those who do not always get everything they want, and those who do not want anything. Those in the latter category are quite obviously fools. And those in the former lot, who do not readily accept the fact …"

"I suppose that would be us," Chutney says.

"Hmm … I was going to say fools …" Lester says, grimacing and rubbing his chin, as the pipe slips from his jaws onto the floor. "Shit."

Chili points discreetly at Lester and says quietly to the others, "We need some damage control."

"Good idea!" Lester says, suddenly at attention and pointing back at Chili. "Damage control, yes, I'm glad someone finally brought that up!"

Chapter 24

Sylvia and her boys are seated around the kitchen table, which is piled with stacks of letters and envelopes. They have a little assembly line going, with Anthony stuffing the envelopes, Michael sealing them and Sylvia applying mailing labels. One letter will go to each and every union member, asking for their vote in the upcoming election.

As if someone has called his name, Michael's eye is drawn to the window, where The Pyramid glows in the night sky. Its lighthouse-style beacon winks at him every three seconds and he stares at it, transfixed, interrupting the workflow.

"Come on, Mikey," Anthony says, "You're holding us up."

"Hey mamma," Michael says, ignoring his older brother.

"What is it, sugar?" Sylvia says, squaring off a pile of envelopes.

"Is The Pyramid watching us?"

"No, of course not. That's just a light, so planes don't run into it."

"Oh."

"Hey mamma," Anthony says, taking the opportunity to pose a question of his own. "You think you're gonna win the election?"

"Not if we don't get these letters out," Sylvia jokes.

"What do you get if you win? You get to order people around and stuff?"

"No, people get to order me around, because I'll be representing their interests. I'll get a lot of responsibility, which will also mean a lot of extra work. So you and your brother need to prepare for that."

"Will you get paid more?"

"No."

"That's stupid. Why you want to be president then?"

"It's all about power and clout," Sylvia says.

"What's clout?" Michael says.

"It's like respect. It means people are more likely to listen to what you have to say. They're more likely to take you seriously and give you what you want."

"What do you want, Mamma?" Anthony says.

"What do you want? I represent your interests, too."

"I don't know."

"Come on, everybody wants something."

Now Anthony's eye drifts to the window. "I want to live in The Pyramid."

"How about you?" she asks Michael.

"Yeah!" he says.

"Well, me too," Sylvia says. "So we'll just have to see what I can do about that."

Chapter 25

After a few years of living in his very specialized environs within The Pyramid, which are opulent, clean and futuristic, Lester decides that his apartment in Queens, although small and antiquated, was his true comfort zone. It wasn't the ideal living space, but he made it work. He knew in which shoebox, drawer, cubby or crevice everything was located. He could find his way in the dark, even with sunglasses on and tennis rackets lashed to his feet and music blaring in his ears. And quite frankly, since moving into The Pyramid, he's had a rather hard time coping with all the space – and the fact that his relatively few original possessions are spread out so widely in that space – making it difficult to stay organized.

To solve this little problem, Lester does what he considers the logical thing and he has an exact replica of his Queens apartment built within his living quarters. It takes up very little space in his bedroom quadrant alone and is rendered down to every conceivable detail – the Velvet Cave, the lofted kitchen, the coffin coffee table, the bunk bed, the driftwood chandelier ...

But to say it's an exact replica would be inaccurate. Perhaps highly inaccurate, because no photographs or floor plans were available, only memory. And, as one might imagine, Lester's memory tends to alter reality to a certain extent due to chemical imbalances and brain cell malfunctions of various kinds. And Tim's is hardly any better when it comes to environmental observations. He has an enormous propensity to remember names and dates and titles and obscure facts, but precious little else.

Lester paces back and forth across the worn gray carpet in the old living room, as per his usual habit before staff meetings. He's all alone with two dozen cats and, of course, his thoughts ...

I can't decide if The Unions are good or evil. It's a sad case indeed when you can't even classify something as good or evil. That is, assuming good and evil are the only two categories from which to choose. I mean, these days they take the thumb twiddlers and say, you know what? I think the government should give us some more money, the company we work for, or the government, or both, should give us more money because we're wearing out our thumbs with all the twiddling. Because we're wearing out our bloody thumbs with all this twiddling! You know what I mean? Our members may need operations at some point to keep their thumbs in good twiddling order. Maybe not now, but there's no telling when those thumbs might give way. So we need some money so we don't have to struggle, right? Because as it is now, we're putting aside part of our hard-earned thumb twiddling paychecks to cover these expenses and it's not fair at all! I mean, what if we weren't so sensible and then when our thumbs gave out, the public would be deprived of our thumb twiddling services. Sure, you could find other thumb twiddlers, but they're not legitimate. They're not licensed. They're not card-carrying members of The Union! So there's only one answer. We've got to keep our thumbs in good twiddling order so we can keep on twiddling. Right? We've got to keep on twiddling because otherwise we wouldn't be thumb twiddlers anymore, would we?

Now, the exception is a strike, because then I say I'm going to withhold my twiddling services, not for personal or selfish reasons but for important political and legal reasons. Now we're talking about rights, you see? As soon as you're talking about rights then you've escalated the issue by sheer virtue of rhetoric. It's all rhetoric! It's all rhetoric, whether you're trying to convince yourself, as in my case, or trying to convince a nation of a billion people. You may think it's something else but it's not, it's still rhetoric. But it's also policy, although policy is really just a glorified sort of rhetoric. So you'd also be right if you said policy. Or if you said it's all rubbish, because you always reserve the right to say something's rubbish, even if it's clearly not. Now, you can't overplay the rubbish card or else you'll come to be known as a rubbish man with no concrete ideas of his own, right? Many have been successful doing this, for sure, but few have been well-respected at the same time. That's the rub, see? The rub with the rubbish. That's so bloody clever!

We never should have made it known to the Inhabitants that we had such a thing as the mainframe computer, that we depended on it, right? As soon as the knowledge is acquired that says every routine function of life depends on one thing, one computer no less, albeit a network of computers, but the whole of it is in fact held together, integrated as they say, by the mainframe itself, which resides in one undisclosed location ... that was totally irresponsible, totally unacceptable, but we must accept it, mustn't we? No, of course not. Because it can only result in negative behaviors amongst the populous, such as paranoia stemming from a feeling of helplessness, of powerlessness over one's own destiny.

Now, we know of course that machines can make errors because they are built by humans, and humans certainly make errors. Until machines are made entirely by machines, that is to say that they're at least three or four generations away from man, so that you've got a machine made by a machine made by a machine, and that machine, the great grandfather machine if you will, was made by a human ... then you could have what you may call a pure machine, which would make no mistakes. But we're not there yet, are we? And the other piece of the puzzle of course is the programming of the machines, the protocols that are burned into them, which is handled by humans as well at the present, and which is very important indeed, just as important as the preciseness of the circuitry and so forth. It's critical! And Dr. Katz, as talented as she is, may have made a mistake somewhere. But enough! We've thought about it enough and mapped out a reasonable, if not field-tested, contingency plan for the scenarios we could conceive of, and what else can we do? Besides, it's dependent upon a lot of other factors, a lot of other factors beyond our control, The Union being one of them and I daresay our nemesis, Mr. Jipt, being one of them as well. But there are many other factors as well and there's really no point worrying about one of them and it's too burdensome to worry about all of them so that leaves the rubbish card again. We won't bother with any of it.

We'll simply enjoy ourselves because we're only here for a certain amount of time, a certain and also uncertain amount of time, right? We don't know for sure what's next, so we'll enjoy ourselves in the meantime. But we've got people depending on us, that's the problem! We can't turn our back on them after all the promises and insinuations that have been made. I can't think of myself, and in doing so I've violated the cardinal rule in operating the equipment that is the human body, right? You've got to look out for your own body, right? You've got to be programmed to look round for any wild creatures with sharp teeth or pianos or anvils dangling from ropes above your head. Your ingrained protocol must be to look before you step to make sure there isn't a gaping hole. But it doesn't stop there. You've got to look out for your other interests as well, your social and financial and political interests as well. Some rely on The Unions to do the dirty work for them but I choose to rely on myself.

But it's all rubbish! It's all rubbish because I'm no different, am I? I'm the leader of a union, aren't I? The rhetoric may be different, I may call it a society, but it's still rhetoric! It's still a union! But it's a good one, I know it is, and anyone who says different is full of rubbish! The question is, have my powers of persuasion been too persuasive? The hypnotism is certainly a factor in all of this and one could argue that it has the effect of revealing the truth, whereby someone else could argue the opposite. Perhaps both of these arguments are valid simultaneously, because each person's perspective is different, and then again perhaps it's all rubbish. But whether it's rubbish or not, it's not rubbish to me, and if I can convince other people it's not rubbish

then it's not rubbish, is it? I think I'll eat a sandwich. And drink a beer.
Drink a beer and eat a sandwich.

* * *

As he's washing down the last bite of sandwich with the last few gulps of beer, a fly buzzes into his mug and causes quite a stir. Caught off guard, and terrified that he'll swallow the nasty bug (all bugs are nasty in his opinion), Lester drops the mug. But it doesn't break. He also spits beer onto the mural portraying Jimmy Changa the dwarf, in knight's armor, riding a sea horse and jousting against a giant swordfish. He takes a brief opportunity to admire how well it embodies the original before taking chase after the winged perpetrator.

Not thinking to close the door or the window – or better yet, both – Lester travels in a circular pattern: through the living room into the kitchen, into and out of the bathroom, into the bedroom, through the window and back into the modern Master's Chambers, then looping around, back into the "old apartment" through the front door.

After several uncanny laps in this way, in defiance of chaos theory it would seem, the fly's behavior becomes more erratic. And as a direct result, so does Lester's, his anger building like he's a steaming hot espresso-cappuccino dispenser. He stomps and claps his hands in attempt to crush the fly from both sides at once. He picks up any sorts of swatters he can find, like magazines, socks and spatulas. These having failed him, he moves on to smashers like history books (very large and absorbent coasters), tennis racquets and brooms. But the fly proves too quick. Too small. And most importantly, too random.

"You are such a bloody fool!" Lester shouts, as the fly buzzes around the spacious new Master Bedroom. "You have this supreme power to be a perfect fool, a perfectly random creature, but you're still a fly! And I will smote you. You will be smitten!" Lester sets the grapefruit down and takes up one of his many swords from its wall-mount above one of his many beds. He unsheathes it and assumes a fighting stance, as the fly bumps repeatedly into the windows. "Get away from there, you coward!" Lester says. And then, as if enraged by his affront, the fly bounces off the window and heads straight for his mouth. Like a snake, Lester's muscles tighten and he coils for attack. Slowly, he raises his sword behind him, the blade pointing above his head at an oblique angle, and then ... *Swoosh!* The air is a'blur with his steel, and the wall above the bed is marked by a tiny black dot. "Dead!" Lester says, with only the tiniest shred of remorse, and only the tiniest shred of pride. The apparent improbability of his feat is lost on him.

Lester sheaths his sword and returns it to its wall-mounting. Tuckered out from his adventure with the fly, he decides to gather his potency and attend to business in one fell swoop by sitting at his antique secretary. He rolls the top back and takes out the mail that arrived a few days ago. After shredding the rubber band in a violent fashion, turning it into a rubber string, he sorts through a stack of postcards, each with his handwriting on the back. Often he's written or drawn on the front as well, such as one from Miami depicting a woman with a gigantic, cellulite-rumpled derriere floating above the skyline like a blimp. The caption says, *Moon over Miami*, but Lester had scratched it out and written, *Exercise daily and never go to Miami*. He does not recall having penned the phrase, and he wonders aloud, "Surely this photograph was doctored. I mean, there couldn't possibly be a woman floating above the city. Unless she were on a wire. I don't see any wire. Well, it could be a hidden wire. Good point. Even still, it doesn't seem plausible. Oh, so you've downgraded it to plausible now? Shut up you bloody sot."

He notes the official and very distinctive Pyramid postmark in the upper right-hand corner, which is partially covered by the more recent postmark from Queens, New York. The round trip to Pedro's and back took seventeen days. In the margin of the calendar desk blotter he scratches the number seventeen with a dull pencil. Then he scratches the equivalent of tick marks in bundles of five, three bundles and two loners. He does this primarily because he fancies the symbolism on a number of different levels, such as the parallels to bundles of mail and prehistoric cave drawings.

He picks up the elephantine antique telephone receiver and stretches the short, straight wire to its limit with a quarter-turn in his chair. "No, I'm sorry. At the moment I'm hunched over my secretary." He turns smartly back to his forward-facing position and places the receiver back on its undersized cradle. "Ha ha! Sounds rather depraved, doesn't it? Hunched over my—" The phone rings with forceful percussion of the bells inside, and the combination of the volume and surprise rocks Lester out of his chair. He tumbles sideways like he's been flicked by the index finger of a 20-foot-tall infant. He scampers back and answers the phone. "Hello?" he says in a mildly paranoid tone, even though he's 99.9 percent sure it's just Squeakins.

"You rang, sir. However, I daresay I couldn't glean the overall jist of your message, sir," Squeakins says.

"Right, nothing a'tall, boy, nothing to worry about a'tall. I was just babbling on and happened to pick up the phone by accident, you know."

"Perfectly understandable, sir. Anything else, then?"

"No. Yes! How long has it been taking, on average, for my personal mail to reach my desk … from the second it enters The Pyramid?"

Perhaps what Lester appreciates most about Squeakins is his lack of hesitation at such complex queries, and the confidence with which he disseminates information. "My best estimate is eight to ten hours, sir."

"My god! Why so long, boy?"

"Well, the large deliveries come at night, when we have a smaller staff in the mailroom."

"Support from the volunteer ranks must be flagging."

"Indeed, sir. I daresay twenty percent since our first month of operation."

"Hmm, that is troubling … but I suppose eight to ten hours is acceptable. I assume anything marked urgent or confidential or something of the sort would be expedited?"

"Of course, sir."

"Good, good … just one other note, then. We may want to think about changing the base period to all the time up until now, minus the part before opening day."

"Very well, sir. I'll have the staff perform some calculations."

"And another thing …"

"Sir?"

"I forgot. Oh, now I remember! I propose there's a correlation between the total amount of time my postcards take to boomerang around to me, you follow? Seventeen days, for example. And the state of affairs in the world-at-large. The better the news, the longer it takes. Of course, I haven't been paying much attention to the news lately …"

"I believe the facts bear out your theory, sir. The past two weeks have been dominated by stories of corporate victory over government regulation, and a reinvigoration of the stock market. I can get you the full stories if—"

"No, no, that's quite all right. Why spoil a perfectly good synopsis, eh?"

"Thank you, sir. Is that all, then?"

"Yes, I believe now it is."

"Then forgive me, sir, but I feel obligated to remind you again about lunch. Svetlana has been waiting on The Lanai for nearly twenty minutes now."

"Right, right! Thank you boy!" Lester sings, clunking the phone down again. But, as if the conversation never happened, he returns his attention again to the postcard on top of the stack. He turns it over and it says: *Dear Lester, Ate some questionable fish today. Caused some extensive delays on the digestive superhighway, if you get my meaning. It could have been the tartar sauce, but I doubt it. Be wary and vigilant. Yours in confidence, Pepe*

"I don't know who this Pepe is," Lester says with great reverence. "But he sure is a gem of information. An information diamond! All that carbon is like his knowledge and it's just pressure-packed in there with un-bloody-believable force!"

Feeling a sudden pang of self consciousness about looking like a caveman, hunched over his secretary like that, Lester removes a pair of half-glasses from the center drawer and balances them on the bridge of his nose. He flips to the next card, from London, that has a picture of old ladies sipping tea in a picturesque English garden. The caption says simply, Tea Time! and on the reverse side Lester has scribbled in bright red crayon, *Dear Lester, I have two splendorous words for you: lingonberry preserves. Goes brilliantly with cinnamon scones! And can you guess the color of this crayon? Lingonberry! It's really quite astounding. You must have Jean-Sebastian whip some up, tout suite! Cheers, Jolly Boy.*

"Once again, I been deprived of the pleasure of meeting this Jolly Boy fellow … I'm quite fond of his taste!"

Lester flips to the next card, from an undisclosed location, featuring a rather horrid maritime scene. It's a gloomy, rough sea, churning with foam, and from below the surface a hand is extended, as well as a broken oar. The paper has a variegated finish, and when he angles it back and forth the light plays tricks with the image. In the depths he can barely make out a body that's been chewed ragged, perhaps by sharks or killer whales. There is no caption.

"That's ridiculous," Lester scoffs. "Like the sea monsters wouldn't feast upon his hand as well! There's some good meat left."

He turns it over, and it reads: *Dear Lester, Do not let the absurdity of this artistic rendering distract you from the message, which is this: He who reaches out to the heavens will not have his hand bitten. But he who is not self-reliant will have the remainder of his body in the bellies of the fishes! Learn it as the truth. Believe it as a fact. And live it like an animal. Tootles, Mrs. Pickwick.*

"For goodness sakes, I feel like a broken bloody record here, but thank you Mrs. Pickwick! Very salient information, indeed. My compliments and utmost appreciation go out to you!" Lester says, teetering a bit in his chair as if drunk.

* * *

Svetlana finds Lester not hunched but slumped over the secretary, unconscious. "You like statistics, so how about this one?" she says angrily, as he jerks awake. "You've stood me up ten times in the past month."

"Svetlana ..." he says, looking both shocked and amazed by her appearance. "I'm terribly sorry, Svety, I just—"

"That word is making me sick."

"I apologize."

"You apology is not accepted," she says, businesslike. "You would not accept such performance from one of your staff, would you?"

"By the way, have you been using my statistical staff?" Lester says in a flip manner, not comprehending to what depths he has sunk in the proverbial swampland of marital inharmoniousness.

"Don't try to change the subject. It's unacceptable behavior and you know it. Unless, of course, our marriage is not important to you."

"That's not the way to think of it a'tall – I mean, I'm just saying ..." Lester backpedals. "Of course it's important to me. But marriage is nothing like a business and it's not the holy matrimony that's important."

Svetlana's eyes widen as if ready to swallow up his forthcoming statement with maximum power, as if she's simultaneously daring him to say something stupid and praying that he won't.

"No. It's you. You are what's important, Svetlana. Your feelings and your happiness." He approaches her smiling, seeking no approval, and throws his arms around her. He squeezes and she doesn't resist. In fact, her body is limp and cold.

Chapter 26

Sylvia refused Jipt's proposal to meet in The Casino, before her shift (as section supervisor), which would have meant wearing her uniform. Clearly his intent had been to demean her and remind her that she's subservient to people who are subservient to him – not even worthy of direct subservience. Or at least that's what she's been telling herself over and over, to get pumped up in anticipation of the meeting, like a boxer or football player or bullfighter readying for battle.

If the discontinuity over a choice of meeting location had been any harbinger, it would have been a spirited battle indeed, but thus far the conversation between Sylvia, Jipt and Hawkins has been nothing if not amicable and patronizing. This would suit Sylvia fine if decisions had been made (in her favor), but they have not. In fact, consumption has won out over concession altogether since the entrées arrived.

At first, Sylvia was irked about the choice of restaurant because it was clearly a "good ole boys" establishment that Jipt had described as a "nice quaint little place with a variety of choices." But what irked her more was the accuracy of his account of the place, called Molly's. It *is* quaint, in a hunting lodge sort of way. It *is* little, having only five tables, all of which are empty (on purpose, she assumes). And the menu *does* offer a variety of different choices, it just so happens that they all had hooves at one time. Steak, buffalo steak, lamb, pork, venison and some other animals Sylvia has never heard of. She's no vegetarian, and no conservationist either, but the list

146

seems a bit excessive. Mistake number one was not scouting the place first. Mistake number two was convincing herself that Jipt is always spewing lies. But she has to admit, at least to herself, that her *chateaubriand* is tender and succulent beyond belief. She just hopes Jipt is picking up the tab.

What also irked Sylvia, at first, was the fact that Jipt brought his sidekick Hawkins with him. Again, Sylvia chose to believe this was intended to humiliate her and tilt the playing field in his direction, when really he was just exposing himself as her intellectual inferior. And not only that, but exposing his fear of it, of her – of her power. After all, she expects someone like Jipt is wary of opposing powers above all else, perhaps even death itself, because he fears losing his own power. And, worse, he fears not gaining any *more* power.

However, in the case of Hawkins, his charm and effortless diplomacy have appeased her ire, much like the *chateaubriand* has satisfied her taste buds. And he's certainly not difficult to look at either, despite the fact that Sylvia has always preferred black men. "Delicious," she says, clinking her fork down on the plate. She intends to give no credit to Jipt for satisfying her appetite.

"That's corn-fed beef from Texas," Jipt says, as if to enhance her appreciation of its taste or price.

"So, Seth," Sylvia begins, before Jipt cuts her off.

"Sylvia, I'm sorry, but before you get to your agenda and tempers rise, I just wanted to say—"

"Who said tempers were going to rise?" Sylvia says to Hawkins, as if he were an impartial mediator.

Hawkins displays one of the many nonpartisan expressions he's honed over the years, a graceful combination of slights. A slight eyebrow-raise accompanied by a slight furrow, a slight smile and a slight tilting of his head to one side, in this case away from Jipt.

"You're right, Sylvia, they shouldn't have to," Jipt says. "And for my part I'll do my best to avoid it. But before we talk turkey I just wanted to congratulate you on your reelection and on all your accomplishments. Sure, I may not have agreed with you all the time, but it's my job, as mayor, to counterbalance The Union. Just like it's your job to counterbalance me."

"It's also in your best interest, personally, to oppose The Union."

"Sylvia," Hawkins interjects, "I think what Seth's trying to say is that we want to reach some common ground with The Union, because ultimately what's good for The Union is good for the community of PyraVegas on the whole, you understand."

"Yes, of course I do," Sylvia says, almost apologetically, before turning back to Jipt, steely-eyed. "Seth, you know our demands, so I'm not going to restate them. They're the same issues you and I have been discussing for over a year now."

"They're the same issues we've been discussing for the past seven-plus years," Hawkins adds, and Sylvia mistakenly thinks he's bolstering her point.

"And there's a good reason for that," Jipt intervenes, taking his cue. "I don't have a magic wand I can wave and create living space in The Pyramid, Sylvia. I wish I did, but we're dealing with a third party here—"

"I know. Lester Ginn, Lester Ginn, Lester Ginn," Sylvia says, making it clear that she's tired of the excuse. "I can't go back to the members with that bullshit again. They're sick and tired of it and they're near the breaking point."

"You mean a strike," Jipt says, not unlike a child trying to make his parents feel guilty for sugarcoating bad news.

"Have you even talked to him, as you promised umpteen times? You supposedly have this rapport with him, yet you've met him, what? A handful of times?"

"That's more than most people can claim," Hawkins says. "And you have to believe us when we say it's not easy. Well, you know, having tried yourself to contact him."

Sylvia wants to deny it, but she figures Hawkins has done his homework so she doesn't want to risk insulting his intelligence. "Yes, I know he's very secretive. But I get the impression that you're not taking us at face value, Seth. You mention the word strike to Lester Ginn, and I guarantee you his ears are going to prick up."

"I'll give you that," Jipt says. "But I still don't think saber rattling is the way to go, here. What I *do* know, from meeting him face-to-face, is that he's an unbelievably ..."

"Mercurial?" Hawkins offers.

"What the hell does that mean?

"Means his behavior is real erratic."

"Yeah, except I was thinking of ...

"Volatile?"

"I don't know, volatile, mercurial – hell, Sylvia, it's pretty clear the guy's got some problems, okay? In the head. I mean, the look he can get in his eyes ..."

"So you're afraid of him."

"No!" Jipt says, banging his fist on the table, causing a clatter of dishes and silverware. But he quickly recovers. "No, I'm not afraid of him. I'm afraid of what he might do, you understand? There's a difference."

"What about the hotel?" Sylvia says. "I don't believe that you can't spare a few thousand suites."

"It's not that I can't spare them," Jipt says, trying in vain to sound sympathetic. "It's just that any major decision like that would have to be cleared through–"

"So you're saying you couldn't absorb it through your end of the profits alone."

"It's not that I couldn't. But we'd need to make cuts somewhere."

"That's bullshit and you know it."

"Look, I'm not making as much of a killing on this deal as you might think," Jipt says, finally setting his own fork and knife down and wiping his mouth crosswise with his napkin. "I mean, I'm operating on fifty percent of what I should really have. Not to mention that this casino is ten times more expensive to operate than any other in the world, you understand? We'd need to make some cuts somewhere."

"So it goes back to Lester Ginn, again," Sylvia says, squaring her jaw.

"I'm afraid it does."

"Well, I can't go back with that."

There's an uncomfortable moment of silence before Hawkins asks her, "If a vote were taken today, on the strike ..."

"It would be close. And if the pro-strikers lost ..."

"There's no telling what might happen," Hawkins finishes for her. Jipt is staring at the pool of blood and butter left in the void once occupied by his 20-ounce porterhouse, shaking his head slowly.

"And I'll tell you this, straight up," Sylvia says, businesslike and matter-of-fact. "I'm not taking the blame, uh-uh, no way." She points one of her long, red fingernails at Jipt, and he can't help but admire her cuticles. "The blame follows my finger, and it's going to be pointed just like this."

Jipt massages the loose skin between his eyes, which is hairless thanks to his Tweezing of the Eyebrows ritual. He suddenly looks tired, old and haggard. "If I support the strike ... and Ginn pulls some kind of crazy goddamned—"

"Then he'll take the blame, won't he?"

"We'll have to make sure of it," Hawkins says. "Which shouldn't be a problem, since the press is largely on our side. But that's worst-case. I don't think Ginn wants a strike any more than we do, and I bet he opens up to discussion at the very least."

Jipt closes his eyes – in agreement with everything except the last part. He does not think Lester will open up to discussion. Rather, he thinks it may cause him to shut down even further, if that's even possible. He knows that a lengthy strike will probably put more of a burden on PyraVegas, and him personally, than on Lester, and that he stands to gain nothing in the rare instance that Lester actually buckles. On the other hand, he knows he'll look like a bad guy if he opposes the strike, and that he'll be left on an island if it goes through without his endorsement. Besides, part of him holds out hope that Lester might not only buckle under the pressure, but break. "All right," he finally says, opening his eyes again. "I'll issue a statement that—"

"No. The Union needs to hear it from you personally. I'm going to stage a rally."

"We'll need to have some of the other community leaders there, too," Hawkins says. "To create a unified front. Chief of police, school superintendent, various corporate leaders."

"I think we can get a pretty decent coalition together," Jipt says, more to himself than to Sylvia or Hawkins.

"Then it sounds like you two need to make some phone calls," Sylvia says, inching her chair back from the table and extending her hand toward Jipt. "Do we have a deal then?"

Jipt wraps his giant white paw around her delicate black hand and squeezes firmly, without uttering another word.

Chapter 27

Because Tim has never met any of the inhabitants, never appeared before them or mingled amongst them, he is free to roam about the lower levels anonymously, and the City Level is far and away his favorite. Like an idealized version of Queens, it reminds him of kicking around the streets as a boy. Plus, as a bonus, he can patronize any number of establishments rife for merriment and carousal, namely bars, pubs, saloons and taverns, which are known for serving up music and liquor in vast quantities, and hosting impromptu games of cards and dice. Thus far, Tim has kept these nocturnal debauches from Lester, and for good reason. There's no doubt he would express vehement disapproval on grounds of safety and security, if not moral decency.

On this particular evening Tim has chosen a spot called Dixie Dungarees, which features bouncy jazz, highballs and Texas Hold 'em. The game is in full swing, the felt table littered with multicolored plastic chips, and the players around the table are a motley, jocund bunch, laughing and drinking and otherwise having a grand time of it. Although they've just met, one might easily mistake them for old drinking buddies reunited for a wild weekend in New Orleans. Wearing Lester's infamous LUCKY LADIES tee shirt, Tim is nestled between a plump redhead named Frances and a goateed fellow in a wheelchair, who's not much younger than him, named Zeke.

Tim studies his hand, which is tinted green by the brim of his cheap plastic visor. A pair of sevens and a pair of twos, king high – which he figures is good enough to win since the betting has been light so far. He puffs on a clove cigarette and flips two red chips into the pot, an imaginary thousand dollars. The woman directly across from him, an unattractive spinster in her forties called Rita, throws her cards down in mock-disgust. "I got nothin'," she says in a New Jersey accent, her hole-riddled attempt at a flush splayed out next to her towering stacks of chips. "Can't win 'em all, I guess." She leans over and nudges Doreen with her shoulder, perhaps too flirtatiously, winking in a manner that might be taken as a proposition.

"Call," says Zeke, reluctantly, shrugging his palsied shoulders.

"Call," echoes Kenny, the old Rastafarian to Zeke's left.

"I'll call," says Doreen, the lithe young brunette who might be a model if it weren't for her slightly bucked teeth.

"I'm out," Frances says with a sigh, apparently having agonized over the decision.

"All right, then," Tim says. "Let's see what you suckers got."

Everyone turns their cards over and the closest hand is Kenny's, with two jacks, ace high.

In a celebratory gesture, Tim takes a heavy puff on his cigarette and a heavy swig of his Tom Collins. "Come to papa!" he says, raking in the pot with both hands, the cigarette dangling precariously from his moist lips. "It's a bloody good thing you folks are banned from The Casino, eh? You'd be licking Seth Jipt's boots after five bloody minutes! Ha ha!"

"Who the hell is Seth Jipt?" Rita says, and the others look at Tim, waiting for an answer.

"Come on, you're pulling my leg," Tim says, trying to catch the attention of the bartender, Carlos, a mildly retarded albino Spaniard. He is facing the other way, busy mixing some martinis, so all Tim can see is the back of his head, which is covered with thin, curly hair like a baby girl's. "*Garçon! Monsieur Carlos!*" Tim says, mistakenly thinking he's French. "Oh, what's the bloody use …"

"Seriously mon," Kenny says, dreadlocks dangling in front of his face. "Who dis Jipt character anyhow?"

"You people really don't know fuck-all, do you? He's The Casino man, you know, the head shot-caller down there."

"I thought Lester was in charge of The Casino," Zeke says.

"Yeah," Rita says.

"Well what gave you that bloody idea?" Tim says, fearing he's already conceded too much. "You're sorely mistaken. What difference does it make anyway?"

"This Seth Jipt, how'd you know about him though?" Doreen says nonchalantly, snapping her gum.

"You find a way round da filter, mon?" Kenny says (referring to the filter on the HoloVision that precludes inhabitants from viewing any material pertaining to The Pyramid, such as news articles and advertisements, of which there are surprisingly few to begin with).

"No, of course I didn't," Tim says with an air of condescension, still trying to flag down Carlos at the bar and debating on whether or not to wipe the sweat from his brow. He decides against it. If he weren't so drunk already, he probably would have made the mistake of bolting from the table in panic at this juncture, but the liquor has boosted his confidence. And besides, he's on a roll. "They went over all of this in orientation, several times as I recall. It's no wonder you forgot the name though. In fact, I don't know how I managed to retain it," Tim says, rambling. "After all, he's totally inconsequential. Just some corporate type, you know." Tim raises his empty glass, jingling the ice cubes like a bell, as if trying to distract a group of housecats sharpening their claws on the furniture. "Hey, Carlos! Mr. Collins has dried up on me over here. Let's go, *toute suite*, man!"

* * *

Lester sits up in bed, scrutinizing a large table of numbers printed on green and white computer paper. The column headers represent monthly averages for the past 27 months, and the rows represent specific metrics, such as the gallons of water consumed, the number of cubes that docked for replenishing and so on.

As he scans the data, the row that jumps off the page is one denoting PEAK TIME: CITY LEVEL, meaning the daily time at which occupancy of the City Level reaches its peak, on average.

"Listen to this," he says to Svetlana, who has fallen asleep with her head on his lap. "The average peak time, City Level, in month one was half eleven, a.m. Well, twenty-four past, but close enough. And it's gone up and up and up, until this past month, when it was almost midnight! That's rather startling, isn't it? Well, isn't it?"

"Huh? What did you say?" Svetlana says groggily.

"Ah, look there at my Russian buttercup! She's fallen asleep," Lester says, half doting and half admonishing her.

"I thought you were going to play with my hair and tickle my back?"

"How do you know I wasn't? You were asleep."

"I would know."

"Well … speaking of that, listen to what I know, thanks to this handy little report here."

"I don't want to know."

"Sure you do, listen."

"No," she says, stubbornly pleading. "It's time for bed. Bedtime."

"I'm *in* bed," Lester says.

"Sleep time, sleepy time," she says, her voice weakening.

Lester sings in a campy lullaby tone, "Sleep time, sleepy time. Time to sleep o' love of mine. Sleep deep ... sleep deep." This appears to have done the trick, as Svetlana's lips are barely parted, her delicate breaths coming at long, even intervals. Lester pats her gently on the head and looks around for his electronic butler, Morris. Morris assumes the persona of a cantankerous old Irishman, which ensures that Lester only calls on him after hours, or when Squeakins is otherwise detained. "Morris!" Lester says in a loud whisper. "Where the devil are you, man?!"

"I'm doon here you stupeed eejit!" Morris yowls from beneath the covers. Lester rustles around under there and produces the sleek little device, which couldn't stand in any starker contrast to Morris' cumbersome, abrasive personality. "Right, well, I'd like a graph of this data for peak time, city level immediately. A two-dimensional graph would be fine, seeing as though we haven't anything to plot on the z-axis ... although, I suppose we could—"

"Are you bloody feeneeshed?!"

"Yes, just give me the graph!" Lester snips, trying to keep his voice down and glancing at Svetlana just to be sure. She's still out of it. The graph appears at center-screen on the far wall, a scattering of dots meandering up and to the right at roughly the same clip. "A line. Give me a line. The average. The mean average." The line appears, which turns out to be slightly logarithmic in shape, ultimately favoring north instead of east as the direction of choice. "My god, just look at that!" Lester says, before shushing himself. "Shhh. Sh Sh Sh. Just calm down. This is much worse than we thought! But perhaps it's not. Perhaps it's an aberration. Morris, show me The Grid." A schematic of The Grid appears on the HoloVision display, the yellow trapezoidal image floating just off the foot of the bed. From this perspective, the interior volume sparkles like glitter on black construction paper and also moves enigmatically, shifting and rippling in such a way that one might think he sees a pattern, just before it disappears. "Zoom in on one of the Elevator Stations," Lester says, eagerly. "The center station." The view tightens down such that individual cubes can be seen, although there's a contiguous cluster around the station itself that's growing larger by the second. "Son of a … it's a bloody logjam down there! And it's nearly – what time is it, anyway?"

"Five after eleven," Morris says.

"It's nearly half-eleven, and they're only now lining up!"

"It's a bit after eleven, not nearly half-eleven you crazy fecker!"

"Oh, shut your bloody pie hole and prepare my chariot," Lester says, referring to his special Executive Elevator. "Destination … City Level!"

"Hmm," Svetlana utters, nuzzling and balling herself into a fetal position.

"Shhhh … Shhhh," Lester says, taking her unused pillow. He thinks for a moment about how he must slide his left hand under her head and slide himself out from beneath her while inserting the pillow in place of his thigh. A complex maneuver, but he's executed it brilliantly on a number of occasions recently and tonight is no different.

* * *

Lester disembarks the elevator and turns to admire his appearance in the metallic doors as they close, his body appearing from both sides and meeting in the middle to complete the picture. He is wearing a black Victorian-style suit, complete with frilly cravat, top hat and cane. He fiddles with the cravat, tips the hat slightly to one side and then applies some spittle to the blatantly phony handlebar mustache with his index fingers. He turns and twirls the cane before proceeding down the secret corridor, which is long and barren. His polished boots clap smartly against the floor, and upon reaching the end he exits through a door.

The door leads to a small room that is also barren, except for a red telephone on one wall, a sink on the opposite wall, and a second door on the wall opposite Lester. Without hesitation, he crosses and goes through that door, which places him in a narrow alley where a silver bumper car is waiting. He hops in and mashes down the pedal.

The traffic out on the streets is heavy but moving, and having just a smidge more power under his hood than the other drivers, Lester weaves to and fro with ease, in the direction of the main entertainment district. In spite of his garish attire, he goes virtually unnoticed by the other drivers, who look a bit odd themselves.

Once the grocery stores, pharmacies and laundromats start giving way to restaurants and bars, Lester pulls over to the curb and gravitates toward a mountainous Samoan waddling down the sidewalk. "Excuse me, good sir," Lester says, looking especially ridiculous leaning out of the tiny car, tipping his hat with the handle of his cane. The Samoan stops and turns around, which takes a rather long time, and looks Lester over without a trace of bemusement, amusement, wariness or suspicion. In fact, he looks quite drunk, his chubby eyelids drooped at half-mast.

"Yeah?" he says.

"I daresay I've never been to this part of town, and I was wondering if you had any place to suggest? In the way of a watering hole, you know," Lester says, raising his eyebrows twice and imitating the quick sip of a beverage for effect.

"What'chu lookin' fo' mista," the Samoan says, his voice deep and thick. "Like some dancing, or a place just to chill or what? Card games or what?"

"Yes! Card games!" Lester says, figuring this will present the best opportunity to crack open the psyche of the average inhabitant – to lay his finger directly on the proverbial pulse of the masses.

"Well, there's Tijuana Tina's ..."

"I despise the name Tina."

"Okay. Then you've got The Fox Hole, it's pretty fun, or Dixie Dungarees, I hear that place has some good action lately."

"Good action, yes, that's precisely what I desire. Point me in the direction of Dixie Dungarees."

"It's just around the corner here, two or three blocks down on your right."

"Splendid. Thank you, good man. Cheers!" Lester says, speeding off. Less than a minute later he pulls up in front of Dixie Dungarees, where jazz is pouring from the open door, robust with horns and piano.

Finished in cracked plaster to look like a dive, and not much bigger than the Golden Horseshoe back in Queens, the place is packed nearly elbow to elbow, and Lester squirms his way to the bar, politely saying "Excuse me," "Pardon me," and so on. He notices the poker game, where a man in a green visor is drawing all the attention. He has one arm around the pot, raking it toward himself clumsily, and the other arm around a promiscuous-looking young woman, who's perched on his lap. Lester can't hear anything over the din, and can't see the man's face from his vantage point. Even if he were expecting to see his son there, the mannerisms might not tip him off. After all, the man with the green visor is shamelessly drunk, and he is smoking a cigarette. As far as Lester knows, Tim does not partake of this vulgar habit.

"How about a frosty lager?" Lester says, catching the bartender's attention.

"Name's Carlos," the albino says in a Spanish-accented lisp, flashing a gap-toothed smile.

"Splendid," Lester says in a patronizing tone, as if this was the last piece of information he wanted to hear. "How about a lager, Carlos?"

"We serve only gin."

Lester curses the Samoan under his breath for withholding this information. "Only gin, fine. Make it a Tom Collins then."

As Carlos turns to prepare the drink, Lester turns back around to watch the poker game. He figures that, if he's to infiltrate the game, the gatekeeper will be the man with the green visor, who's really holding court with the others now. He appears to be telling some sort of humorous story, which, judging from his animated hand gestures, may involve both a fast-moving, horse-drawn sleigh and some kind of Sasquatch creature with vicious claws. Yes, he's pissed drunk for sure, but Lester has to give him credit on at least one account. Even from a distance, from behind, he is enormously entertaining.

Tim guzzles the remainder of his fourteenth Tom Collins and slams down the empty glass. Only, he misses his mark by a few inches and it glances the edge of the table, shattering everywhere. The room collectively gasps and the music even stops while everyone turns to see.

Like a hawk, Lester spots the blood gushing from the man's wrist. "My god!" Lester says, slamming his own drink down on the bar and rushing toward him, pushing several onlookers brusquely to the side. "This man is critically injured!" He gets there as the man is losing consciousness, just in time to catch his head as it pitches forward on a collision course with the glass-strewn tabletop. Lester pulls his head back, and when he exposes his son's face he almost faints himself, but he doesn't. "Get off of him you filthy strumpet!" he screams at the scantily-clad young woman, who's still on Tim's lap, frozen in shock and spattered with blood, but apparently unhurt. Rita jumps up from her chair and helps the girl to her feet, and Lester clamps his hand around Tim's wrist in attempt to stop the bleeding. With his other hand, Lester shakes him, wanting to call his name – wanting to say, "Son! Wake up, son!" – but somehow he maintains his discipline and instead says, "Sir! Wake up, sir!" After all, the first priority may be saving Tim's life, but that doesn't mean the second priority cannot be upheld as well. Their identities must not be revealed.

Tim opens his eyes and shrinks back at the sight of Lester. The words dribble from the corner of his mouth like post-coital urine.

"Hey, what're you doing here, Da—"

Lester jams his other hand into Tim's mouth, cutting him short, which draws curious reactions from the onlookers. Thinking fast, Lester says, "I think his airway is obstructed!"

"I'm a doctor," a drunk man says from the bar. His hair is disheveled and he's spilling his cocktail on the woman in the adjacent stool.

"Hey!" she says, "Watch out!"

"No! There's no time!" Lester says, ripping the cravat from his neck with bloody hands and tying it around the wound. He hoists Tim up over his shoulder and turns for the door.

The crowd parts, except for a stout woman in a flowered dress who looks terribly sober – and terribly concerned. "Wait," she says. "I'm a nurse at the clinic over on Northeast Faithful, just a few blocks away. He needs medical attention."

"Don't worry," Lester says urgently, resisting the urge to steamroll her, on account of her compassion. "I'll take care of him."

"But where are you going?" she persists. "The closest place is—"

Lester's eyes narrow and he bares his teeth, not unlike a perturbed chimpanzee, as he snaps, "I told you I'd take care of him! Now, please step aside!"

"Okay," the woman says, backing away more out of fear than compliance, and Lester sprints out the door.

"That guy sounds really familiar," Zeke says rhetorically, and the room buzzes with conversation. The band starts up again with a blare of trumpet and trombone.

* * *

Lester bursts through the door from the alley into the safe room, the dead weight of Tim's body still draped over his shoulder. He dashes for the red telephone, out of breath from having run all the way. "Hello! Boy! … It's Tim! He's bleeding terribly! … No, I'll bring him up myself, just alert the medical staff immediately!" Lester hangs up the phone and bolts out the other side of the room, into the corridor, and Tim leaves a trail of dripping blood all the way to the elevator. Lester careens inside, bashing into the wall, and leans there for support. He kicks the button for Executive Level One, where The Infirmary is located, and the elevator lurches upward, as if sensing the peril.

Unable to stand any longer, Lester slumps down the wall, leaving a red streak from where Tim's blood has soaked into his clothes. Tears begin to well up in his eyes and he bites his lip, looking straight up. It's as if he can see through the entire Pyramid and into the heavens, searching for mercy, begging for a god to exist.

Chapter 28

Over the months and years since Anna and Tim's estrangement as lovers, the awkwardness has ebbed and flowed from their rapport and ultimately evaporated. A platonic friendship has resumed. However, the emotional void left by their prior relationship has been filled not so much by familial love but instead by unrequited sexual desires. As a remedy, Tim has chosen to seek alternative outlets for his lustful energy, namely masturbation and tennis, while Anna has accepted the unspoken advice of nuns, scholars and widows, arming herself with weaponry the likes of reason and principle. In other words, she has chosen to suppress the feelings, while Tim has chosen to redirect them.

Anna sits at Tim's bedside in The Infirmary's recovery wing, a perfect balance of comfortable furnishings and medical technology, and she is acting strangely coquettish. Her ensemble is even more revealing than usual, a shrunken white tee-shirt with embroidered butterflies, which leaves both ample cleavage and midriff exposed, a short pleated skirt and Italian-made shoes with four-inch heels, a chic design of cork, leather and woven hemp. She crosses and uncrosses her legs, which have been tanned and toned to near-perfection, and flips the rope-like French braid over her shoulder. But all these cues are lost on Tim, who remains staring at the video wall in front of him, which shows an old American football game played before facemasks and instant replay.

She places her hand over Tim's and finally breaks the long silence. "What can I do to make you feel better? I would have baked you cupcakes or something, but I don't really know how."

"Cupcakes are easy," Tim says, distractedly, without turning or even blinking. "From a box, at least."

"I don't think we have any."

"Oh."

"I don't like that word."

"Box?" Tim says, turning, one eyebrow slightly raised.

"Yeah. It's so crude."

"I suppose. I mean, there's a box, or boxes, and then there's—"

"I know. Box."

"Right," Tim says, smiling naughtily.

Anna gets up from her chair and sits on the edge of the bed, one leg tucked beneath her, the other on the floor. Her red skirt drapes in front like a theatre curtain, poised to rise at any moment. She takes his hand and places it on her thigh, just above the knee. "So. What can I do to make you feel better."

"I don't know," Tim says with an adolescent shrug. He has unknowingly anesthetized himself against her wiles, and it hasn't been easy.

"Nothing at all?" she coyly persists, now moving her hand to the drawstring of Tim's pajama pants. She fiddles with the loops and ends but leaves the knot intact.

Tim's eyes dilate and his mouth is suddenly bone dry at the sight of Anna's fingers playing so close to his genitals. And all at once, as if a gauzy veil has been removed from his eyes, he is assaulted by the vividness of Anna's sexuality, by every detail from her painted toenails to her upper lip, pinned delicately above her smile. Not to mention a number of unmentionables in between, of course. He is very close to being, quite literally, breathless.

Anna begins loosening the bow, causing one of the loops to shrink like the very opening Tim has to avoid a terrible mistake. That is, as he sees it. Or *wants* to see it. Or *thinks* he wants to see it. Or thinks he *should* want to see it.

"I've got to get out of here," Tim whispers in a panic, ripping the IV tubes from his arm and wriggling away from Anna's touch.

Startled, Anna gets up again, this time back in the familiar persona of concerned family member. "Tim, I don't think that's a good idea. Look, I'm sorry. I shouldn't have—"

"No, no! It's quite all right!" Tim avoids eye-contact, taking up his electronic butler from the nightstand and tapping the screen with fake commands. "You wanted to make me feel better."

"Well, yes, but—"

"Let me guess. You also wanted to make yourself feel better?"

Apparently Anna doesn't want to admit it.

"Well, I think that's only natural," Tim says. "But personally, I'd rather feel so-so all the time than feel really good and then really bad again, okay?" He starts for the door, but Anna blocks his path.

"You don't really feel that way, do you?"

"Yes, I do. I think so, anyway."

"You're thinking too much, exactly what you told me not to do, remember?"

"Fine, so I'm a hypocrite then. Who isn't?"

"I'm not saying that, I'm just saying … fine. Go. I'll talk to you later."

Tim wavers noticeably, resisting the urge to hug her and tell her he's sorry. But he's not sure what to be sorry for. In fact, he's in a such a state of emotional vertigo, having been flipped round so many times by all the complexities, that he doesn't want to risk saying anything else. So he bolts out the door.

Chapter 29

It's not so much a courtyard as a narrow swath of grass between apartment buildings, and in the center is a row of eight stadium seats. Lester sits in an end seat and Tim in one of the center seats, listening to a Yankees game on the radio. The remaining seats are filled with scarecrows, which are connected to a rigging of ropes, pulleys and rods overhead. Next to Lester is a basket of baseballs and a high-powered jugs pitching machine aimed straight up, its wheels spinning at top speed.

The play-by-play announcer calls the action. "The two-two pitch to Renfro ... swings ... foul ball."

Lester takes a ball from the basket, loads it into the jugs machine and *Shoomp!* The ball rockets skyward out of sight.

"There it is, son!"

Lester pulls a rope which causes the scarecrows to stand up all at once. Tim stands up too and tracks the flight of the ball, his baseball glove ready. He jostles between the newspaper-stuffed bodies and finally the ball comes back down and *Thunk!* Right into his glove. Lester releases the rope, sending the scarecrows back into their seats.

"Got it!" Tim says.

He takes the ball from his glove and holds it up to show the imaginary crowd.

"Brilliant, son! Good show! I think you're almost ready."

"Really? To go to a game?"

"That's right. You might even have to miss a day of school."

"Yippee!"

"Right, well first things first. It's time for our afternoon exercises."

They retire inside to the apartment for said exercises, which always include some combination of mental and physical challenges – but no two sessions are the same. Sometimes Tim is made to recite poetry while running in place. Other times he is quizzed on multiplication tables while fencing. The idea originates in a renaissance view of personal identity and self-improvement combined with a Darwinian view of survival in Lester's mind. In other words, the belief that well-roundedness of body and mind is key to one's longevity and success.

Today, Lester has Tim squat halfway to the floor and hold an unabridged dictionary above his head while answering rapid-fire questions.

"What's the capital of Sri Lanka?"

"Colombo."

"What's the square root of eighteen?"

"Three radical two."

"Who wrote the Heart of Darkness?"

"Joseph Conrad."

"Name an element heavier than Cesium."

"There isn't one."

"Very good. Requiem was the last composition of …"

"Wolfgang Amadeus Mozart."

"What was the first satellite?"

"Sputnik."

This goes on for another fifteen minutes or so and Tim doesn't miss a single question. His legs, however, eventually fail him and he collapses to the floor in exhaustion.

"Just one more question!" Lester says, kneeling down beside him.

"No! I can't!"

"Who's the greatest dad in the history of civilization?"

"You are."

"And who's the greatest son?"

"That's two questions."

"Never mind that. Who's the greatest son?"

"I am."

"Correct again," Lester says. "That's my boy … You know, there are two kinds of people in this world son. Those who believe in themselves and those who believe in nothing. The latter group consists primarily of invalids and thieves."

"I believe in myself," Tim says.

"I believe in you, too," Lester says, as he wraps him in a warm, suffocating hug.

Chapter 30

It takes Lester over two hours via bicycle to find Admiral Bernard Porsley's office, which is tucked deep inside a labyrinth-like Bronx neighborhood. Fortunately, he has allotted three hours – and, thus, he can utilize some idle time in the waiting room to partake in leisurely reading. Even more fortunate is the fact that they have his favorite periodical (just edging out Robotic Butler Magazine), Primate Sports Illustrated. On this month's cover is a particularly adroit chimp who is dunking two basketballs at once. *If only I could do that*, Lester thinks, before delving into the feature article.

The office is located above a pizzeria and the smell of baking pies is making Lester's stomach churn. The general décor looks quite well-suited for a hack private investigator but certainly not an Admiral. The furniture is old and chintzy, but comfortable, the lighting dim. A ceiling fan turns far too lazily overhead to stir the hot, muggy air in the room. Pleasantries have already been exchanged between Lester and the receptionist, a 50-ish-looking woman with beautiful chestnut hair done up in an old fashioned hairdo. Her hair is obviously dyed but lustrous nonetheless and she is very becoming for an older woman – her eyes bright, her skin virtually unwrinkled and her bosom quite ample. On her desk is an electric typewriter, a large black telephone, a crank-style pencil sharpener, a carousel holding various ink stamps, a dagger-like letter opener and a pile of mail. Lester peeks over the top of his magazine every so often and admires the efficiency with which she performs her duties, first sharpening an entire boxful of pencils without pause and then opening the mail and stamping each piece with at least two different stamps. One looks like a date stamp, with three dials on the side, but Lester is curious about the other stamps. He does not want to break her routine, however, so he refrains from edgewise comments. The phone does not ring once and there are no discernable voices or stirrings behind the frosted glass door that says ADMIRAL BERNARD PORSLEY, RETIRED. Lester is in no hurry, as he has cleared the afternoon docket for this meeting, and therefore is quite satisfied to read his magazine in a leisurely manner for another half hour or so. Aside from the profuse sweating, he could not be more comfortable. When the clock on the wall says 3 p.m., the prescribed time for the meeting, the phone rings once and the receptionist picks it up. She listens for a brief moment, then hangs it up and says, "Mr. Ginn, Admiral Porsley will see you now. You can let yourself in."

"Splendid, thank you," Lester says, and he neatly returns the magazine to its place among the others fanned out on the coffee table. Then he stands and smoothes the front of his corduroy sport coat before crossing to the door.

The small office is sparsely furnished with cheap brass lamps and paintings one might find in a motel room or on the set of a low-budget porno film. There is one window and the sunlight illuminates a tremendous amount of dust floating in the air. There is no ceiling fan and it is beastly hot, at least ten degrees hotter than the waiting room. The Admiral is a frail-looking old fellow, seated behind a desk in his full Royal Navy blues, which are adorned with decorations, medals, epaulets and the whole works. He is much too well-dressed and well-groomed in contrast to the tackiness of his surroundings and, as a result, he appears somewhat tragic or otherwise pitiable. Upon closer inspection, Lester sees that his desk is a wooden door mounted atop two wooden filing cabinets, such that there is nothing to obscure the Admiral's spindly lower extremities. He is busy tinkering with a half-built model pirate ship of intricate detail but stops to greet Lester in a stately English accent as they shake hands.

"Mister Ginn, I do thank you for coming, especially under such mysterious circumstances," he says. "Please, have a seat." He gestures to an upholstered arm chair placed squarely in front of the desk, and Lester sits, still mesmerized and dizzy from the heat. The Admiral is exceedingly pale, his hair white as confectionary sugar, and as a result Lester is surprised by the firmness of his handshake. "You must be curious about the purpose of this meeting so let me get to it straight away. Now, I've got several things to tell you, and some are more shocking than others."

"How shocking are we talking about?" Lester says. "Like, aliens have been discovered on the moon? Or, aliens have been discovered here on earth – in fact, you and I are not really men a'tall, but aliens? You'll have to pardon me, Admiral, but you see, I don't tend to handle shock very well. Especially if it has to do with aliens."

"Yes, I see. Well, we shall just have to push through as best we can, because the information must be imparted to you without delay. Very well, then?"

Lester squirms in his seat and loosens his hideous paisley tie. "Perhaps some water might help … with the swallowing of information, you know. Besides, it is a bit warm in here."

"Of course," the Admiral says, picking up the phone. "Ms. Tiddybar, please bring some water for Mr. Ginn … Thank you."

"I'm sorry, did you say … nevermind."

The receptionist, Ms. Tiddybar, appears with a tall glass of ice water and hands it to Lester. He chugs it down, dribbling all over himself, and hands the empty glass back to her.

"Thank you Mrs. – thank you. Another would be smashing, if you would be so kind. You know what they say, Admiral, it's best not to ration your water when severely dehydrated. All at once they say!"

"Yes, well let me begin with the information I must impart, Mr. Ginn. As mentioned in the letter, I served with your father in the Royal Navy years ago. However, ours was a special mission – veiled in the highest level of secrecy – though not militarily related, per se, but more along the lines of exploration."

"Exploration for what?"

"Anything useful really, anything potentially valuable. And what your father's team discovered was just that. A new element in fact, the specific properties of which I will spare you the details of, but which was eventually key to a number of scientific breakthroughs."

"Breakthroughs, eh?"

"Indeed. You see, you may not have been aware, but your father was a brilliant chemist and engineer, and he used this material to produce super-efficient and transparent solar cells, which could be applied to glass. The resulting genesis, or breakthrough if you will, was the solar window, so commonly used today as a source of energy that we take them for granted. Prior to his death, your father secured a patent on this technology, and thus secured enormous royalties for his estate. And I, Mr. Ginn, was granted the responsibility of managing this estate. Until now, that is."

Lester is lost in thought, transfixed by the millions of dust particles suspended in the air. A substantial pause ensues, as he slips deeper into the illusion that the room itself is submersed in water, deep below the surface of the sea, and that the dust particles are actually tiny organisms swimming around, searching dumbly and blindly for food.

"So the light is … the cells are … what was that last part?"

"You mean the subject of your father's estate."

"Right, right, right. I thought the house in Perth was long-since sold."

"Not that kind of estate, Mr. Ginn. It's a term for an all-inclusive collection of assets."

"Hmm. I see. But it's been so long. The will didn't mention anything about ..."

"Yes, well, he wished you to – how shall I say – experience those aspects of life that wealth inevitably precludes. To learn from common struggles I suppose. Now, this is the part you may find rather shocking ..." The Admiral opens one of the filing drawers and produces a single-page document. He hands it to Lester. "Now, if you'll refer to that statement, it indicates the value of the estate, as of the market's close yesterday. The left-hand column indicates the general category of investment – stocks, bonds, treasury bills, precious metals, real estate, cash reserves and so forth – and the right hand column indicates the amount in U.S. dollars. Of course, this is but a cursory synopsis – I have the detail for you here, in this report."

The Admiral hefts a gigantic three-ring binder onto the desktop, the impact of which causes the bowsprit of his ship to come unglued. "Oh my," he says, fretting over the model for a moment. He sighs heavily, in a very childlike manner, before recomposing himself and turning his attention back to Lester, who is staring at the document as if it were written in Sanskrit. "As I was saying, it's all detailed in this report. But, for the sake of time, I thought a high-level summary would be easiest to digest, as you say. So, the total amount shown at the bottom of that page is now – unofficially at least – yours, Mr. Ginn. There are of course some legal necessities, notarized signatures and so forth but—"

Like the masts of a foundering ship, Lester's head lists to one side. His eyes roll unnaturally inward and his mouth falls agape in a state of torpor, a bead of saliva dangling perilously from his lower lip.

"Mr. Ginn, are you feeling all right?"

Just then, Ms. Tiddybar returns with another glass of water.

"I'm sorry for the wait, Mr. Ginn, but – oh my stars. Is he ill?"

"He'll be fine. His father had a similar propensity for catatonics … under extreme duress, you know."

The document flutters out of Lester's hand and he slumps forward in his chair, now fully unconscious.

"Right. Well, I'll have that water please, Ms. Tiddybar, as long as you've gone to the trouble of fetching it."

Chapter 31

The next day, Admiral Bernard Porsley arrives at his office and finds Lester fast asleep on the couch with Tim – exactly where he left them the previous evening. He decides to let them wake by their own volition, but does not bother to tiptoe around. He turns on the overhead lights, opens the blinds and heats some water for tea in a small microwave oven. The microwave sits atop an end table pushed up against the couch, near Lester's head, and it's the series of beeping sounds that finally rouse him.

Clearly disoriented, Lester rolls off the couch and frantically scrambles beneath the Admiral's desk.

"Duck and cover! Duck and cover!" Lester shouts. "It's going to blow!"

"Dad, what are you doing?" Tim says, sleepily.

Without the slightest change in temperament, the Admiral casually removes his mug from the microwave and sets it atop his desk. Then he leans over to make eye contact with Lester.

"It's quite all right, Mr. Ginn, I'm just fixing some tea. Would you like some?"

"Admiral Porsley?"

"Yes."

"What bloody time is it?"

"O' six-hundred."

"In the morning?"

"Yes. I trust you're well-rested. It appears you slept for almost fourteen hours."

176

"How about that." Lester says, standing up and looking around the room as if he's never seen it before. "Tim! Thank goodness you're all right!"

"I'm fine," Tim says. "Are you feeling better?"

"Sorry?"

"They said you were sick. That's why they brought me here yesterday."

"Oh, yes, yes, I'm fine, son. Not to worry about me. I've got some very exciting news, I mean ... say, Admiral? That conversation ... about my father and whatnot ..."

"Was not a dream, if that's what you're asking. Perhaps this document will jog your memory," the Admiral says, taking the financial statement from his top desk drawer and handing it to Lester – as he did the previous day.

Lester's eyes widen upon the total listed at the bottom.

"Yes, I see ..." he says.

"Perhaps you should have a seat. Have some tea."

"No, thank you, Admiral, I've squandered quite enough time already! Must get going!" Lester says, stuffing the document in his pocket and then engaging the Admiral in a vigorous handshake. "Thank you! Thank you for everything, Admiral! Come on, son, I'll explain everything on the way home."

"You're quite welcome," the Admiral says, and by this time Lester already has one foot out the door. "Mr. Ginn, perhaps you'd like to know—"

"Hey, Admiral!" Lester says. "One more thing. How do I ..."

"This checkbook will allow you to draw upon the amount listed as discretionary cash reserves," the Admiral says, handing the checkbook to Lester. "As we discussed yesterday, the entire estate is now under your control. However, at the risk of sounding presumptuous—"

"So you'll continue to manage it for me, then? Mind all the P's and Q's?"

"Yes, it would be my distinct honor, Mr. Ginn. Perhaps, once you've had some time to fully assess things, we can schedule another meeting to discuss your short- and long-term plans."

"Can't wait!" Lester says. "I'll be in touch. Cheers then!"

"Goodbye, Mr. Ginn. And congratulations."

Lester leaves the office, dragging Tim along, and gets halfway down the stairwell before deciding that he just can't wait to tell Svetlana. He runs back up to the Admiral's office and pounds on the frosted glass so hard that it's a wonder how it doesn't shatter under the duress.

"Come in."

"Admiral," Lester says, out of breath. "Do you … mind if I … use your phone?"

"By all means. Feel free to use the one on Ms. Tiddybar's desk. Dial nine to get out."

"Mrs. who? Never mind, I remember. Thanks."

Lester puts his foot up on the desk and dials the number, which is printed in permanent ink on his inner-ankle. It takes a few moments to switch through, but then it starts to ring …

Chapter 32

Sergei raps on the door to Svetlana's office and then opens it, popping his head inside.

"Hey, you hungry?"

"Oh my god, I totally forgot about our lunch!" Svetlana replies. She is definitely more upset than she should be for simply forgetting about their date.

"No problem. I just reminded you, didn't I?"

"No, I mean I can't go today. Anna's sick – my daughter – she's home from school and I promised I'd check on her at lunchtime. I'm so sorry. I meant to come and find you this morning but—"

"Don't worry about it, Svetlana, really," Sergei says, stepping inside. "You've got your priorities in order and that's nothing to apologize for. Lunch is a long-standing institution that will probably endure for years to come. So we can try for another day."

"Thank you."

"How are you getting home?"

"The metro."

"Let me drive you. I could drop you off, pick up something to eat, and come back for you afterwards."

"You're very kind, but—"

"But what? Which station were you going to?"

"Just to the Smolenskaya."

"Oh, that's so close, and you have to change trains. Driving will be much quicker, and you can save yourself the fare."

"You're very persuasive."

"I wanted to go into politics after the violin thing fell through. But the connections just weren't there."

"Thank you, Sergei."

* * *

It is raining heavily outside, and the windshield wipers on Sergei's compact, French-made sedan are barely keeping up with the onslaught. Traffic is somewhat bogged-down as a result, and they find themselves trapped behind a hulking sanitation truck.

"Perhaps the metro would have been faster, after all," Sergei says, in a lighthearted way.

"What is it, Murray's Law?"

"I think it's Murphy's. Good day to be home sick though, I guess. If there is such a thing."

"I hope she's all right," Svetlana says.

"Some kind of bug, eh?"

"Vomiting and fever. Very nasty. I think it may be food poisoning."

"Just started this morning?"

"Yes. And she ate with friends last night – a birthday party at some place near the *Bolshoi*."

"Are you sure she wasn't …" Sergei says, tipping an imaginary bottle up to his mouth.

"No, it was chaperoned. She was definitely sober."

"What did she have to eat?"

"*Rasstegai*. Take a left at the next intersection."

"Okay … Could be bad fish," Sergei says.

"She also had potatoes. It could be the potatoes."

"Listen to us. Like two hack doctors trying to make a diagnosis."

"I wanted to be a doctor once," Svetlana says.

"Too much school."

"Yes. But I also can't stand the sight of blood."

"Ah," Sergei says, chuckling, "I think that's what they call a barrier to entry. I had a similar situation – wanted to be a pilot but—"

"You're afraid of heights."

"Deathly so."

"You can pull over there, next to that … what the …?

"Ha ha! Looks like a man with a wig strapped to his … my goodness, I hope that's not your doorman."

"No … on second thought, why don't you pull into that space right there."

"Okay. Looks like he's moving along. Although you have to wonder where a guy with a skin-colored bodysuit and a wig strapped to his crotch is going in the middle of a weekday."

"I need to get out of this neighborhood. The rent is cheap, but …"

"So you want me to pick you up here in about an hour?"

"I hate to put you through the extra trouble. Would you like to come up? I think I have some food in the refrigerator we could eat."

"Not the *rasstegai*, I hope."

"No," Svetlana says, giggling.

* * *

Svetlana turns the last of three deadbolts and leads Sergei into the apartment. The curtains are drawn and it reeks of vomit, but neither acknowledges the fact. Svetlana crosses to Anna's bedroom and peeks inside.

"Anna?"

"I'm in here," Anna says. "The bathroom."

"It's dreadfully dark in here, honey," Svetlana says, heading to the bathroom around the corner. She turns back to Sergei. "Please make yourself at home. And feel free to open those curtains."

"Sure," Sergei says, opening the curtains and sitting down in a ragged armchair.

Svetlana finds Anna on the bathroom floor in her pajamas, propping herself up between the toilet and the wall. She looks very pale and her hair is matted to the side of her head.

"Oh, Anna," Svetlana says. "Poor baby. I hope you're feeling at least a little better than you look."

"Ha ha," Anna says, sarcastically. "I feel like shit ... Is someone else here?"

"Yes, it's a friend of mine from work, Sergei. He was kind enough to drive me home."

"Sergei, huh? You never said anything about a Sergei."

"There was nothing to tell, honey, I just met him yesterday."

"Do you like him?"

"He's very sweet."

"You like him."

"What do you mean?"

"I mean you like him."

"This is a silly conversation," Svetlana says, trying to glaze it over with a smile.

"Has he asked you out?"

"No. Well, yes, sort of. He asked me for lunch today but it wouldn't have been like a date or anything."

"You shouldn't feel guilty about it."

"I don't."

"Yes you do."

"There's nothing to feel guilty about."

"Exactly," Anna says.

"Are you hungry?"

"I can't really tell. I feel hungry but I'd probably just barf it up again."

"I could fix you some broth."

"Mmm, broth, my favorite," Anna says, again with the sarcasm.

"It's something. You need something in your stomach."

"Okay. I'll take it in my room."

"Here, I'll help you."

Svenlana bends down to help Anna to her feet and, as she does so, the phone rings in the other room.

"Sergei? Can you answer that please?" Svetlana calls to him.

"No problem," Sergei says. "Just tell me where – ah, there it is."

"It's probably your grandmother calling to check on you," Svetlana says to Anna as they leave the bathroom.

"Hello?" Sergei says. "Hello? ... Hello? No one's there."

He hangs up the phone just as Svetlana and Anna are passing through to Anna's room.

"Must have been a wrong number," Svetlana says, betraying her concern with the raised tone of her voice.

"Or not," Anna says.

"Sergei, this is my daughter, Anna."

"Nice to meet you," he says. "I hope you're feeling better soon."

"Thanks."

"You're lucky to have a mother like her to take care of you."

"Yes, I am," Anna says, exchanging a look with Svetlana as if to say, "He's very handsome and charming, isn't he?"

"Well, let's get you back into bed, sweetie, and then I'll fix you that broth," Svetlana says, ushering her into the bedroom and then whispering, "Not a word out of you, understand?"

"You have to tell him eventually."

"Not yet."

"Okay," Anna agrees.

Content with their pact, Svetlana does her best to clear Lester from her mind before she passes back into the living room, smiling – and Sergei smiles back, blissfully unaware of the torment raging inside her.

Chapter 33

It's a wonder Tim has resisted temptation for this long. Although, in fairness, perhaps he doesn't deserve quite so much credit, seeing as though he was conditioned to believe – from the very start – that infiltrating The Casino was impossible. The notion was drilled into his head on a regular basis as doctrine, gospel, an accepted fact, like man's inability to flap his arms and take off like a bird.

Tim has reached the point many people reach – some earlier in their lives, some later, some many times and some never at all – where he has begun to question everything. For every *why* there's a *why not*. For every *how*, a *what if*. And by this way of thinking, impossibility itself is the only impossibility.

The answer was laughably simple. While it's true, one cannot enter The Casino from above, hundreds of thousands of people enter from below every day. And it was even easier than Tim thought to ascertain the skeleton code, which enables one to reach the central train station by means of a secret Executive Elevator. Knowing his father's mistrust in others, as well as his own memory, Tim guessed that Lester wrote the code down somewhere. Furthermore, he correctly guessed it would be somewhere obvious, so he wouldn't forget where he wrote it down – such as on the desk blotter at his favorite secretary. But there was something else Tim needed, which could have been much more difficult to acquire had it not been for his forethought, his craftiness and his confidence in not being caught ...

* * *

Also a believer in obvious and clichéd hiding places, Tim bends back the corner of his mattress. For an instant he laments the passage of time since Anna slept there, but he is distracted by the coveted item – a bundle of crisp $100 bills.

Chiefly because he is drunk and determined, he resists doting upon the inky aroma or exquisiteness of the cash and tucks the bundle snugly in the interior coat pocket of his leisure suit. The suit is olive green with wide lapels and he turns toward the mirror to inspect its symmetry. He tightens his mustard-colored tie and peers down at his reflection in the matching patent-leather shoes. He lifts his feet up and down as if walking – marching actually – up to himself, ripping the amber sunglasses away from his face with purpose and saying in a generic American accent, "Hi there. The name's Wesley Witherspoon and I would like to exchange these bills for chips, please."

Tim knows he should have chosen a more forgettable, believable name, like Mike Jones or John Smith, but he likes the sound of Wesley Witherspoon because it requires so much more vocal acuity than Tim Ginn. And moreover, Wesley Witherspoon is – in almost every way – the polar opposite of Tim Ginn. He is utterly decisive, self-assured and compassionless, thinking only of satisfying his own basest desires.

He pivots on one foot with military-like smartness, takes three long strides to the nightstand and guzzles the remainder of the gin straight from the bottle. "Hot damn!" he says, still in the hokey all-American character of Wesley Witherspoon. "That's smooth!" He slams the bottle down and takes up a banana. He peels it and squishes the whole thing in his mouth, chews twice and swallows mightily. "Whoa! Not so bloody smooth!" he says, pounding his chest.

* * *

Tim mingles into the crowd bustling on the Central Station's main platform. He follows the masses, as well as the signs and arrows pointing toward The Casino, and within seconds he is funneled onto an escalator with unusually large steps, each roughly the size of a shuffleboard court and capable of holding about 50 people. He stands and looks around at the scene through his amber sunglasses.

The escalator tube is well-lit but sparsely decorated – however, that soon begins to change. The transition is gradual, like the color of the sea as one approaches the surface from below. Everything grows brighter and more vibrant, as well as larger in general, as the tube expands wider and wider, higher and higher. The lights decrease in size but increase dramatically in number, shimmering, blinking and winking in a thousand different colors. Tim gawks and grins uncontrollably, not unlike the tourists around him, and has the sense that he's traveling up through the spinal cord of a computerized leviathan, the lights swirling and rippling like data en route to the nerve center.

The escalator tube finally spits them out into another cavernous room, which exemplifies the theme of glimmer, glitz and gaudiness the creators obviously intended. The Pyramidal ceiling is encrusted with millions of faux gemstones, while millions more hang from invisible threads at varying lengths and the whole contrivance is aglow with colored laser beams criss-crossing and zig-zagging every which way. With the exception of The Pyramid itself, the first time he laid eyes on it, Tim has never seen anything so breathtaking in his life.

Down below the laser-light spectacle, also suspended in mid-air, is a comparatively antiquated digital sign flashing WELCOME TO THE PYRAMID CASINO. Expansive neon archways line the perimeter of the room, and though them Tim catches his first glimpse of people engaged in the sport of gambling. They pull levers and touch video screens, screaming and hollering as the machines blink and flash and ring and whistle. Although a terrible cacophony, it is proverbial music to his ears.

Approaching the center of the lobby, the crowd in front of Tim begins to disperse and he notices a series of escalators located between the arches, which dip down below the floor. Above each one is a digital sign advertising what Tim can only assume are different thematic zones of The Casino, as they include names like RIVIERA, WILD WEST, CLASSIC VEGAS, HAWAIIAN PARADISE, WINTER WONDERLAND, TIJUANA TOWN ... there are 21 in all, which is surely no coincidence. He approaches one called OUTER SPACE and debates between the archway and the escalator for a moment, before choosing the latter. After all, he figures if he's going to explore this unknown frontier, then what better place to start than outer space?

Where the previous tube had taken him up and had become brighter, this one takes him down and grows steadily darker. Black-lights eventually prevail, along with fluorescent stars. As Tim steps into The Casino, he is greeted by a similar racket of bells and whistles, and once his eyes adjust to the darkness he finds the layout very similar to that he had seen through the archways. Slot machines as far as the eye can see, which is difficult to judge because of all the mirrors and lights and juxtaposed angles. In fact, the way everything glows white under the black-lights, including the teeth and clothing of many of the patrons, it seems almost as if he's looking at a negative film exposure of the world above.

Tim walks between two rows of slot machines and takes a cocktail from the tray of a passing waitress, who's dressed in a tight-fitting silver jumpsuit. She doesn't even notice and, coincidentally, it's a gin and tonic – just what he wanted. He gulps it voraciously as he walks, and when he tilts his head back further this affords him a splendid view of the accoutrements above, which include revolving planets and miniature rocket ships spewing real fire.

Penetrating deeper into the maze, he is frustrated by the inability to walk in a straight line for more than a few steps before being forced to turn left or right, and the music starts to sound more like noise. Similarly, human features seem to melt from the faces around him – except for the mouths, which contort in shape and babble incoherently, as if fighting against the volatility of the giant radioactive choppers inside of them. He is equally amazed and revolted.

* * *

Tim finds The Aquasino much more conducive to his senses. Bright and airy in spite of the lack of natural light, The Aquasino's predominant color is a refreshing turquoise, manifested in the pools, streams and waterfalls that abound in every direction. Rows of palm trees and various tropical plants, fake but carefully rendered, separate different patio areas where slot machines are mounted within outcroppings of artificial rock. And there are even slot machines and gaming tables half-submerged in the water itself, allowing patrons to half-submerge themselves while playing. All the waitresses are clad in blue-silver, scaly bikinis to look like mermaids, while most of the dealers are hunky men with chiseled physiques, wearing only tight swimming trunks, bow ties and starched cuffs.

Tim stops short of the first set of pathways winding between the pools, and watches a game of blackjack. He assumes they're using some kind of waterproof cards, and he spies on a few of the players' hands, deciding whether he would hit or stick based on his cursory knowledge of the game. Basically, whatever he's been able to glean from movies, as any gaming-related news or information has been filtered from the HoloVision. He hears a woman's voice behind him, but assumes she's talking to someone else.

"Excuse me, sir?" she says, waiting a moment before tapping him on the shoulder and repeating herself in a slightly different tone. "Excuse me, sir?"

"Yes?" Tim says, a bit startled as he turns round. It's one of the mermaids, a curvaceous peroxide blond with silver lipstick and glitter on her eyelids.

"Can I get you a drink?"

"Yes, please. A gin and tonic," he says, removing the bundle of cash from his pocket.

"No, it's no charge," she says with a glittery wink, as if extending him a special courtesy. "You can change your money right over there, though, and also get a bathing suit." With a silver-tipped finger she points to a gazebo painted white to understate the iron bars. "I'll be there in just a minute."

"Great," Tim says, shuffling off in that direction, reciting the line in his head. Hi there. The name's Wesley Witherspoon and I'd like to exchange these bills for chips, please.

* * *

Two hours and eight gin and tonics later, having tried his hand at aqua poker, aqua blackjack, aqua roulette, aqua craps, aqua baccarat and even some aqua slots, with little success, Tim's resources have dwindled to a thousand dollars. But he's had a *whale of a good time*, as The Aquasino's mantra promises.

As it turns out, Wesley Witherspoon is a real likeable guy. He's mingled and bullshitted with people from all over the world, from Tokyo to Timbuktu, Seattle to Sidney, and has been extended a number of propositions, among them investment opportunities, party invitations, job offers and come-ons, just to name a few. But he's turned them all down. After all, he's just a hard-working, god-loving barber from Queens, New York, who's not looking for any favors – just a whale of a good time.

The decision to be a barber, as opposed to a banker, butcher, baker or candlestick maker, was not premeditated. In fact, he had been surprised to hear the words come out of his mouth for the first time.

"So, what do you do for a living, Wesley?"

"I'm a barber."

Perhaps it was something he remembered his father having said years and years before, when he was just a boy. Something about barbers plotting to take over the world. He had said something like, "Don't you think it odd, son, that you never run into barbers on the street? Never see them at weddings or on television game shows?"

He could not have foreseen it, but *barber* seemed to be the ideal answer. Everyone seemed to know exactly what a barber's duties entailed and thus it sparked no further inquiry, just an "Oh," or a "Great." Because, while Tim enjoyed the exchange of banter, he preferred to be the one making most of the inquiries.

Cutting his losses at the tables, Tim heeds the advice of a seasoned gambler and goes to the sports book next. After all, it's football season in America and, unlike games of cards and dice and spinning wheels, he knows something about football.

The main aqua sports book consists of a large amphitheater facing a wall of video screens, which display every sporting event currently being broadcast worldwide. The only sound, however, apart from the cheering and groaning of bettors, and the faint tinkling of slot machines, is the water cascading from above, over each tier, and finally collecting in a pool at the base of the video wall. It just so happens that Tim's favorite team, New York, is playing their arch-rival, Los Angeles, and the game is being shown on the marquee screen, front and center. Tim approaches the betting window, which he's having difficulty locking into focus. He's so drunk that he's forgotten his real name altogether.

"Yello! What's the score of the New York game?"

"You mean the L.A. game?" the young black man says with a smirk. "Twenty to six, L.A. Second half just started."

"Dammit! Two field goals?"

"Blocked extra point."

"Dammit! What kind of action you got?"

"On New York?"

"Yeah, of course."

"I've got eight to one, straight up, and to cover, two and a half to one. Spread's thirteen—"

"Thirteen points?"

"Maybe you forgot how L.A. whooped up on y'all in the playoffs last year."

"Yeah, but we've got Duckworth back healthy," Tim says, referring to New York's star tailback.

"He ain't a hundred percent, I'll tell you that. Besides, I don't make the odds, I just report 'em. I ain't even s'posed to be discussing the games and whatnot." He glances up at a tinted dome above his head, which assumedly houses a camera.

Tim slaps his two $500 chips down on the counter. "Give me New York, straight up."

The amphitheater is packed with hairy-chested men, many of whom are smoking cigars and wearing baseball hats proclaiming their allegiance to one team or the other – which makes for a rather odd scene, all these half-naked men packed into what looks like a sort of bizarre congressional kiddie pool. Much to Tim's chagrin, the only vacant seat is between two L.A. fans.

192

"This seat taken?"

"Depends," says the larger of the two, a biker-type covered with piercings and blotchy, amateurish tattoos. "Who you for?"

"New York."

"Then it's taken," the man snorts, splashing one of his grotesque legs over the stool.

Without hesitation, Tim brushes his leg aside and takes the seat. "Whatever."

"Fine. But you're going to lose!"

"Yeah!" the guy on the other side jumps in.

"We'll see about that," Tim says, rattling the ice cubes in his empty glass, trying to catch the attention of a nearby mermaid.

* * *

Tim's puffy, black and blue eyelids flutter sickeningly and open about half way to reveal his bloodshot eyes. Either the room is spinning or *he's* spinning, one of the two, so he can't determine exactly where he is – but the absence of turquoise means it can't be The Aquasino, and the harshness of the naked fluorescent tubes in the ceiling would rule out anywhere above the line (of demarcation). The anesthetizing effect of the liquor makes this more disconcerting than alarming, however, even though he has every reason to be alarmed.

"Sir. Sir! Can you hear me?" a blurry figure says.

"Huh? Who are you? Where the bloody hell am I?" Tim says, having sloughed off the Wesley Witherspoon persona during his brief spell of unconsciousness. Rubbing his eyes, the blocky shapes around him gain some definition. He's in a small office with a bank of video monitors on one side and a bookshelf full of three-ring binders on the other side. He's sitting in an uncomfortable plastic chair, his swimming trunks still dripping wet, and not one but two men are standing before him, big white guys in crew cuts and black suits who look like they want to beat the living bejesus out of him. In fact, judging by the pain in his face and chest – not to mention his spotty memory – Tim is quite sure they already have.

"You're in a security office at The Pyramid Casino. Now, let's start with your name," the guy on the left says, who's evidently the ranking officer.

"Are you men or mouses?" Tim slurs, wiping some blood from the corner of his mouth, where his swollen lips meet like two overcooked hot dogs.

"Sorry? You'll have to repeat that," the guy in charge says, an implicit challenge for Tim to insult him.

"Wait a second … you're not mouses … you're too big! Ha ha ha ha ha!"

"The guy's totally hammered," the sidekick says. "I'll bet he doesn't even know his own name."

"Of course he knows his own fucking name!" the guy in charge snaps. "You don't—" He whispers, and Tim can hear him, he just can't understand. "You don't plant an idea like that in a perp's head, get it?"

"Yeah, right, sorry about that. Geez, you don't have to give me the third degree in front of the guy."

"Of course I know my own name you stupid wankers!" Tim blurts out.

"What did you call us?" the guy in charge says. "What did he call us?"

"I think it's like a jerk-off where he's from."

"Wanker. To wank oneself silly at all hours of the day and night. Also a very stupid person," Tim says with a cockeyed smile. "Hey! Whatcha gonna do? Beat the piss out of me again?"

"We didn't do anything of the sort. But you're pushing your luck."

"Oh yeah, then who busted open my bloody face, eh? My ribs hurt too …" The combativeness has left Tim's voice, such that he appears like a child complaining to his mother about the bullies at school.

"Our men on the floor. Now, if you want my suggestion, I suggest you cooperate so things don't have to get ugly, you understand? I don't think you want to get yourself in any more trouble, do you? Okay, now are you going to answer my questions?"

"You answer *my* questions …"

"I have been answering your questions, but you haven't been answering mine."

"We could take turns."

"Carl? You going to put up with this crap? I say we just throw him in the tank and do this tomorrow. We're off in like ten minutes."

Carl turns and glowers at his subordinate. "Get ready to document this," he says, pointing to the empty chair behind the desk. "On the computer."

"Yeah, sure, Carl, the computer. No problem, no problem."

"Okay, can I start? Since I answered your question?" Carl says, shifting toward Tim with the exaggerated smile of a torturer or a party clown.

"I guess."

"Great. What's your name?"

"But what have I done?"

"See, now that wasn't the deal, and now you're starting to get on my nerves. You're causing me *irritation*, and I don't make good decisions when I'm irritated, you understand? Now, I'm going to ask you one last time, and if—"

"Timothy S. Witherspoon. The third. There, are you happy?"

"i-t-h-e-r?" the second guy says, fingers poised over the keyboard.

"You have any I.D.?"

"Huh?"

"Driver's license, something like that?"

"No."

"You an American citizen?"

"No. I mean, yeah, of course. Yeah."

"Which is it?"

"Yes, I'm a citizen. I'm a barber from New York."

"A barber, that's great. You have an address in New York?"

"Yeah, of course." Tim says. He wants to lie but all he can think of is the old apartment. His bunk bed with the steering wheel on top, the view of the alley from his window, the Velvet Cave, where he would hide in the cabinets. The address just comes out by accident, as if he didn't think he'd remember. "Thirty-one seventy, forty-fifth street. Queens."

The sidekick pecks away at the computer. "Three-one-seven-zero."

"No. Three-one, dash, seven-zero," Tim corrects him.

"Oh."

"You staying here at The Casino or in Pyravegas?" Carl says, crossing his powerful arms and leaning back on the edge of the desk.

"Hey, it's my turn! You've had too many turns! I mean ... I just want to know what's bloody happened."

"We've taken you into custody, Mr. Witherspoon, on charges of disorderly conduct, assault, battery and destruction of property."

"All that?"

"Why don't I refresh your memory. Cue the tape ... Gene! Cue the fucking tape!"

"I am, I am!"

Carl turns to the bank of video monitors, live feeds from The Casino along with a few blank screens, and one of the blank screens flickers for an instant before switching to an aerial shot of the sports book amphitheater. He points to a figure at lower left, who's stomping his feet in the water and pointing fervently at the video wall. The men on either side of him are also standing, with fists clenched above their heads in victory.

"I believe that's you."

"The ball clearly broke the plane!"

"So that gives you the right to go on a rampage?"

"The game is under protest! What rampage?"

"Have a look for yourself."

On the video, Tim now appears to be arguing with the biker guy. They point fingers in each other's faces and then, with surprising dexterity and quickness, Tim punches him. The camera zooms in.

"Uh-oh," Tim says, almost flippantly.

The biker guy reels back and slumps off his stool into the water, clutching his face where the blow struck. Meanwhile, his buddy lunges at Tim from behind. But Tim sees him and ducks down, almost beneath the water, and then explodes upward as the much larger man stumbles. The result is that the assailant is flipped upside down and then driven head-first down into the water, where his noggin assumedly collides with the concrete below.

"Uh-oh."

Some of the other spectators have begun to scramble out of the gallery and Tim exchanges words with a few of the remaining ones before exiting his row and running down the stairs onto The Casino floor, where a man in dark swimming trunks tries to corner him while holding his finger to his ear and shouting. Tim holds his hands out as if to say, *Whoa! Whoa! Take it easy. I'll cooperate.* A second man with dark swimming trunks shows up and points to Tim, and then at the floor. Tim raises his hands further and says something."

"You see there? I'm not rampaging a'tall."

"Keep watching," Carl says.

Tim turns to the cage, where he had placed his bet earlier, and shouts something at the attendant.

"He called me names! Disgusting ones!"
The two undercover security officers approach Tim cautiously and each grab hold of an arm to lead him away. He complies, turning away from the cage and walking with them.

"See? Look at that."

"Keep watching."

The camera follows along for a few paces before Tim suddenly breaks free. Before the officers can restrain him he grabs a stool from a nearby table and hurls it at the cage. It bounces off and the officers tackle him to the ground as he lunges for the bars. There is a skirmish of flying fists and knees and elbows, which is difficult to follow, and finally Tim is subdued on his stomach, with an officer's forearm on his neck and his own arm twisted up behind his back awkwardly.

"Seen enough?"

Tim sulks again as before, blubbering as if he's about to cry. "Yes, I suppose so ... the ball was over the plane ... it's not fair ... and they were calling me disgusting names and ..."

"Hey Carl? I'm not getting a Timothy S. Witherspoon having ever lived at that address."

"No?"

"No. But I think you're gonna want to take a look at this."

Realizing the terrible mistake he's made, Tim's fear begins to permeate his drunkenness and is subdued only by his anger at himself. *Stupid! Stupid! Why did you give them the real address? Because I couldn't think of any other bloody address! Then you should have given a fake one! They still would have figured it out! Not if you were smart about it!* He's suddenly aware that his mouth is pasty, his palms sweaty. His stomach jumps up into his throat as if he's in a freefall.

Carl shoots Gene a look that says, *This had better be good.* He circles around the back of the desk and puts on a pair of silver-framed glasses. He looks at the screen. "Well, I'll be damned."

"Looks like we got a prankster on our hands, Carl."

"Oh, I think we got more than that, Gene." He swings his spotlight gaze directly upon Tim. "Your name isn't really Timothy S. Witherspoon, the third, is it?"

"Yes."

"No it's not! It's Timothy *Ginn*, isn't it?!"

"No."

"Admit it!" Gene says, angry from having been duped.

"He doesn't have to," Carl says, picking up the phone and dialing four numbers. "Just look at him. He's a spitting image of his old man."

"I guess," Gene shrugs. He's somewhat enthused, but Carl is downright tickled.

"Yes, I'd like to speak to Seth Jipt please … this is Agent Carl Richter with The Aquasino Security Division … Aquasino. It's one of the divisions of The Casino. The one with water … yeah, yeah. The call is regarding a perpetrator we have in custody, who may be of interest to Mr. Jipt … Gone for the day? Well, can you try him at home, or on a cell phone perhaps? … No, it's not an emergency. But trust me, he'll be much more upset if you *don't* give him this message … Yeah, that's what I'm talking about. Just tell him we have Lester Ginn's son in custody … yes … I know. So you'll call him? … Yeah, sure, I'll hold." Carl looks over at Tim, again with the unsettling smile. "She's going to try him at home." Then he turns to Gene. "Jipt's secretary. Sounds like a real ditz."

Tim is distracted, already rehearsing the confrontation in his mind – but not with Seth Jipt, with Lester. He can't get beyond the inevitable question of why he did it in the first place. The only answer he can think of is, *Why not*. He knows this won't cut it. In fact, it may get him hurt even more seriously. His father has never hit him with a closed fist before, but perhaps only because he hasn't had a good enough reason. Tim imagines his face getting pummeled, but he can't imagine himself fighting back.

"Okay, great," Carl says, back on the line. "Hello, Mr. Jipt, sir, this is Carl Richter with the— ... Yes, we do have him, sir ... Yes, of course, sir, we're making sure of it ... Meet in twenty minutes at your office here in The Casino, sir? ... I'll be there – I mean, we'll be there, sir ... Okay, good ... bye, sir." Jipt has clearly hung up in the middle of his goodbye. He sets the phone down. "Guess what? You get to meet Seth Jipt. He's our boss."

"Can I go?" Gene says, and his cheery tone belies his sudden nervousness. "I'd rather not ..."

"I know who he is," Tim replies dreamily in response to Carl. He touches the side of his face and winces in pain.

* * *

Jipt leans forward in his chair, elbows on desk, hands folded as if he's about to pray. His expression is composed, even marmoreal, like the bust of an ancient king. They are alone, the door closed. "So, Mr. Ginn, what did you think of The Casino?"

"Huh?" Tim says, stalling. Despite Jipt's affable manner toward him, he is quite clearly intimidated. Perhaps because this is the opposite of what he had expected, based on Jipt's reputation as a hothead. Whatever the reason, it seems that meeting the man face-to-face has brought the gravity of his dilemma into full light. He feels utterly crapulous, like something scraped from a bathtub drain. A ball of pubic hair, lint and scum. Any reserves of legerity he was able to wield against Carl and Gene are gone, smothered by his nausea.

"The Casino. It was your first visit, was it not?"

"Yes."

"Well, what did you think?"

"It was okay, I guess."

"Just okay? I hope you enjoyed yourself ... at least until things got out of hand."

"I guess I did for a while, in the water place."

"Ah, yes, The Aquasino is one of our most popular attractions."

"I didn't even remember what happened until they showed me the tape. I'm really sorry ..."

"It's nothing, really. Happens all the time. Are you okay?"

"Yes, I think so."

"Might want to get some ice on that lip when we're through."

"Okay."

"I won't keep you much longer, Mr. Ginn. To be honest I just wanted to meet you, and to ensure – personally – that you get back home safe and sound."

"Thank you."

"Should we try to contact your father, in case he's worried about you?"

"No, that's all right."

"Right, of course," Jipt says, clearly pretending to be surprised at his answer and sensitive to his wishes. "After all, you're a grown man. How old are you now?"

"Twenty-four."

"Mmm-hm. I remember when I was about your age. Damn near thought I could walk on water. Well, no need to bother him, I suppose, over such a trivial matter as this."

"No."

Jipt unfolds his hands and slaps the desk lightly with one hand as he rises. "Fair enough. We'll just keep this our little secret then, eh?"

With sleepy reluctance, Tim nods his head a few times before allowing his neck to slacken altogether, his body slumping forward in the chair.

Chapter 34

"Man, that's crazy stuff," Hawkins says. He has been shuffling papers around in his briefcase, on the seat next to him, but now he gives Jipt his undivided attention. They are alone in the calfskin and burled walnut confines of Jipt's limousine. The sun is down. "Your little secret, eh?"

"Fact is, the kid would sooner chop off his own dick than let his old man find out what happened."

"He wasn't supposed to be in The Casino?"

"Like a fox ain't supposed to be in the chicken coop," Jipt says jovially, revealing a mouthful of ultra-white teeth.

A loud commotion is audible outside the car now as it pulls to a stop, and the blazing floodlights from dozens of news cameras can be seen through the tinted windows. The Southern baritone voice of the driver crackles over the intercom. He has the cool, almost comatose, delivery of an airline pilot. "Looks a little hairy out there, Mr. Jipt, but there's a large police presence and your security team is moving into position. Just let me know when you're ready."

"Thank you, Pete."

"You've got the speech, right?" Hawkins says.

"Got it."

"You don't think the ending is too soft? I feel like it's still not convincing enough."

"Relax, Tommy. It's not my job to be convincing. We'll leave that to Sylvia King."

"Yeah, you're right Seth."

"I mean, damn. Sometimes I think that woman could convince a tumbleweed to sit still."

"She's a dynamo."

"More like dyno-*mite*," Jipt says. "But people like her, and you can't argue with that, I guess …"

"No stopping for questions on the way in," Hawkins confirms.

"Hell no," Jipt says before pressing a button on his armrest. "Let's roll, Pete."

"Roger that, sir."

"Roger that," Jipt says mockingly.

A moment later the door opens, unleashing a deluge of light and sound. Hawkins steps out first, followed by Jipt, and riot police struggle to keep the noisy crowd at bay. Many are holding professionally made signs that say STRIKE or NO SCABS. Others have merely penned their own slogans on cardboard, such as JIPT = JOKE, DON'T GET JIPT, UNION 1 JIPT 0 and several others, which are even more convoluted.

They walk briskly through the narrow pathway carved out by men in blue, Jipt now out in front, his head up, wearing the politician's smile for the cameras. He appears undaunted by the chorus of jeers and epithets directed at him. A harried newswoman manages to slither through the fracas, between two police shields. It's Tina Franco.

"Mayor Jipt! Will you endorse The Pyramid workers' strike?"

"Sorry Tina, you'll just have to wait and see," Jipt says, winking at her. Judging by her expression, she is just happy to have prompted any response at all.

A stocky bald man from a rival network pushes through on the other side of the barricade, "Mr. Mayor, can you confirm rumors of human rights violations within The Pyramid?"

Jipt ignores him altogether and heads straight for the field house, where one of his men is stationed to open the back door for him. Ordinarily used as a recreation center for PyraVegas University, with ten basketball courts and ten tennis courts, as well as batting cages, a track and a climbing wall, the building is large enough to hold about 20,000 people. It's currently flirting with that capacity, packed to the rafters with a crowd that represents nearly a third of all union members. Flanked by Hawkins and a bevy of security guards, Jipt takes up a position at the end of a row, the first of five being maintained by police in accordance with fire codes. The room buzzes with thousands of conversations and only a few people in the immediate area seem to have noticed his arrival. Everyone else's attention is on the small stage way at the opposite end of the field house. Barely readable from Jipt's vantage point is a banner on the wall behind the stage that reads: PYRAMID WORKERS / UNITED AGAINST INEQUALITY!

Having just received her cue, Sylvia strides up to the podium, radiating self-confidence. She is dressed sharply in a gray pinstriped suit that accentuates just enough of her voluptuous curves.

Her hair is pulled back into a tight bun, like a racecar gearshift, and her lips are glossed with bright red lipstick. She waves to the crowd.

As she steps behind the podium, the buzz gets louder, accentuated by some screams and applause, and then begins to quiet down. "Good evening, hello ... Hello!

"Hello!"

"That's more like it. Thank you for coming tonight, you're looking good! I'm looking around at all the faces out there, old and young, men and women, so many diverse colors ... and I see one commonality ... Hope. Hope for a better day, that's all. We don't ask for much, do we? We don't ask for the stars and the moon because we're humble people, aren't we? We're respectful people and we're grateful people. But we're also *just* people. That's right ... You know, when I was writing my speech the other night I didn't think of those words having two meanings ... Did you think about that? We're *just* people, as in, we know the meaning of justice, right? And not only that, but we have confidence that we're standing *behind* it, aren't we? Or else we wouldn't be here tonight. But, on the other hand, we're just *people*. We don't have any saints among us, I'm sorry to say. Yes, even you Reverend Palmer!"

A largely black section of the crowd containing the reverend and a group of his parishioners erupts in laughter and applause.

"I'm sorry, but it's a fact. We're just *people*, and we carry all the baggage that goes with it. Notice I say the baggage and not the sin, reverend. Freedom, equality, aspiration? These aren't sins, they're *rights*. Like a mountain of solid rock. Immovable. But not impervious. They've been chipped away, haven't they? They've been chipped away by policies and regulations, but they've also been chipped away by *excuses*, haven't they? With *rhetoric*. Like *quid pro quo*. Have you heard that one? They say concessions go with the job, because so many people want it. *Quid pro quo*, my ass. They say this is the best we can do. They say this is all the economic model will allow. They say we're better off than most in our profession. Maybe so. But we're the best of the best!"

There's some sporadic shouting and hollering throughout the field house.

"We deserve more. And I think it's got a lot to do with that word up there behind me ... inequality. It's a big word. And it's got even bigger consequences when you're at the low end. The reason we're here tonight is because we are at the low end, people! Not because we chose to be there and not because we deserve to be there ... but because we are being held down!"

"It's oppression!" a particularly rotund, feisty black woman screeches from deep inside the crowd.

"You're damned right it is! It may not be the worst oppression that was ever recorded in human history, I'm not going to stand up here and say we're slaves, but it is what it is. An *injustice*. And we don't have to stand for it. In fact, we have to do something about it, don't we? For our families and for ourselves and for those who will come after us. Why should we carry the burden? Why should we sacrifice our own interests for a society of freeloaders? We shouldn't and we won't!"

The loudest-yet approval is voiced by the crowd, in the form of cheers, whistles and applause.

"Our hand is being forced, plain and simple. We're being forced to act. We're being forced to make hard decisions. I don't think there's a person in this room who *wants* to go on strike. Who *wants* to risk everything we've already attained. Who *wants* to cause pain and suffering to anyone else. Because if there is, I'll tell you right now you're with the wrong organization. We have pride in what we do. Pride in the good way of pride. Or maybe pride isn't the right word, but you know what I'm saying. We enjoy making a contribution to something important, don't we? And, if anything, we want to give more. We're willing to *give* more to *get* more. But we have to be given the opportunity first. We have to be empowered to make a difference!"

The crowd explodes, even louder this time, and Sylvia patiently waits for them to calm down.

"Now, listen up people. We've been doing a lot of talking here – hell, I love to hear myself talk." (laughter and applause) "I do. But the time for talk is over. It's time for action. It's time to make that hard decision."

"Strike!" someone yells, and soon the crowd is chanting in unison. "Strike! Strike! Strike!"

Sylvia leaves the podium and mingles with some people in the front row, smiling and nodding her head and hugging and shaking hands with them. It's too loud for conversation.

Jipt chuckles to himself and leans over to Hawkins. "You think they're convinced yet?!"

"I just hope we're not making a big mistake!" Hawkins says, but Jipt is already heading for the stage.

As people along the row begin to notice him, the chanting becomes increasingly undermined by boos and catcalls. He had expected this, just as he had expected Sylvia to deliver a rousing speech. After all, The Union members expect him to bandy about words like "scab" and "layoff," which they fear. And fear is almost always an acceptable excuse for irrational behavior in Jipt's book. Not nervousness. Not trepidation or deep concern, but outright fear. Like the fear of not being able to feed one's children. He turns the corner and crosses in front of the stage. Sylvia is still working the crowd and he wants them to witness a pleasant greeting.

He rests a well-manicured paw lightly on her back and she turns around. "Hey, Seth, how you doing?!"

Jipt thinks about hugging her but decides it's too risky. They shake hands instead. "Great! Hey, great job up there!" Jipt says, his voice failing to carry over the din.

"What?!"

"Great job!"

"Thanks! Well, I guess they're all yours! Watch your step!"

"Thanks!" Jipt says, taking a deep breath and bounding up onto the stage as the boos intensify. He avoids the temptation to look sideways before reaching the podium. Once there, he turns, and his expression gives away nothing but the notion that he's willing to wait as long as necessary, like a scientist documenting the movements of a tree sloth.

Like a marble rolling round and round in a bowl, the pandemonium stubbornly winds down to a murmur, and this is good enough for Jipt. He speaks – and contrary to Sylvia's style of taking long pauses he tries not to give the crowd any opportunity to respond. He also tones down his Southern drawl just a fraction. "Thank you, I know Sylvia said the time for talk is over, but I hope you will let me say a short piece, and I really will keep it very short." (boos) "I think you'll be surprised actually, at what I have to say. I know I've been opposed to a strike all along, and Sylvia's exactly right about the excuses, I've made my share of them, and maybe that wasn't the right thing to do."

In the back, Hawkins chews on his thumbnail. Jipt is not following the speech. In fact, he hasn't even taken it out of his pocket.

"Problem was, I wasn't hearing one voice coming from The Union. I was hearing one voice coming from the *other side*, and you know who I'm talking about, although you probably don't want to hear his name anymore, as it's become an excuse in itself, and I don't blame you. But I'm hearing one voice from our side now, and a lot of that is thanks to the hard work on the part of the leadership, especially Sylvia here. You're lucky to have a leader like her because she's convinced me that justice is on our side and that the time really has come to make a hard decision."

The murmuring continues, but the boos have stopped completely and it seems they're beginning to realize his position has changed.

"It's been a hard decision for me personally, like I said, because I didn't have all the perspectives, and I was thinking too much about the business end of things. I'll admit that I'm a businessman, and a pretty good one I think, but I'll also admit that there's one basic principle I often overlook, relating to people. And it's true not only in business but in politics, education, you name it. Every great business, every great city, every great family, is built on great people. You are those people, not me, not our customers, and especially not those deadbeats living up there in that Pyramid."

The growing buzz reaches a crescendo, and Jipt pauses for a moment. He contemplates taking the speech from his pocket, but doesn't want to ruin his momentum – or worse, appear disingenuous in any way.

"Now, I'm real proud of what we've accomplished so far, and I know there have been some tough times, but believe me when I say that those will soon be behind us. If we send a powerful message, and by that I don't just mean a strike, but a strike that's ninety-five to one-hundred percent unanimous, I think we can remove some of the barriers. It's our best chance, and we may only have one shot at it. And if we remove some of the barriers, then I think we can take this thing to another level, and if we do that, then we all stand to profit, that's what I'm saying, and I think ultimately that's what everyone wants."

"You got that right!" a man yells from the Reverend Palmer section.

Jipt takes the speech from his pocket now, opens it and shows it to the crowd. He knows for a fact that even those in the front row can't read it. "In the next day or so, each of you will be receiving a copy of the letter that will be sent to Lester Ginn, stating the specific demands of The Pyramid Casino Workers' Union. I think you all have a good idea of what those are, and rest assured that Sylvia and I worked very closely together on the specific language. That letter is your ballot. If you wish to participate in the strike, you'll simply sign that letter and drop it off in one of the ballot boxes, which will be located at all union offices, and in all break rooms at The Casino for the next couple of days. Friday is the deadline. If you haven't received a letter by Friday, talk to your departmental chief or call Sylvia or I personally." Jipt pauses again. He knows that he should have said, "me" instead of "I" and worries that he may have gone too far by inviting them to call him personally.

"We'll have the votes tallied by Sunday afternoon, and with a two-thirds majority we'll send the letter to Mr. Ginn on Monday morning. At that point, he'll have forty-eight hours to respond. If he fails to respond, or if he refuses to meet any of our demands, the strike will begin first-shift on Thursday. If he agrees to some of the demands, but not others, we'll reconvene for an emergency session, where another vote will be taken on the spot, very straightforward. Of course, if he agrees to all our demands, which I hope will be the case, a strike will be avoided altogether, and we should all be happy. After all, let's remember what it is we really want. Like Sylvia said, we don't want a strike, we want what the strike can give us." Having set the paper down on the podium, Jipt picks up in the final paragraph. "Short-term sacrifice for long-term gain, that's what it's about. Standing up for something you believe in, being a part of something great ... that's what it's all about, and we're all in this together. So support each other and believe in each other, and trust in your leadership and trust in your cause. This will enable you to persevere, and ultimately, this will enable you to prosper. Thank you."

Jipt looks up and witnesses a beautiful sight, thunderous applause sweeping through the field house like a tidal wave. It buoys his spirit and, at the same time, washes away his latent guilt.

Chapter 35

"I smell them!" Lester says good-naturedly, bounding up the double-helix staircase to the Apex Conference Room.

"Maybe so, but I taste them!" Ping says, as he crams an entire cookie in his mouth at once. "Ha ha!" He spits out crumbs onto the coffee table.

"Nice," Chutney says with the driest hint of irony, like the cardamom in the cookies.

Lester makes a beeline for the petite wicker basket, where the still-hot cookies are snugly wrapped in a checkered napkin, but he stops just short of the table. His hands are frozen in the act of reaching, like a cartoon bear whose animator has just taken lunch break. "No! No, no. Let's make this fair, chaps, what do you say? In light of my tardiness."

"You mean your pattern of tardiness?" Chutney says.

"My pattern, yes. We do fall into patterns, don't we? For better or worse … Habits, you might say. Now then, about the challenge! Well, it could *escalate* to a challenge, but it must be issued by a party other than myself. Granted, I am a party unto myself …" Lester says, waiting for the pun to soak in. However, the reaction amounts to nothing but more crumbs spewed onto the table by Ping, who, incidentally, is pissed drunk – blotto, as they say.

"Very nice," Chutney says, her irony a bit more effervescent this time.

"Right, so as I was saying," Lester continues, "I'll issue a decree, or an affirmation, and then—"

"Just get out with it!" Schnitzelhaus says, frazzled, although he tries to cover it up with a humorous facial gesture reminiscent of a (frazzled) groundhog looking for his shadow.

"Here it is. I'll guess every ingredient in those cookies! Jean-Sebastian *did* tell you the ingredients, didn't he?"

"I think you made it part of his job description," Katz jokes.

"Yes … and I'll guess them all!"

"And the amounts," Chili says.

"Do you know the amounts?"

"No, but we could ask him."

"And go through all that trouble? What? You don't think naming the ingredients is enough? Sight un-bloody-tasted mind you! I'm relying on olfactory prowess alone, man!"

"Fine."

"Fine?" Lester says, crestfallen.

"I don't think you can do it!" Schnitzelhaus huffs, laying the gauntlet Lester desires, but it's difficult to tell whether he's serious or not.

"Oh yeah? Is that a challenge?"

"The same."

"Wait a second," Chili says. What's the wager? What's on the line, here, anyhow? Otherwise it just ain't interesting."

"If I lose … I can't eat any cookies."

This statement jettisons Lester's mouth like an ejected fighter pilot and drifts down to the center of the table, into the basket of cookies, where everyone's looking.

Chutney responds first. "How about … if you lose, you can't eat any cookies, *ever*."

Lester's eyes widen with burning speculation. So wide, in fact, that it appears he's trying to gobble the cookies, basket and all, with his orbital sockets. "*Ever* ever?"

"At least until you die, how about that?" Chili says.

"Until … I don't like the turn this has taken a'tall," Lester says somewhat queasily.

"What's the matter? Are you afraid?" Schnitzelhaus says, openly taunting him now.

Lester turns slowly, mechanically, toward Schnitzelhaus, like a killer robot leveling its death ray. He pauses long and hard. "Sugar, brown sugar, eggs, baking soda, vanilla extract …" He takes a breath. "Unsalted butter, old-fashioned dried oatmeal …" He cocks his head straight up now, toward the apex, as if trying to examine The Beacon for lens imperfections. He closes his eyes. He wafts his hand in the air, gently corralling atoms into his nasal cavity. "Dried currants!"

"Mmm, dried currants!" Ping says, popping another in his mouth.

"Impressive," Schnitzelhaus says. "But you still have a few more to go."

Lester wafts more vigorously. "Cinnamon, of course … allspice?"

"Yes!" Ping says.

"Was there allspice?" Chili says, questioning the inebriated Ping as a matter of course.

"Yes, there was," Katz says, "I remember."

"Me too," Chutney says. "But you're not there yet … No more cookies for the rest of your *life*."

"But eat all you want when you're dead, of course," Katz says.

"I know, I know," Lester says, exposing a slight waver of doubt. "I know this … it's …" He leans over the table, between Chutney and Katz, and they exchange knowing glances off the flank of his polyester-clad derriere. "It's cardamom!"

"What's car-om-om?" Ping mumbles.

"That's right," Chili says. "Good 'ole cardamom."

"Well done," Schnitzelhaus says, his taut German lips softening into crooked smile.

"Yes!" Lester exclaims, pumping his fists. "He's done it, ladies and gentlemen, and now he shall claim his bounty!"

"Not so fast," Chutney says, sliding the basket away. "You forgot flour."

"Aaah!" the others say (minus Katz), realizing they've made the same mistake.

Lester's expression changes from elation to panic like a strobe flash, and he clutches the sides of his head. "No! But flour is a given. Flour holds it all together. All cookies are made of flour for heaven's sake!"

"Interesting, isn't it? That you forgot the main ingredient?"

"I should get to eat half a cookie," Lester pleads.

"You might as well eat them all. It's not like you're going to give them up, anyway."

"Yes I will!" Lester says, banging his fist on the slab of onyx tabletop. Despite the force of the blow, it hardly produces an emphatic *Bang!* as had been the intended effect. He closes his eyes again, tighter than before, and groans lightly, throatily, almost like a snore, as he tries to assuage his own defiance. It appears to work. When he opens his eyes he is calm, detached, even solemn. "I made a promise and I have every intention of keeping it."

"We were just playing around, Lester, no big deal," Chili says, hoping to diffuse the situation. "Go ahead, try one."

"Car-om-om?" Ping mumbles to himself.

"No, it's fine, really. I've already taken two key measures to ensure the deal is kept. Number one, I've convinced myself that cookies are bad for me. Bad in every way. Nutritionally, psychologically and otherwise. Don't worry, they're okay for you, but bad for me. Terribly bad. And number two, I've reassured myself that other goods may be substituted for cookies. Cakes and donuts, for example, which I also enjoy."

Chutney takes one of the perfectly round cookies from the basket and bites into it. "Mmm, but there's nothing quite like a good cookie. So crisp and chewy …"

Ping shoves yet another whole cookie in his mouth. "Warm and gooey!"

Lester smiles. "I'm unaffected by your rapture, as well as your rhymes. You see, I've fully accepted the fact – embraced the fact! That I will die having not eaten another cookie. Just as I accept the very fact that I *will* die."

"So you finally admit it?" Katz teases him.

"Yes. But that doesn't mean I have to think about it every minute of the day, does it? That doesn't mean I need even be aware of my own mortality. I've disconnected that particular synapse, because that's all it is … Life requires all my attention! Yes indeed. Now then, we haven't gathered here on this glorious afternoon to discuss cookies, have we? Or by all means, *death*. I mean, please. We've come here to discuss …"

"The letter," Schnitzelhaus says, holding up the original sheet of paper for Lester to see.

"Right! Of course, the letter, I've read it several times with increasing … obstinence."

"Obstinacy?" Chutney asks.

"Yes, that too, I suppose … Would everyone agree that conceding to these demands is highly undesirable?"

"Yes," everyone says, but with varying degrees of conviction.

"Good. Now, would you also agree that conceding to these demands would, in effect, nullify our very purpose for building this magnificent structure, and for standing atop it today? Standing and sitting, that is?"

"Yes."

"And that such an act of concession would entail breaking a promise, not only to ourselves but, more importantly, to the inhabitants who placed their faith in us?"

"Yes," everyone says again.

"But," Chili says.

"Ladies and gentlemen, a *but* has made its first appearance in the proceedings!"

Ping giggles, covering his mouth to prevent the discharge of more crumbs.

"I thought you'd like that one, Ping."

"Lester," Chili says. "I'm just saying we need to think about a contingency plan, for a strike."

"I gather you already have."

"Well, yeah. It's not too pretty, but ..."

"But?"

"It's a plan," Chili says.

"And like all plans, it too is contingent upon contingencies."

"I guess you could say that, yeah. If we shut down The Casino tomorrow, we'd have sixty to ninety days to either get it running again or find an alternate source of revenue."

"Two sub-plans, if you will," Lester says, pleased with what he's hearing.

"Exactly, which I would suggest we execute simultaneously."

"Simultaneously, yes, of course. In case one fails."

"Either way, though, we've got to get around Seth Jipt," Chutney says. "Because when it comes down to it, we haven't the faintest idea how to run The Casino."

"A faint idea," Chili says, defending himself.

"But not enough to hire and train a whole new labor force of that magnitude."

"Agreed."

"What? So sub-plan one is already nixed?" Lester says, catching up with the conversation.

"Not necessarily. We have to deal with Jipt is all I'm saying. We can't just fire him and bring in somebody else."

"Why not?" Lester says, excitedly. The thought of sacking Jipt hadn't even occurred to him, for reasons he can't recall.

"The contract," Katz says.

"Right … that blasted contract. If we could have only developed a way to extract water from the air …" Lester says, referring to the water rights issue that gave Jipt equal footing in the original negotiations.

"We could broach it," Schnitzelhaus says. "What could he do, sue us?"

"No, worse. Breach it himself," Chili says.

"He wouldn't dare cut off our water," Katz says. "Would he?"

"There's no telling what he'd do, if he feared losing everything," Lester says.

"That's one contingency we're powerless against." Chutney emphasizes.

"I just don't understand why he's siding with The Union," Katz says. "Maybe I'm just naïve."

"No, of course not, Patricia. Your heart is simply too pure, so you cannot possibly understand such a twisted, depraved state of mind."

"But *you* can!" Ping says, and this joke is well-received by all except Lester himself, because it's true.

"Do you want the short answer or the long answer?" Lester says.

"Short," Katz says.

"Very well. He is siding with The Union because otherwise he'd be siding with us."

"You," Chili says. "We're just behind the scenes."

"Whatever. In other words, he's not really siding with The Union a'tall. He doesn't want his bloody *card shufflers* living here in The Pyramid, with full access to its tempting array of diversions and luxuries. Productivity would go straight to hell."

"Most likely, over time," Chutney says.

"And it would be a sociological disaster, wouldn't it, Chutney? To mix them with our remaining inhabitant population?"

"The gap would be rather startling, in terms of individual contribution levels. And I don't imagine it would take long for The Union to resent their position as the working class."

"I mean, it's all a rather transparent bluff, isn't it? And this coming from a so-called gambling man! Ha!"

"Being a gambling man, though, he must think the odds are in his favor," Chili says.

"And who says they aren't?" Lester retorts. "They might very well be. However, Mr. Jipt has foolishly overlooked one critical detail regarding the odds."

"What's that?"

"That a gambler is always at their mercy. But he will soon learn his lesson. Boy!"

A moment later Squeakins comes shuffling up the spiral staircase. "Yes, sir?"

"I'd like to issue a response to this letter. One copy to Mr. Jipt and another to Miss ..."

"King," Squeakins says.

"Right, The Union leader." He turns back to the others with a rhetorical question. "And you really can't blame *her* for shooting the moon, can you? After all, she's The Union leader."

"What if the strike goes longer than ninety days, and sub-plans one and two both fail?" Schnitzelhaus asks insistently, as if for the second or third time.

"We'll cross that bridge when we come to it – before we come to it – but not right at this moment," Lester says. "Bottom line is whether or not we're in agreement, that all requests must be vehemently denied."

"Yes," they say.

"Then all requests are denied! With the utmost vehemence! And furthermore, we're shutting The Casino down immediately."

"Say what?" Chili says.

"Yes! It's perfect! A little bluffing of our own, right? Shake up the odds a bit, eh? Eh?!"

"Lester," Chutney says, "I don't know if that's such a good idea."

"Do you think Jipt planned for that contingency?"

"Well, probably not."

"Then that's exactly what we should do! And let's make it clear to The Union that their jobs are hardly guaranteed when, and if, The Casino reopens."

"Jipt doesn't know about the sixty to ninety days," Chili offers to the others, as a means of rationale. "For all he knows, we've got a proxy workforce lined up and ready to go."

"Yes, for all he knows," Lester says. "And considering we haven't told him anything, that amounts to diddly-squat!"

"Hmm, preempt the strike with a lockout …" Chutney says, mulling it over carefully. "Assuming they didn't call our bluff, it *would* turn the tables, that's for sure."

Lester glances around the table and receives a nod from each of the Visionaries in turn.

"Very well, sir," Squeakins says. "I'll have a response drafted up for your immediate review." He corkscrews back down the stairs, out of sight.

"Well," Lester says with a pronounced sigh. "I'm glad *that's* settled ... Are there any cookies left?"

Chapter 36

Jipt sits uncomfortably in his overstuffed leather chair, like a 600-pound gorilla atop a basket of robin's eggs. His last bowel movement was before the rally, nearly a week ago, and he can feel his intestines backed up like rush hour traffic on the PyraVegas beltway. All the waiting and stress, punctuated by Lester's most unanticipated response, has not helped in the slightest. In fact, it's the main culprit, despite the fact that Jipt continues to blame his Lynette-imposed diet.

He examines the boxes of several different over-the-counter gastrointestinal remedies, lined up on the desk before him, and from the look on his face one might think he's trying to read the Chinese Bible. A few of the drugs purport to have fiber. Jipt's understanding is that fiber has natural laxative qualities, although the high fiber content in his diet would seem to contradict it. *Yep, it's the stress*, he thinks. *This goddammned Lester Ginn sonofabitch is killing me! Poisoning me with my own shit!*

The intercom buzzes rudely. "Um, Mr. Jipt?" Vicki says cautiously, as if he's a murderous leprechaun hiding in her underwear drawer.

"What?" Jipt barks. Their professional relationship has been tenuous at best since *the letter* arrived (two days earlier than expected).

"Your one-thirty appointment is still waiting … and he's getting, um, a little impatient."

Jipt seethes for a moment in silence before responding. "First of all, I told you not to schedule meetings back to back to fucking back all day long. Second of all, refer to the people by their names. Who's my one-thirty?"

"Um, Art Hogue?"

"Who the hell is Art, fucking, Hogue?"

Vicki's um-frequency increases as she becomes more harried. "Um, he's from a non-profit, um, organization called, um—"

"Get rid of him!" Jipt says. "And stop saying um, goddamn it!"

"Yes, sir, Mr. Jipt, sir." Her phone rings in the background. "Um, I mean, I'm going to get that?"

"Go ahead. But unless it's Sylvia King or the fucking Pope, I don't want to talk to anybody."

He turns his attention back to the laxatives, ranking them by strength level, from *Regular* to *Extra* to *Maximum*. He figures maybe he should start with the regular and work his way up to maximum if necessary.

The intercom buzzes again. "Mr. Jipt? It's Sylvia King on line one."

"How did I fucking guess? I'll pick it up." Jipt says, lifting the thin, effeminate phone receiver off its cradle. He has requested a new one on several occasions, to no avail. "Howdy Sylvia."

"Don't howdy-Sylvia me, Seth. You knew he was going to do this, didn't you?"

"What? No, Sylvia, I—"

"Then help me understand how this shit went sideways. Help me understand how you backing the strike didn't have a direct impact on—"

"Whoa, Sylvia, just hold your horses a second. We didn't know how Ginn was going to react. I've told you a million times, he's a nutcase."

"I didn't know how he would react, but *you* did, didn't you? Yeah, I think you did. You knew he despised you so much that he'd never give in to our demands, or even give us the satisfaction of a strike. And that's why you magically decided to align yourself with us."

"Sylvia, that's ridiculous," Jipt says, truthfully, as that hadn't been the plan at all.

"Is it? Or do I remember you saying something like, you won't be responsible if Ginn pulls some kind of crazy shit?"

"You think I wanted this to happen? Of course not. I just said that because—"

"You *knew* he might do something like this."

"No, not like this, Sylvia, believe me."

"Or *maybe*, he's not so crazy at all."

"What are you talking about?"

"Maybe you both saw this as a way of getting a cheaper workforce. Mexican immigrants, perhaps?"

"Sylvia, that's ridiculous. I told you, I've only met the man a couple times, and that was years and years ago, in the planning stages for chrissakes."

"Mmm hmm," she says disbelievingly. "Funny, I was just reading a newspaper article that says you have, quote, routinely used immigrant labor as both a threat against unions and as a *scab* workforce, often failing to rehire union strikers. Unquote."

"Where did you read that?"

"Is it true?"

"Where did you read that? Did Donnie Betts write that crap?"

"Is it *true*?"

"No, it's not true. I've used scabs on *occasion*, you have to for chrissakes, in this business, and there was one incident with a few illegal aliens, but—"

"I'm running for mayor, Seth."

There's an expectant pause, and before Jipt can say, *What?!* a sudden paroxysm ravages his abdomen.

"You hear me, Seth? I'm running against you."

The pain is so intense now that the entire room is throbbing, bending and spiraling into an invisible vortex just below Jipt belt. He slams the phone down and doubles over in his chair, eyes clamped shut, mouth wide open in a frozen scream. But there's no sound – except the echo of the voice inside his head saying, *Why? Why is all this happening to me? I don't fucking deserve this.*

Chapter 37

Tim wears the headgear his father used to wear – the leather football helmet with the speakers lashed to the sides – not only as a means of projecting his voice to his pupil, but also as a means of protecting himself *from* his pupil, should he decide to revolt. This is not altogether irrational, considering his pupil is Escobar, a full-grown male chimpanzee.

Tim's interest in Escobar came as a surprise to just about everyone. However, what surprised them even more was the instant rapport the two seemed to develop. As a deposed alpha male, Escobar would figure to have a problem with authority, chimpanzee or otherwise, but instead he seemed relieved, perhaps even grateful, for having been liberated from the stress and conflict of hierarchical society. Granted, his new regimen of anti-psychotic drugs may have served as a proverbial shoehorn in this transformation. Yet, in looking at him, one cannot help but anthropomorphize, perhaps envisioning a weary corporate CEO who secretly relishes in his ouster by a hostile takeover, with the knowledge that his golden parachute will land him safely on his feet. And for Tim's part, he's exhibited a degree of patience and sole-mindedness that no one thought he possessed, by sheer virtue of his heritage. First in a sequestered area of The Habitat, under careful supervision of Svetlana, and then in his own cube, Tim has worked with Escobar on almost a round-the-clock basis. And as a result, after a period of only a few weeks, the two carry on like old friends.

Among other interests, such as eating bananas and bouncing up and down on the bed, Escobar shares Tim's affinity for watching American football.

"Oh! Big hit! Big hit!" Tim says, in reaction to a particularly violent play in which a linebacker has almost decapitated a wide receiver. The receiver coughs up the ball and flops to the turf like a waterlogged scarecrow. "Well, it looks like this game is well in hand for the good guys ... so, time for another lesson, eh? Yardley, cue the slide please."

Replacing the game on the video wall is a photograph of *The Heinousmeistress*, with superimposed arrows and terms labeling the various key components of the ship, such as the main deck, quarter deck, bowsprit, main mast and so on. Tim then methodically recites the various terms and points to them with the tip of his sword. Escobar nods after each term, as he has been trained to do for Tim's benefit, so he can move on to the next one.

"Next slide, Yardley."

The next slide is identical to the previous one, only without the labels. Then, in a supreme display of confidence and faith in Escobar, he hands over the sword and has him point to the various parts as he announces them in random order.

"Gunwale. Bowsprit. Hawes hole ... Frunkenschmidt."

Escobar stops and signs: *None.*

"Very good," Tim says. "There is no such thing as a Frankenschmidt." He thinks about how Lester used to employ trick questions so often with him as a boy, as a means of vetting his command of a given subject matter, and the fact that Lester's image appears on the screen at this very moment shakes his belief in mere coincidence. Startled in his own right, Escobar grunts and drops the sword.

"Son? Are you there?"

"I thought we agreed about not popping up like that."

"What's the matter, catch you in a private moment, did I?"

"No," Tim replies childishly. "I happen to be working."

"Well, turn on the video then, so I can see you."

"Yardley," Tim says, and having monitored their conversation for just such purposes, the electronic butler instantly confirms the video is on.

"Oh," Lester says, "Hello there Mister Escobar! Sorry to interrupt your lesson but this is rather important … Tim, it's time to rehearse the final scene."

"The final scene?" Tim says, confused. "But I thought we already—"

"That wasn't the end."

"The Captain and young Archibald defeat the rival band of pirates and sail off into the sunset. That's not the end?"

"No. Well, I thought it was, but it's not."

"I just don't understand—"

"There's nothing to understand!" Lester snaps. "Just present yourself on deck immediately!"

Tim looks to Escobar for a moment, as if the chimp might provide an adequate excuse. The fact is, he was extremely disappointed by the way the story ended, with Archibald still playing second fiddle to the bombastic Captain. And in similar fashion to the way he compartmentalized his feelings for Anna, after their initial estrangement, he's done everything in his power to forget the business of the play entirely. So now his instinct is to rebuff Lester's request – but at the same time he can't ignore the curiosity gnawing at his artificially constructed will. On one hand, he doesn't want to be disappointed again, but on the other, he entertains the hope for a better outcome.

"I think you'll be pleased with it," Lester says more calmly, as if sensing Tim's inner turmoil.

"All right," Tim says. "But Escobar comes with me."

* * *

The Ship Room is quiet, except for the guttural food vocalizations being emitted by Escobar, who's gorging himself on grapes up in the crow's nest. Tim finishes reading the script and looks up, raising his eyebrows to Lester as if to say, *Really? This is really how it ends?*

Lester nods curtly. "Need to look over it again before we start?"

"No, I think I've got the gist of it."

"Ready, then?"

"I think so," Tim says, checking the fit of his costume with nervous hands – the boots, the belt, the vest, the headscarf.

"I think you are. Very well." Lester gives the thumbs-up to Schnitzelhaus, who's perched in his directorial chair atop the port-side scaffolding.

"Okay!" Schnitzelhaus says, clapping his hands together once for effect. "Act three, scene twenty nine. The battle has been won by the crew of *The Heinousmeistress*. However! Because the captain he was wearing the red battle shirt, yes? The crew is not aware that he was badly wounded. So, when the scene opens, the Captain's strength finally gives out. Okay? Places …"

Lester climbs to the quarter deck and Tim remains on the main deck, tending to some loose hitches. Ping works the hydraulics, causing the ship to roll gently.

"And action!" Schnitzelhaus exclaims.

A grimace slowly creeps across Lester's face. He takes one hand off the wheel and clutches his stomach before collapsing with a noisy groan.

"Captain!" Tim cries, rushing to his side. He rolls him onto his back and pulls his hands away from the imaginary wound. "My god, sir ..."

"Oh, it's not so bad, Archibald," Lester says laboriously, wincing and even twitching a bit to understate his lack of control. "You see, I've got real guts after all. Ha! Ow! That bloody hurts!"

"Take it easy there, Captain. You're going to be just fine ... Why didn't you—"

"Say something?"

"Yes."

"The same reason you just lied to me."

"But I ..."

"You told me what I needed to hear, Archibald. No fault in that."

"Nonsense, we can make landfall by morning if—"

"No! A man deserves to die in his own home. This is my home," Lester says, gazing into the distance as if to mean that the sea, and not the ship itself, holds this distinction.

"You're not going to die!" Tim says desperately, losing his composure. "You're not going to die ..."

"Yes, I am, Archibald. And I'll tell you why. Because I'm *accepting* of it. After all, it's the only pure truth, isn't it?"

"No."

"What else, then?"

"I don't know ... everything."

"Everything, eh? Well, we've already established that lies exist. I lied to you and you lied to me. So wouldn't that mean everything's a lie, then?"

"Maybe it is all a lie! But we can also lie to ourselves, can't we? And therefore pretend things are true – the things we want to believe?"

"*Touché* Archibald, *touché* ... ahh!"

"Captain!"

"It's nothing, just a wee bit of pain ... it's the ultimate test of your theory, Archibald. The problem is, it's damned hard to believe the pain doesn't hurt, you know?"

"Is there anything I can do, Captain?"

"Yes, as a matter of fact, there is ..." Lester pulls his sword from his scabbard and offers the hilt to Tim, who just stares at its sharkskin grip and ornate silver cross-guard. He is equally captivated by its beauty and confounded by the gesture. "You can finish me off."

"What? No, I couldn't."

"You can, and you will. You want to be Captain, don't you?"

"I ..."

"Well? Don't you?"

"Yes, but—"

"If you let me die, Archibald – suffering miserably in the process, I might add – you'll have a power struggle on your hands."

"I don't—"

"No? Don't think so, eh? You fool! The ship would be in utter chaos! And why? Because you didn't follow your Captain's last order."

"You're not going to die!"

"Stop saying that, dammit! Now, either you take this sword and run it through my heart ... or you can walk the bloody plank!"

"You wouldn't."

"Wouldn't I?"

"No."

"And why not?"

"Because it would be unjust."

"Unjust? Ha! Ow! Bloody hell, that hurts. Unjust you say? Perhaps you forget that we're bloody pirates, mate."

"We still believe in justice, even if it's our own particular brand."

"You're killing me, you know that? You're killing me slowly and – aaaah! – painfully, with this bloody rhetoric. So why don't you just do the job quickly with the steel. Go on, now, take it!"

"No."

"Don't make me get nasty with you."

"Do your worst."

"You know what, forget it. I'll get Fowler to do it. I always thought he'd make a better captain than you, anyway. And now you've just proved it."

"You're lying!"

"I'm not! I wanted to believe you were the man to replace me, but as you say, I was lying to myself. You're nothing but a yellow bastard, Archibald! You make me bloody sick!"

"Stop it! You don't mean that!"

"Yes I do! You're a pathetic little mongrel is what you are! A putrid, repulsive, sniveling—"

Tim grabs the sword and, without hesitation, drives it through Lester's heart as he cries out, "Noooo!" At least that's what it looks like from Schnitzelhaus' vantage point. Caught up in the drama, he's going through the motions himself, wielding an invisible sword.

Tim pulls the sword out quickly, as if hoping to retract his decision, and his expression changes from intense rage to horror. "Oh Lord, what have I done?"

Lester gasps. "You see there? … That wasn't … so hard, now … was it?"

"Captain!"

"No … just call me Goodfellow … You're the captain now."

"But—"

"And I didn't mean … all that other rubbish … I just …"

"Said what I needed to hear."

"That's right … You're a good man, Captain Archibald … Godspeed to you." Lester's eyelids flutter and then close, his head listing to the side to indicate his final passing.

Tim kneels down at his side and lowers his head, weeping silently.

"And cut!" Schnitzelhaus says. "That's a wrap, people."

Chapter 38

Anna and Cleopatra sit close on the sofa, a portrait of polarity, yin and yang, Anna in black silk pajamas and Cleo in white. They're watching an old movie on the video wall, a sappy love story that each claims as her childhood favorite, although neither can remember how it ends.

Anna is aware of Cleo's hand on her thigh. The gesture seems benign enough, a common display of affection among girlfriends – that is, girls who happen to be good friends – but it feels different somehow, like a tacit understanding or a forbidden pact. All she knows is that her skin tingles and her heart flutters with anticipation.

But anticipation of what? Does she want Cleo to seduce her? She's never experienced these kinds of feelings in the company of a woman before. Then again, she's never met a woman like Cleo before – a woman who looks like a goddess yet walks and talks like a man's man, often sporting motorcycle boots and a penchant for vulgar language. Her straight, jet-black hair is cut at mid-neck, as if by a laser beam, and the ends bow inward, framing her triangular face. She wears bangs, also geometrically precise, and her blue eyes stand out like crystalline mountain lakes viewed from an airplane window. Her eyelashes are voluptuous, her nose self-effacing, and her mouth seems to drip with sexual appetite. In fact, her incisors seem unnaturally long, vampire-like, so it's not difficult to imagine her lunging for one's neck at any moment.

Anna met her a few months ago on the Rec Level tennis courts. The family foursome had long-since dissolved, and Tim refused to play her head-to-head after being humiliated on more than one occasion. Fresh competition was badly needed. As it turned out, she found more freshness than competition in Cleo, whose athleticism could not make up for her poor ground strokes. Off the court, however, the two sustained marathon rallies of conversation and laughter, becoming fast friends.

At first, Anna was concerned that class differences might cause a rift between them, Cleo being an inhabitant and her being – well – someone who lived above the inhabitants. But upon learning that Lester Ginn was her stepfather, Cleo hardly batted an eye. Indeed, she proved easily amused but not easily impressed, which suited Anna just fine. Besides, they had a lot in common. Like Anna, Cleo had recently suffered an estrangement from her boyfriend under tenuous circumstances, citing "chemistry issues" (in addition to his lackluster performance of cunnilingus). Like Anna, her subsequent advances were callously rebuffed. And, like Anna, she blames herself for complicating matters in the first place. But unlike Anna, she's decided that men, in general, aren't right for her. Anna just doesn't know it yet.

Cleo gives Anna's thigh a quick squeeze before removing her hand, and Anna feels a chill run from the voided spot through her leg and up her spine. "So when am I going to meet your Tim? You've been hiding him from me."

"I have not," Anna lies, smiling to give herself away.

"You have, you sneaky little *minx*. Why else would we hang out here all the time, as opposed to your penthouse suite?"

"I like my cube … you know, today is kind of our anniversary – or would have been, if …"

"You were still together."

"Right. I don't know why, but I had this feeling he was going to do something, you know, to try and get back together."

"And you think that's what you want?" Cleo says with one eyebrow raised.

"You think it's not?"

"I don't know, Anna, you just seem like you're in a good place right now."

"I guess."

"Hey, you still didn't answer my question," Cleo says with a smirk. "When am I going to meet him, anyway?"

"I don't know. Sometime."

"You're just afraid I'm gonna to kick his ass."

"Well …"

"Don't think I couldn't do it. How big is he?"

"I don't know, bigger than you."

"Strong?"

"Pretty strong. Not a musclehead or anything."

"I could take him," Cleo says. "It's all about the element of surprise. Stand up."

"Why?"

"Just do it."

"Fine."

"Okay, you pretend to be him. Pretend you have a shriveled little excuse for a phallus between your legs and a brain about the same size. Are you in character?"

"Sure."

"I don't believe you. Scratch your balls."

"Come on, Cleo."

"Scratch your fucking balls. And spit. Okay, just pretend to spit."

Accepting that resistance is futile, Anna humors her, scratching and hawking up some imaginary phlegm.

"Hi Tim, I'm Cleo," Cleo says, extending her arms for a hug. "I've heard a lot about you – all good, of course."

Anna reluctantly enters her embrace, wary of Cleo's next move, which comes quicker than she expected. Her right leg darts behind Anna's left leg and she pushes, flipping Anna backward onto the sofa. Then, an instant later, Cleo is straddling her, pinning her wrists into the cushions beneath the small of her back. It's a position of total helplessness, yet she's unable to contain her laughter – even though Cleo persists in the charade, looking genuinely spiteful.

"What's so funny, Tim?"

"Stop it," Anna says, struggling and giggling at the same time.

Cleo gets right up in her face now, their noses almost touching, and Anna's giddiness is supplanted by an exhilaration so poignant and sexually charged that it leaves her breathless. She wets her lips, ready for the kiss that now seems inevitable.

"What's the matter Tim? Anna's not good enough for you? Her breasts aren't big enough for you? Her pussy isn't tight enough for you, is that it?" Cleo stares directly into Anna's eyes for a moment, her pupils dilated, and then she breaks the spell, smiling mischievously. She releases her grip and rolls onto the sofa beside her. Anna takes a long-awaited deep breath – or rather, a series of short gasps that betray her ragged nerves. Part of her is disappointed, the other part relieved.

"We need some fucking ice cream," Cleo says.

"I'll get it," Anna says.

* * *

Tim waits for his cube to home in on Anna's, brushing some lint, as well as cat and chimpanzee hair, from the lapels of his tuxedo.

He is nervous. At his feet, Mister Zippy Do-da seems to warn him against carrying out his plan, meowing loudly.

"I don't care what you say, I'm bloody doing it," Tim says. (meow) "Well, I don't need your endorsement, do I?" (meow) "No, I don't. Look, it's really quite straightforward. It's been exactly three years since I professed my love for her, so it seems apropos to reaffirm that love and—" (meow) "What if she doesn't believe me? Well, that's what the flowers and the tuxedo are for, to convince her once and for all." Tim takes the bouquet of roses from the kitchen counter and shows them to Mister Zippy Do-da. He sniffs them warily, stretches and yawns. "Right. I told you it was a cunning plan. Now if we could just get there, Yardley!"

"Docking in less than one minute, Mr. Ginn."

"So the override code is going to work?" Tim asks, referring to the code he obtained from Dr. Katz, which should allow him to circumvent standard protocol and dock with Anna's cube without her permission.

"Yes, of course."

"Yes, of course," Tim repeats. "Why wouldn't it?"

"I can't speculate."

"Right, speculation … what separates man from machine."

"Docking to the north in three, two, one …"

"Back!" Tim shoos Mister Zippy Do-da back from the doors as they open. Then he stands up straight, holds the flowers behind his back and musters the warmest possible smile. His face falls, however, when he sees the dark-haired young woman on the sofa painting her toenails candy-apple red. Anna doesn't have many friends, so he's relatively certain it's Cleopatra. She eyes him coquettishly, and her bright cerulean irises render him speechless.

"Well, are you coming in?" she says, leaning over to blow on the wet nail polish.

"Yes. No, perhaps I'll – I mean, yes, I was planning to, but—"

"It's okay, she'll be back in a minute. She just stepped out for some ice cream."

"Ice cream?" Tim says, reluctantly stepping inside. The doors whoosh closed behind him, blocking his means of escape.

"Yeah, sounds good, doesn't it? I don't know what I'd do without the stuff." She screws the cap back on the nail polish bottle and rises, walking over to Tim. She is tall and carries herself like a runway model. Stopping just short, she examines him from top to bottom as if he were made of stone. "So what's with the getup? Ooh, are those flowers for me?"

"Sorry, but …"

"They're for Anna."

Tim nods in a hangdog sort of way, embarrassed by his chivalrousness.

"You could have played along. Isn't that sweet of you, though. I'm Cleopatra by the way," she says, extending her hand. "You must be Tim."

"Yes, nice to meet you," Tim says, and the next thing he knows he's flat on his back with the lithe vixen on top of him, her knees pinning his wrists to the floor. "Jesus Christ!" His mouth falls open in an expression that's equal parts surprise and desire. She moves in close to him, just like she did with Anna, and Tim strains to pull his head back. The floor doesn't give, and he can't help but peek down the front her loose-fitting pajama top.

"You men are all so pitiful," Cleo says. "That thing between your legs is like a parasite, *sucking, sucking, sucking* away all your good sense."

To his own chagrin, Tim is further aroused by her use of the word *sucking* in this context. "I love her," he says.

"Oh, do you? Then why do you want to fuck *me*?"

"What?"

"I can feel it struggling to get out of your pants."

Tim closes his eyes in an effort to subdue his penis by telepathic self-debasement. Because the fact is that she's right, he *does* want to fuck her. All kinds of different ways. "It's a biological reflex, like a knee jerk," he says, eyes still clamped shut to avoid her acerbic, yet irresistibly beguiling, stare.

"Like I said, pitiful."

"Do you ... know if she still loves me?" Tim says, wincing in expectation of another scornful rebuke.

Cleo doesn't answer immediately. Instead she backs away, sitting up straight as if on horseback. She sighs. "Look, I've been messing around with you – fine, I've been a total bitch to you. But I'm going to be straight with you now, for Anna's sake, okay? ... I wish the answer were yes, but ..."

Tim feels like his chest is about to cave in, due to everything inside being hollowed out by her words. "I should go."

Cleo dismounts him and presses the DOOR OPEN button on the wall in lieu of verbal concurrence. She picks up the ruffled bouquet of flowers and hands them to him.

"Thanks," Tim says dejectedly walking back into his cube.

"Hey, Tim."

"What?"

"Maybe the three of us could hang out sometime."

"Sure."

The doors close behind him and, almost simultaneously, the doors open on the other side of the room. Anna bursts in, spirits high, carrying a paper grocery sack. "I couldn't decide between Fudge Fantasy and Praline Paradise so I just got them both."

"Both is good," Cleo says, her eyes falling to a lone rose petal at her feet.

Anna turns her back at the kitchen counter and takes some bowls out of the cupboard. "They're different kinds of sweet, but I think they'll be good together, don't you?"

Cleo picks up the rose petal and lays it on her tongue like a communion wafer. It disappears into her mouth. "Good together? I think it'll be a fucking match made in heaven."

Chapter 39

Major General Vernon Bossy (ret.) bears disturbing resemblance to the culinary tour de force known as Turducken. Only instead of a chicken stuffed inside a duck, stuffed inside a turkey, one might imagine a moose cow stuffed inside a hippopotamus, stuffed inside a fire-breathing dragon. Needless to say, the man is appallingly unattractive, not to mention a real surly, vociferous bastard – and of all things his nickname is The Desert Hawk (due to his hawkish ways, which led him to several victories in the Middle East).

Since retiring from military service, he's entered the consulting field, planting his corpulent rump across the table from notorious CEOs and politicians both in the U.S. and abroad. It seems his repute for Machiavellian problem-solving has made him an invaluable resource to those faced with situations requiring a combination of brute force, laser precision and utter secrecy (his track record of success is far too long, and too lurid, for tasteful description within these pages).

At present, however, Bossy's corpulent and ever-shifting rump is seated across the table from Seth Jipt and Tommy Hawkins. Elbows on table, he scratches his taut, mustachioed face like a savage while disgorging tobacco into his coffee mug. Jipt and Hawkins lean back in their chairs as if forced by an opposite-poled magnet inside Bossy's bulbous, clean-shaven head.

For his part, Jipt is fighting off a rising tide of anxiety and nausea after having heard Bossy's rather impudent proposal. It's not the idea – after all, it was originally his own – but instead the vivid, coldhearted fleshing out of the idea that has turned his already-sour stomach.

"So, start to finish, this operation would take ..."

"Two hours. Three tops," Bossy says, spitting again. He has no discernable accent, just a thickness to his voice that sounds like unabashed gluttony.

"What if he's planned for something like this?" Jipt says, aware that he sounds whiny. "Surely he's planned for something like this. What if your men get trapped in there? For chrissakes, I can't afford to have any blood on my hands." Jipt conceals his hands below the table, lest Bossy take notice of his impeccably manicured fingernails.

He doesn't of course. Instead, Bossy just chortles and wipes the excess spittle from his lower lip. "No one does, Seth. That's why I'm here, to do this thing right."

"Or not do it at all," Hawkins says, unable to hold his tongue any longer.

"Sure," Bossy says, with an air of indifference. "But in my experience, Mr. Hawkins, people only call me when doing *jack squat* ain't an option anymore. Would you say that's about the position you're in, Mr. Jipt?"

"We've got to do *sump'm*," Jipt says. "I'm just not sure this is the way to go about it. I mean, there's a million different ways shit could hit the fan."

"There would be some unknowns," Bossy concedes, spitting.

"*Some* unknowns?" Hawkins says incredulously. "The whole Pyramid is an unknown for god sakes. We may have a rough blueprint, but we don't know what's around every corner."

"Besides," Jipt says, "even if we *could* get Ginn out of there ..."

"What would we do with him? Pack him off to Siberia?" Hawkins says, finishing the thought. "It's just insane. Not to mention illegal."

"But the fact is that you do need him out of there, correct?"

"That's debatable," Hawkins says.

"We need him out of there," Jipt affirms, glancing sidelong at Hawkins. "Soon. Before the election."

"What happened to calling his bluff? He can't survive without The Casino any more than we can."

Jipt broods silently, probing his left ear for wax. There's none to be had. He wishes he could make Bossy disappear, make Lester Ginn disappear, make Sylvia disappear – make this whole quandary just disappear. He knows the election is as good as lost if he doesn't get The Casino running again. And he also knows if he loses the election, The Casino might not be his to run anymore. With Sylvia in office, the balance of power would swing heavily to The Union, making him a puppet at best. With that in mind, he imagines Sylvia literally reaching up his ass and manipulating his jaws like a puppeteer, and it has the simultaneous effect of amusement, revulsion and – perhaps most unexpected of all – sexual arousal. He crosses his legs in attempt to smother his growing erection.

"So what I'm hearing is that you need to smoke him out somehow," Bossy proffers, breaking the awkward silence. "Something less direct."

"Hmm? Yeah, smoke," Jipt says. "Smoke is better than fire."

"But you know what they say, Seth. Where there's smoke ..."

"Well, what in the hell do you suggest then, Tommy? And don't say wait it out, 'cause there ain't time for that."

"Well, I just think it's ill-advised to do anything without giving diplomacy a shot first. You, Ginn and Sylvia sitting down together and just working through the issues."

Jipt starts his rebuttal with a fuming head of steam, as if launching into a diatribe, before the abdominal cramp cuts him short. "Goddamn it, Tommy–" He hunches forward slightly, wincing.

"What is it Seth? You okay?"

"I'm fine," he says, straightening up again. "It's nothing."

"Way I see it," Bossy interjects. "You need to fire a shot across the bow. Let the guy know you got his nuts in a vice. For example, what if the main power line into The Pyramid got cut? Accidentally, say."

"There aren't any power lines," Hawkins says. "It runs entirely on solar power."

"Well, shit. What about water, then?"

"Water's a touchy subject. Seeing as though we're in rationing mode already, I don't think the sight of water gushing into the desert's likely to please the average taxpayer. Regardless of where it was headed."

Staring at the massive globular dome above Bossy's eyebrows, Jipt's eyes suddenly light up. "Hey Tommy, remember that big 'ole balloon we used for the Diamond Ball promotion, way back?"

"Yeah, I remember, Seth," Hawkins says, clearly having no idea where this is headed.

"What ever happened to that thing?"

"Gosh, I remember we tried to sell it back to the manufacturer, but they wouldn't take it, since it was a custom job. So we just stashed it away in one of the basement levels. I'd reckon it's probably still down there someplace."

"Find out, would you?"

"Sure. But why? You're not thinking we could …"

"Well, Major Bossy, it looks like we may not need your services after all," Jipt says, his smugness returning out of the blue, like a runaway mutt long-since given up for dead.

Chapter 40

The Corporate Wars began as a result of many slow, macroeconomic, socioeconomic and sociopolitical changes in the global landscape occurring over the course of many years. Like tectonic plates shifting and rubbing against one another, they caused friction and the occasional flare-up of trouble, but little to worry about – yet, all the while, an immense pressure was building beneath the surface.

Extraordinarily complex forces were at work that we shall not attempt to analyze but merely summarize. Companies became larger and larger and, at the same time, underwent increasing pressure to streamline their operations. Competition stiffened and the lines between one company and other became horribly blurred, in fact, many companies formed alliances that were kept secret from investors, consumers and regulators alike. Arrogance and hubris and fear ran rampant through company boardrooms and executive suites. Then, at some point, companies became so desperate and disillusioned that they resorted to sabotaging each other in hopes gaining an advantage in the marketplace. Telecommunications lines were cut. Warehouses were burned. Food was contaminated. But the most visible battles, and those with the gravest consequences, were fought in the transportation and logistics industries. Fleets of trucks and trains and planes were commonly known to suffer catastrophic mechanical failure or simply to explode en route. Many people perished, and few were ever brought to justice for it.

However, today, for Lester, it is merely a tremendous inconvenience that such an incident has occurred, halting all worldwide air traffic and stranding him in Amsterdam.

The most anguishing part of the situation for Lester is that his travel itinerary never included Amsterdam in the first place. The plan had been New York to Paris to Moscow, but between the language barrier and a half-dozen cognacs at Charles de Gaul, everything went sideways. How he was allowed to board the wrong plane is still a mystery to Lester, as the cognacs washed away his memory of the boarding incident during which he identified himself as an undercover diplomat with top secret "microfish" (not microfilm or even microfiche) hidden inside his pancreas.

But truth be told, Lester finding himself in Amsterdam is not exclusively the most anguishing part of the situation. It's the fact that his suitcase and the handcrafted, engraved gold, platinum and titanium alloy, three-carat diamond and ruby-studded engagement ring inside of his suitcase have been sent to Moscow. For fear of being robbed or heavily taxed, not to mention fear of his own irresponsibility, Lester had decided it best to check the ring through as opposed to carrying it on his person – a most foolish decision he's ruing now along with his decision to wear a wool suit, an alpaca overcoat and a fox-fur *ushanka* (large, furry Russian hat) in anticipation of the blisteringly cold Russian winter. He still hasn't straightened out the global seasonal scheme in his mind and, of course, it's late summer in the northern hemisphere. Blisteringly hot.

Sweaty, drunk and belligerent, Lester interrogates a handful of polite, but curt, airport employees.

"Why have you sent me here?!" he says. "What have you done with Moscow?!" He says, among other less-than-pleasantries.

Finally, the true story is revealed, and he takes it very hard. Indeed, the throes of despair grip him so violently, shake him so vigorously, that he falls to his knees and begins to weep. He imagines stout Russian policemen guzzling vodka straight from the bottle and slashing open his suitcase with rusty knives. They bang their club-like fists on the table and then paw at the contents of his suitcase: the fine silk robes, the jars of peanuts and cans of beer, the toiletries ... and then, in a velvet box stuffed inside a sock stuffed inside a shoe, they find the ring. And they laugh. They laugh like barbarians on acid.

Lester's *ushanka* has fallen to the floor and a man picks it up. His face looks old and weathered, yet amiable. His voice is friendly and English.

"Excuse me, sir? You are going to Moscow, is that right? I overheard you speaking in the terminal."

Lester stares at the man's finely polished shoes, unable to think of any words.

"To be afraid is only natural in a situation such as this. Who knows when the violence will stop. And all the governments, they must be profiting somehow, don't you think? Otherwise they would use their power to stamp out this injustice."

The man's even-tempered rant has the effect of a finger down Lester's throat and like vomit he spits out a response.

"Corrupt bastards," Lester says.

"My name is Dennis. Dennis Sepins. But most people call me Squeakins," the man says, extending his hand. "Rather a long story I'm afraid."

"Squeakins?" Lester says, shaking with him and allowing to be helped to his feet. Upon taking a full look at Squeakins for the first time, Lester sees that he is exceedingly tall, probably six-three or four, and old – 75 or 80 if he's a day. He is clean-shaven, bald, and most of the snow-white hair on his head is concentrated in his thick eyebrows, which run together in the middle and hang over his eyes like a wooly awning. He wears pressed linen trousers and a taupe dress shirt, and holds a tweed hat and a leather valise in his free hand.

"Yes, it's rather a long story. My impression is that you must have a few of your own," Squeakins says.

"Bloody hell, yes."

"Well, I too am headed for Moscow. I am a butler by profession, you see – have been in London, but recently my master was hauled off to prison. That's the short of it, anyway," he says, chuckling a bit. "Well, I managed to get a letter of recommendation out of him, but the rub is that this new man's in Moscow. He's English, but living there for the time being, you see. A writer apparently, researching his latest book."

"England hasn't any men in need of butlering services?"

"Yes, well, at my age you can't afford to diddle about too long without a steady income. So I go where the work is. And I do hope it is satisfactory ... well, enough of my troubles. We're here for at least another twenty-four hours so why don't we find ourselves a hotel. What do you say, good sir?"

"Grand idea. I could use a cold shower. Something to eat would be good too."

"I know just the place," Squeakins says. "We shall just have to catch a taxi to the city proper."

"You're a sharp one, Squeakins."

"Thank you, sir. Knowledge of foreign cities has proven quite advantageous in my professional experience. And what may I call you, sir?"

"Right, right! My apologies. The name's ... Quimby. Quimby Miles," Lester says. "I'm an attorney. I have some depositions in Moscow tomorrow but I guess that's out the window!"

Sitting in the cab, Lester sweats profusely despite having stripped down to his undershirt. Squeakins is up front with the driver, discussing local restaurants. There is no air conditioning, but this has not deterred Lester from demanding it repeatedly.

"For God's sake, man! Can you turn that bloody air on?!"

Having already explained the situation several times, the driver ignores him, turning up the music – a frenetic techno beat that is like a thousand wet noodles lashing at Lester's delicate psyche. He stares out the window at the flowery Dutch countryside rolling by and, slipping into a state of delirium, he babbles to himself in a childish sing-song tone. "Lolly pops and gummy drops … mommy drops the yummy sauce, tummy moss, funny boss, honey claws …" Then, as one might expect, he slumps unconscious.

* * *

Lester is sprawled facedown, gripping the bars on the headboard as if the bed were being dragged behind a speedboat. His hands are covered with ink stamps from nightclubs, and on the nightstand sits a plastic bag full of marijuana and various pills. Already dressed, Squeakins opens the curtains and then taps Lester on the shoulder until he awakens.

"Mr. Miles?"

"Huh? Who?" Lester says.

"It's Squeakins, Mr. Miles."

"Mr. Miles … the ring! Where's the ring?"

"Your luggage is waiting for you in Moscow. I phoned the airline and they say it's safe and sound."

"We're not in Moscow yet?"

"No. Our ride to the airport will be here shortly. Would you like to get some breakfast?"

"My head … I think I may be sick."

"Why don't we get you to the bathroom, then. Up we go."

Squeakins helps Lester to his feet and escorts him to the bathroom, where he proceeds to vomit profusely in the general direction of the toilet. His accuracy, however, is less than perfect.

"There you go, Mr. Miles. That ought to help."

Squeakins is right. It does help to get some of the impurities out of his system. Lester sinks to his knees and retches a few times, having completely emptied his stomach. Then he stares at his vomit in the toilet bowl and at his own mottled reflection, and he finds a certain clarity that is most often found either through religion or dissoluteness.

"Mr. Squeakers?"

"Squeakins, Mr. Miles. Just Squeakins is fine."

"Squeakins," Lester says, his head still bowed, "What would you say about coming to work for me?"

"I appreciate the offer, Mr. Miles, but I have a commitment to—"

"My name's not Miles ... it's Ginn. Lester Ginn. And you see ... I know I haven't put a good foot forward here, but ... I have some very big plans when I get back to the U.S., and I think you could be of great service."

"Again, I thank you, Mr. Ginn but—"

"I'll pay you whatever that writer guy was going to pay you, plus I'll give you a horse, how about that? No, I'm just kidding, I'll give you ten times the amount – and the horse!"

"Well, I suppose excuses could be given."

"You'll do it then?"

"Yes, I'll do it," Squeakins says. "Now, I suggest you bathe yourself before we go to the airport, sir."

"Fantastic! That's the spirit! Welcome aboard, Squeakins! I've got a lot to tell you, so I hope you can ... if you know what I mean," Lester says, pretending to lock his mouth and throw away the key.

"If I couldn't keep a secret, sir, I wouldn't have lasted a day in this business, much less fifty years."

"Very well then, I'm not sure where to begin so I'll begin at the beginning …"

"Perhaps you should shower first."

"Yes, good idea," Lester says. "I do smell rather … great mother of Pete! Bloody rancid. What is that?"

"It may be petrol," Squeakins says. "And vomit. I'd suggest we dispose of that shirt altogether, sir."

"Right, good idea," Lester mumbles, stepping gingerly into the tub.

Chapter 41

Seth Jipt is a man who relishes spinning yarns about past injuries, but is squeamish at the most incidental presence of blood — especially his own. In pounding his fist on the edge of the conference table for no apparent reason, his hand glances off the edge and he rips off a sizeable portion of his thumbnail. He does not wince or yelp in pain, having trained himself well in this regard, but he merely grits his teeth and struggles to bear it.

"Ouch," Tommy says, "You all right there, boss?" He does not approach, probably in fear of appearing womanly, but also in fear of a violent outburst from Jipt.

"Yeah, yeah, I'm fine. Just nicked that ligament in my thumb," Jipt lies. "You know, the one that got all jiggered by the barbed wire … I never told you that story?"

"I thought the barbed wire messed up your eye."

"Well, it did that too," Jipt says, reinforcing a prior lie he cannot remember telling. "No, but this was after that, when I was about sixteen or so. I was way out on the outskirts of the ranch, mending some barbed wire with Lyle."

"So he was eight or nine?"

"Yep, and as usual, he was monkeying around and generally raising hell. He had this mini-bike we'd carry in the truck for him, and he was scooting around on that thing, jumping scrub and so forth, you know. And then, like the true moron he was, he decided to jump the fence."

"He didn't make it."

"He made it half way, but that landed him smack on top of the fence. Well, the wire, it jerked right out of my hand, right through the glove and – you know."

"Ripping the tendon in your thumb," Hawkins finishes.

"Hurt like a sonofabitch."

"I can imagine."

"There was blood spurting everywhere too, but that wasn't the worst of my problems. Lyle cracked his head on a rock, just like a hardboiled egg. It was all dented in on the side, and after I wrapped my hand to prevent from bleeding to death I set about – what is it?" Jipt says, watching Hawkins fidget with the buttons on his suit jacket.

"Sorry to interrupt you, Seth, but Manny Mojo's out there to discuss the last-minute details before the fight."

Jipt swills the remainder of his scotch and water. "Sonofabitch is late."

"Actually, he was—"

"And don't call him that. Manny Mojo. Granny Mojo's more like it," Jipt says. The sophomoric insult makes no sense and clearly betrays his drunkenness.

"I don't know his real name, to be honest with you," Hawkins says.

"Shit, I don't either … you know the difference between scotch whiskey and bourbon whiskey?"

"Scotch is barley-based and bourbon is corn-based," Hawkins says, as if recalling a fact learned in childhood.

"Hey! That's right! How'd you know that?"

"Oh, you know, barstool talk," Hawkins says, neglecting to mention the umpteen times he and Jipt have discussed the topic.

"Well, all right fine, send him in! I suppose he wants to talk about the fix."

"I'm not sure," Hawkins lies.

"And tell Trixie in there to get me another one of these," Jipt says, raising the glass and then accidentally losing hold. It shatters all over the hardwood floor. "Son of a fucking bitch!"

"You mean Vicki … don't sweat it, Seth, I'll have her clean this up lickity-split."

"Fuck it. Go ahead and send that two-bit con-artist in here," Jipt says. "Get it over with."

"You sure?"

"He ain't barefoot, is he?"

"No, I don't imagine … no problem, Seth," Hawkins says, leaving the conference room.

Jipt immediately inspects the damage to his thumb, fretting over the rough edge of the nail. He digs an emery board out of his coat pocket and begins the repair work, his back turned to the door.

Then Manny Mojo comes bursting through in all his gold-laden, neon-pinstriped glory. He has the unnatural energy of a cartoon character, his arms and legs, torso and neck constantly moving in all directions. His face is pimpled and pock-marked, his English just as obscene, rooted in the former Latino ganglands of Las Vegas.

"Yo yo, Sethie J. *Que pasa*, my friend?" Manny says, his yellow and black wingtips crunching across the floor. "What's dis shit, man? You have a hebe wedding in here or what?"

"Yeah, you got me," Jipt grumbles, stealthily returning the emery board to his pocket. "Sit down and let's tie up our business."

The men shake perfunctorily, and as Jipt turns away he wipes his hand over his tie, which is coated with an antibacterial residue. One of his many little hygienic secrets.

"Jew cranky, man. Whassa matter, you no dip your pen in the pussy today?"

"You mean *ink*."

"No, I means *pussy*."

"No, you mean *ink* you stupid piece of—"

"Eh-hem," Vicki interrupts, clearing her throat from behind the half-open door. "Um, Mr. Jipt?"

"Yeah, what?" Jipt barks. "This had better be about my drink."

"It is," Vicki says, meekly, holding the glass out but remaining behind the door, as if to avoid sporadic gunfire.

Manny checks the condition of his greased-back hair – a personal habit prior to doing someone a favor – and then facilitates delivery of the cocktail.

"Jesus Christ," Jipt huffs. "You got that spic-grease all over it."

"You're fucking welcome," Manny replies, amused rather than offended by Jipt's discrimination, largely because he's higher than a crack whore on payday. "You got to quit that shit, man. Eets no good for your heart and shit, das what I read."

"You read," Jipt chuckles dryly, taking a gulp. "God damn it, how many times do I have to say just a splash of water!" He does not expect a reply from Vicki, who has already slinked out, and he receives none. So he whines to himself, "How many times do I have to say it?"

"Maybe perhaps one times more," Manny says, as if trying to sound astute and sarcastic at the same time.

"For chrissakes, what's the goddamned fix?"

"Shit, man! Don't be saying that shit. Jew need to use the code, man, remember?"

"No, I don't remember it."

"You say, what's the weather forecast."

"Why do we always have to do this at the last minute," Jipt gripes. "There's no tape recorders in here you paranoid dopehead, so just get on with it."

"Okay," Manny says, "Jew listening?"

Jipt just stares at him and takes another contemptuous gulp of water and scotch.

"Okay," Manny whispers, "It's going to be sunny for nine days."

"Which guy in the ninth?"

"Shit, man! The white guy, okay?"

"Of course it's the white guy. What's his name, Robbins?"

"Thompson. He's the challenger. Psycho Robbins is the champ. My boy. Don't you know nothing?"

"I don't give a – hey, I'm told your people are dragging their feet with the stake money."

"They no put it up?"

"Not as of five minutes ago," Jipt says.

"That's weird," Manny says, rubbing a finger underneath his nose and sniffing.

Jipt eyes him with suspicion. "You went through someone else, didn't you?"

"No."

"Who was it? Vertuzzi?"

"I don't know."

"Bullshit you don't know. I handle it, that's the deal," Jipt says.

"Eets no biggie," Manny says. "I owed some monies so I go through him. One time."

"Owed him for what? Hell, I don't give two craps. Just get your goddamned greasy Mexican ass out of here."

"Panamanian ass. And I ain't greasy, just slick. Ha!" Manny says, spinning all the way around in his chair before jumping to his feet. "I see you down there, man."

* * *

Jipt settles into his ringside seat like a pile of bologna sandwiched between two slices of bread, with Lynette on one side and Hawkins on the other. The narrow seats and the garish charade of the title bouts usually put him in a foul mood and, generally speaking, tonight is no exception. His anxiety has been temporarily drowned out by the liquor, however, and therefore he's not nearly as concerned as he should be about Manny.

The standard deal is that he handles all the bets – indirectly of course, through a variety of complex laundering syndicates – to prevent Manny from changing the fix at the last minute. And it's worth pointing out that Manny has a history of doing this, to secure himself a greater share of the action. Jipt has never fully trusted him, not just because he's Hispanic and not just because he's in the boxing business either. Manny is a dynamic businessman if nothing else, with several side ventures including a modeling agency, a record label and a specialized private eye service.

The latter is his pride and joy, because he devised the whole idea himself – offering women the means to test their husbands' fidelity, using tantalizing "actresses" well-learned in the art of seduction. Manny's devious twist is that the women are all prostitutes, porn stars and habitual sluts, who often have sex with the men irregardless of their agreements with the wives to gather circumstantial evidence only. Granted, in some cases the outcome is devastating to the marriage, especially if the wife figures everything out. But in most cases she doesn't. In fact, her trust is often solidified by the results of the experiment. As Manny likes to say, "She get piece of mind, he get piece of ass – and everybody live happy ever after." Some might argue that a mogul in the gaming industry shouldn't cast stones. But in Jipt's mind, his business is squarely planted on one side of the moral decency line, Manny's on the other.

Normally, Jipt would have pulled out of his bets under such questionable circumstances. But he needs the cash badly at the moment, the Corporate Wars having eroded his profits in recent months. The rash of incidents lately has indeed caused widespread jitters in the tri-state area, which supplies the majority of The Casino's patrons – and it doesn't look to be on the up-tick again anytime soon. So, in essence, he's decided to take a gamble of his own, largely on credit. $10 million worth.

The ring announcer introduces Danny "The Tank" Thompson and then J.J. "Psycho" Robbins, as the crowd of 10,000-plus vocalizes their support and objection. Incidentally, Jipt considers this perhaps the most objectionable aspect of boxing overall – the way the fighters emerge from the wings in their silk robes, with their ridiculous entourages of thugs and freeloaders, and the way people cheer for them. This strikes him as absurd and sickening, and he turns his attention to Manny, who's in the front row of the adjacent section yelling and carrying on like a fool.

The tawdry hype-fest winds down at last, and the actual boxing is set to begin. The round card girl holds up a number one and saunters around the ring in her sequined bikini and high heels.

"I'd do her sideways and upside down," Jipt says to Hawkins underneath the din of crowd noise.

"Yeah," Hawkins says, hoping to leave it at that. He glances over at Lynette, who pays no heed to the comment. In fact, she's cheering and clapping herself, in anticipation of some good clean violence.

Unlike her husband, Lynette loves the fights. Perhaps because she thinks the best man really does win – at least most of the time. And it's not the violence that excites her, but the power. The tangible force of a punch landing square. That noise it makes, an explosion of air and rippling of flesh. She delights in all the carnal stimuli – the grunting, sweating and bleeding.

The bell rings. Bristling with energy, the two men dance and prance circles on the canvas more than they punch each other. Commentators might say they're sizing each other up, feeling each other out, but it's all an act. An exceedingly simple yet well-choreographed act designed to create the most entertaining spectacle possible, while generating the most amount of money possible.

While Lynette sees two finely tuned machines clashing in the ring, all Jipt sees is dollar signs. In fact, J.J. "Psycho" Robbins' shorts have dollar signs on them, which he finds rather odd. A psycho being preoccupied with money, that is. He stares at the little green patches embroidered on the white shorts and thinks about money. Having it, not having it, wanting more of it. The dollar signs blur together, but Jipt snaps them back into focus. He wishes he had another drink.

In rounds two through eight the action intensifies. First The Tank scores a barrage of points by getting in too close for Psycho to use his trademark jab. Then Psycho reverses the onslaught, backing tank into the corner and jabbing him silly.

Round nine begins with Psycho living up to his name. He browbeats The Tank like a man possessed, backing the challenger into one corner after another until he is forced to scuttle the attacks with bear hugs and headlocks. The referee steps in repeatedly to separate the fighters, as Jipt looks nervously back and forth between the ring and the clock, now at one minute left in the round.

"Come on," Jipt says to himself. "Go down already you bastard."

But amazingly, The Tank stays on his feet and takes punch after punch without so much as a wobble. 45 seconds remaining. Psycho's vigor starts to flag, as evidenced by the way he's draping himself over his opponent. The two men stagger around the ring in that sort of bizarre, vaguely homosexual waltz that occurs when neither fighter has anything left. 30 seconds. Jipt's anxiousness is personified by the spectators around him. They've fallen silent, with the exception of a few hecklers and enthusiasts trying to spur their favorite to victory.

"Punch him goddammit!" Jipt roars, drawing an amused glance from Lynette, but no action in the ring.

"15 seconds!" Psycho's trainer yells from his corner, and the champ musters a few tired jabs before The Tank locks him up again. And by the time the referee pulls them apart, the bell has already rung. The men are positioned opposite their corners, and as The Tank crosses, Psycho belts him right in the nose with a sucker punch. The crowd erupts and The Tank charges like an angry bull, driving his assailant into – and over – the ropes, clear out of the ring.

"Jesus Christ!" Jipt bellows, standing in unison with the rest of the crowd. "I'm going to kill that cheating sonofabitch!" Wild-eyed, he looks over to where Manny was sitting, but he's gone.

All hell breaks loose in the vicinity of the fighters, as their respective entourages swarm each other in a blur of fisticuffs. After all, such melees justify their being on the payroll – a revelation completely lost on Jipt at the moment, whose world is starting to spin – literally. He slumps back into his seat, gasping for breath and clutching his chest.

"Hey, Seth, you okay boss?" Hawkins says, only somewhat concerned. All Jipt can do is shake his head no. "Lynette!" Hawkins urgently taps her.

"Seth, what's wrong? Seth?! My god, baby, you're white as a ghost! Tommy, call nine-one-one! I think he's having a heart attack!"

Chapter 42

Jipt feels like a sissy in his baby blue, polka-dotted hospital gown. Holding down the button on the remote control, he loops around the television dial for the hundredth time today as Lynette attempts to shave the last bit of scruff under his chin.

"Hold still," she says.

"Why don't you just slit my throat," he says.

"You'd like that, wouldn't you?" Lynette says sardonically. "The easy way out, is that it? Leaving your poor wife to clean up the mess you've made of everything. There, all done. That wasn't so bad now, was it?"

"Mmm."

"What do you say?" Lynette says, as if addressing a young child who's just received a birthday present.

"Thank you."

"The doctor says you'll be back on your feet in no time. So cheer the fuck up, will you? You're driving me crazy."

"I'm hungry."

"Well, dinner's not for another hour."

"I can't eat that goddamned dog food any more," Jipt moans. "Can't you bring me some fried chicken or something?"

"You must be delirious," Lynette crows. "That's how you got yourself here in the first place. That and the booze. And the stress. And lord knows what else."

"Come on, Lynette, please."

"Forget it. Maurice did make some wonderful vegetable lasagna, though. If you play your cards right, I might could smuggle you in some of that."

"Aww."

"Fine, I won't then."

"No, I want it."

"You want it, what?"

"Please."

"All right, then," Lynette says, satisfied but not smug.

There's a knock at the door, and Hawkins pokes his head in.

"Hey Seth – oh, I'm sorry, Lynette. Didn't know you were here. I'll just drop by later."

"No, come on in, Tommy, I was just leaving," Lynette says. "I think I've had enough sunshine for one day."

"Thanks," Hawkins says, cracking a smile.

"You boys talk business, or whatever you need to do. No arm wrestling though. Doctor's orders."

"You got it."

Lynette gathers up her enormous, faux-leopard skin purse, which is about the size of a small leopard, and breezes out the door.

"She's a real pistol, huh Seth?"

"Yeah, right," Jipt says. "I wish she would just pull the trigger and get it over with."

"Aw, come on, she's just dishing out some tough love, you know that."

"I guess."

"Well, anyway, I just came by to give you a quick update on everything that's going on … unfortunately, there's not a lot of good news at this point."

"Give it to me."

"Well, I had to finagle a little to make that bond payment."

"Finagle?"

"Sell some assets."

Jipt closes his eyes and takes a deep breath, as if praying or readying himself for a cannonball to the stomach. "What?"

"It was the only way Seth, without losing interest in any of the properties themselves."

"What then?"

"The Lucky Lady, for starters."

"That boat was a goddamned money pit anyway. What else?"

"The G-Five."

"Hell of a plane. But also a money pit. Is that all?"

"Your share of LunarLight Technologies."

"Remind me what the hell that was?"

"That company that wants to project advertisements onto the moon? Remember that Indian fella you met at the tech convention last year?"

"Patel?"

"Yeah, that's the guy."

"Crazy goddamned dothead. Fine, is that everything?"

"Well … there is one more thing," Hawkins says, looking at the floor.

"Not the ponies."

"The thing is, Seth—"

"No, Tommy, you didn't!" Jipt says, lurching forward in an vain effort to sit up.

"Easy boss," Hawkins says, reaching out but not touching him. "I hated to do it, believe me. But they're in very good hands – a fella by the name of Scott. David Scott, a real enthusiast. He's in oil incidentally."

"Which is where I would be, if I had a goddamned lick of sense. Tell me you at least kept Mud Slinger? Please."

"Of course, Seth. Him and a couple of the other riding horses. Jackpot, Fancy Fred, Helen of Troy … a couple others I can't remember."

"Chestnut Charlie?"

"I thought he was dead."

"Not yet."

"Yeah, then I'm sure he's still around."

"Good, good … what about Lester Ginn? What's that crazy sonofabitch been up to? Anything?"

"I, uh … didn't realize you still wanted to keep an eye on him. You know, I thought we wrote him off as a nutcase."

"Yeah … he is a goddamned nutcase," Jipt says. Got to give him some credit though, I guess. That Pyramid Casino is one hell of an idea."

Chapter 43

"Lester. Lester, wake up," Svetlana says.

Lester has resumed his habit of drinking whiskey late at night, after Svetlana has gone to bed, which makes the transition to consciousness a lumbering affair. His faculties protest all the more because it's still dark in the room – even though the curtains have been drawn.

"Lester, please wake up. You need to see this."

Lester's eyelids flutter and open ever-so-slightly, just enough to reveal his bloodshot sclera, and then he clamps them shut again, as if to avoid excessive bleeding. "See what? It's still dark."

"Yes, but it's nine o'clock in the morning," Svetlana says, rolling Lester over so he faces the windows.

"Huh? It's just a lunar eclipse. Go back to sleep."

"I don't want to go back to sleep. And that's not the moon."

"How do you know?"

"Because it has ropes attached to it, going to the ground. Look."

"Hmm, so it does. What the bloody hell is that?" Lester rolls out of bed with a thud and crawls across the floor to the windows for a closer look. "Boy! Boy!"

"Lester, please. Why can't you just use the phone. It's right there."

He reaches for the phone just as Squeakins appears in his pajamas, holding a pair of high-powered binoculars. "Sir, have you fallen by accident or—"

"On purpose, boy, not to worry."

"Very well, then. My apologies, sir, for my unseemly appearance as well as my tardiness. I would have notified you earlier, but I just now awoke myself. I'm usually up with the sun, you know."

"What the hell *is* that, boy?"

"I'm afraid I don't know for certain, sir."

"Let's relinquish absolute certainty for now, boy — and by all means, we must not be afraid! Now, have you any thoughts on the subject? Hypotheses, as it were?"

"Well, it appears to be some sort of balloon, sir. I've spied it through my field glasses, and it appears tethered to four large vehicles out in the desert, perhaps a few miles outside the perimeter of the city. I'd venture to say it's designed to move with the sun along its prescribed arc."

"Diabolical bastard ..."

"Here, see for yourself, sir. You might want to step out on The Lanai though." Squeakins opens the sliding door and a blast of cold air rushes in. He takes note of Svetlana bundling herself in the down comforter. "My apologies, Mrs. Ginn."

"It's quite all right," Svetlana says. "The fresh air actually feels rather good."

Chapter 44

The rhythm emanating from the portable stereo is quick and funky, and Sylvia's hands dart around her body like tropical fish skirting a reef. She dances when she needs to think – and has no problem doing it in the company of her staff.

The centerpiece of her deliberation, of course, is the giant orb hanging in the sky, which has already been dubbed "The Black Balloon" by local media – many of whom, incidentally, have amassed outside her campaign office.

The song ends with an abrupt, inharmonious guitar chord and Sylvia taps the STOP button with one of her long red fingernails. "Talk to me, George."

"Well, if this mayoral thing doesn't work out, you've got that to fall back on."

"I hope you don't mean my ass."

"Your dancing."

"Talk to me, George. What's going on out there?"

"So far no one's claimed responsibility."

"You tried Jipt's office again?"

"No dice."

"So he hasn't said anything public yet?"

"Nope."

"You sure?"

"I've been glued to the TV all morning. They're broadcasting live outside Jipt's house and so far there's no sign of him."

"Hmm."

"Mostly they've been doing man-on-the-street interviews, you know, to fill the time."

"So what's the man on the street saying?"

"Actually, most people assume we're – The Union's – behind it."

"And?"

"About half say it's a good idea, it's about time something was done, that sort of thing. One or two say it's a public nuisance, and the rest don't really know what to think."

"And for once they have a good excuse."

"They've had a few experts on, too. Solar energy guys. The consensus is basically that it might take a few weeks, but it could force The Pyramid to use up all its energy reserves."

"Interesting. What else?"

"So we're having a press conference in … five minutes?"

"I had to buy some time," Sylvia says.

"No, that was smart. Question is …"

"Jipt is obviously the one behind this."

"Well, yeah," George agrees.

"And he wants us to fire off some accusations before he takes any credit."

"But why?" George says.

"So he can then accuse *us*."

"Of doing it?"

"Of doing nothing."

"Are you saying what I think you're saying?"

"I need to know what it's made of, what's inside of it, etcetera, etcetera. If I launched the thing, then I should probably know something about it, don't you think?"

"Right."

"You know what the funniest thing is, though?"

"What's that, Sylvia?"

"If you tell anyone, I'll crack your head open like an egg."

"Fair enough."

"Well, believe it or not, I haven't always been the trim and shapely Sylvia King you know today."

"No."

"Oh, yes. Growing up, my momma fed me fried chicken, fried okra, all kinds of greasy chitlins, biscuits and gravy, you name it. And that's not to mention the pies, bless her heart. Mmm-mmm-mmm, she could make a mean pie. Point is, I was a chunky little monkey until I got to college and had to pay for my own meals. And you know what they used to call me?"

"What?"

"The Black *fucking* Balloon."

Chapter 45

The atmosphere in the Apex Conference Room is dim and quiet, as a pot of tea and a basket of shortbread cookies make their way around the table. Lester steals a glance at Chutney before guiltily placing one cookie on his plate and two more under his napkin. Without diverting her attention from the task of honey-stirring, Chutney says, "I saw that."

"They're biscuits really," Lester says.

"Then why are you sneaking them?"

"What do you mean?"

"Under your napkin."

"Napkin?" Lester says incredulously, peeking underneath. "Oh my goodness, will you look at that!"

"It's The Union," Chili says through a mouthful of cookie. "Sylvia King announced it at a press conference about half an hour ago."

"Hmm," Lester says, examining both sides of his cookie. "I thought it seemed a bit too imaginative for Seth Jipt. How's it affecting our power situation?"

"We've got about half as much as usual," Ping says. "It's enough for daytime but—"

"Our peak consumption hours are at night," Schnitzelhaus finishes for him.

"Right, so we'll have to use the battery reserves."

Lester rises from the table, glowering at the balloon as if it just spit in his face.

"And how long will that last?" Katz says.

"It's hard to say for sure, but I think about two or three weeks," Ping says.

"I can program some energy-saving measures."

"We can fire up the generators," Chili says. "But with the price of gas so high and our cash flow next to nil …"

"Perhaps we could build a sort of supercharged harpoon," Lester says.

"To shoot from here?" Schnitzelhaus says. "That would be like trying to harpoon the moon!"

"Hmm, I suppose you're right."

"Don't the Indians have a small military force?" Chili poses. "They might help us out."

"Yes, I believe they have a tank or two," Lester says, loudly stroking his chin-stubble, which has been allowed to grow unchecked for almost a week.

"I don't know," Chutney says, setting down her teacup. "If we start shooting tank shells around willy-nilly, this could easily escalate to something much nastier."

"True, they might not let us just waltz in there and blast the sucker," Chili adds.

"Nobody said we'd *waltz* exactly," Lester says, although it's clear he's given up the idea, arguing only for argument's sake.

"We could do the funky chicken!" Ping blurts out, along with some cookie crumbs.

"What did I tell you about talking with your mouth full?" Chutney says, her tone not entirely jovial.

"We could mount the harpoon on a helicopter," Schnitzelhaus says.

Lester continues staring at the balloon for another moment or two before closing his eyes. He can still see it, except it's much bigger now, looming above him like a pregnant mother ship. With a dagger clenched in his teeth, he climbs the rope like a chimpanzee – like a machine – higher and higher. Reaching the top, he stabs at the belly of the proverbial beast, piercing the balloon's rubbery membrane again and again.

"I've got an idea," Tim says, having ascended the stairs unnoticed.

"Does it rely upon the use of tanks or harpoons?" Chutney asks, deadpan.

"No. It relies upon surprise, deception and about the only thing we have left to rely upon," he says with a histrionic brand of aplomb, as if he's been an understudy rehearsing the line for years. "And that thing is human courage."

Lester turns from the window to his son, looking him straight in the eyes. Indeed, they are aglow with the very courage in reference and, at this, Lester can't help but swell with pride.

Chapter 46

Tim has just executed the first phase of his plan, which he dubbed Operation Boll Weevil. He has never seen a Boll Weevil in person, in a photograph or even an artist's rendering for that matter, has never read about them in books or heard their eating habits discussed at cotton farmers' conventions. Instead, he's chosen the name strictly on phonetic and emblematic grounds. It's a trick he learned from his father (who learned it from *his* father), to set very specific and very attainable goals and to use catchy operation names for purposes of troop morale and motivation.

In hindsight, Tim thinks that perhaps Flush n' Ferret might have been more appropriate, if not quite as catchy as Boll Weevil, as the operation entailed all his personal effects being located (ferreted) and extricated (flushed) from their respective hiding places – drawers, cabinets, bags, boxes – and strewn about his quarters in plain sight. Although he reasons that Operation Ferret n' Flush would be more accurate, it doesn't meet his phonetic requirements either.

Confident that he named his first operation correctly, Tim begins the moniker postulation process for phase two, in which he will circulate his quarters and stuff giant black garbage bags with only those items deemed viably necessary beyond all reasonable doubt. He's not sure what this means to the letter, but, again, it sounds good. It sounds important. The overarching plan, or mission, must embody goodness and importance, so everything seems to be locking into place. He decides on Operation Gobbling Goblin.

Crawling around on his hands and knees, Tim scours the motley morass of belongings in a punitive fashion, snatching items and ramming them down the proverbial throat of the black goblin, which soon grows plump and cumbersome. He ties it off and starts anew with an empty bag. He is appalled by his own degeneration into materialism, and only wishes he had the courage to leave it all behind. After all, if he could leave The Pyramid itself behind, leave Anna behind … speak of the devil.

"Tim, why are you doing this?" Anna says, marching into the room with a look of aggravated perplexity. "It's insane, not to mention dangerous. I'm begging you, please don't."

"Oh, I see … you've reduced yourself to begging now? Pardon my saying so, but it doesn't suit you well a'tall. Begging, my dear, is only appropriate for two kinds of people, the shameless and the desperate. And perhaps the greedy. But, by nature, they're usually shameless."

"Oh, spare me the two kinds of people bullshit. Talk about desperate – I am fucking desperate, Tim! And so are you! This proves it once and for all."

"Nonsense … What am I desperate for?"

"Oh, I don't know. How about your own identity?"

"My own—"

"Separate from your father's."

Tim doubles his working pace, stuffing frenetically, and it's clear his mind has strayed from the task because he's now including superfluous objects like a stapler, a yo-yo and a big foam cowboy hat.

"It's true, isn't it?"

Tim stands up and looks at her defiantly. "Well, as long as we're playing *this* game, I'll tell you what you're desperate for, Miss I-know-everything-about-everybody."

"What? Go ahead, tell me."

"A dream."

"Ha!"

"Eh? Mmm?"

"No. Wrong … Besides, dreams are overrated. Either they don't live up to expectations, or they never come true at all."

"How can you believe that?"

"Personal experience."

"So I'm right."

"No."

Instead of dropping the subject, Tim has the temerity to push her. "So what's your dream, then?"

"Just forget it. You're right, okay? You're always fucking right."

"If you're afraid to answer then …"

"To live a normal life, Tim! That's my dream. To live a normal life like a normal fucking person, and to be happy."

"Normalcy. Talk about overrated."

"Look, I'm not going to argue with you anymore. I just wish you could explain why you're doing this. I just wish you could help me understand."

"Because I can make a difference. That's why I'm doing it."

"A difference to what? The Pyramid?"

"Yes, The Pyramid."

"I hate to break it to you, but it's a lost cause, Tim. I mean, half the people don't even want to be here anymore. And the other half are probably just too scared to say anything."

"Bollocks."

"Did *he* put you up to this?"

"Absolutely not. It was my idea."

"It's just – it's totally nuts. Do you realize that?"

"I think you're just jealous."

"Jealous? I'm jealous of you?"

"Because I'm taking control of my life. Because I have a purpose."

"Sure, a purpose you created for yourself. It's a fucking illusion, Tim."

Tim brusquely ties off another gorged goblin and hurls it across the room. "Yes, you're exactly right, I chose to create this purpose for myself. I *chose* to, of my own free will. And maybe it *is* an illusion. Maybe so. But it's mine, and I'm going to pursue it with everything I've got. Why do you care so much, anyway?"

During the course of Tim's little speech, Anna's expression has undergone a stark transformation from anger to despondency, evidenced by her vacant stare at the floor. "I don't know why I care so much, Tim. I thought I … I don't know, I thought maybe we … apparently I was wrong though."

"Wrong about what? You thought maybe we *what*?" Tim says, suddenly feeling sick to his stomach at the thought of another missed opportunity. He's afraid to say too much though – afraid of leaving himself exposed.

"Nothing. Nevermind. You know, maybe you're right. Maybe I *am* jealous of you, after all."

"Really?" Tim says, with an air of suspicion.

"Yeah. I don't want to stand in the way of your dreams. I just want you to be careful and come back safe."

"I will, I promise."

"Okay," Anna says softly.

"So we're okay?"

"Yeah, we're fine."

Tim spreads his arms and Anna folds hers to her chest, elbows down, fists to chin, submitting to his embrace like a tree about to be pulled from the ground by a terrible machine.

Chapter 47

In Lester's opinion, the foremost problem with modern culture – American culture, specifically – is that it's all but devoid of ritual and ceremony. For example, the average American is likely to cite eating turkey on Thanksgiving or watching fireworks on July 4th as meaningful events in their lives, even though most can't distinguish one year from the next. Indeed, few have experienced a moment as poignant and rich with latent consequence as the one Lester has planned for his son this afternoon.

With the muted diligence of a tradesman, Lester polishes the blade of his father's sword with a calfskin towel, admiring the gold inlay for what he reasonably expects may be the last time. It's not that he believes Tim will fail to return from his mission, but simply that he will soon claim ownership rights to the sword – and it's not considered appropriate to fawn over another man's sword, even if that man is your own son.

Satisfied with its luster, he sheaths the rapier and places it back in its decorative wooden box. The blood-red velvet interior serves as a dramatic backdrop and, in spite of his best efforts, Lester cannot quell the emotions stirring up inside him. After all, he's saying goodbye to an old and trusted friend. Granted, she had never been called upon to defend him against his enemies – but she had always been at the ready, and Lester has no doubt that she would have performed brilliantly.

When Svetlana enters the bedroom, Lester reflexively slams the box lid shut and rubs his eyes, just in case any tears have escaped.

Showing no interest in his activities, however, she crosses to her dressing table and slides a gold watch onto her wrist.

"I forgot to put my watch on this morning."

"You came all the way up here just for that?"

"No, I'm having lunch with Chutney."

"Why aren't you having lunch with me?"

"Because Chutney asked me, and you didn't."

"Right ... I don't see how you can stand that thing."

"What, my watch?"

"Yes. I'd imagine it's so heavy it would pull you round in circles."

"It's not such a burden knowing what time it is," Svetlana says, fiddling with her hair. In a fine show of dexterity, she untwists it and then twists it up again. "You might find it helps to avoid being late for everything."

"My internal clock works just fine," Lester says, tapping the side of his head. "Let me guess, it's half eleven."

"Not even close. Try one-fifteen."

"Really?"

"The watch doesn't lie."

"Damn. I was supposed to meet Tim at one."

"So you're going to let him do this?"

"Yes, of course. I don't see how I could stop him."

"You could."

"Well, sure, I *could*, but ..."

"Why don't you just give those people what they want? If they're capable of blocking the sun, then who knows what else they'll do, Lester."

"Is that what Chutney told you to say?"

"Chutney? No. She's got nothing to do with it. This is about our family, Lester. I'm worried about Tim. And frankly, I'm worried about you."

"I'm fine."

"Now. But what if something happens to him? He doesn't deserve to be caught up in this."

"Don't worry, Svety, he'll be fine. Besides, he'll have Escobar with him."

"I don't like that one bit, either, and you know it."

"I know, I know," Lester says. "But you're just so beautiful when you disagree with me."

* * *

In the privacy of his cube, Tim works with Escobar in the final stage of his training. The ceiling is dappled with volleyball-size black balloons, each with a tail of white string. One after another, Escobar pulls the balloons down and pops them with a dagger, for which he is rewarded with a morsel of fruit-flavored candy.

* * *

Chutney probes her Caesar salad for bits of chicken, looking remiss that she didn't order something else. "He said that? He really thinks I put words in your mouth like that?"

"Weird, isn't it?" Svetlana says, chewing her club sandwich. "You want some of mine?"

"I don't like bacon."

"You could pick it out."

"No that's okay. I'll just have a snack later. Maybe an apple and some peanut butter."

"You and your peanut butter."

"I can't believe he said that. It's so unlike him," Chutney says.

"You don't think he should compromise, then?"

"Well, I did at first. Like before the strike even started. But now ... I'm not really sure. It's a dodgy situation out there. Complicated, you know? I mean, it's not even clear who we'd be compromising *with* anymore."

"I thought it was The Union."

"Right, well that's one possibility. Then there's this Seth Jipt character, who's got his own motives I'm sure. He's sort of aligned himself with The Union, but it doesn't make any sense. Something's not right about it. I mean, for god sakes, The Union leader is running against him for mayor!"

"Shouldn't he be aligned with *us*?"

"You would think. Thing is, though, it's fairly obvious that he's always resented Lester – for his idealism, shall we say. It's about ego and power and money all that stuff men have waged wars over for thousands of years."

"That's what I'm afraid of," Svetlana says.

"I think that's what Lester is afraid of, too. But you know how touchy he is about the F-word."

Chapter 48

"Mom, I feel ridiculous," Anna says, looking at herself in the bathroom mirror and fiddling with the giant white feather in her cap. "You know I hate costume parties."

"Oh, come on. I think that hat is a good look for you."

"Your mom's right," Sergei calls from the living room. "I think you look dashing."

"Really?"

"Absolutely. Both of you do."

Svetlana returns to the living room, followed by Anna.

"I'm not wearing the mustache though," Anna says.

"Did I mention there's a costume contest?" Sergei says. "Five thousand rubles first prize."

"Let me see that," Anna says, holding her hand out to Sergei for the mustache. "Besides, people are less likely to recognize me."

"Oh, heaven forbid," Svetlana says, mockingly. "Hey, these are real swords."

"They're fencing epees, actually," Sergei says. "The point is blunt, but you could still take someone's eye out. So I wouldn't recommend bandying it about too much."

"Are you into fencing?" Svetlana says.

"Not much lately. But I used to be an alternate on the national team."

"Wow," Anna says, genuinely impressed.

Svetlana lightly pokes Anna in the rear-end with her epee.

"Hey! You heard him, no bandying. Unless of course you want to eat steel."

"Oooh, I'm scared," Svetlana says.

"Okay, ladies. I can see I'm going to need to keep an eye on you two."

"I'm sure you'd rather keep both eyes on her," Anna says, shooting Svetlana a mischievous look.

"Anna."

"Should we get going?" Sergei says, breaking a somewhat uncomfortable silence. "You know the way people are at an open buffet. The food's liable to be gone before eight o'clock. So what do you say? All for one?"

"And one for all," Anna says, poking Svetlana again with her sword.

Chapter 49

In general, citizens of non-English-speaking countries – especially those in low-wage positions of authority – tend to become irritated when someone insults them in English, screams at them or otherwise acts in an accusatory or confrontational manner. By no means is this a phenomenon unique to Russia. However, upon finding the lock on his suitcase broken, and upon not finding the ring in his toiletry kit, where he thinks he put it, Lester behaves in exactly this manner toward the greasy-haired, gap-toothed airline representative in charge of lost baggage.

"Where is it?!" Lester shrieks, rising to his feet and kicking aside a pile of sweaters he flung out of his suitcase in search of the ring.

Squeakins steps in and attempts to mediate, but to no avail. "Mr. Ginn, I suggest we—"

"Let me handle this, Squeakins," Lester says in a moderate tone, although through clenched teeth.

"Very well, sir."

"So where is it?! Hey! Boris! I'm talking to you!" Lester continues, even though the man's name badge clearly says MIKHAIL. "You can't play dumb with me, you stupid wanker! You thieving vermiculate bastard! Give it to me before I make mincemeat of your bloody face!"

Mikhail stares icily at Lester for a brief moment before responding in Russian, not with a raised voice but with his country's trademark flair for expressing utter disdain and contempt. It seems that, with each word, he's spitting out shrapnel from a proverbial grenade that's just exploded in his mouth. Translated: "You pathetic degenerate Englishman. You are foolish to think I will help you, now that you have insulted and disrespected me personally, as well as my country. Rot in hell."

"So you deny it!" Lester exclaims. "You will not get away with this, you greasy worm! I want to talk to your supervisor!"

At this point, Mikhail displays his gap-toothed smile and raises a walkie-talkie. "Security to lost baggage please."

"That's right," Lester says, "You're going to pay."

"What's this?" Squeakins says, picking up a sock from the floor with a square lump in it.

"Let me see that!" Lester says, snatching it out of Squeakins' hands and removing the red velvet box. He turns away from Mikail and opens it – then lets out a huge sigh of relief upon seeing the ring in all its hand-crafted, engraved gold, platinum and titanium alloy, three-carat diamond and ruby-studded glory. Then he whispers to Squeakins, "He could have switched it out for a fake!"

"Doubtful," Squeakins says, eyeing two soldiers across the terminal, who are heading toward them. "Now I suggest we take leave, Mr. Ginn."

"Sure, sure," Lester says, stooping to gather his clothes off the floor.

"Now," Squeakins says, with a subtle nod in the direction of the soldiers.

"Oh, right!" Lester says. "Well, sorry for the misunderstanding … Mikhail. Cheers, then!"

He takes one step before realizing that Mikhail has a hold of his arm.

"Unhand me, swine!" Lester says, ripping away from him. Mikhail doesn't bother to give chase but instead says something into his walkie-talkie that prompts the soldiers to start running – with their Kalashnikov assault rifles in tow.

In the midst of the confusion, Squeakins has managed to commandeer a nearby vehicle – the kind used to ferry passengers between terminals – and Lester jumps on the back. Luckily, it has more pickup that the ones typically seen in U.S. airports – and it doesn't make that awful beeping sound either – but nevertheless, the soldiers are gaining on them.

They swing around a corner and then through a set of automatic doors leading outside, as people scramble to get out of their way. Squeakins deftly steers them into the road and pulls behind a parked bus, where they disembark and jump into a nearby cab just as the soldiers are leaving the terminal. The cab driver looks back and asks where to, and there's a very tense split-second of indecision before Lester blurts out the first thing that comes to mind.

"To the Kremlin! Go! Go!" he says, and the driver responds to the sense of urgency by mashing down the gas pedal. Perhaps he thinks they're an important foreign delegation in a terrible hurry, but for whatever reason he peels out of there and makes several death-defying weaves through traffic to get clear of the terminal traffic. It does not appear as though they're being followed.

"Whoa! That was a mighty close scrape back there, eh Squeakins? Where'd you learn to drive like that anyway? That was bloody brilliant."

"If the truth be told, Mr. Ginn, I was something of a hoodlum in my younger days, involved in my share of mischief, you know."

"You don't say. I never would have guessed it by the looks of you. Well done though, old boy!"

"Thank you, sir."

* * *

It's late – nearly midnight – by the time they reach Svetlana's apartment. Lester hands the driver a wad of bills – roughly $200.

"Do you take dollars?" he says.

"Does ze frog's ass keep out ze water?" the driver says, taking the money and bearing his browned teeth. "But I must give change in Rubles."

"No change! By all means. For those maneuvers you pulled, I only hope we can call it square."

The driver laughs. "You can call it whatever you want."

"Lovely," Lester says. "Well Squeakins, old boy, I thank you for your services, and look forward to our future business relationship." He tucks another wad of bills in Squeakins' pocket. "That should get you back to the U.S. in fair shape. You have my number?"

"Yes, sir."

"You'll phone me up then, when you arrive?"

"Yes, sir."

"Smashing. I'll need your help coordinating the festivities and whatnot. Do you have any experience with that sort of thing?"

"Yes, sir."

"Smashing! Well, I'm off then. Cheers!"

"Good night, sir, and good luck."

Lester enters the building and takes the staircase up to the third floor in search of Svetlana's apartment, number 303. He finds it and knocks lightly, waiting a moment before trying again with more emphasis – but no response. He takes the piece of paper out and as he is double-checking the number, an old woman emerges from apartment 304 across the hall. She seems almost as wide as she is tall and has a gruff, gravelly voice, which makes the Russian sound like a broken record played backwards.

"You are looking for Svetlana?"

"Svetlana, yes," Lester says, recognizing that one word. "Svetlana no home?"

"She went out with her daughter and a man. Come, you can wait in here," she says, waving him over.

"She come back tonight?"

"We can have tea and cookies. I made the cookies myself, not that crap from the store."

"She come back soon?"

The old woman comes up to him now, takes his hand and leads him away. He does not resist as they enter her apartment. It is painted yellow and smells like mothballs. She seats him at a small kitchen table, and Lester finds it odd that she already has a kettle whistling on the stovetop and a plate of cookies on the table at this late hour. He chalks it up to a cultural anomaly, even though it's nothing more than a personal eccentricity, and he begins eating cookies. They do not taste good – in fact, they have the general flavor and texture of rabbit food – but Lester is so famished that he devours them one after another.

"Oh, you have a little bunny rabbit," Lester says, pointing to the cage in the living room.

"It's a rabbit," she says.

"Rabbit," Lester says.

"Rabbit," she says.

"These cookies are delicious," Lester says, holding one up and smiling for effect.

"I make them from rabbit food."

"Delicious. You'll have to give me the recipe."

"Here, have some tea," she says, pouring him a cup. "It is special tea mixed with rabbit piss."

"Tea and cookies, hard to beat that!" Lester says, taking a sip. "Whoa! That's got a little bite to it, eh? Delicious though, really."

"He he he," the woman laughs. "It will make you strong and bounce high like rabbit. He he!"

As the woman's cackling subsides, Lester hears another laugh out in the hallway – a beautiful and melodious sound that could only emanate from his dear Svetlana. He rushes to the door and looks through the peephole. It's her – but there's a man with her and his arm is around her waist! And they're both dressed ... like musketeers. Lester is frozen, rooted to the spot with hesitancy and confusion, and he can do nothing but watch and listen. Of course, they too speak in Russian, so he cannot understand – only infer.

"What happened to Anna?" Sergei says.

"I think she lagged back on purpose," Svetlana says, unlocking the deadbolts.

"Oh, I see. Well, I guess this is goodnight, then," he says, turning toward her.

"Your clothes ... you're not going to come in and change?"

"No, I was just going to go home like this – yes, of course I should change. Silly me, I forgot," he says, laughing, and Svetlana laughs too as she opens the door. They disappear inside, and Lester continues to watch at the peephole.

"She is with another man," the old woman says, from the kitchen.

"Shush you hag! Keep quiet!" Lester says, maintaining his vigil.

Soon Anna appears, but before her hand reaches the doorknob, Lester reaches her. With the proficiency of an assassin, he covers her mouth and drags her across the hall into the old woman's apartment. He closes the door, taking care not to slam it, then he turns

Anna around so she can see him. He gives her a moment of recognition before he removes his hand from her mouth.

"My god, it's you," she says.

"It's me."

"What are you doing here?"

"I came to see your mom."

"Just to see her?"

"No ... to talk to her."

"Yeah. Well, your timing isn't so good."

"Who is he?"

"A friend of hers from the zoo."

"Are they ..."

"Dating? I think you need to ask her that question."

"This is not good, Anna. Not good at all," Lester says, beginning to pace.

"Not good for you," she says.

"Is he rich?"

"He works at the zoo."

"Is he handsome?"

"He's pretty good looking, in a Russian sort of way. But look, Lester, I really don't want to get in the middle of this so ..."

She turns to leave.

"Wait a second! Wait a second, please," Lester says, rubbing his forehead, his mind racing to develop a plan. Then it hits him. "Is that a real sword?"

"It's a fencing thing, yeah."

"Even better. I'm going to need that. And your costume."

"Are you crazy? Of course you are, what am I thinking? No, I'm not giving you my costume. I don't have anything to change into."

"You can have my clothes."

"Oh, there's a fair trade. You smell like piss."

"Maybe Mrs. Whatchakov over there can lend you one of her robes, or a burlap sack or something."

"Lester, forget it."

"Anna, please. I was always kind to you, wasn't I? I took you and Tim to Coney Island."

"You got us kicked out of Coney Island."

"That clown was harassing us – and he tried to fondle you!"

"I know … I hate clowns."

"But you don't hate me, do you? I may have made some mistakes, but I'm only human. Not like a clown."

"No."

"So you'll give me the costume?"

"Well … all right. I'll admit I'm curious to see where you're going with this."

* * *

Having changed back into his street clothes, Sergei emerges from the bathroom, takes a seat on the couch and switches on the television. Svetlana is still in her bedroom, changing out of her costume. The door flings open and Lester the musketeer bounds into the room, startling and surprising Sergei on a number of different levels. He obviously expected a more subdued entrance, with Anna under the feathered cap instead of this wild-eyed man.

"Who are you?" Sergei says, rising to his feet.

"Do you speak English?" Lester says.

"Yes. Who the hell are you and where is Anna?"

"Shut up! And listen carefully. Anna is fine. And you'll be fine too as long as you leave immediately."

At this point, Svetlana appears from her bedroom wearing pajama pants and a tee shirt. "What's going — oh my god, Lester. What in the world …"

"Svety, thank heavens you're all right! I've come to save you from this … this ruffian."

"Lester, he's—"

"Look, *Lester*," Sergei interjects, with a discordant emphasis on *Lester*. His eyes narrow and his face tightens. He is the cheerful, happy-go-lucky Sergei no more as he continues, "I don't know who you are or how you know Svetlana, but I think she should decide who stays and who leaves."

"No, I … where's Anna?" Svetlana says.

"I'm right here mom," Anna says, meekly presenting herself in the doorway, dressed in a robe with big white rabbits on it.

"Svetlana," Lester says, "I know you're too hospitable and kind-hearted to throw a guest out of your home, so I'll take the liberty of doing it for you."

"You will do no such thing," Sergei says, in an even more unyielding tone than before.

"Well then, if that's how you want to play it, I see only one recourse … draw your sword!" Lester exclaims, drawing his own epee from its scabbard.

Without hesitation, Sergei takes his epee from the couch and draws.

"Please stand back ladies," Lester says.

They cooperate, being familiar enough with Lester to know the hour for diplomacy has passed. Once Anna has crossed the room and taken up a position with Svetlana in the threshold of her bedroom, Lester turns on his adversary. He makes three quick attacks and is surprised by the ease with which Sergei parries them.

"You are not a stranger the art of swordplay, I see," Lester says, making three more attacks with the same result.

"You are not so bad yourself," Sergei says, staging a counter attack. Lester repels him and the battle ensues with the utmost vigor from both sides, as the two men drive each other back and forth across the room, the air resonating with the comparatively feeble *tic-tic-tic* of the epees striking one another.

Lester jumps up on the coffee table to gain an advantage – and for a moment it appears to work, as his thrusts come closer and closer to landing on Sergei's torso. But Sergei sees an opening and exploits it, going back on the advantage and causing Lester to retreat quickly – so quickly in fact that he trips and falls to the floor. His back hits the hardwood first, followed by his head with a sickening *Thump!* and his eyes flutter open just in time to see Sergei above him, delivering the victorious blow to his sternum. Lester gasps as if he's actually been run through, releases his sword and then slowly regains his feet, stumbling and reaching out for the wall to support himself. He looks at Sergei with bewilderment, then at Svetlana in utter humiliation before he slinks out the door.

* * *

The hardened late-night patrons of the Crustok Bar tend to become quite ornery after five or six straight hours of drinking unfiltered vodka and lamenting their bitter defeat in the cold war, as they do every night of the week. Without fail, the conversation quickly degenerates into a stale, circular and altogether incoherent rant among the same three or four men. These are stalwart, barrel-chested men with hands like 60-grit sand paper, mouths like bear traps and eyes like jellyfish. And they are not accustomed to newcomers – especially Englishmen dressed in tights and feathered caps.

"Bartender! I need a beer! Beer! You understand?" Lester says, hoisting an imaginary mug.

The bartender does understand. But he, too, is drunk and ornery and in no mood to be bossed around by an English fool such as this. He says nothing for a moment, sneering at Lester like a condemned killer sneering at the family of his victim across the courtroom. Then, still sneering, he speaks in Russian to a group of men at the other end of the bar. "What have we here, my friends? The tooth fairy? Did anyone lose a tooth?" he says, erupting in vociferous laughter along with the others.

"I need some teeth!" one of them says, pounding his fist on the bar hard enough to rattle the glassware. "Perhaps I take some of his!"

"He looks like a peacock!" another says. "And I bet his cock is the size of a pea! If he has one at all!"

"Maybe we should put that feather up his ass! Then he will really look like a peacock!"

"Excuse me? Yes, I'm talking to you!" Lester says to the bartender. "I would like a beer please."

The men burst out in laughter again.

"A beer … I just want a beer," Lester says with a grimace, as if bracing for tears, his voice trailing off. "I just want a beer."

"Don't give him a beer if it makes you feel better, Gustav," Svetlana says in Russian, having sidled up unnoticed in the midst of the hubbub. "But give me two. Unless of course you want Tanya to know about your little gambling habit."

"Yes! Of course Ms. Svetlana! I didn't know this man was a friend of yours."

"Svetlana!" Lester says, wide-eyed, as if she were a winged angel descended from the heavens. "How did you find me?"

"Well, let's see. This is the only bar in the neighborhood, and the only place open at this hour so—"

"That was a stupid question ..." Lester says. There is a long pause, as they struggle with the awkwardness – the uncertainty about each other's feelings and to what extent time and distance has eroded them. Lester wants nothing more than to take Svetlana in his arms – to literally sweep her off her feet – but he knows he cannot.

"Lester, about Sergei ... I'm sorry—"

"No no, please, Svety, don't be sorry for anything – especially to me. I'm the one who owes you an apology. More than an apology though, so much more for what I've done ..."

"Two beers," the bartender says, sliding the glasses in front of them. "On the house."

"Thank you," Svetlana says, and Lester tips his cap.

"Shall we sit?" Lester says, motioning to a nearby table.

"Yes."

They sit, and Lester gazes down at the table for a moment, collecting his thoughts, before he looks up at Svetlana. Gone from his eyes is any sign of mania or fear, sorrow or desperation. And when he speaks, his voice is filled with humility. "Svety, it's so good to see you."

"It's good to see you too, Lester."

"I'm sorry I just dropped in like this, but it's so difficult to talk on the phone, you know, without that face-to-face element, and I love your face so much. Your face is so beautiful, you're so much more beautiful even than the idealized images I made in my head ... I have so much to tell you that I don't know where to begin."

"Why don't you start at the end, then?" Svetlana says.

"That's right, I remember. You always read the end of a book first, don't you?"

"Just the last sentence."

"Then the first sentence?"

"Yes. By then I can usually tell if I'll like it or not."

"Are you usually right?"

"Almost always."

"Very well, then … this isn't how I had this planned, mind you, if my appearance isn't proof enough of that," Lester says, with a sheepish grin. "But here goes."

He reaches for the pocket of his blazer, but of course the pocket is not to be found – and, therefore, neither is the ring.

"Oh, no! I left the — damn it, I've botched this whole thing."

"The what, Lester?" she says, growing suspicious.

"Wait here, I'll go get it," he says, starting to rise.

Svetlana grabs his hand.

"No," she says, "whatever it is, you don't need it."

"And you're sure you want me to start at the end? Maybe I could start in the middle and explain a little about—"

"No, tell me the last sentence."

"Well, actually, I hope it's the next-to-last sentence."

"Why's that?"

"Because it's a question," he says, taking both of her hands in his, sliding out of his seat and taking a knee in front of her. "Svety … will you marry me?"

"Yes."

"I promise I'll—"

"Yes. I said yes."

"You said yes? You said yes! Oh my god, Svety, you've made me the happiest man in the world!"

He stands and pulls Svetlana into a tight embrace. The men at the bar begin to clap and cheer but neither can hear the sound. It's as if they are the last two people on earth, standing amidst the charred rubble of the apocalypse, a barren wasteland of humanity, and they know their only hope – their only chance for survival – is to stick together until the very end.

Chapter 50

Jipt hasn't slept well for months, but his dreams have been more vivid and provocative than ever. In this morning's feature, he walks down a palatial hallway lined with guards. They are dressed in ornate red and gold uniforms and hold giant battle axes at 45 degrees on either side, creating a smaller archway through which to pass. He does so alone, making eye contact with no one as he approaches the giant wooden doors, which seem to be miles away.

The doors open to reveal an unbelievably ornate throne room. Inside, Lester sits high on the gilded throne, flanked with more guards and beautiful women of every race and complexion. He holds a gold, jewel-encrusted scepter that appears to glow with ethereal radiance.

Jipt wants to turn back, but he can't. It's as if he's on a roller coaster slowly cranking higher and higher, gaining potential energy for the ensuing thrill-ride. Continuing toward the throne, his eyes locked on the scepter, he feels a baleful chill run along his spine. When, at last, he reaches the throne, he drops to his knees and kisses Lester's sandaled feet with the profusion of a leper.

* * *

Jipt awakens with a start to find himself in bed alone, and he fumbles on the nightstand for the remote control. After pressing two buttons, the curtains on the enormous picture window automatically draw open and a radio turns on. He gets up and heads straight to the bathroom to begin the morning's hygienic regimen.

The staid intonation of the news anchor's voice fills the room all at once, as opposed to light from the windows, which trickles in slowly as the curtains draw farther apart.

"—in Washington, I'm Charles Grant. After a decade marred by corruption and violence, the Corporate Wars have officially ended. At a summit meeting earlier today in New York City, leaders from more than 100 companies signed a peace treaty and vowed to usher in a new age of ethics and responsibility in the business world. A group of protestors gathered outside The Plaza Hotel, calling for workers' and consumers' rights, but the ceremonies continued uninterrupted. There were three arrests ..."

The bathroom also affords a window-view of The Pyramid, but Jipt is too busy silently critiquing his teeth-brushing technique in the mirror to notice what's different today. On the right side of The Pyramid, silhouetted against the dawn, a grand sailing ship inches its way down the slope. It looks like a prop cut from black construction paper, but of course it's not. It's none other than *The Heinousmeistress* herself.

"Eight coalition soldiers, including five Americans, were killed in Seoul, South Korea, late last night by an alleged suicide bomber. Eyewitnesses say a man riding a bicycle slammed into a roadblock and detonated the powerful explosion, which also wounded dozens of civilians in a nearby café. In response to this, the latest in a string of insurgent attacks on the Korean peninsula, President Franks sent his condolences to the families of the victims, but also said the coalition would not be deterred in its efforts to return stability to the war-torn region."

Jipt moves on to The Shaving of the Face, which is a two-step process involving a state-of-the-art electric razor followed by a blade for maximum closeness.

"A U.S. cargo ship sunk in the East China Sea early this morning after allegedly striking an explosive mine. A fishing boat in the area was able to save the twelve-man crew of the doomed ship, which was carrying Chinese-made consumer goods. As of yet, no one has claimed responsibility for the mine, but U.S. officials say a thorough investigation is already underway."

Next up is The Cleaning, Emulsifying and Moisturizing of the Face, utilizing a cornucopia of expensive creams, balms and lotions, most designed especially for women.

"In economic news, third-quarter unemployment figures were announced today amid increased optimism on Wall Street. At nine-point-eight percent, it's the first time unemployment has reached single digits in nearly a decade. Earlier this week, other key domestic indicators like housing starts and consumer confidence also hinted at a break in the latest recession."

Feeling the sudden need to urinate, Jipt pivots toward the toilet – and the window – at which point he freezes. He blinks several times in attempt to clear his vision, as if the anomaly before him is merely a bug on his proverbial windshield. The simple fact is that he cannot comprehend what he's seeing, and thus wonders if perhaps he's still asleep. After all, he often experiences nightmares about his various maintenance routines – usually involving lacerations, his hair falling out or his skin turning grotesque colors, but nothing like this.

Because pinching himself seems too clichéd, he bites his tongue instead. It hurts, which he takes to mean he's indeed awake, and which is both reassuring and disconcerting at the same time. He can't seem to muster another step, however – even when he feels the warm trickle down his leg and sees the revolting yellow puddle gathering on the Italian tile.

Chapter 51

Due to its virus-like commercial growth over the years, PyraVegans have, in essence, become inoculated to overblown exhibitions, extravaganzas and publicity stunts of every kind. What they are seeing today, however, compliments of Tim, Escobar and *The Heinousmeistress*, is something altogether new and different.

Sylvia holds her boys close as they jostle amidst the throng of people gathered on Commerce Boulevard East, one of the city's major thoroughfares. Ordinarily snarled with traffic, this morning it's been cleared by local authorities as a parade route. That is, for lack of a better term, they're calling it a parade. Without a doubt it's a spectacle. The media is everywhere – in the street, on the rooftops and buzzing overhead in numerous helicopters.

Having wiggled his way to the front, trailed by Sylvia and Anthony, young Michael squeezes his head through the police barrier and looks up the Boulevard.

"Michael! You're going to get your head stuck," Sylvia warns, but it's already too late.

"Momma! Momma! I see it! It's coming! Look!"

"Where?! Where?!" Anthony says, trying to lean over the metal fencing. "Lift me up, mamma."

"You're crazy."

"Come on."

"No, and it's not a matter of won't. It's a matter of *can't*."

"Sure you can."

"Have you looked in the mirror lately? You're built just like your – you're big, okay. You'd squash me like a grape."

"But I can't see."

"Here it comes!" Michael says again.

Sylvia can't suppress her curiosity any longer and leans out, balancing on her tip-toes to catch a glimpse. It's a pirate ship all right, which is being nudged along by a squat, boxy vehicle, like those used at the airport to push aircraft back from the gates. She can't make out the figure at the helm, but perched high on the center mast is what looks like a chimpanzee donning a bright crimson headscarf. For some reason, this doesn't strike her as odd, perhaps because the context itself is so incredibly weird to begin with. The real question is: *What the hell is this all about? Is this Lester Ginn's idea of a diplomatic envoy?*

Nearby, up the street, Sylvia spots Tina Franco preparing to deliver a live report. She conceals herself behind a man in a cowboy hat, lest Tina want to interview her, but tunes her ears to the shrill timbre of the reporter's voice, hungry for any new details that may have emerged.

"And three, two, one ... This is Tina Franco with PyraVegas 5 News reporting live from Commerce Boulevard, where a sort of impromptu parade is taking place behind me. As you can see, the centerpiece is this ship, which looks like – and I'm no expert mind you – but it looks like a pirate ship. In fact, it's actually flying a skull and crossbones flag, in addition to American and British flags. By now you probably already know that this ship emerged from high in The Pyramid early this morning and actually rolled down the side, all the way to the ground, where it proceeded to the inner city limits. As for the man at the helm of the ship, PyraVegas 5 News has just learned, from a very reliable source inside The Pyramid, that he is Tim Ginn, son of the infamous Pyramid Overlord, Lester Ginn. His mission? A gesture of solidarity, albeit a bizarre one, with The Pyramid Workers' Union, whose recent plans to strike were preempted by his father, in what some considered to be underhanded political dealings, possibly involving Mayor Seth Jipt as well. Furthermore, sources tell us Tim Ginn's destination is the Black Balloon, launched earlier this week by The Union in protest of the lockout, which he intends to protect from those who have threatened to destroy it. Needless to say, this story is still unfolding, so stay with us here at PyraVegas 5 News for the latest … Well, the ship has almost reached us now, so I'll step aside here and see if we can get a closer shot of it for you …"

Sylvia cannot believe she just heard that right. *Protect the balloon? Solidarity with the Union? Supposing he was, in fact, at odds with Lester, how could he pull off such a feat behind his back? Of course, it all goes back to the Lester Ginn wildcard, as usual. Either he's a legitimate madman or he's a fucking genius, keeping such a low profile for all these years, not challenging any of the allegations that he's a madman. As a result, it's damned near impossible to guess his motives. It should be to our advantage if the story's true. But if it's not true, then what the fuck is he doing here?*

"Michael! Get your head out of there right now before you break your neck."

"I can't! I'm stuck!"

Sylvia can tell he's not really stuck, but that extrication will require a bit of ear-ruffling. "Stop squirming for a second."

Becoming hysterical, Michael doesn't comply. Instead he squirms even more vigorously and blubbers for help.

Sylvia softens her tone in an attempt to mollify him. "Just be still, baby. I'll get you out."

This time he cooperates, and the instant Sylvia feels his muscles slacken she jerks his head back through the bars. He lets out a brief yelp but then falls silent, as if amazed it didn't hurt more.

"Dumb ass," Anthony chides him.

"Anthony. You want me to stick your head between those bars?"

"No."

"Then shut your mouth."

"You okay, baby?"

Michael nods his head and wipes away the tears.

"Good. Now what did we learn? Not to stick our heads in places they don't belong?"

Michael's eyes widen and he nods more emphatically, as if understanding the allegorical implications of the lesson he's just received.

Chapter 52

It's been over a month since Sandeep enjoyed his last glass of orange juice, which had become a staple of his diet not only in the morning but throughout each day. Beer and bread have also been in short supply, but the orange juice deficiency has impacted him the most, in terms of his daily energy level. After checking every market in The Grid to no avail, he started asking around.

To his dismay, most of his initial inquiries proved fruitless, so to speak. In fact, the most common response was, "No, I haven't seen any. Have you seen any (licorice, ketchup, aspirin, etc.)?" It seemed the hoarding problem had grown to epidemic proportions, and eventually he learned that the only way to obtain these items was to win them. So Sandeep has descended to the City Level tonight, to the purported epicenter of this black market economy, Five Card Studs, where poker tables cover almost every square inch of usable space like lily pads on a frog pond.

As of yet, Sandeep hasn't found anyone with orange juice, but he has managed to win a few hands, turning five measly chocolate bars worth of equity into a modest nest egg.
A case of wine, a few dozen sticks of butter, some shampoo – all represented with paper IOUs of course, as opposed to the actual products, which would be burdensome to tote around. And by the account of fellow gamblers, thus far the system has been relatively devoid of malfeasance.

Having just folded his second straight hand, Sandeep feels a tap on his shoulder and turns around to see that it's Felipe, a man he had met earlier in the evening. Felipe is a plump, gregarious Mexican with an eye patch and a tremendous poker face. He, too, had a hankering for orange juice, as well as a supply of cookies to his credit, so they had agreed to join forces and split whatever winnings they could accumulate over the course of the evening.

"Sandeep, my friend," Felipe whispers. "Our man has arrived. He wears the orange cap."

Felipe turns and Sandeep follows his eyes to an orange baseball cap, sitting atop the head of a handsome, clean-shaven, athletic-looking young man – the stereotypical American frat boy. He has a cigarette behind each ear and looks cocky, raking in a pile of IOUs.

"You sure?" Sandeep says, although it occurs to him that the man's chosen hat color must be a sign.

"Yes. I seen him take over five-hundred gallons last night."

"Okay, let's go."

"Wait," Felipe says. "We must get a drink first."

Sandeep follows his lead over to the bar, where Felipe asks the bartender to make sure "his friend," the man in the orange cap, never sees the bottom of his bourbon and soda. Then they order non-alcoholic drinks for themselves and Felipe explains the signal system they will use to maximize their chances for success.

"You got it?" Felipe says.

"I think so."

"Good. I'll go over first, and then you come after a few hands."

"Okay."

So they set the plan in motion, and it's Sandeep who hits a lucky streak first, winning more than half the hands over a three-hour time period. Meanwhile, the man in the orange cap has been getting sloppy, his judgment eroded by the merry-go-round of bourbon cocktails. But there's one problem. He has kept his orange juice close to his vest, instead wagering with other assets – among them mouthwash, cold medicine and even ladies underwear.

The game continues, hour after hour, with a steady flow of players coming and going from the seats around Sandeep, Felipe and the man in the orange cap. In the process, Sandeep loses most of what he gained before, but Felipe's luck starts to pick up instead. By this time it's nearly five in the morning and Sandeep is dead tired, running off the fumes of his residual determination and hope.

Finally, about an hour later, they get the man in the orange cap right where they want him. He looks to be holding something good (they can only hope it's not *too* good, or that he's bluffing), and he decides the time has come to recover his losses. He spikes the pot with the 500 gallons of orange juice – actually 500 cans of concentrate, each capable of producing one gallon of juice – and for some reason it just now occurs to Sandeep that his refrigerator-freezer must be packed to the gills with the stuff, leaving room for little else.

Sandeep takes another look at his cards, even though he knows exactly what's there. Two pair, jacks and sevens. Not as strong as he would have liked, especially since Felipe's elbows are on the table, meaning he's got nothing. Felipe folds, and by Sandeep's estimation he can't have much of anything left – assorted sundries, maybe some herbs and spices, all of which are in low demand. After Felipe, there are calls all the way around to Sandeep, who has no choice but to toss in his last slip of paper, 10 bags of potato chips, and call as well.

"All right, let's show 'em," the man in the orange cap slurs merrily.

Sandeep looks at his cards, blinking several times to clear his vision, to make no mistake about what he's seeing. Two pair, queens and threes. Sandeep feels the rush of adrenaline synonymous with victory, which is then sucked out of him an instant later by the horrified look on Felipe's face. It's the old woman with the puffy hair between them. She's smiling like a mongoloid in the glow of her full house, three kings over two queens.

"Lucky ladies!" the old woman cackles, and she encircles the pot with her skeletal arms like a young girl hugging her first teddy bear.

Chapter 53

If Seth Jipt had a tollbooth on his sphincter, the past 24 hours would have represented a major financial windfall. Indeed, the high dosages of prescription-strength laxatives finally kicked in with unbridled vengeance, wreaking havoc on his digestive system. So much diarrhea passed through him that, at times, he feared his intestines themselves may have been liquefied. And then there was the smell – the unspeakably ripe stench that, in wave after wave, exploded from his bowels like a poltergeist, steamrolling him to the brink of nausea time after time …

But, of course, no such tollbooth exists, and thus the only blessing hidden in this fecal cataclysm for Jipt was the abundance of quiet, personal bathroom time it afforded him. In between labor pains he had an opportunity to meditate and deliberate on a number of salient topics, and he even reached a few decisions.

First off, he decided – or convinced himself, as the case may be – that his loss to Sylvia in the mayoral election will actually turn out to be a good thing. Why? Simply because, now that he's out of the political spotlight, his every move will not be subject to media scrutiny and public opinion – at least not to the same degree. And that's not to mention the newfound void of accountability. Which, in turn, led him to the second decision of note, to call another meeting with The Desert Hawk himself, Major General Vernon Bossy.

* * *

"I've read the same articles you guys have," Bossy says, chewing on his ubiquitous wad of tobacco. "And you ask me, the story's got horseshit written all over it."

"Even if the Ginn kid *was* in a spat with his old man, why would they release a story like that?" Hawkins says, probing the issue further.

"They wouldn't," Bossy confirms, planting both elbows on the oak conference table, left hand wrapped around right fist. "Unless, of course ..."

"What?" Jipt says, diverting his attention from a rogue strand of knuckle hair he evidently missed in the plucking process.

"Ginn's not in power anymore."

"An internal *coup*?" Hawkins says.

"Happens all the time in the real world."

Jipt tries to pinch the hair between his thumb and index finger, but his nails are too short. "He's still up there ..."

"You're probably right," Bossy says. "And we'll find out soon enough, soon as we get our hands on the son."

Hawkins swivels his chair toward Jipt. "We don't even know if the balloon is having any effect, right? Chances are, it's not. So, if we think he's going to bring it down, why not let him? It's going to play as The Union's loss anyway. Maybe *they'll* try to stop him and we won't have to get involved."

Jipt tries to pull the hair out with his teeth, but only succeeds in cutting it shorter. He wants nothing more than to excuse himself, to get some tweezers, but he's paying Bossy an exorbitant hourly rate for his services and doesn't want to retain him any longer than necessary. "How do you reckon he's planning to bring that sucker down, anyway?" Jipt says to Bossy, inadvertently glossing over Hawkins' comments. "Some kind of harpoon?"

"My guess is he'll just try and cut the ropes, let the thing drift away on its own."

"That makes sense," Jipt says, reverting to his fingers again as a means of extricating the dastardly knuckle hair.

"At the rate he's going, my calculations indicate he'll reach the target in the next eight to ten hours, so we've got to get the wheels moving."

"What wheels are those?" Hawkins says.

"The blocking force," Bossy says, his tone implying a forgone conclusion.

"You'll have to excuse Tommy," Jipt says. "He couldn't join in our phone conversation earlier, so this is all new information."

"It's very straightforward," Bossy says, unfolding a map from his pocket and jabbing at it with a plump finger. "Two vehicles, eight men. Intercept him about here, take him into custody and transport him here, to the temporary outpost."

"Outpost?" Hawkins says.

"Double-wide trailer," Jipt says. "Very comfortable, he assured me."

"He'll be treated with the utmost dignity," Bossy says, spitting in his coffee mug. "Like a prince ... or whatever he is."

"How is that not kidnapping?" Hawkins says.

"He'll be trespassing," Bossy says.

"So what? We use him as a bargaining chip?"

"With any luck we won't have to. The first step will be to find out what's really going on in Pyramid Land."

"And what makes you think he'll cooperate?"

Jipt raises his eyebrows in a gesture of, "You know why."

"Oh yeah ... I don't know, though, Seth. It still seems like we'd really be sticking our necks out awfully far on this."

"I value your opinion, Tommy, I do. But we've been straddling the fence for long enough, trying to please everyone. Well, now we don't have to do that anymore, see? We're free to pursue our own interests. Besides, a man straddles that fence long enough and all he gets is—"

"A sore crotch. I know, Seth, it's just that … ethically, you know, this just doesn't feel right."

Bossy jumps in. "Every aspect of the plan will be handled with utmost—"

"Please, Major General, this is between Tommy and me. Look Tommy, don't piss down my back and tell me it's raining. You're just going to have to trust me on this."

"That's the problem though, Seth. I'm not sure I do, anymore."

Jipt opens his mouth – maybe to rebut him, maybe to admonish him, but nothing comes out but a breath of hot air. He's not sure how to respond because no one ever had the balls to tell him that before, to express their mistrust in him. In fact, he never even had the balls to tell himself.

Chapter 54

The Pyramid represents something of a personal, if not public, embarrassment for The President of the United States. After all, it's been built right under his nose – construction started in the prior administration but finished in his own – and thus far he's chosen the path of least resistance with respect to policy. In fact, he's barely even acknowledged The Pyramid's existence, having been tied up with a barrage of more immediate concerns, namely wars (in addition to the Corporate Wars) that have raged on nearly every continent – Western Africa, Eastern Europe, the Persian Gulf, Southeast Asia, Korea, Central America … the list goes on.

Despite initial outcry from the media and from a small segment of the American population, The Pyramid quickly became a back-page story (or more commonly, a no-page story) by simple virtue of a lack of available information. The Pyramid's complete identity became enveloped by The Casino and Hotel, and thus it was treated no differently than the newest mega-colossal theme park. Sure, these glitzy, adrenalin-pumping wonderlands are exciting at first – but if nobody dies, if they don't catch fire or none of the rides collapse, they're essentially just dots on the map, glossy brochures displayed in motel lobbies – nothing newsworthy about them really.

In the case of The Pyramid, this below-radar flying was largely attributable to the keen strategy employed by Lester – and moreover, Chutney – in the area of public relations. Or rather, the lack of any relations with the public whatsoever. During construction of The Pyramid, for example, Lester remained very secretive and inaccessible. Yet more importantly, he refrained from openly misleading, challenging or otherwise toying with the media as he was wont to do in the past. So in a sense, he and the president took similar approaches, similar paths of least resistance. However, all paths that are not parallel must intersect at some point in space and time – and these paths intersect at the present, in the Apex Conference Room.

So why is President Gerald "Buddy" Franks here? What does the world's most powerful man want from our poor Lester? He wants concessions. He wants assurances. And to a certain extent, he wants regulatory authority. Part of the impetus for his visit is the embarrassment issue – the public perception, and that within his own party, that says he's too rhetorical, too old and too conservative – even for a republican. But more powerful than that is the political "firestorm" that has erupted in congress, largely due to a few rabble-rousing democrats who are desperate for any advantage possible going into the next general election.

As everyone knows, partisan politicians have never been above speculating wildly, even starting unfounded rumors, with the purpose of damaging an opponent's credibility – or, at the very least, giving him a severe headache. And this is precisely what has happened. The speculation: That The Pyramid is a non-regulatory, tax-free haven for enemies of the state. In fact, the president's adversaries have gone so far as to draw oblique connections between very distant and enigmatic dots. And in doing so, they've created a picture of his alleged "devious plan," which includes varied stages of wrongdoing and conspiracy leading to a dramatic political victory. In other words, he's accused of letting the problem grow unchecked for the sole purpose of eradicating it. The whole business has gotten very ugly, very fast.

With all that said, the president remains a powerful figure, and a proud one. Furthermore, he knows that the best way to get what you want, whether it's a cookie from grandma's cookie jar or a multi-billion-dollar foreign policy budget from congress, is to try being nice first. If all else fails, kick ass – but at least try being nice – especially with a wildcard like Lester Ginn. As dictated by his job requirements, the president knows how to put on a friendly face, how to press the flesh, pump up egos, play to sympathies and weave his agendas into the fabric of seemingly casual and benign conversations. And this is the tact he chooses with Lester from the instant they shake hands.

For his part, Lester is quite tactful and cordial as well, having been coached and lectured extensively over the past week by Chutney, and Admiral Porsley, and Squeakins and everyone else who could get a word in edgewise. The overarching theme: Say as little as possible. Be as congenial and non-confrontational as possible. And finally, remember to take the prescribed medications beforehand. He has taken this advice, as well as the attire recommendation provided by Svetlana – a black suit and shiny gold necktie. As a result, he looks and feels sharp.

Lester's first impression of the president is that he appears even older in person than he does on television. In fact, Lester is repulsed to a certain extent by his face, which hangs with enough excess skin to cover a basketball, and which is caked thoroughly with makeup, giving it the general complexion of a used prophylactic. His hair is thick and full, but looks and smells as if it's been colored with black shoe polish.

We will skip over the pleasantries, the exchange of commentary on weather, the mutual eating of tea cakes and so forth, and get right to the meat of the meeting, as it were, which is instigated by Lester's decision to suggest a game of horseshoes be played. Somewhat reluctantly, the president agrees, and with the president's entourage of security and advisory personnel in tow, they head down to the Rec Level.

The Rec Level is indeed a sight to behold, especially on a bright and sunny day such as today, albeit dampened somewhat by the presence of The Black Balloon. As a pleasant coincidence, the cherry trees are in full bloom, reminiscent of Washington in the springtime. Lester points this out, as well as the fact that there are over one thousand species of flora and fauna on the premises – cross-pollinated by just one very industrious society of bees.

The president's eyes widen upon stepping off the elevator, and one can tell he is genuinely bowled-over – as opposed to at the Apex, where his imagination could have forecasted with reasonable accuracy what the view might look like. He turns all the way around and then looks straight up at the ceiling – or rather, at the miles of blue and white fabric hung in such a way as to obscure the ceiling and simulate the natural texture of clouds and sky. He is speechless, which suits Lester just fine. They walk along one of the many footpaths and Lester narrates perfunctorily and without embellishment, like a car salesman highlighting the standard features for an impatient customer – power windows, door locks and mirrors, cruise control and so on. They stroll past the lake where a regatta of remote-controlled sailboats is taking place, past the tennis courts and the basketball courts, the swimming pool and the par-three golf course, all of which are being thoroughly and quite enthusiastically patronized by inhabitants. Finally, they arrive at the horseshoe pitch, which is tucked away behind a grove of willow trees out of view from everything else. Lester hands the black shoes to the President and keeps the gold for himself.

"Before we get started, there's one other question I have to ask you, out of personal curiosity," the president says.

"Fire away."

"Your son. And the pirate ship. What's that really all about?"

"Want to take a few practice throws?" Lester says, ignoring the question.

"No, that's alright," the president responds without a hitch. "I've thrown more than a few of these in my day. Is this regulation length?"

"Forty feet exactly, stake to stake. Would you prefer to throw first or last?"

"You go ahead."

"Very well, then," Lester says. "It's funny, isn't it, how they say close counts in horseshoes? While the fact is you either finish first or last. Last isn't anywhere close to first in my book."

"I suppose it's in reference to the scoring of the game itself."

"Right … Shall we go to twenty-one?"

"Sounds good," the president says.

Lester is not the slightest bit inclined to lose the match, and therefore plays to the best of his abilities, throwing ringers in three of the first four innings as he jumps out to a 9-1 lead. The conversation during this time is sparse and focuses primarily on the various technological marvels incorporated in The Pyramid's design – its state-of-the-art solar panels, its unique transportation system (within The Grid) and its general structural integrity, just to name a few. Lester's explanations are, by intention, overly simplistic, as if directed to a child. However, his manner of speaking, his intonation, conveys the sense that his own limited scientific knowledge precludes further detail. In other words, it doesn't seem as if he's *dumbing it down* for the president but merely telling him the facts as he understands them. Of course, this is all a very cunning deception on Lester's part.

The president's questions cease during a particularly tense walk to the other end of the pitch, as both men detect a possible turning point in the match, a proverbial swing of momentum from

Lester to the president. Upon closer inspection, it is confirmed that the president has won his fourth straight inning on a ringer, drawing the score even at 11.

"Good show! That ties us at eleven, I suppose … Tell you what," Lester says. "Before we talk about why you're here – and I appreciate your tastefulness in not coming right out with your demands – before we get to your demands, or shall we say, your requests, I'd like to better understand your general position, Mr. President. I'd like to cut through the rhetoric, if I could, and understand what keeps you up at night. You know, worrying and so forth, about this great nation of ours. Yours, I mean."

"Fair enough. Well, the Corporate Wars, as they've been dubbed, although now officially over, continue to have an impact, economically and socially."

"Mmm hmm. At least the violence has stopped. Oh! That was close!" Lester says, his final exclamation of course in reference to his throw – it looked like a ringer at first but actually spun around the stake and landed clear of it.

"Yes, I've – my administration has been able to control that aspect of it, thank god, but there's still an awful lot of damage being done – to the system in general. Take the stock market for example. Investors still haven't come out of their shell."

"Right, right. And if the pearl stays in the oyster, then it's not worth anything a'tall, is it?"

"It's a turtle metaphor, actually. About having the courage to stick your neck out. Looks like your point."

"Right, the investors are a frightened little turtle. Got it. Yes, that was close, but definitely my point. Okay, what else?"

"Well, healthcare is another issue. You've got the drug companies and the insurance companies and the HMOs all wrangling for their own interests, and meanwhile it's the average person that's stuck with the bill."

"Mmm hmm. Too much fast food and cigarettes. Damn! Unkindly bounce!"

"I suppose that's part of it. Anyway, then there's the energy crisis. And the associated foreign policy issues. The fact is, despite advances like your father made with solar energy, we're a nation dependent on foreign oil. And most of that oil comes from countries with less-than-spotless records on human rights, weapons of mass destruction, and so on. I believe that's a ringer for me."

"Mmm, yes. Oil is for suckers. Pay the leaders, choke the masses, isn't that it? How about education?"

"Don't even get me started. Our schools are in ruins. We don't have enough teachers and those that we do have are overworked and underpaid. Not to mention under-qualified."

"No incentive."

"Exactly. Crime is down over the past three years, but it's still out of control if you ask me. Our inner cities are basically breeding grounds for drugs, gangs, prostitution – it's a real mess."

"I see. That is rather a lot to think about. So how can I help you solve any of those problems?"

"You can't. But you see, these are historical problems, Mr. Ginn. And with a nation this size, you're always going to face them. It's the status quo, and when it comes to winning elections, all you have to do is say you'll try your hardest."

"Confounded rhetoric."

"See, these may be the big issues, the important issues, but they aren't the ones that win and lose elections."

"No?"

"No. And regardless of what anyone tells you, every politician's top priority is to win elections."

"If you lose, then you're not even a politician anymore, are you?"

"That's exactly it. It's like a survival instinct, that's why it gets so cutthroat. That's why politicians spend a lot of time and energy trying to create new issues out of nothing. Like character attacks, mud slinging. Or like this place, for example."

"Two points. That makes it what? Seventeen-fifteen?

"I've got sixteen."

"You must be mistaken."

"No. From eleven I had a ringer plus one for fifteen, plus another one in the last inning."

"Hmm. What about it?"

"What?"

"The Pyramid. You said issues are being created."

"Well, Mr. Ginn, I'll be perfectly frank with you. I've let you carry on your business out here – including your little sociological experiment, or whatever you prefer to call it – for a few reasons. Number one, you're not hurting anyone, at least not that we know of."

"Certainly not."

"And number two, we haven't had a legal leg to stand on, with these being Native American lands, technically. Now, that was a fair-and-square deal after the Yucca disaster but, nevertheless, you're within the borders of the United States of America, and rumors have begun to circulate."

"Let me guess. That we're a bunch of communists plotting to take over the world."

"Or simply overthrow the government, yes, that's a big part of it, Mr. Ginn. In all fairness, nobody knows exactly what's going on in here. And although you may not present any immediate threat, you're an unknown. And as an unknown, you present an inherent threat all the same, understand? Now, I've got to do something about that, otherwise somebody else is going to beat me to it. And even if they don't find a smoking gun, any direct evidence of sinister activities, it can certainly be made to look otherwise."

"First of all, you have my assurance that nothing remotely sinister is going on here. And secondly, with all due respect, Mr. President, why exactly is your reelection campaign my problem?"

"It's not. But I'll tell you what may be your problem. And again, I'm giving it to you straight. Last I checked you're still an American citizen, so a treason charge is a very real possibility."

"Is that a threat?!"

"No. Listen, Mr. Ginn. This can all be avoided if you trust my discretion. I just want to probe around a little, send in a team of experts to take some pictures and write up some reports – produce documentation – so I can say with some degree of confidence that these allegations are ridiculous. On the other hand, if it's left to my political enemies, they'll tear this place apart. It will happen, Mr. Ginn, mark my word on that. They'll find loopholes. Or they'll introduce special legislation if they have to."

"You can veto it."

"Let's not get ahead of ourselves. I sympathize with you, Mr. Ginn, I really do. You're caught in the middle here but-"

"I didn't ask for your sympathy!" Lester snaps, recovering his poorly thrown shoes from the outer edge of the pit. "Sympathy is best reserved for orphans and refugees."

Perhaps it's the medication wearing off or the fact that the president has taken a 20-19 lead that's causing him to become irritable. The perimeter of security draws a step closer.

"I understand," the president says, unflustered. "But if you really have nothing to hide, then I don't see what the problem is."

"I'll tell you what the problem is," Lester says. "My legal or political obligation to assist you is outweighed by my responsibility to protect the best interests of my people!"

"Please lower your voice," the president says, gesturing to a security agent who has slipped his hand inside his coat. "You're making them a little jumpy – and they have guns."

"Right, right, I apologize. Allow me to attempt a salient comparison. You used to be in business right?"

"Over thirty years."

"So you had your share of hiring employees then, right?"

"Absolutely."

"Great. So when you hired people, did you make a practice of sending out notice to all the losing candidates, outlining the salary and benefits they'd be missing out on?"

"Of course not."

"Why?"

"Because it's cruel and unusual, that's why. You'd be asking for trouble."

"And you don't want any trouble."

"Of course not."

"Then you get my point."

"No, Mr. Ginn, I'm afraid I don't."

"I can't spell it out any clearer! Okay, okay, everything's fine. Let me try another point."

"Mr. Ginn-"

"Let me try another point, damn it!"

"Okay, fine."

"I assume you brush your teeth?"

"Yes, I brush my teeth."

"They look pearly white, by the way. Do you have a preferred brand? Don't tell me what it is!"

"Yes, I have a preferred brand."

"Now, is it safe to say that part of the reason you prefer that brand is because it leaves your mouth feeling cleaner and fresher than other brands?"

"Sure, I suppose so."

"All right, well let's say it's your job to market that toothpaste. You could probably get four out of five dentists to agree with you, right? To put an actual coefficient value on the state of freshness, mind you!"

"I suppose so."

"Well, I bet I could get four more dentists to say your dentists are quacks! Eh?! To say your study's rubbish – that your toothpaste isn't fresh a'tall!"

"Mr. Ginn, I really don't see what you're driving at."

"Fine! Let's say you own a restaurant, and I say I saw a rat scurry into the kitchen wearing a little bowtie and—"

"Mr. Ginn, please," the president says, and at this point he throws the second of his two horseshoes. It's a leaner. One point. "Ha! How about that! Well, Mr. Ginn. It was a pleasure …"

"Excuse me, but I think you must be mistaken, Mr. President. I have my horseshoes left to throw."

"What are you talking about? It's first to twenty-one, plain and simple."

"It's not over until the last half of the inning is played. Like baseball."

"I'll have one of my men look up the rule right now."

"Look it up? Where? You know as well as I do that no abundance of documentation can settle this dispute. It's a matter of principle. And if your desire is to prevent my final throw, I'd suggest it's out of insecurity. Perhaps even cowardice!"

"Fine, go ahead and throw then."

"Thank you, I will." Lester says, and proceeds not only to knock the President's shoe off the stake but to land his own in a perfect, three-point, game-winning ringer. At least he's almost certain this is the case. He doesn't want to celebrate prematurely, in risk of compromising his bargaining position. Instead, he walks calmly and silently to the other end with the president.

"Son of a bitch!" the president says.

"Well, I hope you fare better in your reelection campaign," Lester says, extending his hand. "Good match."

The president begrudgingly shakes with him and then gestures to one of his aides hovering nearby.

"We'll be in touch," the president says. "In the meantime, I'd reconsider your position."

"I'd consider reconsidering, but I'm afraid I cannot. Due to other considerations."

"We'll be in touch," the president says again, before his entourage whisks him away, leaving Lester alone.

"Well ladies and gentlemen," Lester says to himself. "If they don't have a legal leg to stand on, I suppose we'll have to cut their arms off as well. Just to be safe. Mmm hmm ... yes ... Our safety must be preserved at all costs ... I've got it! That's the analogy! It's like a spacecraft, right? Even if you put the tiniest pinprick in its fuselage, the whole thing will implode! Explode? Implode. Yes ..."

At this, Lester decides to play another game of horseshoes against himself. If nothing else, he figures he'll learn to accept victory and defeat simultaneously – and on equal terms.

Chapter 55

In Bayonne, New Jersey, Sandeep Ganesh tries to improve the reception on the one station his short wave radio will accept. This station broadcasts only in Chinese. Sandeep does not speak or understand Chinese but he finds the broadcast entertaining in a purely acoustic sense. By manipulating the antenna and an elaborate aluminum foil appendage, he is successful in clarifying the high-pitched incantations of the female broadcaster. He imagines that she is relating vitally important information specific to him personally, Sandeep Ganesh, and that he is bound to absorb some of the key details by listening carefully.

He hunches over the electric hot plate, where his chunk of processed meat-food is cooking, and he flips the homogeneous pink slab with a spatula. Somehow a fly must have gotten underneath, because its black body is an aberration seared on the crust formed by the various oils and other impurities in the meat-food. He makes a half-hearted attempt to scrape it off with the corner of the spatula, but quickly abandons the effort, thinking that the extra protein could only help him.

Sandeep turns the heat off, deciding to let conducted heat perform the remainder of the cooking duties, and he flops onto the bed. One selling point of this apartment is the convenience of having the bed within flopping distance of the kitchen (hot plate), as well as the toilet, bathtub and door. Actually, it's not an apartment but a room within an apartment, and the other selling point is that it's dirt cheap. These two selling points go a long way for someone like Sandeep, who has only one arm and one leg – and no job.

Sandeep is somewhat learned, however, and can read quite well with the help of his glasses, large and very unfashionable horned-rim glasses that make him look like a turtle. The only reading material within reach is the Creaky Hinge, a locally produced newspaper featuring classified ads for jobs and apartments as well as various genres of merchandise ranging from automobiles to rare antiques to any other junk people want to get off their hands. His attention is drawn to some previously circled items, and he's curious as to why he would circle, for example, a rather wordy listing under *WANTED* that reads as follows:

INHABITANTS

Do you believe in the impossible? Unable to overcome disadvantages yet have a penchant for optimism? Have uncontrollable forces derailed your ambitions? Yearn for the day when the oppression of economic survival will miraculously wane before your eyes? Do you feel lost in the system? Do you fear the future? Do you inherently trust other people but distrust their motivations? Do you seek refuge from the revolution instead of weathering its violent storm? Do you want to die a fool or, at best, a martyr? (the martyr is overrated, one might argue, because he is dead) Finally, do you love yourself enough to elevate safety to a level of chief importance? If you answered all these questions correctly, you may qualify to inhabit a place that defies even your wildest preponderances. This place will shelter you, feed you, clothe you, sustain you, nurture you and keep you safe from all the world's evils. You will learn the true meaning of citizenship, of selflessness and trust. But one final question! Can you say goodbye to the world as you know it? Families up to six welcome, but all must be over 18. Submit credentials to: The Pyramid Foundation, P.O. Box 28902, Queens, New York.

Sandeep is highly confounded by the listing, as he only knows about half the words, but he cannot ignore it. He cannot ignore it because it's so different than the others, which beckon to *self-starters* and *team players* with big, bold phrases like, *Big $$$ Opportunities!* and *Get your career in the fast lane!* He reads it a few more times and thinks about his answers to the various questions. He worries that he will not be able to afford to live in this place, whatever or wherever it is, but his preponderances are indeed wild.

He imagines a remote island oasis, perhaps somewhere in the Pacific, where beautiful women would cater to his every desire. He sees them as tanned and oiled, with tiny seashells strung loosely over their erect nipples. They would feed him fresh pineapple and massage his loins. With this vivid image in mind, his eyes now closed, Sandeep reaches under the elastic waistband of his underpants and pleasures himself to orgasm.

Having worked up a hunger for breakfast, Sandeep eats his processed meat-food with gusto. And now, with both his sexual and meat-food appetites temporarily satisfied, Sandeep can truly apply his analytic faculties to the subject at hand. This leads to several questions of his own, namely: What is this Pyramid Foundation all about? Is it some sort of apartment building or is it a job? He thinks perhaps it could be both, as he's heard of factories or hotels offering living arrangements for their workers. On the other hand, he thinks it could be a scam. Or worse, some sort of evil scheme in which he would be used as a pawn or a patsy. He has heard these terms in movies and knows he wishes to be neither. Sandeep knows a sizeable gamble is involved with this decision. However, he's been wagering on credit for some time now, like an over-indebted card player whose wantonness prevails in the face of impending ruin. So there's not much more to lose in other words. And besides, he figures he's about due for a jackpot.

Sandeep reaches for the typewriter shoved under his bed and it requires some considerable effort to hoist it up – with just the one arm. He found it in a dumpster, and it still works, although the network of rods, levers and springs is rusted and stiff, making it absolutely devastating to the fingers, which must be used like battering rams to depress the keys. If nothing else, this requires Sandeep to keep his letters brief and to the point, or else spread the typing process over a couple of days. He retrieves a box of fine stationary that he found in a different dumpster. The paper is cream-colored and thick, with a generic-looking coat of arms at the top, and he rolls a sheet into the machinery of the typewriter. He stares at the coat-of-arms and wonders what type of credentials he ought to include since he does not really have any.

* * *

Sandeep's childhood was very light on promise, as he was born into the streets of an Indian slum in the state of Gujarat. His leg was trampled by a donkey when he was only five years old and had to be amputated. This was messy and extraordinarily painful. Sandeep can remember the pain to this day. Shortly thereafter, his mother sold him to a factory owner from Bombay who was organizing a child (slave) labor force. The factory produced cheap machetes and the work was very dangerous. Sheets of metal the size of tractor trailers were bathed in hazardous chemicals, then shot at high speed through a series of rolling, stamping, cutting and sharpening machines. The machines were loud beyond belief and required continuous oiling. This was Sandeep's job, to oil the machinery, and it eventually resulted in the irreparable mangling of his right arm. Like his leg, it had to be amputated and, again, this was done in a very crude manner as the factory owner wanted to avoid any inquiries.

Shortly after returning to the factory, Sandeep decided he could not afford to lose his other arm, so he escaped. He stowed away on a ship to the Philippines, then to Japan, China and finally to America, where he was taken immediately into custody by the authorities. He spoke no English, had no identification papers and was severely malnourished. Considering him more trouble than their low government wages could compensate them for, the calloused immigration officers released Sandeep onto the streets of Los Angeles with nothing more than the filthy clothes on his back and just over a dollar in loose change. Little did they know they were doing him a favor.

He panhandled for a few months and lived under a bridge, enduring routine beatings and molestations. Mainly, his colleagues in the begging industry were jealous because he was something of a novelty, being so young and having only one arm and one leg. He was clever too, and squirreled away his money in a secret place, and when he had enough for a bus ticket he headed off for New York. He seemed to remember from his days at sea that the various smugglers talked highly of the place. He worried though, if the city had yet fully recovered from the attack of the giant gorilla he had heard about.

In New York, he faced many of the same challenges but also caught a few breaks. He met a kind old man who ran a delicatessen in Bayonne and he gave Sandeep a job – first sweeping and cleaning and then making sandwiches. Sandeep was very grateful to the old man, and very loyal, and he worked at the delicatessen for the next 20 years of his life. Then the old man died and the delicatessen closed. That was six months ago. Sandeep is now 30 years old.

* * *

Sandeep's arm and index finger move to action now, the finger pecking at the keys like the early bird after the worm:

Dear Mr. Sir:

I apply to live and work in your place written in newspaper. It sounds good and nice. Please choose me. I answer questions yes, yes, yes, yes, yes, no, yes, yes, no, yes, yes. I am from India and come to America. I come because in India I lose my arm and leg and if I stay I die very soon of something. I want safety and not die so I come to America. I have no family or friend. I have no job. I have no school but read and write. I hear and talk English too better than read and write. I can work good and help with things. I can clean and sweep floor and make sandwich. Good sandwich with meat and cheese. But I can do other thing too. I can write letters.

Sandeep stops and curses himself for this last sentence, which is obvious and stupid. He considers starting over but fears his breakfast of processed meat-food has not afforded sufficient energy to do so. He is too anxious and cannot wait until after his dinner of processed meat-food, lunch being omitted from the schedule due to lack of resources. He dabs his throbbing index finger on his tongue, blows on it to prevent overheating, then begins typing again:

I can write letters for business. I have only one arm and one leg but I can move fast around and do things. I am 30 years old. I am healthy. Please choose me.

Sincerely,
Sandeep Ganesh

Sandeep cools his fingertip again and surveys the letter. He feels all his applicable credentials are present and agrees with the form and flow of the correspondence. He notices the two mentions of his one arm and leg and hopes it will not hurt his chances. He wonders if there is anything else he should include along with the letter. He knows nothing of the résumé and therefore does not think to include one. He thinks a photograph might be a nice addition, but he doesn't have any. Finally, he folds the letter using his hand and foot in concert, seals it within his only envelope and addresses the outside. Having sealed the envelope (and his fate), his misgivings begin to awaken from their proverbial catnaps and run rampant everywhere in his thought process. This annoys Sandeep and he expresses himself as such by floundering around on his bed and moaning in lieu of pacing. After all, pacing with one foot is just silly.

When he tires himself out he sits up and decides he will ask his landlord, Mr. Bubbakis, to review the letter, as he tops off the short list of candidates. The other options are Mandy, the morbidly obese, retarded girl who sublets the room to him, and Mrs. Chung, the old lady who lives next door and speaks no English. Mr. Bubbakis is certainly no rocket scientist, but is more coherent than Mandy or Mrs. Chung for sure.

Sandeep reconsiders getting the second opinion since he's already sealed the envelope. He contemplates not opening it and then opens it. He finds some trousers on the floor and slips into them. The empty leg is stuffed with newspaper and tied off at the end with sisal rope, as per Mr. Bubbakis' suggestion. Mr. Bubbakis is always touting the versatility of sisal rope and has a side-venture peddling the stuff from his apartment.

Sandeep hops out of his room and past Mandy, who is sitting on the couch with a large, buzzing massager held firmly and shamelessly between her legs. She is watching cartoons.

"Rent's due!" she slurs, and Sandeep ignores her – as he's learned it's best to do.

He continues into the hallway, which is littered with chicken bones and watermelon seeds. A mangy dog sleeps inside a rusted-out dishwasher, wheezing loudly. Sandeep hops around the corner to apartment 1-A, which has a gold placard on the door that says LANDLORD. Before his third knock, Mr. Bubbakis jerks the door open to the extent the security chain will allow and stuffs his puffy Greek face into the aperture. He has a bushy moustache and one bushy eyebrow.

"Ah! Mr. Sandeep!"

"Hello, Mr. Bubbakis."

"Wait a minute, boy!" Mr. Bubbakis says, closing the door to remove the chain. He opens it again, revealing piles of sisal spools and tangled rat's nests of loose rope strewn everywhere. He smiles broadly, displaying his browned, irregular teeth, and then introduces a new use for the sisal rope. Mr. Bubbakis boasts a new use for sisal every day without fail. At least, that's his claim.

"Just in time! Just in time, Mr. Sandeep. I have a man coming to look at ze zizal and my newest demonstration is a two-man job. I believe if ve verk togezer ve can cut zis mattress in two!"

Mr. Bubbakis heaves the mattress off his bed and stands it up on its side.

"But why—"

"Look here, Mr. Sandeep. You take zis end of ze rope, I take zis one, and ve go like zis, zhoop zhoop zhoop zhoop," Mr. Bubbakis says, gripping Sandeep's wrist and moving it back and forth in a sawing motion with his own.

"Yes, I see, but—"

"See? Zhoop zhoop zhoop zhoop!"

Sandeep realizes he has no choice but to cooperate and wholeheartedly applies himself to the destruction of his landlord's mattress. After several minutes of effort, the rope begins to penetrate the exterior fibers and Mr. Bubbakis exclaims, "Ve can do it!" just prior to dropping the rope. He gasps for air, doubled over his heaving belly. He huffs and puffs for a moment and then straightens up to his full height again, which only reaches Sandeep's shoulder.

"Heee! Zhat's hard work, eh?"

"Mr. Bubbakis? I wanted to ask you to read a letter I made."

"You are making letters now? Perhaps you write letters for me about ze zisal, yes? Ve can say zis about ze zizal and zat about ze zizal. It can tie to doorknob to open, it can tie prisoners, tie furnitures to each other, cut mattress!"

"Why do you tie the furniture again?" Sandeep asks.

"So ze prisoners don't steal zem!"

"Oh, right. Well, Mr. Bubbakis, will you read my letter?"

"Give me zis letter."

Mr. Bubbakis greedily snaps it up. Sandeep notices his grubby, sweaty fingers smearing the letter as he paws at it, finally smoothing it open upon his bedside table as he plops down on the box spring. He reads far too quickly for a man with elementary level reading skills and turns to Sandeep.

"You are joining ze army?" he says.

"No, not army," Sandeep says.

"Vell … zis letter iz good, zen."

Sandeep is no more confident than before but decides to cut his losses before the letter is manhandled any further. He thanks Mr. Bubbakis and hops out the door.

He thinks being a landlord must not be such a bad job. After all, it doesn't seem to require a lot of brains.

Chapter 56

Normally she'd run the dishwasher, but it's broken and they can't afford to fix it so Sylvia King scrubs the dishes in a panicked frenzy – yet she's conscientious about removing every last bit of grease and caked-on food. Her husband Rodney likes the dishes clean when he gets home, and he's due home any minute. He also likes his dinner ready, so Sylvia dashes over to the cupboard in search of palatable ingredients, of which there are few – lima beans, pumpkin, corn, tomato paste – it looks like the dregs of a canned food drive for the homeless, however, she manages to find some black beans and flour tortillas. Cradling them in her soapy hands she flings the refrigerator door open. "Please be there," she says, addressing the salsa and cheese that will allow her to make some half-decent burritos. "Please, please, please."

Meanwhile the water is still running in the sink and it overflows onto the linoleum tile floor. "Shit," she says, dumping the salsa and cheese on the counter along with the beans and tortillas. "Damn!" She hates it when multitasking backfires, but it's too late now so she turns off the water and preheats the oven to 350. Then she scrubs the remainder of the dishes, rolls the burritos and slides them in the oven just as it reaches critical temperature.

* * *

Sylvia has been overcoming obstacles all her life. She lost her father and role model at the age of 12 and was forced to raise her two younger sisters while her mother worked multiple jobs to support them. She defended her sisters against the predators in their poor Atlanta neighborhood – gang-bangers, drug dealers and pimps. She took a swing shift at a rubber factory during her senior year in high school to save money for college. Then she became the first woman in her family to attend college, and afterwards she went to work for a satellite television company and climbed through the sales division ranks in spite of bigoted managers who tried repeatedly to sabotage her efforts. The fact was, they could not dispute her results. Her unique combination of tenacity and charm made her the consummate salesman, while her shrewdness and judgment of character made her an effective manager. Her career was on the so-called fast track, and she even met a bright, handsome young man who shared her drive for success.

Technically he was a co-worker – a contract agent in the purchasing department – but their jobs didn't overlap so Sylvia felt comfortable ignoring the adage about fishing off the company dock. Besides, Rodney was quite a catch, with a huge personality to match his huge body. At 6'5", 275 pounds he cast a large shadow indeed, but he had a gentle touch in those days. He courted Sylvia in the most gentlemanly fashion, spoke softly to her and treated her like a delicate object of art. He brought her flowers and candy unexpectedly and professed his amorous feelings for her often. They married and everything was perfect. They bought a house and a new car. They took exotic vacations. They made love almost every day.

Then Sylvia got laid off from her job, yet another side effect of the Corporate Wars. So she decided to take some time off and go back to school for a business degree, which left Rodney supporting them both, and finances became a point of regular contention. He worked longer hours and it wore him down. It took a toll physically but also mentally as he became obsessed with meeting his ever-increasing targets for cost-savings and efficiency. Between the rigors of his job and the perpetual fear of losing it, Rodney's personality gradually became snuffed out, and the void was filled by episodes of depression and rage – the brunt of which was felt by Sylvia most of all.

The first time he hit her, she threw him out of the apartment and vowed never to let it happen again. But it did, and she couldn't fight back. In fact, what scared her most wasn't the pain or the suffering but her rationalization for why Rodney was doing it. After all, he *was* shouldering a heavy burden. She believed him when he said he couldn't help himself, that the pressure was too much for him to bear, that it wasn't his fault. She believed things would get better.

It was like being married to two completely different people, and she loved the one so much that she coped with the other the best she could. And thus, when the thoughtful, sweet-talking Rodney resurfaced she welcomed him back time and time again. But things didn't get better, they got worse, and bit by bit Sylvia became consumed by the pathos that it was her fault, that she could have been a better wife, a better lover, more understanding, more accommodating to his needs, until she lost touch with her true identity altogether. All the strength she had built over the years was suddenly gone, all the self-confidence gone like a mighty sand castle washed away at high tide.

* * *

She hears Rodney coming up the stairwell, his signature *thump-thump-thump* like one of those giant hydraulic mallets used to drive in telephone poles. For a fleeting instant, she considers jumping out the window and running away. It's only a second story apartment and there's a grassy courtyard below. She has seen parachute jumpers landing on TV, rolling smoothly from feet to hip to shoulder in order to spread the impact over a greater surface area. She could make one roll and be back on her feet and just run and run and run into the darkness. She could disappear, never looking back.

"Hi honey, how was your day?" she says, greeting him at the door with the smile of someone about to be kicked in the teeth.

"Aw, you don't want to know," he says, his eyes distant, his arms hanging loosely at his sides like two massive salamis.

"Sure I do, sweetie. Tell me what happened."

Rodney yanks his shoes off without untying them and crosses the living room en route to the kitchen, stomping over her Ethics in Management book and some notepads as if to make a point. Sylvia follows close behind him, silently cursing herself for leaving the place untidy. "One of the grounds crew got caught smoking dope in the parking lot," he says.

"So he got fired?"

"Oh yeah, he got fired all right. Problem is, he worked for a subcontractor, which just so happens to be black-owned, and now the prime is cutting them loose."

"Can they do that?" Sylvia says.

"Sure can. And they blamed me for recommending the sub in the first place. Like it's a fucking *race* issue. What's for dinner?"

"Burritos."

"I had tacos for lunch," Rodney says, as if to say wrong answer.

"So the prime contractor—"

"Damn it, Sylvia! I don't want to talk about it anymore!" He opens the refrigerator and slams it shut. "No beer?"

"We're out."

He trudges over to the oven for his habitual look-see, crossing through the puddle of dishwater in the process. "Jesus!" he says, dancing an impromptu jig in his wet socks. "What the fuck?"

"I'm sorry, some of the dishwater—"

"Damn it, Sylvia, you're here all fucking day and you can't clean this place up before I get home?"

"I did! The water is from the washing the dishes, most of which are yours anyway you big jerk! And it's not like I've been sitting around eating bon-bons and watching soap operas all day. I studied for eight solid hours, Rodney, and I'm tired too."

"Why the hell are you in school, anyway? All it's gonna do is make you over-fucking-qualified for whatever jobs are left out there. Besides, it's costing us money. I mean, shit, Sylvia, for the price of one of those books we could get a fucking maid."

"We're not getting a maid," Sylvia says firmly, in hopes that stating the obvious will diffuse the argument.

"You're damn right we're not," Rodney says, before leveling one of his thick, cigar-like fingers between Sylvia's eyes. "Because you're dropping out of school. So you'll have plenty of time to clean this place and get dinner on the table before I get home. Not in the oven, understand? On the fucking *table*."

For a black woman, there is hardly a greater insult than a finger pointed in her face, regardless of who's doing it. In most cases she'll either notify the person that his finger may get bitten off, or she'll simply bite it off without warning. Ironically, Sylvia used to think she'd rather be punched than pointed at, but now she finds herself tolerating one to avoid the other. "Fucking asshole," she mutters loud enough for him to hear.

Rodney grabs a pot from the stovetop and makes a move like he's going to clobber her with it. She shields her face instinctually and he turns and throws it toward the kitchen table instead. It shatters a cheap vase that Sylvia had arranged with dried flowers – the last flowers Rodney brought her, two months earlier.

"You can practice by cleaning that shit up. I'm going to get a fuckin' burger," Rodney says, incredulously, before marching past her and slamming the door behind him.

Sylvia begins to cry. It makes seeing the tiny shards of glass especially difficult, but she gets down on her knees and tries to pick them up with her bare hands anyway. She finds a piece about the size of a razor blade and thinks about cutting herself – one quick slash right across the wrist – and it should all be over in a matter of minutes.

Chapter 57

S queakins finishes chopping the carrots and potatoes and ferries them up to Lester on the dumbwaiter, which he cranks by hand.

Like a quarterback braced for the snap of the football, Lester holds his hands out in eager anticipation and leans over to retrieve the bowl as soon as possible, in an effort to save Squeakins' energy and also valuable time. For the reception Lester has chosen Indian food, which due to the varied ingredients and cooking methods can test even the seasoned professional. Yet it's not the degree of difficulty that concerns Lester, since he considers himself a seasoned professional, but the inflexible constraint of time – less than 24 hours until the wedding.

"I suppose it just goes to show you, boy," Lester shouts above the sizzling and boiling sounds, as well as the music blaring from his trusty headgear (blues-inspired rock and roll). "You just can't cram twenty pounds of shit into a ten pound box."

"Don't worry sir, I believe we shall meet our deadline with time to spare. It's been going faster since we fixed the dumbwaiter," Squeakins says, even though it's been going much slower. At the start, Squeakins just handed the bowls of ingredients up to Lester, but after one missed exchange Lester decided the system would not endure. So he sent Squeakins out in search of a dumbwaiter and managed on his own for the interim. How Squeakins was able to procure a dumbwaiter in less than two hours – in an unfamiliar city – is a genuine testament to his indispensability as a butler, especially for someone like Lester, who tends to operate outside the bounds of common reason and expectations.

"Time to spare! That's right, boy, the key is to sustain morale. And the dumbwaiter! The dumbwaiter has been an absolute godsend, if such a thing exists," Lester says, lifting two sauté pans at once, and adroitly flipping them to turn the vegetables over. "I won't ask you to state your position on the issue of religion, because I have a good idea of where you stand."

Lester flips the pans more vigorously and a lone wedge of potato tumbles overboard, bouncing over the side of the range. Lester shuffles closer, trying to pin it with his thigh, but it falls to his knees. "You stupid bastard!"

"Sir?"

"This potato! Stupid bastard just jumped out the pan and pitched himself over the ledge! Give me your blade, boy."

Squeakins picks up the long, pointed chef's knife and turns the handle toward Lester.

"No, don't hand it up. Toss it."

"Sir, I—"

"Just give it a light toss, no rotation. Success in this feat will give us the will to redouble our efforts! Momentum, as the sportsmen say. Come on now, boy, toss it here," Lester says, turning to face Squeakins and holding his hands out palm up – wrist up.

"Very well, sir, but please be so kind as to turn sideways again … back up from the stove a bit … there. Now, if the blade rotates you can simply pull your hands away."

"Like a matador's cape!"

"Yes, exactly like that, sir. Are you ready?"

"Ready."

"Here we go," Squeakins says, executing a perfect toss. Lester fields it cleanly and then raises it in the air with his right hand. "We did it!"

"Indeed we did, sir."

"Wasn't that invigorating?"

"I must say that it was, sir."

"Now where did that bastard of a potato go?"

Just then, Svetlana and Anna enter the apartment, but Lester fails to notice them right away. "Ah-ha!" he says, spearing the escapee with the knife. "There you are, you coward! You're a bloody fool to think you could escape!"

"Lester, I think you need to take a break from this," Svetlana says, dropping two fully loaded bags of groceries to the floor. "Shit, the eggs weren't in there, were they?"

"No, I've got them," Anna says. "Lester, haven't you ever heard of catering?"

"And that helmet thing … it's so silly," Svetlana ads. "You look like an elephant."

"Well, good day to you two lovely ladies as well!" Lester says, removing the headgear and setting it down on the platform behind him. "Thanks for dropping by for the nag session! In all seriousness though, we haven't got a moment to spare so let's get the assembly line going here, chop chop."

"We just get the stuff," Anna says. "We don't do the chop chop."

"Anna's right," Svetlana says. "Why don't we just cater the reception like normal people."

"I know I needn't remind you of how very far we have strayed from normal already! And how we can't turn back now!" Lester says. "And besides, we owe our esteemed guests the assurance of quality – and more importantly, of safety."

"You're paranoid, dude." Anna says.

"Some might call it astute caution – dude."

"Couldn't you at least rent out a normal kitchen somewhere?" Svetlana says. "This one is so absurd."

"Absurd? Is that better or worse than silly?" Lester chides her. "It has been nothing but an essential resource for years! You seem to have forgotten all the meals it produced for you, which were so savory and enjoyable to consume – delicacies fit for royalty! Handcrafted especially for you, with love."

"I remember," Svetlana says, smiling, and it's apparent that she and Lester are mentally undressing each other.

"Mom, save the bedroom eyes for your wedding night, eh?"

"Party pooper," Svetlana says, mock-pouting.

"Where's Tim?" Anna says.

"Probably editing his wish list," Lester says. "I mandated a fifty percent reduction across the board."

"Iron fist," Svetlana teases.

"Tim!" Lester says. "I'm outnumbered by women here and I need help! Help me, son!" Lester turns off his music, which allows them to hear the music coming from the bedroom – some Latin American concoction of guitars and horns.

"I'll get him," Anna says.

The sight she sees upon opening the bedroom door causes her to react in an unexpected way – a spit-second prevalence of instinct over reason in which she steps inside – as opposed to retreating outside. Tim is on his top bunk, hunched over some sort of ladies' undergarment catalog, masturbating like a fiend, and Anna just stands there with her back to the door, staring wide-eyed for a moment before Tim notices her. He scrambles around like five stoned Mexicans in a Chinese fire drill trying to get back into his pants – tumbling off the top bunk much like the potato tumbled off the range out of the scalding hot oil in the frying pan. The bed affords a soft landing, but then bounces him onto the floor with a *Thud!*

"What was that?!" Svetlana calls from the other room.

"Nothing mom! Tim was just horsing around!" Anna says over her shoulder. Then she whispers loudly to Tim. "Get your pants on, now!"

Tim capitulates with the utmost diligence and speed, but he remains on the floor, in the grips of embarrassment. Anna walks over and stands above him. Her expression is severe but not accusatory. "This never happened," she says.

"Easy for you to say!" Tim says.

"Shush. I'm not the one who was—"

"You have to show me yours."

"Bullshit I do."

"That's the only way to even things up," Tim says.

"I'm not buying it," Anna says. "Nice try though."

"What are you, afraid?" Tim says.

"Again, nice try."

"Come on."

"Fine. How about if I give you a quick flash under my shirt."

"Under the bra?"

"No, over. And that's my final offer."

"Okay."

Anna lifts her shirt to reveal her flat stomach and still-developing breasts, small and firm beneath the plain white bra.

"There. Are you satisfied?"

"No," Tim says.

"Too bad," she says, dropping her shirt again. "This whole thing is just gross. Now let's go. You can help chop vegetables, since you're so good with your hands."

"Ha ha."

They join the group in the kitchen and form an efficient assembly line, with Svetlana peeling potatoes, carrots and onions, Anna chopping them and Tim cranking the dumbwaiter to Lester while Squeakins cleans up the apartment a bit.

"Excuse me, sir, but it appears you have a message." Squeakins says, while dusting around the telephone answering machine. It is an old and antiquated variety, using a tape as opposed to a computer chip, and the message light blinks red in an exaggerated fashion, as if warning of some impending catastrophe.

"That's odd, it must have come in while you were out after the dumbwaiter. Well, let's hear it," Lester says.

Beep. "Lester, it's Chutney … about three o'clock and I have everyone here at the Horseshoe like you suggested – including, I might add, an exceeeeeeedingly drunk Dr. Spoon Ping."

"Lester!" Ping shouts in the background. "Where Lester go? Lester go … somewhere! Ha ha ha!"

"Yes, well, as I said … You were supposed to be here at two. So get over here tout suite or call me on my cell, love, okay? Okay, bye then. Hurry." *Beep*.

"Damn," Lester says, I totally forgot. "Squeakins, please do me a favor and—"

The door opens and in walks Chutney, along with Ping, Chili, Schnitzelhaus and Katz.

"Never mind. Why look! There's the gang now!" Lester says. "The whole gang's here."

"Gang!" Ping slurs. "We gonna pop cap in you ass!"

"Right … Listen, Chutney, I'm so sorry. I just got all caught up in the whirlwind here … let me get this batch into the freezer and then we'll all sit down for a minute."

"I can take care of that, sir," Squeakins volunteers.

"You cook too? Man, I tell you what, Squeakins. You're an absolute godsend."

"Me and the dumbwaiter, sir."

"You more than the dumbwaiter though. There's nothing dumb about you, that's for sure boy!"

"Thank you, sir," Squeakins says, helping Chutney flop Ping like a rag doll into one of the armchairs.

"By the way, you don't mind me calling you boy, do you? It's easier than Squeakins, you know."

"Not at all, sir. In fact, I find the irony quite amusing."

"Me too."

"We should get going mom," Anna says. We've got to pick up the dresses and everything."

"We'll be back soon," Svetlana says to Lester. She climbs up the ladder and they share a brief but passionate kiss.

"Gross," Anna says.

"Don't look then," Svetlana says. Tim and Anna look at each other for a moment and Tim looks away first.

After saying a quick round of goodbyes to everyone, Svetlana and Anna are out the door, allowing the Visionaries to speak in private – almost.

"Tim," Lester says. "Do us a favor and run out for some ice cream sandwiches. Is anyone else craving an ice cream sandwich? Creamy ice cream, chocolaty cookies …"

"Me!" Ping says, suddenly coming to life like a marionette.

"I'll have one too," Patricia says.

"That's three … Chutney?"

"Sure."

"Schnitzelmeister?"

"Why not."

"Chili?"

"Dig."

"Six then ... boy?"

"No, thank you sir," Squeakins says.

"Come on."

"Very well, if you insist, sir. An ice cream sandwich does sound refreshing."

"Seven then, plus however many you want," Lester says, handing Tim a wad of cash. "You do want some delicious ice cream, don't you son?"

"Yes."

The moment Tim leaves, Lester gets right down to business.

"All right, ladies and gentlemen, again, I apologize for the inconvenience – how are you Dr. Ping? You look vibrant!"

"I smell chicken!" Ping babbles. "Bock bock bock!"

"My goodness, you are bollocksed beyond belief, aren't you? Well, in the words of Admiral Bernard Porsley, we must push through. It all started with Admiral Porsley in fact, when out of the blue I received—" There's a knock at the door. "Son of a bitch," Lester says. "Who in the bloody hell could that be?" He stomps to the door and leans down to the peephole. "Yellow trousers," Lester says to himself, knowing they belong to his neighbor, Mr. Odenwilder. He opens the door. "Mr. Odenwilder."

"Hello there, Mr. Miles," Mr. Odenwilder says, standing up high on the balls of his feet, as if trying to see over Lester. This is Mr. Odenwilder's distinguishing characteristic – outweighing even his habit of wearing yellow pants – with most people referring to him as "the guy who walks up on the balls of his feet."

"What can I do for you today, Mr. Odenwilder?"

"Do you have an O-ring approximately one half inch in diameter?"

"How many centimeters?"

"One, I think."

"Hmm ... O-ring ... you just may be in luck, Mr. Odenwilder. I'll confess, I hoped to rule out any possibility of having such an O-ring. But because I cannot, I feel obligated to search for it. Please come in ... Quickly!"

"Oh, I didn't realize you had company," Mr. Odenwilder says, bounding into the room. "I can come back later."

The Visionaries, minus Lester and Ping, are engrossed in a heated debate about black holes and don't even pay heed to Mr. Odenwilder, in spite of his garish yellow pants. And Lester doesn't pay any heed to the Visionaries, muttering to himself as he sets out for the junk drawer, located in the Velvet Cave.

Once inside the Velvet Cave, Lester turns on the red light and empties the drawer onto the counter. Then he sifts through the jumble of items with his fingers, like two giant mechanical claws used to dismantle razed buildings. There are far too many items for Lester's brain to process and categorize, but he attempts to do so anyway – chains and wires, clasps and hasps, nuts and bolts, batteries, birthday candles, keys, writing implements, miscellaneous papers ... and the O-ring.

"Ladies and gentlemen! The system works! The system works!" Lester says, bursting from the Velvet Cave with the o-ring in his clenched fist – or so he thinks. He rushes up to Mr. Odenwilder, extends his fist and opens his hand. "Ta-da!"

"I don't see it," Mr. Odenwilder says.

"That's because it's not there!" Lester says. "Where the ... it's got to be ..."

"It's okay, really. Don't trouble yourself any further," Mr. Odenwilder says, growing uncomfortable as a result of Lester's erratic behavior.

"Just hang on a second!" Lester pleads. "We can't give up now … we can't give up," he says, crawling around on his hands and knees. "In situations like this, I like to pretend that my eyes are actually cameras on the underside of a miniature helicopter … hovering above a miniature landscape …"

"Me too," Mr. Odenwilder says, after an awkward silence. He's clearly lying of course, but only because he couldn't think of another response.

"So, you see, your little O-ring is really about the size of a bicycle tire … shouldn't be too difficult to – there she blows! We're lowering the claw!"

He lowers his hand as if it's dangling from a cable and scoops up the O-ring. "There you go," he says, proudly handing it over to Mr. Odenwilder.

"I think that's too big," he says.

"Flapdoodle!" Lester says, dismissing the argument out of hand.

"Or maybe not," Mr. Odenwilder says, all-too-eager to correct himself.

"That's the spirit," Lester says. "Now good day to you."

"Thank you very much. Thank you, really," Mr. Odenwilder says, bounding back out the door as Lester holds it open for him.

Lester slams the door and sighs heavily. "Jesus H. Christ on a unicycle! I'm sorry about that, mates. Now, as I was saying before, it all started with this Admiral fellow, Admiral Bernard Porsley," Lester says, trying to imitate the Admiral's deliberate cadence and meticulous pronunciation in stating his name.

"Lester," Chutney politely interrupts. "I told them."

"About the …"

"Yeah," Chili says. "About *that*."

"And …" Lester says, in a moment of extreme suspense.

"We're in."

Lester's expression does not change until he looks to Schnitzelhaus with raised eyebrows.

"In like Flynn," Schnitzelhaus says.

Like a lawn sprinkler, Lester rotates around the circle counter-clockwise.

"Me too," Katz says.

Chutney nods, and in a split-second they exchange a meaningful look embodying hope for the future, embodying optimism.

Ping is out cold, so Chili speaks up for him.

"He's down with it, Lester. We all agreed."

"So we're all agreed?"

"Yes," everyone says.

"About building The Pyramid?"

"Yes!"

"I'm sorry," Lester says. "It's all just so …"

"Surreal?" Katz says.

"No," Lester says. "Well, yes, but not what I was thinking of."

"Fucked up!" Ping yells, suddenly awake again and flapping his arms around like a marionette again.

"Yes, but no. It's so …"

"Fortuitous," Chutney says.

"Yes, fortuitous! That's exactly it! It's also rather … dizzying," Lester says, fainting into Squeakins' waiting arms.

Chapter 58

Sandeep looks at the painting on the far wall of Lester's makeshift office. It is an oil-on-canvas rendition of a chimpanzee trundling a large, flimsy-looking baby carriage across a meadow. A stork's head is poking out of the carriage, and in her beak is a crucifix wrapped in swaddling cloth. Sandeep has no earthly idea what this scene might represent.

Because the office was thrown together on the spot, it is furnished rather tastelessly in a number of competing styles and motifs. However, this makes no difference to Sandeep at the moment – or to Lester, who is fast asleep in his chair, also facing the wall adorned by the unusual artwork. He has been interviewing candidates practically round-the-clock ever since he and Svetlana returned from Thailand about a week ago. So even if he had been keeping to his regimen of vitamins and anti-psychotic drugs, he might still be unhinged on account of sleep deprivation.

Lester's secretary, an unattractive Long Islander in her late twenties named Sarah, enters wearing a hideous lime-green pantsuit. Without trepidation, she taps Lester on the shoulder. He spins around in his chair.

"What?! Damn woman! I was dreaming about the future and now I don't know what will happen! Who's this?" He is wearing a heavy brown cloak and he peers at Sandeep over half-glasses.

"Your three o'clock appointment," she says, eager to return to her nail-painting.

"Oh," Lester says, shuffling through the papers on his desk. "My apologies ... Ms. Pemberton?"

"It's Sandeep Ganesh."

"Sandy who?"

"San-deep Gan-esh."

"Oh, right, right, right ... Pakistan?"

"The north of India," Sandeep says, shifting uncomfortably in his chair.

"Wendy, how about some lemonades?" Lester calls to Sarah as she's leaving the room. "In frosted glasses!"

"Whatever," she says over her shoulder.

"Lemonade and cookies!" Lester says, having missed her comment. He yawns protractedly, removes his glasses and rubs his eyes so hard that Sandeep worries he may dig them right out of their sockets. "Ugh, sleepy ... Excuse me just a moment." Lester rises and walks over to a meat freezer in the corner. He lifts the lid and thrusts his head into the frosty cloud billowing out. Then he reaches inside and shifts some heavy objects around, perhaps large chunks of meat, and produces a football helmet. He puts it on his head, and this seems to reenergize him like a surge of electricity. "Woooooooooh-we! Yes indeed! Woooooooooh-we!" Lester removes the helmet and puts it back in the freezer. "Thermo-cranial stimulation! Does wonders for my synapses. Now then, lets get started ... I saw your file around here somewhere, Mr. Ganesh ... there she blows! Okay, now, let's see ... childhood in India ... some unfortunate accidents, which would account for the ..." Lester motions to Sandeep's missing arm and leg.

"Yes."

"Right. Lived in Bayonne, New Jersey ... As much as I'd enjoy the exchange of pleasantries, I have quite a few of these interviews to conduct, in light of the overwhelming response to the ad – which was rather catchy, if I do say so myself – so I'll get straight to the review of your questionnaire." Lester turns the page over. "Question number fourteen, true or false, death is bad and must be avoided at all costs."

"True." Sandeep restates his answer with confidence.

"Please understand that there is most certainly a right and wrong answer."

"Yes."

"Yes then! You're correct! Please elaborate a bit."

"I think true because, if false, death is good, yes?"

"Go on," Lester prods him like a schoolteacher.

"Then people they do not enjoy life as much."

"Yes, keep going."

"And if life is bad ..."

"Then life is bad," Lester bails him out.

"Yes."

"Then you've solved it, mate! Kudos to you."

"Thank you."

"Well, two questions remain. Linda!" Lester says, smashing down the red button on the desktop, which is not connected to anything. "Where the bloody hell are those lemonades? I mean, for heaven's sake, Mr. Ganesh, one would think we had ordered platters ceremoniously garnished with fresh fruit and cheese. It's her headaches I think, some kind of a condition. Well, we must press on. Question number twenty-three. Are there any people or places you deem essential to your overall well-being? In other words, what in your current life are you unwilling to abandon?"

This phraseology is confusing to Sandeep, and he thinks for a moment before responding, "Nothing."

"Everything?"

"No, nothing I think."

"You think right again! Just one more question, which was not on the list. Tell me, Mr. Ganesh, can you imagine living in a place where you are submersed in a culture of acceptance? And where futuristic technology makes all your handicaps and disadvantages melt away? Yet! It is such that your contact with the world-at-large is also virtually eliminated forever! Mr. Ganesh, allow me to cut straight to the quick of the matter. Keeping in mind that certain sacrifices will be required, are you willing and prepared to embrace the idea that utopia is possible?"

"Yes." Sandeep says without pause, because utopia is a word he knows – and he has believed in it all his life.

Lester stares at Sandeep intently over his half spectacles, thumbing the woolen fabric of his cloak – so intently that one might think he is trying to read newsprint between Sandeep's eyes. "Very good, then," he says in a mellow tone. That's good to hear, Mr. Ganesh … well then! Just three more questions. My sincerest apologies, but I neglected the part about how I may change the rules at any time, to suit my whimsy. Believe it or not, I once knew a man named Whimsy. Daft bastard. About as much sense in him as a bacterium. This is more of a rhetorical question but, since your mind seems so open to possibility, tell me this, are bacteria capable of lurking? That is, with the premeditated intent of attack? Say, from underneath one's fingernails?"

"What is lurk?"

"To lurk is to conceal oneself and lie in wait for something. For example, a lion may lurk in tall grass before pouncing on a wildebeest."

"Okay. Bacteria do not have brains I don't think. So it cannot be possible to lurk."

"Mmm-hmm, mmm-hmm, I agree," Lester says, as if Sandeep has changed his mind by force of argument. "You are a sharp one! Of course, in the case of a sword, sharpness can be very useful but also dangerous … we shall never find out for sure though, shall we, Mr.

Ganesh? Find out what motivates those dastardly bacteria to perform their nefarious work?"

"It may be possible."

"You think?"

"Perhaps with help of computers," Sandeep says.

Lester stares at him again, and after a short time begins nodding in rapid succession. "Yes! With computers! There's no telling what we might accomplish with computers! But they, too, may also be quite dangerous. Do you think computers might be dangerous?"

"I think no. People can be dangerous but not computer."

"Interesting opinion. Very … something, I don't know. One more question. If we assume this utopia exists, once there, would you embrace those you encounter as compatriots?"

"What is compatriot?"

"Like a countryman. Or a brother, if you will."

"Yes."

"Without question?"

"Yes."

"I believe you, and not merely because I want to. You see, I am rather patriotic myself, just not so much about this country anymore …" There is a long pause and Lester's head bobs forward slightly, as if he has lost consciousness for just a instant but recovered. "Which reminds me, where is that lazy, no-good woman with our sliced fruit and cheese platter?" Lester mashes down on the red button again. "Francine!"

"My name is Sarah, you fucking nut!" Sarah screams from the other room.

"Oh, thank god!" Lester says, expressing relief with a deep sigh and a whistle. "I can't stand anyone named Francine."

Lester stands now and scans the room blankly before another outburst surfaces. "Aaaaah!" He bellows, clutching his head in hands.

He stumbles forward and collapses to the floor at Sandeep's feet. Sandeep recoils in alarm, pressing himself deeper into the overstuffed chair. "Can't you see I'm malnourished!" Lester writhes around on the hardwood floor like an earthworm that's been cut in half. "It may be scurvy ... aaah ... I'm just asking for a little help here!"

"Are you okay?" Sandeep says, reaching out to him.

Lester scrambles to his feet and suddenly appears stricken with paranoia and fear. "Is everyone okay?! Mr. Ganesh, are you hurt?"

"I'm fine," Sandeep says, hoping temperance will placate the madman before him. He wonders what sort of a business would hire such person to serve as their representative – whatever it is that he's representing. As one might expect, Sandeep is wary of the situation he has gotten himself into. But he's also curious, not to mention desperate.

"Well, thank Jehovah and his witnesses you aren't badly hurt. That was a close one!" He presses the button on the desk again. "Woman, call the state department and let them know only minor damage has been sustained and no fatal injuries — I think you'll pull through, Mister ..."

"Ganesh," Sandeep says, perplexed at how the man could have forgotten his name after repeating it so many times during their conversation. He figures it's best to attempt a coup upon the proverbial rudder at this point, which is now clearly jerking about, unmanned. Otherwise, the outcome of the interview may become mired in uncertainty. Or worse, his hopes will be sunk along with this foundering fool, who is obviously insane.

* * *

From her seat in the waiting area Sylvia can hear everything. And like Sandeep, she's beginning to question her decision to apply for this … whatever it is. Amidst the distractions, she's been trying to complete the questionnaire. Do you smoke? No. Are you a paramedic, a doctor or nurse? No. She cannot help but think all the negative answers are hurting her score. She circles back to a few questions she skipped the first time around, such as number eleven: Are you willing to be hypnotized? Sylvia's uncertain about that one. After all, she's heard about people being led to believe some crazy things under hypnosis. She skips it again and goes to number nineteen: Financially speaking, do you have a problem with someone else's loss being your gain?

"Excuse me," Sylvia says to Sarah, who's blowing on her nails to dry them.

"Yeah?"

Sylvia lowers her voice to avoid being overheard through the paper-thin wall. "I was just wondering, what is it exactly that I'm interviewing for?"

"You don't know?" Sarah drones, as if trying to stultify her on purpose.

"Well, no. The ad didn't say exactly."

"Beats me. All I know is that he's not paying me enough to put up with all this bullshit."

"You don't have any idea?"

"Come to think of it, I've heard of him talking about some pyramid. That might have something to do with it."

"Ah," Sylvia says, more to herself than to Sarah. "The Pyramid Foundation, of course. So he's The Pyramid guy."

The door opens and Sandeep pops his head out, looking a bit frantic. "Miss?" he says to Sarah. "He say he wants some cookies from vending machine down the hall?"

"They're not on a platter though so he won't eat them," she snips.

"I *will* eat them!" Lester proclaims from the other room.

"Alright, alright, I'll get him the cookies. But I ain't going out for no fruit or no cheese. The streets are all blocked off 'cause of the riot."

"Okay, thank you," Sandeep says, closing the door without fully processing the bit about the riot.

* * *

"Did she say riot? My god!" Lester says, turning the giant oak desk over with a flip, nearly smashing Sandeep's one remaining foot. He throws himself behind it like a soldier diving behind a wall of sandbags. "Get down! Gunfire! Get down Mr. Ganesh!"

Sandeep is paralyzed from the thought that he just came within mere inches of being footless. He reaches down to touch the foot and this makes him feel better, and by now Lester has heroically crawled to the window and peeked over the sill.

"I see multicolored umbrellas! I see smoke! I see chicken feathers! It's a bloody melee! Dammit Mr. Ganesh! Get yourself down!"

"I did not hear gunshot," Sandeep says, as yet unmoved.

As a byproduct of the Corporate Wars, violent protests and even outright riots have become rather perfunctory events in New York and a host of other U.S. cities. Most result in little damage being done – perhaps a few broken windows and minor injuries – and in general they're broken up swiftly, either by heavily-armed police or by soldiers.

With this in mind, along with the fact that he has yet to hear any commotion whatsoever from outside the window, much less gunshots, Sandeep is not concerned. He is curious, however, so he gets up and hops over to the window for a look. But before he can catch a glimpse of anything, Lester grabs hold of his belt and drags him down behind the desk.

"You fool!" Lester shouts, covering Sandeep's body with his own. "You'll be killed!"

At first, Sandeep feels unnecessarily affronted. That is, until an explosion occurs and a chunk of asphalt crashes through the window at high speed, bouncing off the desk before punching a sizeable hole in the wall. All of a sudden shocked and relieved, he looks into Lester's piercing green eyes, and for the first time since he can remember, Sandeep truly feels safe.

Chapter 59

Drunk and jolly, Tim clambers up on deck of *The Heinousmeistress* with a mischievous look in his eye. Spurred on by Escobar's shrieking from the crow's nest, he negotiates the ladder to the quarter deck and, taking the wheel in hand, pans the horizon for signs of trouble. While he's been sailing for less than 24 hours now, the experience has already lacquered him with an intrepid self-assurance not uncommon to grizzled veterans of the sea.

"What sees you on yonder horizon, mate?!" Tim says, assuming Escobar's agitation is a result of their close proximity to The Black Balloon – and one of the four utility vehicles tethering it to the ground.

Escobar continues to sound the alarm, pointing over Tim's head, over the stern of the ship, where a truck approaches at a high rate of speed.

Tim levels his antique brass mariner's telescope at the vessel, which appears as a blurry, vibrating box on wheels.

"Ah, we have company indeed. The nature of which I'd venture to say is barbarous for certain! Prepare the cannons!"

Escobar swings through the rigging down to the main deck and Tim cuts the wheel, turning the ship broadside. She rolls along the smooth black glass surface without a sound except for the sails rippling in the wind.

"Prepare to fire on my command!"

The cannons are not operational, nor does Escobar understand Tim's instructions. He bolts straight back up to the crow's nest and resumes his prior state of excitability. Meanwhile, the truck is closing fast and Tim has become distracted by Anna's voice, which is echoing inside his head saying, "Tim, please don't go. I'm begging you. I'm begging you. I'm begging you." (Prior to this instance, Tim had considered the presence of voices, much less echoing voices, inside one's head to be a product of filmmakers and other cliché mongers.)

The rumble of the truck's engine snaps Tim back to the moment and he draws his sword out of its scabbard lightning-quick. "Very well, then," he hollers to Escobar, "I suppose we'll just have to kill them in person!"

Slowing down, the truck pulls alongside *The Heinousmeistress* and from a hatch on the roof climbs a military-type in black fatigues. He's equipped with some sort of unwieldy elephant gun, and he barks out, "Drop your weapon Mr. Ginn!"

"Give me one bloody reason!"

"Because you will not complete your mission!"

"I suppose you're going to stop me?"

"Yes. Now drop your weapon and no harm will come to you!"

"What kind of gun is that, anyway? It looks ridiculous."

"This is your last warning, Mr. Ginn!"

"Consider me terrified," Tim jeers.

The assailant fires a net in Tim's direction and he ducks, allowing it to become ensnared in the rigging behind him. Then, as if he's rehearsed it a thousand times before, Tim cuts one of the ropes securing the main yard (crosses the main mast), sheathes his sword, and uses the rope to swing down and deliver a two-footed kick to the man's chest, knocking him overboard.

Tim's dismount onto the truck's roof is comparatively graceless, as he lands heavy and clattering like a stack of metal folding chairs. He recovers quickly though, scrambling to his feet, anticipating the hatch to yield another wave of men. Instead, he suddenly finds inertia tossing him onto the hood of the truck and subsequently the ground, due to the driver having slammed on the brakes.

The fall knocks the wind out of him, and by the time he wriggles free of its suffocating grasp, he is surrounded by five more thugs in black fatigues. To his surprise, they don't have firearms but instead wield police-style nightsticks, apparently with the intention of beating him into submission.

Tim sucks in a few nourishing breaths of air before regaining his feet. He reaches for his sword but freezes as the perimeter tightens around him.

"This doesn't have to get ugly, Mr. Ginn," says one of the thugs.

Tim looks closely at the man's face. His nose is crooked and he has a long scar under his left eye. "By the looks of *you*, it's already too late for that."

"You're coming with us one way or the other. So why don't you be a good little boy and just lay down on the ground."

"Lie."

"Huh?"

"Lie!" Tim draws – and a flash of steel later, the brute sinks to his knees with a matching scar under his right eye, squealing like a distressed piglet. As the remaining heavies lunge at him, Tim wheels this way and that, ducking and dodging clubs and fists while introducing all four of them to the business end of his sword. After all these years, his education is finally paying dividends.

As the last militiaman falls to the ground, spurting blood and crying out in agony, Tim takes a moment to admire his handiwork. He is equally awed and repulsed by the sight, endorphins swarming in his head like angry hornets and his teeth clenched so tight his jaw aches. The sword throbs like a life force in his hand, as if goading him to finish the job. He imagines thrusting the blade through skulls and ribcages, hacking and slashing until nothing remains but a bloody pile of meat. He nearly vomits before his nausea is trumped by fear – as a shadowy figure appears in his periphery – and then by pain, as a tranquilizer dart whizzes into his thigh.

"Aaah!" Tim charges toward the source, a man in khaki fatigues and mirrored sunglasses holding a rifle. He's about 10 strides away but Tim collapses after five or six.

Bossy lowers the rifle and shakes his head, expressionless. "Medic!" he hollers over his shoulder. Another man emerges from the truck carrying a red duffel bag and rushes to the aid of his fallen comrades.

Bearing the distress of these unforeseen consequences, Jipt circles around from the passenger side of the truck. He takes a step toward Tim but Bossy holds him back.

"Don't do it, Seth. He might be playing possum," he says, before loading another dart in the rifle.

"How about your men?"

"They'll be all right. This wouldn't've happened though, if they'd been properly armed."

"Jesus Christ," Jipt mutters, "I just didn't want any shooting … hey, what's that monkey up to?"

Jipt points and even the wounded men turn their heads to watch the hunched figure of a chimpanzee scamper across the desert floor, making a beeline for the utility truck. With a dagger clenched in his jaws, Escobar leaps onto the giant spool of cable (which is designed to give slack as the sun rises, and reel it back in during the sun's descent) and he begins to climb.

"Shit," Bossy says, "He must have trained the little bastard. Here, hold this." Handing the dart gun to Jipt, Bossy steps up into the cab and hops down a moment later with an assault rifle. He snaps a round into the chamber and takes aim at Escobar.

"What the hell are you doing?" Jipt says.

"What does it look like?" Bossy growls. "I'm gonna shoot that monkey 'fore he pops your balloon."

Oddly enough, these words tumble from Bossy's lips in a perfectly natural way, like green turds from a horse's ass, like he's reaffirming the existence of gravity or poverty, one of life's universal truths. And perhaps this explains Jipt's dumb acceptance of them, just as he has begun to accept his own preposterously dumb fate.

Chapter 60

Still groggy from the tranquilizer, Tim's eyelids plunge like a velvet theater curtain as he recalls the third grade and something his crotchety old science teacher, Ms. Farwahr, once said to him. He had been alone with her in the stark classroom, only half-finished with his multiple choice quiz on photosynthesis, the other children running and screaming outside on the playground. "I wish I didn't have to go to school anymore," Tim had said, and then Ms. Farwahr had looked at him with a more grave expression than usual and said, "Be careful what you wish for, Tim."

At the time he didn't understand what she meant – that, for instance, he might be run over by a train or be abducted by aliens and, therefore, not have to attend school anymore – but he does now. He knows all too well. That's because he's handcuffed to a bed.

Sure, he's wished it on occasion – fantasized about it – except the details have always been very specific with respect to who's doing the handcuffing. Typically it's Anna, clad in tight black leather, but recently it's been Anna and Cleopatra together, both clad in tight black leather, or Anna and various permutations of movie stars, clad in tight black leather. The point is that women were always involved, clad in tight black leather. Therefore, since Seth Jipt's henchmen are neither women, nor clad in tight black leather, the Wishmaster must have a selective memory. Otherwise it's all rubbish, that old bag Ms. Farwahr was full of rubbish, and he's been right all along. It doesn't really matter what you wish for because only careful choices, sacrifice and perseverance can affect the outcome.

Along with luck, of course. There's always got to be a wildcard, and in most cases it's luck. But you can't wish for luck, that's the rule. Lester taught him that, and he believes it to this day, which is why he wishes that a hole would open beneath Seth Jipt and he would fall down to where he rightly belongs, ass-first onto Lucifer's fiery prick. Check that. He wishes Jipt would uncuff him first, then fall ass-first onto Lucifer's fiery prick.

Tim reluctantly opens his eyes again to the drab interior of the trailer home, which is furnished only with his bed, a desk and two chairs, in addition to the burlap curtains and chintzy brass light fixtures. "I want to talk to my father. Right now," he says, trying not to sound like a little boy crying for his daddy.

"Sure, no problem," Jipt says smugly. "I'll just give him a jingle … although, by way of introduction, I reckon I will have to mention the circumstances of our prior meeting, in The Casino."

"I know what your plan is," Tim says, as if avoiding further discussion of the topic will absolve him of culpability in the blackmail process.

Jipt has been pacing the linoleum floor, pausing every so often to peek through the curtains at the horde of media who have besieged the trailer with their cameras and microphones. He turns to Tim and attempts to veil his anxiety using an altogether shoddy combination of disdain and sarcasm. "Well, shit. I'm glad someone finally figgered it out, cuz I'm stumped. By all means, let's hear it, Mr. Ginn."

"Right, well first of all, you needed to defend your little balloon – your big balloon, I beg your pardon – from the onslaught of my forces, so you could continue perpetrating this charade of yours, which I can only assume is designed to turn everyone into vampires from sunlight deprivation. After all, it's certainly not having the slightest effect on The Pyramid's vast reservoir of electricity."

"I think you're lying."

"And I think you're ugly," Tim says, yanking on the handcuffs to no avail. "But that's neither here nor there. By now my crew has surely eradicated the floating nuisance so — Escobar! What have you done with Escobar?"

"Is that the monkey?"

"Ape."

"He's – he got away," Jipt says, reconsidering the effect the truth might have on his detainee.

"Probably half way to Tijuana by now, lucky bastard … Now then, your plan was not just to stop me from completing my mission, now, was it?"

"No."

"No, it wasn't a'tall. You wanted to capture me, which, so far, you've managed fairly well. Granted, I could bust out of these flimsy shackles anytime I want, but nevertheless … you're hoping to incite my father to make rash decisions, namely abandoning his seat of power and coming to rescue me, his beloved son. Flush him out, as it were, and then swoop in yourself to fill the vacuum."

"Not bad, Mr. Ginn. Not bad. Although I take it you don't think it will work."

"No, and I'll tell you why. Two simple words. Self. Reliance."

"Meaning what, exactly?"

"Meaning one of the key tenets of Lester Ginn's philosophy – one of the pillars – the veritable foundation – the backbone of –"

"Self-reliance."

"Right, self-reliance," Tim says, as he struggles into a seated position, with his back against the wall and his cuffed wrists now idle in his lap. "When I was a boy, perhaps eight or nine, my father bought this car. Well, actually I think he bartered for it with various goods and services, because money was scarce in those days, back in Queens. Anyway, it was a large American car and I loved to play in the thing after school, pretend I was a taxi driver and whatnot. Well, one day I got bored, one thing led to another and I got myself locked in the trunk. So I banged and screamed for help, and eventually my father found out about it. But he didn't let me out of there, no sir, he said, 'You got yourself in there and you're gonna get yourself out.'"

"And you did."

"Well, not straight off. Not until I got the flashlight and the screwdriver."

"Where'd they come from?"

"He gave them to me, along with some water and a candy bar. The man's not cruel."

"Hmm." Jipt rubs his face and then inspects his hands with a look of concern, as if they were covered in blood.

"And he's not stupid. He knows when word gets out about what's going on here, this treachery, I'll be carried back home on a silver platter. Why, I bet the police will kick that door in at any moment. You *do* have police in this godforsaken place, don't you?"

"Sure, we've got police. But at this point, I'm protecting *you* from *them*."

"That's a load of rubbish!"

"Rubbish, eh? You'll be lucky if all my men recover from their wounds – after shish-kebabing them like you did. Besides, if anyone's going to kick that door in, it'll be the goddamned media wanting to know why you refuse to go back."

"Refuse ..."

"Yeah, and why your father tried to kill you."

Chapter 61

In light of the two-hour wait for the Complaint Confessional, Svetlana had every opportunity to change her mind. She had every opportunity to convince herself that matters have *not*, in fact, spiraled out of control – that Lester has *not* become hopelessly anesthetized to the truth of things – and that her love for him has *not* been steadily eroding into a bleak chasm of fear. Yet, with the facts laid bare, these were arguments she could not win, even against herself. And turning back was an option she could not justify, even *to* herself.

The thick, vault-like door swings open and a buzzard-faced man appears from the confessional wheeling an oxygen tank behind him. Like many of those who preceded him, his lips are taut with frustration, his eyes like craters born out of futility. "I don't know why I even bother," he grumbles, sniffling mucous up his giant beak of a nose. "For God sakes, I can't beat my meat no more. I just can't do it no more."

Embarrassed, and anxious to the point of nausea, Svetlana avoids eye contact with the man as she steps into the confessional and shuts the door behind her. While the exterior façade had been sterile and unornamented, giving no hint of piety, the chamber itself harkens to a bygone era, when church and state were unambiguously entwined. As rare as the appearance of authentic wood accoutrement is in The Pyramid, here it's literally all-encompassing. Stained to a deep red finish, the walls, floor and ceiling give Svetlana the general impression of being inside a nutshell.

Unsure at first of what to do, she lowers herself to the velvet-padded kneeler. This brings her face in line with the rectangular gold screen built into the paneling, through which she can see neither shape nor shadow. A wave of panic crashes over her. She puts one foot back on the floor in an effort to stand, but an abrupt noise causes her to resume of the kneeling position. It's Lester – sliding open the tiny door behind the screen, which now glows with an orange-hued light. "Good morning," he says solemnly, and Svetlana freezes up, unsure of how to produce the disguised voice she took days to perfect. "Hello? Anyone there? Don't be afraid, now. Is this your first time?"

At least this allays her fears about him being able to see her through the screen. "Yes," she whispers, holding her breath.

"Well, you don't have to whisper. No one can hear us."

"My throat."

"You have a throat ailment, I see. My sympathies, Missus?

"Thompson."

"Right. I can hear you just fine, though, in fact, the softness of your voice is a welcomed respite from the shrill, piercing blather I've been hearing rather a lot in recent weeks. But yet, I sense that something troubles you very deeply."

"Yes."

"Mmm … indeed. It's not laundry detergent or dinner rolls that brings you here, is it Ms. Thompson?"

"No."

Lester lowers his own voice now, just above a whisper. "Then what? Tell Lester what it is so he can fix it."

"It's my husband."

"Mr. Thompson, hmm? Has he hurt you?"

"Yes."

"With his hands?" Lester says, raising his voice again.

"No."

"Certainly not with his feet."

"No, nothing like that."

"So he hurts your feelings then."

"Yes."

"I'm sorry to hear that, but, you see, I'm not a marriage counselor. So unless there are some environmental factors also contributing to your—"

"Yes, there are."

"It's the rationing of electricity, isn't it? That's a big one lately. We're working the problem, let me assure you Mrs. Thompson."

"No, it's not that."

"What then? The hot water? Again, that's a power issue, which we're working round-the-clock to fix."

"That's it. That's the problem."

"The hot water?"

"No, the working round-the-clock."

"Your husband? Working on what, exactly?"

"The hot water, the power, the laundry detergent, the dinner rolls ... every damned thing that's wrong with this place."

"I don't understand what your husband ... what he has to do with ..."

"Lester."

"Yes?" Lester says tentatively, his voice clearly stifled by apprehension.

"I just wish ... I were as dear to you as your Pyramid," Svetlana says, resolved to accept the consequences. She reaches out with her fingertips and caresses the screen lovingly, as if it were Lester's own skin. She waits for a response from him but receives none – that is, apart from a very quiet, very desperate sobbing that is just audible above the beating of her own heart.

Chapter 62

Anna has never thought metaphorically about tennis, in terms of how it imitates life, but she's thinking about it now, as she runs Cleo along the baseline with her precision ground strokes. *WHACK! Get back to center after each shot. Stay centered. WHACK! Position is everything. WHACK! Anticipate the shot coming and get ready for it. WHACK! Feet. Racquet. Visualize and execute. WHACK!* She drives the ball with a roundhouse swing, deep to Cleo's backhand side, and the topspin eats her up.

"Thirty-love."

It all starts with a good serve. But hard serves often meet with hard returns. No time to appreciate your work. WHACK! Just like I said. WHACK! Wear your opponent down. WHACK! Keep them off-center. WHACK! Keep them guessing. WHACK! Pick your time to charge the net carefully. WHACK! But don't hesitate. WHACK! All or nothing. WHACK!

Only something strange occurs to her. This is not her life, not even close. She's not centered, not ready for whatever comes her way – and what's more, she hardly ever charges the net. Life is supposed to be about competition, but she has no one to compete against and nothing to compete for. There is no ambition and no reward – no fame, no fortune, no sense of accomplishment, self-improvement or dedication to a goal. No hope for the future. Her life is basically just elaborate masturbation, without the orgasm.

Even with regard to tennis, she realizes that playing is about little more than time-consumption. She can play for three or four hours and it seems like nothing, because she thinks about nothing.

Her body just moves back to center on its own, her racquet finds the ball and she hardly ever decides to charge the net. She doesn't play to win, or even "not to lose" as the commentators say, but simply to apply some sort of structure to her life. Five points. Six games. Five sets. Done.

Granted, Cleo is much improved since they started playing together, but she only takes games, sets and matches that Anna willingly concedes. Even when she used to play those heated doubles matches with her mom, Lester and Tim, it was never about winning, it was about making everyone happy. Making it close, making it exciting and, in most cases, letting the other team win in the end. After all, she always found more joy in consolation than in praise – joy, of course, being a relative term.

By this time Anna is thoroughly pissed off at the world and just about everyone in it, namely herself. Grunting from the effort, her jaw set with angry determination, she unleashes another rocket forehand and dashes to the net. Cleo rips a solid forehand of her own, down the line, and all Anna can do is lunge for it, issuing a weak volley back to the fat part of the court. Cleo tees off again, which sends Anna lunging the other way this time. Her racquet barely connects, again leaving the ball down the middle, but short. Cleo charges, tries to lob, but not high enough. Anna applies more torque than necessary to her smash and Cleo screams, cowering with racquet protecting her face. Which is a good thing, too, as the ball glances off the strings and rattles the chain-link fence behind her.

"Jesus! You don't have to take it out on me!" Cleo says with a smirk.

"Take what out?"

"He'll come back, Anna, don't worry."

"Tim?"

"Yeah, Tim. You know, that guy you're crazy about?"

"I don't really care anymore," Anna lies. "I'm over him."

"If you say so. He must be pretty messed up though, after what happened."

"That whole story is bullshit. You know that, right?"

"What, you mean Lester didn't try to ..."

"Kill his own son? Please. He may be nuts, but he's not a murderer."

"So ... I don't get it, then."

"I don't really get it either, to be honest with you. All I know is there's some sort of game being played between Lester and this Jipt guy."

"Okay, so Tim *does* want to come back, but this Jipt guy isn't letting him. And he just made up that story so that—"

"Forget it, okay?!"

"I'm sorry, Anna, I just ..."

"No, it's all right. I'm sorry. Let's just drop it, though. We shouldn't really be talking about this."

"But, why not?"

"Because I don't want to," Anna lies again.

"Fine. That's cool," Cleo says.

They walk off the court and Anna sits down on the bench, where they've left all their spare racquets and superfluous gear. Elbows on knees, she towels off her face, drawing comfort from the temporary darkness. She feels the bench moving and peeks out to see Cleo's bright white tennis shoes planted on either side of her. Evidently she's climbed up on the back of the bench for some reason – which becomes apparent when her fingers begin kneading Anna's trapezius muscles (shoulder/neck). It feels good. Really good. Considerably better, in fact, than Anna thinks it *should* feel.

"You're so tight, sweetie. You just need to relax a little," Cleo says, her voice moist and delicate, like a spider web covered in morning dew.

"Tim never gave me any massages. I begged him, but he wouldn't do it."

"That's probably why, because you begged."

"Yeah, maybe."

"Men … So what do you want to do tonight?"

"I don't know, maybe get drunk, watch a movie and cry myself to sleep?"

"Sounds like a party! Can I come?" Cleo says with over-the-top sarcasm.

"Sure, if you do this again."

"Deal. See, life isn't so bad, is it? You've got your own personal masseuse and everything. Here, lean back."

Anna slouches a bit, raising her elbows and allowing Cleo's warm thighs to slide under her armpits for support. Near the base of her skull she can feel the snap on Cleo's skirt, and this sends an unforeseen tingle dancing up her spine.

"I want to go places," Anna says after a brief interlude.

"Like where?"

"I don't know. Paris, London, Rome, Africa, the Caribbean, lots of places."

"It's not all that, believe me. Well, I've never been to Africa, but I can't imagine, you know. My dad used to be in the army, so we moved like every year or so. It sucked."

"You were just a kid, though. It wasn't like going on vacation," Anna says, closing her eyes.

"It's just not safe these days, Anna. Besides, why travel when you've got everything you need right here at home?"

"You really love this place, don't you?"

"I wish I could get some better shampoo and conditioner," Cleo says with a chuckle. "But yeah, I really do. I never want to leave."

"Don't you want to meet new people?"

"I met you, didn't I?"

"That's not what I mean," Anna says, and by now she has loosened up considerably, her head bowed forward as if she were asleep. But she's not asleep. Instead, she's acutely aware of Cleo's hands moving over her shoulders to her deltoids where they pause, squeezing and rubbing, before sliding under her chin. Anna allows her head to be tilted back, as Cleo's fingers delicately trace down the front of her neck, and a flutter runs through her as Cleo's hands cup firmly under her breasts. She's afraid to move a muscle, even though she knows her implicit acquiescence becomes more of a certainty with each passing second. And she's afraid to open her eyes, because she can feel the warmth of Cleo's breath in her right ear.

"I know you don't love him anymore," Cleo whispers. "That's why I told him. I did it to protect you."

Anna warily opens her eyes and sees Cleo hovering above her, staring back with a lupine intensity. Anna's throat is so dry that the words barely eek out. "What? When?"

"A while ago, before he left."

Desperately trying to reconcile this information, bewildered and aroused and scared all at once, Anna slides forward out of Cleo's grasp and takes two steps away.

"Sweetie," Cleo says, pushing her knees together and cocking her head to the side in a manner of demure supplication. "Don't be upset with me."

"You told him I didn't love him anymore?!" Anna says, her myriad emotions suddenly crystallizing into rage.

"Yes, but—"

"Where did you see him?"

"At your place … he came by one day while you were out."

"He came by? Out of the blue he just came by? After not coming by for, like, two years? Well what the fuck did he want?"

"I don't know."

"Bullshit. What did he want?"

"I don't know. He had flowers. He was wearing a tux. It looked like he was picking you up for the prom, Anna. It was really pathetic."

"I can't believe you did that, Cleo. I can't believe it," Anna says, her lower lip quivering, her anger beginning to unravel into a passionate fretfulness. She thinks about how many times she could have confessed her true feelings to Tim, how many opportunities she let false pride win out over reason, and she literally shivers at the thought that Tim may be in danger as a result of it.

"Sweetie, please, we can work it all out," Cleo says, stepping off the bench, holding her arms open in suggestion of embracing her.

"Stop calling me that! Get away from me!" Anna screams, and she runs away. Like a little girl running from her own imaginary ghosts she runs away.

Chapter 63

Lester remembers with startling clarity the day he drank his first pint of beer. He was fourteen years old, and it's the last memory he has of being with his father.

Down by the navy pier in Portsmouth was a place called The Barnacle, which was a favorite of the officer corps primarily because of its cleanliness, its quaint, traditional décor and its impressive selection of lagers, bitters and stouts from all over Great Britain. Lester would accompany the Commander there whenever he shipped out, and would sit quietly while the men exchanged colorful banter, thrashing out matters of politics, business and, of course, football. On this particular occasion, however, he recalls the conversation being strangely ominous, and his father's behavior uncharacteristically maudlin. Upon setting the frothy pint before Lester he said, "Son, this is a man's drink. It's about time you had one, because you're a man now. You're a man, equal with any of us at this table. Be mindful though, son, with this distinction not only comes great privilege, but also great responsibility. Someday soon, you'll have people depending on you."

Years later it would become apparent what he meant, when he returned from sea in a box draped in The Union Jack, and his mother suffered a complete nervous breakdown, leaving him, the only child, to care for her, to get a job and to support her for the remainder of her life. He wonders if it had not been a mere five years before she died of pneumonia, if he'd still be there, changing her underpants and wiping soup off her face with a crumpled paper napkin …

"Lester? Lester, you've tuned out on me again," Chutney says, sliding his half-drunk pint away from him, at which he's been gazing blankly for some time now.

"Huh? Oh, right. I just got to thinking about my father … and the last time he took me to The Barnacle." Lester glances around the pub, sopping up the details that are meant to be an exact replica of those in The Barnacle – the oak paneling, the ship's wheel chandeliers, the mirrored adverts for lagers, bitters and stouts from all over Great Britain.

"You didn't answer my question."

"Right. What was that again?"

"I don't remember," Chutney says with a bittersweet smile. "Something about The Confessional perhaps? Have you talked to Svetlana since …"

"No, no, of course I haven't," Lester says, again making eye contact only with his beer as he swirls it around in the glass. "It's not a subject that can exactly benefit from argument at this point, is it?"

"Who said you should argue about it?"

"Nobody, there's nothing to argue about. But you can't throw the baby out with the bloody bathwater, can you?"

"I'm not sure what you mean."

"Sometimes responsibility just outweighs privilege, it's just the ghastly truth of—

"Lester."

"Yes?"

"Svetlana was just being honest with you, about the truth as *she* sees it. And now I'm going to be honest with you, about the truth as *I* see it – because I think the others are afraid to be."

"Afraid? Of what?"

"Of letting you down."

"Well, how the devil would—"

"This isn't working anymore, Lester."

"You mean—"

"Everything, yes. It's just not. And it's my fault as much as anyone's, because the assumptions were all wrong. They were myopic and overly optimistic and just plain wrong. You just can't stop someone from wanting more, once you hand them everything on a silver platter for God's sake – if there's no sense of earning it, of self actualization ..."

Lester's eyes start to glaze over again.

"Maslow? Realizing one's purpose? It's the paradox behind every utopia theory yet we were blind to it, Lester, we just looked the other way because ... Lester?"

"I think I miss the air most of all."

"What?"

"The air. I miss the air ... at home, back in Queens, the way it was always so ... thick, so pungent ... with sulfur, exhaust, sewage, rotten fish heads ... it was awful, wasn't it?"

"Yes."

"Why do I miss it then?"

"I don't know."

"Bollocks you don't!"

"You remember how happy we were Lester, back then? Back when this was all just an idea? It was a perfect and harmless idea, and we couldn't let well enough alone."

"We can get things under control," Lester says unconvincingly.

"No, we can't, Lester. We can't control what people think, what they want, what they aspire to, any more than we can control the rising and setting of the sun."

"That bastard is holding Tim hostage!" Lester explodes, pounding the table with both fists in a juvenile fashion. "Hostage!

And not only that, but he's telling people I tried to kill him! Can you imagine, Chutney? My own son!"

"I know, Lester, but he's all right. He's safe and sound."

"Well, I don't give a damn who thinks I'm a ruthless dictator or a tyrant, but I will not be called a bad father! I'm going after him!" Lester says, swinging his legs out of the booth.

"Lester, wait!" Chutney says, grabbing hold of his wrist. "I don't think that's a good idea."

"You don't?"

Chutney clasps Lester's hands together and squeezes them between her own, looking intently into his eyes. "No, I think it's exactly what he wants you to do."

"Yes, perhaps you're right … but what then, Chutney?" Lester says with a desperate urgency, just above a whisper. "I can't just sit on my hands. My son is out there, and I can't just—" He's silenced by the sudden appearance of Svetlana, whose face is bright red and glistening with tears. "Svety, my God, what's wrong?"

She wipes her face with a trembling hand and takes a labored breath. "It's Escobar. He's dead."

Chapter 64

Considering the DNA of chimpanzees is upwards of 99 percent similar to that of human beings, it only seemed appropriate to hold a proper funeral for Escobar. Besides, he was well known by all the Visionaries, as each developed his or her own routine of visiting the Habitat for the purpose of observing the chimps and, perhaps more importantly, keeping Svetlana company in Lester's absence.

So, along with Svetlana, Lester and Anna, they've all convened in The Gardens this morning, where Escobar's gold-trimmed casket has just been lowered into the ground atop a gently sloping berm planted with lilacs. Normally on such a morning, the place would be dappled with bright sunlight filtered through the windows and the upper canopy of foliage, which is much sparser than that of The Habitat, comprised chiefly of palm trees, but instead the Black Balloon casts a grayish pall over the proceedings.

As Squeakins genteelly tosses shovelfuls of dirt into the grave, the semicircular assemblage breaks apart and the Visionaries meander away down one of the cobblestone paths to the reception area, where tea and various baked goods await them. Her eyes still moist with tears shed during her impromptu eulogy, Svetlana appears on the verge of emotional – if not outright physical – collapse. And, as only an ill-programmed robot or a sociopath could fail to recognize this, Lester moves to her. He opens up to her with his arms, as well as his expression, and she slumps forward, grabbing hold of his neck as if he were a lone buoy in a vast sea of nothingness.

"He didn't deserve this," Svetlana says. "It's my fault. It's all my fault."

"Nonsense," Lester says tenderly, stroking her hair. "It's my fault. I shouldn't have permitted it. And as for the coldhearted bastard who—"

"Don't say it, Lester. Please, don't say anything more about it."

A few steps behind Svetlana, looking rather despondent herself, Anna catches Lester's attention by widening her eyes.

"I'm going back upstairs."

"Wait a minute," Lester says. "Svety, why don't you go up with Anna and lie down for a while. I'll be up in a jiff. Are you hungry?"

"No."

"Alright then. Go ahead with Anna and I'll be up in a jiff."

Anna peels her away from Lester and they walk together, arm in arm, along the path cutting the straightest line to the exit. As soon as they disappear around a bend, Lester grips his forehead and turns to Squeakins as if to say, *What have I done?*

Without interrupting the cadence of his grim duty, or even raising his head, Squeakins says, "At least he died free, sir."

"Well said, boy. I suppose it's a privilege we often take for granted. Albeit a gloomy one."

At that, Lester follows the path taken by the Visionaries, and soon arrives at the reception table to find them huddled around, whispering urgently to one another. "What are we plotting?" he says too loudly. "Must be something brilliant indeed from the look of it!"

Chutney is first to separate herself from the clique, with a look of sympathy and embarrassment. "Lester, we need to talk," she says. "But I don't know if this is the appropriate—"

"Time? Place?"

"Yes."

"For talking?"

"Yes, perhaps we should—"

"No no, we're here, aren't we? All of us?" Lester says with an artificial peppiness, looking at each of the Visionaries in turn and then back at his own feet, as though doubts had been raised as to his own visibility. "And you know what they say, no time like the present!"

Chili steps out now, alongside Chutney. "Seriously, it's no rush, Lester. We just need to hash some shit out is all."

"No rush? To judgment you mean? Are we rushing to judgment? Because if we're rushing to judgment then, yes, by all means, there's no rush a'tall. In fact, we could put it off indefinitely, don't you think? Yes, I think we could! After all, it's a nasty, nasty business, rushing to judgment. Nasty as nasty can be."

"It's not that way at all, Lester," Chutney says in a conciliatory tone. "It's been a long time coming for all of us ... and I know, deep down, you know that."

"What, exactly?"

"Lester, please don't make this more difficult that it has to be," Chutney says, the emotional tension now clawing at her still-beautiful face. "It's just time ... we took up our real lives again."

"Oh, I see. Yes, I understand now. How insensitive I have been for assuming! For assuming that we! ... nevermind, nevermind ... there were too many holes to patch up, far too many holes, and as one got patched up, another opened, didn't it? Another and another, and we became so consumed with patching the holes that the whole bloody ship ran aground, didn't it? The whole bloody goddamned ship ran aground!"

"As far as transition plans," Chili says. "We obviously need to—"

"Go on then."

"What?"

"Go on then!" Lester shouts, red faced, pointing in no specific direction. "I just told you we've run aground, so save yourselves! Go on, be gone with you!" He folds his arms across his chest melodramatically and turns his back to them.

The others look to Chutney for direction, and without saying a word she tells them it is okay to leave, that she'll try to smooth things over on their behalf. To a man (and a woman), they appear torn up inside, muted not by the scarcity or temperance of their feelings but simply by their inability to do them justice with speech. They file away two-by-two with heads down, Schnitzelhaus with his arm around Katz's shoulder, and likewise, Chili with his arm around Ping's.

Chapter 65

Sylvia is frustrated to the point of speechlessness, which is a condition she's never experienced before. Up to this point in her life, good-old-fashioned tenacity and perseverance have been enough to achieve everything she's set her sights on – from the pink bicycle she had campaigned for prior to her fifth birthday to the mayoral title recently bestowed on her by the citizens of PyraVegas. But the situation with Lester Ginn is different. It's like catching a black cat in a dark room filled with bar stools. Like finding the truth at a nihilist convention. Like shooting a ghost in the fog.

In retrospect, it had been a dumb idea to claim responsibility for the Black Balloon. Granted, it remains popular with the Union, her key constituency, who believe it's their only hope in forcing Lester to reopen The Casino. But, at the same time, it creates a rather pesky catch-22 because Lester refuses to negotiate while it's still afloat, and Jipt refuses to bring it down on account of Lester.

To make matters worse, Seth Jipt hasn't been much easier to get a hold of than Lester. And, as alluded to at the top, Sylvia is nearing the end of her proverbial rope. She's just called Jocelyn into her office. Well-trained and eager to please, Jocelyn stands there with pen and notepad ready, awaiting instructions. Sylvia taps a fingernail against her front teeth and tries to remember what she had meant to say. Jocelyn is unaccustomed to the silence and, much like a chimpanzee learns sign language by imitation, she taps her own teeth nervously with the butt of her pen. *Tap-tap-tap-tap.*

The phone rings. Instinctively, Jocelyn turns and makes a break for her desk, which is a wobbly, shuffle-footed undertaking in light of the ridiculous heels she's wearing. Sylvia has yet to become accustomed to someone taking the calls, so she doesn't think twice about picking it up herself.

"Mayor King's office," she says, raising her voice an octave while converting some of her poise to pep.

"Hello, this is Thomas Hawkins calling from Seth Jipt's office. Is the mayor perchance available?"

Sylvia's mental block is suddenly breached by a wellspring of thoughts, and it's all she can do to restrain herself for a moment in order to say, "One moment please, Mr. Hawkins ... Sylvia King."

"Mayor King, this is Thomas Hawkins calling from Seth Jipt's office. You may recall—"

"I remember you, Mr. Hawkins. Jipt's right-hand man, the brains behind the brawn, the good cop. I've been trying to track down your boss for over a week now."

"I know. There's ..." Hawkins' voice lowers and Sylvia imagines him looking over his shoulder. "There's a reason why he's been avoiding you, and I just thought you deserved to know."

"Having doubts about our loyalties, are we?"

"I just thought you should know is all, that he has a meeting set up with Lester Ginn. Tomorrow afternoon."

"Well, at least we know what it takes to get a meeting with the man. All you have to do is kidnap his son," Sylvia jokes. "I bet that will be an interesting conversation."

"Look, I've sort of been cut out of the loop, but I wouldn't be surprised if an alternative labor deal is put on the table."

"An alternative to The Union, you mean."

"You know as well as I do, there's no shortage of people who want those jobs, who'd be willing to accept a lot less than The Union is demanding."

"It would only be a matter of time before they'd demand the same, if not more," Sylvia says almost automatically, before she remembers that Hawkins is doing her a huge favor, not to mention risking his own livelihood. On the other hand, she has learned never to apologize in matters of business.

"Be that as it may," Hawkins says, seeming to grow more anxious. "I'm just passing this information along as a concerned citizen, so do with it what you will. I've got to run, now."

"Thank you, Mr. Hawkins, I appreciate the courage it took to do what you've done. And don't run too far. Because when all the dust settles, I think this city will have a use for a man like you," Sylvia says – but, by this time, the line has already gone dead.

Chapter 66

Lester is not as unacquainted with, and indifferent to, the politics and personalities of PyraVegas as many have come to believe. He knows who Sylvia King is, for example, and what she looks like, and he is not the slightest bit surprised that she accompanied Jipt to this afternoon's meeting. Yet, by the same token, he did not invite her to take part in the meeting, so he feels a certain degree of gamesmanship is in order.

Squeakins has already seated the visitors at one end of the Apex conference table, on opposite sides, when Lester tops the staircase in a flourish of corduroy, tweed and polyester. The irony is lost on his audience, but he's wearing the exact same ensemble he chose more than 13 years ago, when first appearing on television to unveil The Pyramid concept to the world. Due to his continued regimen of weight lifting, both the jacket and pants are literally bursting at the seams as he flounces over to the head of the table. Jipt rises, followed by Sylvia, and they approach him for the obligatory handshake.

"So glad you could finally make it," Lester says to Jipt with a straight face. "Is this your secretary, then?"

"No, this is—"

"Sylvia King," Sylvia says, extending her hand. "Mayor of PyraVegas."

"Brilliant! So we've got the old and the new mayors. Mayor mania! In fact, I'm the only one in the room who's never been one, aren't I? Yes, indeed. You know, I used to think there were two kinds of people, but now I think there may be three, all represented in this room! Of course, overall, there are still only two kinds, those who believe there are only two kinds of people and those who don't."

"I think everyone is their own kind of person," Sylvia says.

This strikes him like the lyrics to a song previously misunderstood. "Well, nevertheless, I refuse to let that drive an axe between us, because I still feel we have a lot in common. Allow me to illustrate." Lester corrals Sylvia and Jipt back into their chairs and takes up a standing position at the head of the table, between them. He removes a white-tipped grease pencil from his blazer pocket and proceeds to sketch out a large triangle on the tabletop. Then he divides the triangle into seven layers from top to bottom.

"Now then," he says. "Either of you ever heard of a bloke called Mancow?"

"No. Listen," Jipt says, impatiently.

"You mean Maslow?" Sylvia interjects.

"Yes! That's it. Doctor Johann Maslow, I believe it was."

"Abraham," Sylvia says.

"Right. The point is, he developed this ingenious theory, a hierarchy of man's basic needs, embodied in a pyramid-shaped compartment such as this. It's really quite extraordinary. Now—"

"Goddammit Ginn, I didn't come here to—"

"Quiet! You rude and inconsiderate mongrel! I'm very close to losing my patience with you!" Lester shouts, before closing his eyes and taking a deep breath. "Now, at the base here, we have physiological needs – things like shelter and water, right? Then we have – does anyone know? Mr. Jipt? A chance to redeem yourself ... Safety. The answer is safety. Profoundly important, is it not? Then we have the sort of touchy-feely needs in the middle here – love, affection and belongingness. I personally would rank belongingness and love in a tie, but this is but one minor point of disagreement I have with Doctor Marlowe."

"Maslow," Sylvia corrects him again.

"Maslow, yes. Thank you for keeping me honest, Ms. Armstrong."

"King."

"Right! I'm afraid I have the retention of a bloody sieve."

"I tell you, this is real inner'sting and all, Ginn, but—"

"I'm not finished! Damn it, please!" Lester says, before tempering his anger and again regaining his full composure. "Two needs remain. Here, just below the top of The Pyramid, we have esteem, namely self-esteem, not to be overlooked, eh Ms. King? I can feel the self-esteem radiating out of you. You're afire with it!"

"Thank you."

Clearly disgusted with the turn of events, Jipt sighs heavily and looks up at the beacon atop The Pyramid, watching it turn round and round.

"Which brings us to the very top, the very apex of The Pyramid, where we have self actualization! Now, the beauty and genius of self-actualization is that it has nothing to do with what you've got in the bank, does it? Nothing to do with how you look in the mirror or even what title you have in front of your name."

"It's your belief in a higher purpose," Sylvia says, and Lester gasps and clutches his chest dramatically, as if shot with an arrow. He reels backward and stumbles around the room. Finally, he gathers himself and leans on the table across from Sylvia, looking directly at her.

"Yes," he says with an air of catharsis. "That's exactly it. The belief in a higher purpose ... And it's important you understand that, if not for this belief, The Pyramid would never have been envisioned in the first place, much less actually built."

"Yet, it could be argued that no two people have the exact same concept of their higher purpose."

"Yes … and therein lies the problem, as it were. I suppose democracy was originally envisioned as the ideal solution, however, as we all know—"

"Spare us the ideological horseshit, Ginn. Don't you even care about getting your son back?"

"Funny you should mention it, although you make it sound as though he were a lost puppy or set of mittens found in the schoolyard. I love my son, Mr. Jipt. That is a fact I dare you to refute. But he's a grown man who may return at his leisure and of his own volition. That is, unless someone were preventing him from doing so, yes? By holding him captive, for example? Is that what you're implying, Mr. Jipt, that you're holding my son against his will?"

"I think this is a conversation we need to have man to man."

"Very well. Ms. King—"

"Fine with me, as long as I get a private meeting too."

"Mr. Jipt, is this agreeable?"

"I suppose."

"You see? Now we're really making some progress."

* * *

Yet another premature dusk has fallen due to The Black Balloon, and the Apex Conference room has become a bit chilly, so Lester starts a fire burning in the hearth. With his back to Jipt, he tends to it with the poker in one hand and the shovel in the other hand, poking and prodding the few remaining logs from his once-abundant stockpile.

"The way I see it," Lester says, "the derivation of our problem is not unlike this very fire. You see, it requires a lot of maintenance at the beginning, doesn't it? Making sure the logs have a good burn going on them. The goal is to reach a point where you can sit back and enjoy the heat, right? And ... I'd say we're there now. Yes, you can already feel things warming up a bit. And this fire will now burn for hours, unless of course—" Lester reaches in and catches the flue handle with the hooked end of the poker. Then he closes the glass doors, and it's only a matter of seconds before the flame begins to weaken in the oxygen-poor environment. "Someone cuts off a vital resource ... then all you get is smoke ..." He reopens the doors and, indeed, smoke billows out into the room. He reopens the flue and pokes at the logs until, once again, the fire is burning vigorously.

"Sure, but the fire will go out by itself, too, if you don't throw another log on there once and a while," Jipt says.

"Another log representing what, exactly?"

"What do you mean, representing what?"

"In the analogy."

"To hell with the analogy, Ginn. Let's boil this down. I've got something you want, and you've got something I want, so what do you say we make a deal?"

"And what is it that you want, Mr. Jipt?"

"All I want is to see this place realize its full potential. I mean, for chrissakes Ginn, we're sitting on top of a goldmine here, literally. You take those couple-hundred-thousand units of yours and turn them into hotel rooms, and we'd knock profits out of the ballpark."

"I'm not concerned—"

"I know," Jipt interrupts him. "You're not concerned about profits. You're concerned about the welfare of the people who live here, right?"

"Yes."

"Well, that's understandable, but let me tell you a story."

"Very well," Lester grumbles, turning his back again to tend the fire.

"I once knew a man by the name of Deerfield, who manufactured farm equipment. Deerfield Machines out of Houston. He was a hell of a businessman, could talk a dog off a meat wagon, and he built the company up from nothing. Before long his tractors and threshers were the industry standard, best you could buy. His prices were good, too. Very competitive. Not only that, but his employees loved him. Between the three factories, and the corporate offices, he had about five thousand people and they all loved him because he was honest and fair, not to mention a whiskey-drinkin', pickup truck drivin', good 'ole southern boy at heart. Anyway, a number of years went by and Mr. Deerfield became a very rich man. More money than he knew what to do with as a matter of fact, so he decided to give something back to his people, in appreciation of their hard work. And I'm not talking about a five percent Christmas bonus here, either. I'm talking about doubling and tripling salaries, company cars, company planes, box seats to football games, you name it. The guy went way the hell overboard is my point. And you know what happened?"

Lester gazes into the fire, studies it like he would a creature having emerged from outer space to share the secrets of the universe. Yet, remarkably, he heard Jipt's story from beginning to end – and even more remarkably, it makes perfect sense to him. "Productivity went down," he says in a distant voice.

"Absolutely right," Jipt says, his tone giving Lester credit only for stating the obvious.

"Quality suffered," Lester adds.

"Yup, that too. But he was past the point of no return. He couldn't roll back the benefits otherwise he'd have a angry mob on his hands. So he did the easiest thing he could do to hold the line."

"He raised prices."

"You bet he did. Meanwhile, his customers started dropping like flies, and the ones who stuck with him were riding him like a rented mule. After all, these are farmers we're talking about, who barely scrape by. They didn't take too well to the news that one of Deerfield's assembly line workers was bringin' home more in a month than—"

"Enough already! How does the bloody thing end? No! Let me guess. He sells out to his competition and retires in the tropics."

"No. The board forced him to resign and three months later he shot himself. But, yeah, if he was smart he'd be sitting on a beach somewhere, sipping rum from a goddamned coconut."

Lester wheels on Jipt with a look that could melt glass, a borderline demonic look, as if he's somehow absorbed the energy from the fire, harnessed it, and then unleashed it through his eyes. He crosses to within a few steps of his nemesis, still clutching both the fireplace poker and shovel, and says, "On your feet."

"Ginn, I don't know—"

"On your feet!"

Jipt pushes his chair back and rises, sighing through a visage tailor-made for antipathy. Meanwhile, Lester tosses the fireplace poker into the air, leaving Jipt little choice but to catch it. He does so, and the antipathy gives way to guarded consternation. Lester takes another step closer and Jipt fumbles for the handle, assuming a position of self-defense. "We both know there's only one way to settle this," he says, spreading his arms and arching his back so his chest protrudes between the lapels of his jacket. "Strike me down."

"Forget it, Ginn, I ain't doing it."

"Strike me down, coward! Put me out of my misery!"

"I said I ain't doing it, you demented sonofabitch!"

Like a spring-loaded mousetrap, Lester snaps to action. The shovel cuts a perfect arc across Jipt's flinching body, connecting with the poker near its midpoint. Neither man turns to watch as it clatters loudly across the floor. Then, fearing a backhand strike, Jipt charges Lester and pounds him square in the chest with both forearms at once, like a fullback knocking a linebacker out of the hole. The anterior of Lester's skull hits the floor first, rendering him unconscious, and the force is so great that his limp body slides all the way into the fireplace hearth, where the flames take but an instant to engulf his upper torso.

Upon awakening only a few moments later, Lester finds Jipt sprawled on top of him, frantically snuffing out the last of the corduroy hot spots with his bare hands. Then both men freeze for an instant as their eyes meet with sudden awkwardness, a mutual sense of embarrassment – perhaps even shame – belying their diametrically opposed wrath. They separate quickly, each regaining his feet, and with as much dignity as possible Lester totters down the stairs without uttering another word.

Chapter 67

Lester and Sylvia stand at one end of the now-ill-maintained horseshoe pitch and, incidentally, Lester is fairly unkempt himself, having hastened to wash up and change clothes after his encounter with Jipt. As much as he'd like to do so, he cannot attribute to mere coincidence the fact that he emerged bearing few, if any, noticeable indications of the fiasco that occurred. A partial singeing of the eyebrows. A lump on the back of his head. A painful recollection of Jipt's minty-fresh breath.

Sylvia throws a horseshoe much too low and it bounces a good ten feet in front of the stake.

"Try delaying your release a bit longer. What you want is a nice loft, a gentle rotation and just float it onto the stake …" Lester demonstrates, throwing a horseshoe just as he's described, and it hits the stake with a resounding *Clang!* "Like so. You know how they say close only counts in horseshoes and hand grenades? Well, I beg to differ. Because you have the natural truths of the world, right? Atomic structure, gravity, hunger and thirst – try again."

Sylvia throws her other shoe. It has better trajectory than the first and lands in the pit this time, very close to the stake.

"Ha ha! How about that? Yes … and then you have the metaphorical truths, the abstract truths like those represented in the hierarchy of needs, right? They're pure only in concept, we'll never realize a whole and perfect feeling of any kind – but we can try our best to get close, can't we? You see, this place is designed to fulfill those two base needs as absolutely as possible, so one may focus his energies on fulfilling the remaining five for himself."

"Including the higher purpose."

"Yes, naturally." *Clang!*

"Well, I'm dying to know what that is, Mr. Ginn, for you."

"Please, call me Lester."

"Okay, Lester. I mean, why are you doing this?"

"Go ahead with your other throw, then I'll tell you."

Clang! Sylvia's horseshoe hits the stake dead-on for a ringer.

"Bravo! Well done."

"Well?"

"Why am I doing this? Right. Well, it's about freedom, really. You see, at one time, freedom was largely defined by one's ability to go wherever he wanted, whenever he wanted. To say anything he wanted and to eat anything he wanted and to spend his money any way he wanted. You remember that?"

"You don't think freedom is still defined that way?"

"*Defined* that way, perhaps, yes. In theory. But in practice, it became a different story altogether as our once-vital, once-brave societies were infiltrated by fear, and infused with it down to the core. Fear of losing our basic needs, or worse yet, our very lives."

"You're talking about the Corporate Wars."

"Yes, certainly, they were a major part of it, along with other factors, but the crux of the issue – what I'm arguing here – is that fear itself is the chief agent of subterfuge – the antithesis of freedom – and, therefore, the only way to grant people true freedom is to remove fear from the equation entirely."

"And the only way to do that … is to seal them up in a giant pyramid? Isolated from the rest of society?"

"Well, again … You have to understand that this, too, was but a theory. Which, in practice, has proven round about fifty percent effective to date, give or take."

"Not too bad, I guess, considering," Sylvia says. "But what about the fact that, for every person in here there are literally thousands upon thousands of people out there who are struggling every day, suffering every day, just to make a living. Just to feed their children. And for what? Not for their own higher purpose but for yours, Lester. Think about the fundamental injustice in that."

"Indeed, I have thought about it. Long and hard. And all those individuals I mentioned, who wish to leave The Pyramid, will soon be free to do so."

"And you'll meet all our original demands?"

"Yes."

"Well! That's wonderful news. I must say, this is all very unexpected. I've had this image of you in my head all this time and …"

"I'm not the autocratic madman you thought I was?"

"Are you kidding? I just don't get it, Lester. Why haven't you defended yourself against all these blatantly false claims Seth Jipt and the others have been making?"

"So you never believed that I tried to kill my own son?"

"Not *now* I don't."

"Oh, bollocks," Lester says, rubbing his scalp. "I suppose maybe I should have challenged them … but that's not to say anyone would have believed me."

"You don't know until you try … So, how did your *other meeting* go?"

"With Mr. Jipt?" Lester says biliously. "I refuse to negotiate with scoundrels."

"So you didn't tell him about …"

"Heavens no."

"What are we going to do about him?"

"I don't see why we need to do anything."

"Can't you find someone else to run The Casino?"

"Believe me, if I could just sack Jipt and be done with it, I would have already done so with utter delight. But it's not that simple. You see, ironic as i'tis, Mr. Jipt was instrumental in bringing The Pyramid to fruition. He brokered the deal for our water supply, for one thing, and on top of that he raised a great deal of investment capital."

"But I thought you used—"

"The money I inherited, yes, but it wasn't nearly enough to complete a project of this magnitude. The fact is, we relied heavily on outside investors, and most of that capital was garnered by Mr. Jipt."

"He wants rid of you, Lester, and rid of The Union too, for that matter. We've already seen the measures he's willing to take. I'm just afraid—"

"Please, don't be afraid. I appreciate your concern, but I think it's only a matter of time before Mr. Jipt is exposed for what he really is."

"Yeah, a greedy, cold-hearted motherfucker. Excuse my language."

"Perhaps. But, you know, if there is one frightening aspect to this situation it's that you and I aren't all that different from Mr. Jipt, are we? I mean, think about it. We're all very ambitious people."

"Sure, but—"

"You and I have a higher purpose, whereas Mr. Jipt has no purpose outside of feeding his own appetite for wealth and power."

"Like I said, he's a greedy motherfucker. Well, if there's anything else I can do to help going forward ..."

"Actually, you can answer one more question for me."

"Sure."

"These people you represent, the card dealers, the maids and cooks and waitresses, what makes you think The Pyramid will solve all their problems? After all, it's already failed to do so for a vast number of my original inhabitants?"

"I don't know," Sylvia says. "There aren't any guarantees, but maybe the difference will be in expectations, you know? Because they're not expecting The Pyramid to solve all their problems. Just one or two at the top of the list."

* * *

Meanwhile, back in the Apex Conference Room, Jipt is slumped down in one of the plush chairs, fast asleep. His back is to the staircase, so all Chutney can see is his feet.

"Lester?" she says, although she's never seen him in wingtips.

Jipt wakes up and spins around in the chair. "Huh. No. Uh, excuse me ..." He jumps to his feet, overeager to be polite and clearly intimidated by her beauty. "Seth Jipt, pleasure to meet you."

"Madeline Chutney."

"Doctor Chutney."

"Yes. Sorry to disturb you, but where's Lester?"

"Not really sure. Last I heard he went off to throw horseshoes with Sylvia."

"Sylvia King?"

"Yup. Please, have a seat."

"No, thank you."

"Oh, come on," Jipt says. "I've been sitting here for ..." He looks at his garish platinum, diamond-studded watch. "Over an hour, now. I'm getting lonely."

"Well, all right. Just for a minute, though. I don't think Lester would appreciate me being so friendly, you being his nemesis and all," Chutney says with a straight face. They sit.

"Dr. Chutney, you know Ginn – Lester – you know him well – maybe better than anybody. So tell me, has he always been like this? Had this … tunnel vision, where all other viewpoints – hell, all rational thought whatsoever – is completely blocked out?"

"Lester is … a unique thinker, Mr. Jipt. A visionary some might say. However, he does have a severe – almost fatalistic – case of idealism."

"You care for him a great deal, don't you?"

"Yes, I do."

"So, if you knew he was in trouble, you'd want to help."

"Of course. What kind of trouble are you referring to?"

"Well, first of all, let me say this. If you don't believe what I'm about to tell you, I understand one hundred percent. Lester and I have been butting heads since the second we met, and over the years I've done some things I'm not too proud of. It's kind of like the boy crying wolf, I know, but sometimes there really is a wolf out there."

"Yes, well, I can't promise I'll believe you. But I am listening."

"Fair enough. Now, keep in mind, too, I'm only telling you this for two reasons – perfectly honest. One, I've tried getting through to Lester directly and it's no use. Like I said, the man is stubborn as a – well, he's real stubborn."

"Granted."

"And two, your helping him would be the best thing for everyone involved in this situation, and I'll admit that includes myself. See, the federal government has thought all along they'd be better off keeping their hands clean of our business out here, for a lot of reasons. But recently, they've begun to think otherwise."

"Lester's meeting with the president wasn't exactly a smashing success from what I heard. Although I suppose it's all the rumors, too?"

"Yeah, but the human rights thing is only the public side of the story. Fact is, they want their hands in the cookie jar, tax-wise, which is where I take issue. Now, I still have a few friends in Washington I consider pretty reliable sources, and the word is, they've got some charges trumped up on Lester. Tax evasion, racketeering, god knows what else."

"What does that mean?"

"It means they're going to arrest him. By force if necessary."

"Oh my god, when?"

"I don't know, and I'm not sure that I will. It could be any time."

Chutney takes a long, penetrating look at Jipt. "You told Lester this?"

"Sure did. And he laughed in my face."

"Well, even if I believe it, I don't think that will convince him to leave, if that's what you're asking."

"Well, I kind of guessed as much … so I've got a plan B. Thing is, it involves some degree of subterfuge."

"Subterfuge?"

"Secrecy, tact, and maybe a little luck. Does Lester sleep at night?"

"A few hours at least, maybe two 'til seven or eight."

"You think someone could slip him something, to make him sleep a little better?"

"His wife, I guess. She'd have to be in on it anyway. Then what?"

"Well, the way I see it, I'd send in a team of my own during the night, posing as the feds. That way, if the sedative doesn't work, he's less likely to resist."

"No guns," Chutney says.

"No guns," Jipt says. They'll just scoop him up and y'all can leave together. We'll have a plane waiting at the airport to take you anyplace you want. The Islands, Europe, wherever you want."

"He loves this place."

"I know. But I think this is the only way he'll ever set foot in it again."

"What makes you think the government won't come back for him, if he returns in the future?"

"I can't say for sure they won't, but considering this whole thing is politically motivated to begin with, I'm guessing their window of opportunity is pretty narrow here, you know what I'm saying? In a year or so nobody will give a damn."

"What about—"

"Tim? As you know, he's already in our custody, safe and sound. Call me." Jipt hands Chutney a business card and she takes it, eyeing him skeptically. Then she hears someone bounding up the stairs.

"Mr. Jipt, I think it's time you—"Lester reaches the top of the stairs and is suddenly taken aback upon seeing Chutney and Jipt together. "Got going ..."

Chapter 68

S vetlana rejects Lester's proposal by turning over and nestling deeper into her side of the bed. He had hoped to rekindle the bygone spontaneity and joie de vivre of their "wake up and dance" ritual, and he is disappointed by her lack of willingness. However, what's even more troubling is the notion that he doesn't feel much like dancing himself. It's simply the *idea* of dancing that appeals to him – and, instead of pursuing the idea further, he marches off to the Mail Closet, where he plans to indulge his self-pity with the nastiest, most spiteful and offensive letters he can get his hands on.

It doesn't take long to find just the toxic medicine he seeks, in the form of a note hand-written in crimson ink, or perhaps even blood. It is riddled with fully capitalized and underlined words, profanity and exclamation marks, not to mention egregious misspellings and grammatical *faux pas*. The author wantonly indulges herself in numerous tangents about her own destitute state of affairs – that is, since her application for Pyramid inhabitance was denied – but the general theme is that Lester embodies nothing less than the devil himself.

Another, slightly more urbane, slightly more pedantic, letter draws well-documented parallels between Lester and history's most ruthless dictators. However, most of the allegations are highly circumstantial and speculative to say the least.

Yet another overzealous antagonist credits Lester with triggering the chain of events that will eventually destroy all mankind. And while he knows the facts are on his side, that these opinions are largely grounded in repeated personal failure and subjection to lies, he cannot discount the genuineness of the feelings behind them. The anger and bitterness. The hopelessness and heartbreak. He cannot deny the inherent truth of their existence, and the fact that his legacy will be marred by them. Then again, he thinks, *What difference does it make, anyway? Death is the consummate slate-cleaner.*

With that, he marches back into the bedroom and announces, "Svety, let's go to The Arcade!"

"Huh?"

"The Arcade! We haven't been there in so long!"

"I want to sleep."

"Oh, come on! We can play skeeball! And the game you love with the gopher and the big rubber mallet! Maybe you can win a stuffed animal!"

"Maybe later."

"Oh, come on!" Lester says, bouncing on the edge of the mattress. "It'll be fun! Just you and me! It'll be so much fun!"

"Fine."

"We can drive the go-karts and play mini-golf!"

"I said fine," Svetlana says, rolling over but not bothering to open her eyes.

"You want to?"

"No, but I'll do it anyway."

"Why?"

"Because I love you."

"You do?"

"Sometimes I forget why, but yes, I do."

"Oh, I love you too!" Lester says, kissing her on the neck repeatedly like a woodpecker. "But I want you to *want* to go. For yourself."

"Okay, I want to go."

"You're just saying that."

"Yes."

"All right, well ... let's get our clothes on, then."

* * *

Just a short time spent in The Arcade proves that Lester's enthusiasm is still contagious, and that Svetlana's emotional immune system has yet to develop antibodies against it.

"Hey! You cut me off!" Lester shouts over the ruckus of electric go-kart motors and bouncy pop music.

"And I'll do it again!" Svetlana hollers back, swerving in front of him as they hit the brief straightaway and continue zipping around the track, which carves a figure-eight through the maze of video games, pinball machines and various carnival-style amusements. Lester has given Svetlana the faster car on purpose, because her happiness is the top priority.

After driving themselves to a fever of uncontrollable laughter and dizziness, they move on to other diversions, including the aforementioned game of "Get the Gopher," where the object is to bash the lovable rodent with a mallet when he pops up from a series of holes. Svetlana bests her all-time high and collapses to the plush, carpeted floor, ecstatic yet thoroughly exhausted. Lester flops down on top of her and sweeps a lock of tousled hair out of her eyes. She's laughing so hard that her whole body shudders, so hard that tears begin to flow over her apple-red cheeks.

Lester wishes he could hit PAUSE on a master control panel, he wishes he could freeze this moment in time before it inevitably changes to something else, something more realistic. And before he can finish this thought, Svetlana's disposition makes a subtle, almost graceful, transition from giddy laughter to frantic sobbing.

"What's the matter?" Lester says.

"Nothing."

"Svety, really. What is it?"

"I don't know. Everything."

This is not what Lester had expected her to say, and the sudden poignancy of it strikes a direct blow to his heart, like news of a death in the family. His mind is devoid of words, his skin devoid of feeling and his ears deaf to all but the sound of his own blood flow. Yet he can see, more clearly than ever, the crystalline fear brimming in Svetlana's eyes. It's painfully difficult to look at, yet he can't bear to turn away.

Chapter 69

Since its inception, The Pyramid has represented something of a quandary for the media. On one hand, the dribs and drabs of information coming *out* of the void have been tantamount to an ancient tome, written in a dead language, that only one human being has the knowledge to interpret. In other words, his translation must be accepted as fact. And consequently, vetting and verifying all the accusations directed *toward* The Pyramid has been like trying to catch a school of minnows with chopsticks. As a result, the paradigms of journalistic integrity have shifted to a report-everything-now-and-let-the-public-sort-it-out-later code of ethics. In many regards this has worked in Lester's favor – and in many regards this has worked against him.

With that said, only time will tell which effect this morning's proceedings will have on popular opinion. After all, it's an altogether unique situation, with Sylvia and Jipt having just emerged hours earlier from the unannounced, yet much anticipated, summit meeting with (arguably) the world's most elusive figure, Lester Ginn. Compounding matters is the fact that their respective press conferences are being held simultaneously, in different locations. This not only divides the media but also popular opinion, which, in essence, has been reduced to a popularity contest.

Indeed, as one might expect, the stories being told by the former and present mayors are as different as shit and sugar …

* * *

"Meeting face-to-face with Mr. Ginn simply confirmed my worst fears about his regime of manipulation and madness. I have no doubt that he is a danger to every human being inside The Pyramid," Jipt says, his head bobbing up and down as he recites from a written statement, which was composed with no small amount of help from his wife, Lynette.

* * *

"Lester Ginn contradicted just about every assumption I had previously made about him, based on a series of allegations that I now know to be politically motivated and blatantly false," Sylvia says, making eye-contact with nearly everyone in the room. This is a rare case in which she has written and memorized a statement, because she knows that affability is far less important than quotability in addressing this particular audience.

* * *

"Despite Mr. Ginn's stubbornness and defiance, I was able to negotiate the release of approximately 100,000 individuals who have been living under the thumb of his brutal dictatorship. However, considering his extensive record of deceit, I have little confidence that he will make good on his promise," Jipt says with a frown.

* * *

"I am pleased to announce that Mr. Ginn has agreed to meet all original demands laid out by The Casino Workers Union of PyraVegas. This includes a stipulation to accommodate Union members as residents in The Pyramid, pending the emigration of approximately 100,000 current residents," Sylvia says with a smile.

* * *

"Furthermore," Jipt says. "I have every belief that Mr. Ginn's perpetration of communist indoctrination and brainwashing will continue and possibly even escalate."

* * *

"And I can also say with a great degree of confidence," Sylvia says, "after speaking with Mr. Ginn at great length, that his intentions are, and have always been, virtuous, if not noble. If he can be accused of anything, it's over-optimism and an unwillingness to compromise his principles."

* * *

"No, Mr. Ginn did not deny trying to murder his son, Tim, who has chosen to remain sequestered until further resolution can be brought to the situation," Jipt says.

* * *

"Mr. Ginn vehemently denied these allegations of attempted murder, and personally, I find it curious that his son, the alleged victim, has yet to issue a public statement, instead remaining in the dubious custody of Mr. Seth Jipt," Sylvia says.

* * *

"I have no further comments at this time," Jipt says.

* * *

"I'd be happy to answer more questions later today, once I've had a chance to review the transcript of Mr. Jipt's statements," Sylvia says.

* * *

And thus, the frenzy begins. Among the anchors and pundits, few will deny the magnitude of this day, yet none will predict the drama with which it will end.

Chapter 70

One might argue that it's an inherent trait of human beings – a natural desire – to want to rebuild things of ours that have been destroyed. Sand castles, card houses, teepees, churches, office buildings. And not only to rebuild them as they were before, but to make them bigger and better, especially when the destruction was incurred by other human beings. It is trait that, if sought in a hierarchical classification system, might be found under Ego, with Ego of course being a major subset of Pride.

Assuming one accepts this line of reasoning it is interesting, not to mention salient, in the context of this story, to note that Seth Jipt's ego has been destroyed at least twice over the course of his life. The first perpetrator was his father, a mean, rattlesnake of a man, who began his assault on young Seth's fragile psyche before he could even comprehend the English language. At first, his intentions were not malicious. He simply came from a school of thought that held up proving someone wrong as the key catalyst for ambition. As a result, he (figuratively and, on occasion, literally) beat the idea into his son's head that he would never amount to anything. Then, later in his life, around the time Jipt graduated from high school, he honed the message somewhat. Then it essentially became, *You'll never amount to anything unless you follow in my footsteps.* In other words, taking over his oil business, which, of course, Jipt chose not to do.

So, as he built his career in the gaming industry, he rebuilt his ego at the same time. Then Lynette came along. Through the newlywed period, say two or three years into their marriage, Jipt could do no wrong. She couldn't say enough about how proud she was of him and how successful she thought he could become. But, in fact, enough was never enough. Pretty soon, even before he would reach one career milestone she'd be touting the significance of the next one. Then, when The Pyramid came along, all other milestones fell away, and, as far as Lynette was concerned, assuming total control became an all-or-nothing affair.

Thus, Jipt finds himself wallowing in the depths of his life's second ego trough. And, irrational as it may be, he's decided the only way to restore his ego, and to prove both his (deceased) father and Lynette wrong, is to reach that ultimate milestone – assuming total control of The Pyramid.

In the language of American football, it's "crunchtime." Fourth and goal with only seconds remaining in the game. Which is why Jipt has decided to dial up his secret weapon, Major General Vernon Bossy.

"I sure hope you're serious this time, Seth," Bossy says, spitting into his ubiquitous coffee mug bearing the slogan, COFFEE GOES WELL WITH PEOPLE LIKE YOU, BECAUSE I EAT PEOPLE LIKE YOU FOR BREAKFAST. The phrase is so long that it's taken three meetings for Jipt to read the whole thing, and he's sure that Bossy must have had it custom-made, because surely no self-respecting professional slogan-writer would be so wordy.

"I'm serious this time," Jipt grumbles. "We've got no choice but to do this now, before he releases those people."

"Well, that's good to hear. I anticipated this would be a quick turnaround, so I've had my teams standing by for the past couple weeks now. We'll just debrief 'em one last time, gas up, lock and load, and get this thing done."

"No guns though," Jipt says.

Bossy spits again and sighs as if to say, *Let me tell you something about the guns.* "Seth, we've been over this. These are my men, and I'm not sending them into a hostile environment without firepower. Why don't you ask those guys still in the hospital right now what can happen."

"But I promised—"

"I don't give a rat's ass who you promised. It's my way or the highway, buddy."

Oddly, Jipt is less incensed by Bossy's mulish attitude than he is by being addressed as a buddy. He can only imagine what Hawkins would say about the gun issue, much less the invasion plan as a whole, if he were here. On one hand, Jipt feels terrible about letting him go. But on the other hand, he's relieved, because it's like a part of his conscience has been surgically removed – the part that would have prevented him from making a brazen, unilateral decision such as this.

Chapter 71

Although it would never occur to her, Svetlana's life can be compared to the making of a baseball. She started out as a simple ball of cork, a buoyant child resistant to the flames of social turmoil raging across her native Russia. As she grew older, and more perceptive, she compensated for her lost naïveté by developing a thick skin – a coating of rubber around the cork, protecting her innocence and supplying a much-needed bounce in her step. When she finished high school and started working to support herself, in a series of dead-end jobs, the harsh realities began to wrap her tighter and tighter, like 150 yards of cotton yarn wrapped around her core being. Then she moved to America, to pursue a college degree in biology. The rigors of academia, along with the looming threat of financial peril, wrapped her even tighter – with an additional 219 yards of wool yarn. She managed to graduate, but she did so without aspiration or purpose. The global economy was in shambles, job markets dried up everywhere. She was a useless ball of string about to unravel.

Then she met Lester Ginn. He was borderline dangerous, yet alive with ideas and optimism. He was often preoccupied, yet strangely attuned to her innermost desires. His sentences were often left incomplete, yet he completed her. His unfailing belief in her potential served as the cowhide, and his impassioned love resembled the 108 stitches that held her life together at the seams.

* * *

As contrived coincidence would have it, Svetlana's favorite reading spot of late has been the supple, brown leather chair shaped like a baseball glove. It's located in The Library, which not only offers convenient access to reading materials but also a quiet, cozy atmosphere reminiscent of another time and place altogether. Devoid of all the blinking lights and computer monitors indicative of man's technological advancements, The Library is insulated from the outside world by towering bookshelves stacked floor-to-ceiling with everything from encyclopedias to erotica.

More and more lately, Svetlana has been using books as a means of escape from her own growing anxiety. Mostly romance novels but also some thrillers and horror stories, anything that keeps the pages turning. At present, she's curled up in the baseball glove with an epic wartime love story called Victory's Graveyard. Candlelight and classical music fill the air.

"Does he love her?" Chutney says, leaning on one of the bookcases.

"Oh, hey Chutney, you scared me. How long have you been standing there?"

"About an hour."

"No."

"No, just a few seconds. You seem really wrapped up in that book."

"It's very good. Sad, but good. Have you read it?"

"A long, long time ago. So what do you think?"

"I think he loves her. But with the war and everything, he may not realize it until it's too late."

"Sounds strangely familiar. I don't even remember how it ends. Probably for the best, so I don't spoil it for you."

Svetlana's thoughts have already sunk their hooks into reality again – past and present, but largely the uncertain future. She is aware of the long pause in conversation, her blurred vision and the listing of her head to one side, yet, as if hypnotized, she cannot break the spell without assistance.

"Svetlana, there's something important I need to tell you."

"What? I'm sorry, I …"

Just then, Anna rounds the corner with a book in hand. "Oh, hey mom, I thought I'd find you here. Hey Chutney … What? What's going on?"

"We were just talking about the novel your mom's reading, some dreadful love story," Chutney says with an atypically strained smile.

"Figures. What's yours about?"

"Sorry?"

"Your book."

"Oh, it's about socialism," Chutney says, looking down at the cover as if she weren't sure.

"Like communism?"

"Sort of. Socialism provides – nevermind, I'm sure you don't want to get me started."

"No, really. I've always been confused about the difference."

"Well, simply put, socialism provides according to one's contribution to society, whereas communism provides according to one's needs, irregardless."

"Gotcha … So, what happened yesterday? I heard that Jipt guy was here."

"I was actually just about to share some news with your mom, so I'm glad you're here."

"Is he going to let Tim go?"

"Sort of, yes."

"What do you mean, sort of? I'll kill that son of a bitch if he so much as—"

"Let me explain everything," Chutney says, taking a seat on the heel of the baseball glove, by Svetlana's pink-slipper-clad feet. "Why don't you sit over here, Anna."

"Geez, this must be heavy stuff, if we all have to be sitting down."

"It is. In fact, what I'm about to tell you needs to stay between the three of us. And that includes Lester. Now, Svetlana, I know this sounds rather ... well, husbands and wives aren't normally supposed to keep secrets from one another ..."

"I haven't even seen Lester since this morning," Svetlana says, her voice suddenly glinting with an edge of provocation.

"You haven't?" Chutney asks.

"No. Have you?"

"No."

They turn to Anna. "Don't look at me," she says.

"What time is it?" Chutney says.

"Nine-fifteen," Anna says.

"Okay. We need to find him and have him to bed by midnight, or else we're going to have major problems."

"We don't have major problems now?" Anna says half-jokingly. "I mean, we don't even have electricity most of the time."

"Chutney," Svetlana says, with a tone of pleading now. "I don't know how much longer I can ... you know, carry on like this."

"Me either," Anna says. I don't see why we can't just tell Lester we're leaving unless he—"

"I know, I know," Chutney says. "That's why I'm here. There's a way out, girls, but it's not going to be easy. You've got to trust me, and do exactly as I say ... and even then, we'll probably need more than a little bit of luck, as well ..."

Chapter 72

It's one of the worst nightmares Lester has ever experienced, and he's had his fair share of them. Ogres wielding morning stars. Fiery pits opening up in the earth. Locusts, vultures and sharks. Endless corridors and toothless executioners … the gamut. But, at least in those situations he could apply a modicum of reasoning. Tonight's feature is terrifying because it *defies* reason altogether.

In the dream, Lester sees himself from a third-person perspective, which wouldn't be so awful if he weren't a person at all but a disembodied blob slithering through an endless maze of tubes and circuits. Whether he's a single-celled organism or simply a bead of mercury is unclear. And, since he has no brain, he is not capable of rationalization. He's trapped, cut off from his conscious self and, therefore, unable to open his eyes. Of course, the opiate isn't helping either.

Of the various zones and themes within the bedroom quadrant, Lester and Svetlana have long-since settled into the roomiest and most tastefully decorated milieu. The bed itself is dimly aglow with the lights of PyraVegas twinkling through the windows, and Svetlana lies awake beside Lester, watching the shadows, waiting for something to happen. After some time, a single figure appears from behind one of the partitions – a woman. She crosses to the bed and sits down beside Lester.

"Chutney," Svetlana whispers. "What are you doing here?"

Without acknowledging the question, she says, "Lester. Lester, wake up," as she clasps one of his hands between hers.

"Mmmm … Errrr," Lester moans, trying to claw his way back to awareness.

"What's wrong?" Svetlana says, but again Chutney ignores her.

"Lester, wake up! It's Chutney! Please wake up!"

"Huh? Oh. Chutney, thank god … You saved me from the purgatory of that dream. I don't even know how to recount it."

"Lester, I think I've made a dreadful mistake! Jipt told me the government was coming for you so we should get you out and so his men are coming but I think it's all a lie and I don't know what he's really going to do and – my god I'm sorry Lester! I'm so sorry!" Tears stream down her cheeks and she squeezes Lester's hand.

"Shh shh shh … it's all right. It's quite all right. Don't you worry about it. You were just doing what your heart told you to do."

"Lester, did you hear what I said? He's—"

"Coming to get me, yes. And it's about bloody time," Lester says, laboriously jacking himself upright with a groan.

"What do you mean? You mean you—"

"Knew all about it, yes."

"You knew about it and you didn't say anything?" Svetlana says, although her tone reflects her awareness that she, too, is guilty of keeping secrets.

"Well, I didn't know anything for sure, so I didn't want to alarm anyone. But I had a strong suspicion Mr. Jipt's patience would soon run out."

"When are they getting here?" Svetlana says. "What are we going to do?"

"I'll seal everything off," Chutney says, regaining her typical composure. "I'll just change the access codes."

"No. Let them come," Lester says. "And let's get all our essential belongings together if we haven't already, okay? Cherished keepsakes, heirlooms … we can get new sundries and the like. Svety, I'm afraid you'll have to leave most of your wardrobe behind."

"I don't care about that," she says wide-eyed, her expression a delicate balance of hope and regret. "You mean we're …"

"Yes," Lester says. His demeanor is grave, yet uncomplaining. "I assume Anna is close at hand, so let's get her rounded up and I'll explain the details over tea."

"But there's no time," Chutney pleads. "They're supposed to be here any minute and—"

"Oh, come now," Lester reassures her. "There's always time for tea."

Chapter 73

Sandeep's dream is all lollipops and ice cream cones – metaphorically speaking, that is. He lies flat on his back, snoring lightly. But when he hears the sound of the bell his eyes pop open with animatronic keenness. Lester's image appears before him, as it does every morning. But Sandeep knows it's not morning yet, and his gut tells him something's wrong.

"Please wake up," Lester says, still jingling the tiny brass bell as one might entertain a baby with a rattle. "Thank you. I apologize for the early arousal, but certain circumstances necessitate our meeting without delay. You'll be arriving at The Arena shortly, so please get dressed as quickly as possible. Or don't get dressed if you like, it makes no difference to me. Well, see you soon!"

* * *

The Arena is about a quarter full when Sandeep reaches his seat. Spotlights swirl around the football field and around the crowd, making for an expectant atmosphere. A man in the row behind him leans forward and says, "What do you think this is all about?"

Sandeep swivels around and discovers the Rabbi he met on the very first day. The man is easy to recognize since he's wearing the same traditional uniform. "Hello!" Sandeep says excitedly. "I think we met before, at the pond, remember? You were racing sailboats."

"Yes, of course," the Rabbi says. "How have you been getting along?"

424

"Well, it's been kind of tough lately, but I'm still here."

"Blackouts or no, it still beats what you had before, eh?"

Sandeep nods his head. "I don't know what this is all about. You never really know with Lester though, I guess."

"Some good news is what I'm praying for. Like an end to the strike finally."

"I still don't understand exactly what's going on with that," Sandeep says. "What do they want?"

"I'd imagine the same things we wanted, when we applied to live here in the first place."

* * *

Jipt's paramilitary convoy consists of four bus-like personnel carriers, each holding 50 men, in addition to the armored jeep carrying himself and Major General Bossy in the back seat. On The Pyramid's south side, they've stopped just short of where the train tracks disappear below ground. Bossy has decided to send his teams on foot from here, to avoid having their vehicles trapped in a quagmire, and he barks commands to one of his lieutenants through a two-way radio as he chews on the butt of a cigar.

"We're in position up here," says a voice crackling over the airwaves. "Locked and loaded."

Bossy turns sharply to Jipt. "You ready?"

Jipt nods his head.

"All right," Bossy says, keying the radio again. "Let's make this short and sweet, men. Go, go, go!"

Jipt cracks the tinted window and peers out into the semi-darkness as men in black fatigues, armed to the teeth, pour out of their vehicles and disappear into the tunnel. Despite the fact that he hasn't eaten for nearly 24 hours, Jipt feels oddly bloated, as if all the malevolence and avarice deep inside him has congealed into a noxious slime. He pushes open the door and retches, but nothing comes out.

* * *

The Arena is now close to half-full, which means all remaining inhabitants have arrived (those who had requested to leave were allowed to do so just hours before). The lights go down, and the air buzzes with anticipation for about a minute before the darkness is broken by four stationary spotlights trained on something at mid-field.

It is a sort of canopied alter, with four main posts and a silky fabric draped over top, like a handkerchief over a birdcage, such that only a man's shadowy, silhouetted figure is visible inside. A chant of "Les-ter! Les-ter! Les-ter!" arises from somewhere in the upper deck and proliferates quickly through Sandeep's section. He recoils back through memory to the afternoon of his initial interview, when Lester saved his life, and a sense of fervent patriotism suddenly fills his veins with adrenaline. He pumps his arm in the air and joins wholeheartedly in yelling, "Les-ter! Les-ter! Les-ter!"

"Welcome once again," Lester's voice booms throughout the cavernous Arena. "I appreciate the sacrifice you've all made, of your restful, nourishing sleep, in order to come together here tonight. And I apologize for hiding myself like this, but it must be so ..."

* * *

Elevator vestibule, Master's Quarters: All four sets of elevator doors open in unison and the troops scurry out like cockroaches.

Heavily laden with jangling gear and gizmos, they split up, each taking one of the main corridors.

* * *

"Unfortunately, there is little to gain in this world without sacrifice. We should all be acutely aware of the sacrifices we've made, of the lives we left behind, of the uncertainty we entered into, with only hope and trust and courage to carry us along ..."

* * *

Ruby-red laser beams probe the darkness as a team of about ten men sweeps through the bedroom quadrant, surrounding one empty bed after another. They yap at each other in short bursts of jargon, and mutter to themselves things like, "How many beds does this guy need?" and "I bet he's got a different honey for every one of these."

Finally, they train their sights on the one bed without neatly folded linens. The comforter appears to have been thrown back in haste, and one of the men kicks it to the floor as if Lester might be balled up inside.

"Desert Hawk, this is Rattlesnake Two. Nothing here, sir. There's about twenty beds up here, and he ain't in a single one of 'em."

After a short pause, Bossy's voice ricochets back. "Teams one and two, work from the top-down. Teams three and four from the bottom-up. No stone unturned. Let's go get 'em!"

* * *

"But did we sacrifice for nothing? Of course not. Our sacrifice yielded bountiful rewards. Intangible rewards. Immeasurable rewards. And we are grateful for these. We must be grateful for these or we risk losing the very thing that defines us as human beings – our spirit. Our individual spirit but also our collective spirit …"

* * *

Jipt feels another upsurge of nausea, but he knows better than to embarrass himself further with another dry heave. "If he doesn't want to be found, we ain't gonna find him," Jipt says. "It's like trying to find a needle in a goddamn stack of haystacks a mile high."

"If you were Ginn, where would you go?" Bossy says, spitting into his coffee mug.

"If I were Ginn? Well, let's see … I reckon I'd want to gather all my people together. You know, for one last hurrah."

"The Arena," Bossy says before spitting again and keying the radio. "Teams five through eight, stand by, I'm coming to you."

* * *

"By providence our spirits have united behind a singular purpose here, a singular faith in something much bigger than ourselves. But we do not rest our faith with providence alone, do we? Instead, we rely upon our own free will to guide the choices we make. So let's talk about some of those choices, now. The important choices. The difficult choices. The very choices linked to sacrifice and reward. By virtue of remaining here, you have chosen to give up something for the purpose of salvaging something else …"

* * *

The Apex Reception area is deserted, as is the Apex Conference Room, and the five men who have ascended the spiral staircase cannot help but gawk at the breathtaking, 360-degree view afforded to them.

* * *

"In any society, there is a precarious balance between the power of knowledge and the danger of misconception. Between contentment and fulfillment. Between ambition and morality, self-interest and self-preservation, needing and deserving, instinct and reason, good intentions and bad consequences, love and brotherhood, belief and acceptance, respect and devotion, optimism and fear ..."

* * *

As the teams continue their fruitless search, losing confidence with the passing of each vacant space, they seem more and more distracted by the sheer size and grandeur of the place, which has been shrouded in mystery for so long. In fact, unbeknownst to The Desert Hawk of course, the overall tenor of the mission has changed from one of military execution to one of sightseeing amusement – to The Arcade, The Pub, The Library, The Lounge, The Movie Theater, The Bowling Alley, The Concert Hall, The Swimming Pool, The Habitat, and on and on and on.

* * *

"These various points of balance have been impacted greatly by the choices I've made on your behalf. I am grateful for this tremendous responsibility, which you've bestowed upon me, and I am humbled by the mistakes I've made. And indeed, I've made more than a few. I allowed pride to get in the way of prudence. I chose lofty ideals over practical solutions. And for that, I beg your forgiveness."

* * *

Jipt nervously cinches the straps on his flak jacket and stays glued to Bossy's hip as they march double-time around The Concourse, which echoes with Lester's voice. He fears the impending confrontation and begins to think he should have waited in the jeep after all.

With a series of hand gestures, Bossy orders groups of five to peel off from the main force and position themselves at each of the tunnels leading to The Arena.

* * *

"You have every right to lay the blame squarely upon my shoulders. But please understand, these shoulders already carry the burden of repentance. And furthermore, I beseech you to understand, I have sacrificed everything, including my own happiness and that of my family, to protect you against our enemies. Enemies! Who envy you and wish to destroy what you have built! Who wish to take away what few rewards you have left. So you must make one final choice. A choice between giving up on yourselves, on each other and on the power of your solidarity – and standing up for what you've built! Standing up for what you've sacrificed for! And standing up for what you can still achieve together! With one spirit! With one purpose! Stand up! The future is in your hands! For you are the lucky ones!"

Already on their feet, the inhabitants erupt with riotous howling, whistling and applause louder than any The Arena has seen before, even at full capacity, and, at first, few notice the splotches of black descending to field-level like boulders cascading down an inverted mountainside. However, as they surround the alter, dissecting the gauzy veil with their laser beams, a sudden hush falls over the crowd.

"Mr. Ginn!" Bossy yells, clearly relishing the moment. "Put your hands in the air!" The shadow complies, and Bossy then motions to one of his soldiers, who steps forward and rips the shroud away (in much the same manner Lester once revealed a model of The Pyramid).

A collective gasp is emitted as it becomes immediately clear that the frail, white-haired man with his hands in the air is not Lester Ginn. Stupefied, Bossy turns to Jipt, whose face is burning with mortification and rage. "Who the fuck is *he*?" Jipt doesn't reply, so Bossy turns back to the old man, who looks rather at ease for someone on the business end of that much firepower. "Who the fuck are *you*?"

"My name is Dennis. Dennis Sepins. But most people call me Squeakins," the man says, extending his hand. "Rather a long story I'm afraid."

* * *

Lester sits in the back of the limousine, covering the microphone with his left hand as though trying to keep a genie sequestered inside a bottle. Svetlana sits next to him, fidgeting with the lock switch on the door handle, flipping it one way, then the other. In the seat opposite are Chutney and Anna. However, Anna's turned around, chatting with Ms. Tiddybar through the open privacy window. On Chutney's lap is some sort of instrument panel with various dials and blinking lights.

"You cut the signal?" Lester asks. Chutney nods. He hands her the microphone. "Did that make any sense?"

"Yes, I think so."

"I don't even remember what I just said. It was just, *Whoosh!* right from my head out my mouth and gone. Did that make any sense, Svety?"

"Huh? I'm sorry, Lester, I wasn't paying attention. How long until we get there?"

"I don't know."

"About twenty minutes," Anna says, relaying the message from Ms. Tiddybar.

"Hmm. I don't even know what twenty minutes is anymore," Lester says. "Is that a lot?"

"I do hope Squeakins is all right," Chutney says.

"Yes, me too," Lester says. "I told him we could use a dummy, but he insisted. He said, 'If they shoot me, I just hope they aim well, so I go quickly.' Can you believe that? He's a good man, that Squeakins. A damned good man. Where's my sword? Ms. Tiddybar? Do you have my sword up there?"

"Yes," comes the reply from up front.

"Well, pass it back if you would please. I daresay it won't be needed, but you never know."

* * *

By the time they get back to their vehicles, Jipt feels like his heart is going to explode through his chest. In fact, part of him wishes it *would*, just so he can avoid having to face Lynette, and Sylvia, and the media – and that absurdly simple, nagging question he knows will always smolder inside him: *Why?*

Bossy growls some orders into the radio and the convoy swings around, heading full-throttle back in the direction from whence they came.

Chapter 74

"Here we are," Ms. Tiddybar calls back, as the limousine eases to a stop.

"Holy shit," Anna says, still turned around looking out the windshield at the media mob surrounding the trailer home. It doesn't take long for them to notice the limo and surround it as well. "This is insane."

"I'm scared," Svetlana says. "I don't know if you should go out there, Lester."

"Don't worry, my dear, I'll be back in a jiff. You see, these media types are like any sort of wild animal. If you're afraid, they'll tear you limb from limb. But stand up to them – growl a bit and show your teeth – and they skulk away with their tail between their legs. Right, now where's that sword?"

Arching his pelvis into the air in a rather unseemly fashion, Lester buckles the sword belt around the waistline of his sporty silver track suit. Then he kisses Svetlana on the cheek and winks at Chutney before stepping out into the mêlée of reporters jostling and elbowing for position.

Standing tall, Lester looks over their heads as if they weren't there at all, panning the entire scene from left to right. The sun has just broken over the mountains, and from this vantage point the Black Balloon only blots out half of its intense, dawn-orange light. Some distance away the *The Heinousmeistress'* sails ripple gently in the breeze. "Get back! Make way!" Lester roars. And, indeed, a path opens up before him. "Back! Back!" He snarls, as microphones, tape recorders and cameras jut out toward his face. "All of you, back! Except you." He points to a short woman struggling to keep her head above the fray.

It's Tina Franco, and her face lights up like a Christmas tree. "Mr. Ginn, you remember me."

"Yes, it's Marcy, right?"

"Uh, well—"

"I'm kidding! Tina! Of course I remember you. Follow me. Everyone else get back!"

With Tina and her cameraman in tow, Lester plows straight ahead to the trailer home, where a gorilla-sized man is positioned in front of the door, his tattooed arms folded across his chest, which looks as if it's stuffed with anvils. He reaches for his sidearm, Lester reaches for his sword, and then they both freeze, staring each other down.

"So you're a quick draw, are you?"

The guard just looks at him dumbly, and Lester notices his trigger hand beginning to quaver.

"If you'd like to keep that hand intact, I suggest you walk away. Although, I'm sure these folks would prefer if you shot me in cold blood," Lester says, tossing his head back ever-so-slightly. "You know, in terms of news-worthiness."

After pondering his options for a moment longer, and no doubt recollecting how his comrades were sliced and diced at the hands of Tim, the man raises his hands patty cake-style and disappears into the throng.

Lester flings the door open and is surprised to find no additional opposition between himself and his son, who is handcuffed to a bed with duct tape over his mouth.

"Tim!" Lester calls out, rushing to his side.

"Mmm!" Tim says, before Lester rips away the tape. "Ow."

"Are you hurt?"

"I put up a fight."

"I'm sure you did, son."

"I was outnumbered."

"Of course you were."

"They had guns."

"Not fair a'tall," Lester reassures him, fumbling with the cuffs.

"The keys are in that desk over there."

"Lock that door!" Lester instructs Tina, as he crosses to the desk. He finds the keys and sets Tim loose. They embrace and grin and pat each other on the back.

"Can I ask you some questions?" Tina asks warily.

"Yes, I think we should set the record straight, don't you?"

"Yes. Well, it's hard to know where to begin."

"Did you hear that?" Lester says, pulling apart the window blinds. "Shit. They got here sooner than I thought."

"Who?" Tina says.

"Who do you think? It rhymes with gypped."

"I'll decapitate that son of a bitch!" Tim rages. "Give me your sword, dad. They took mine."

"You will do no such thing," Lester warns him, peeping out the window again.

"They've got lots of guns, don't they?" Tim says.

Outside, Bossy's troops have formed a perimeter around the entire site, but they appear uncertain how to proceed from there. Lester strokes his chin and begins to pace the room. "Mm, lots of guns, indeed … We must reach the limo."

"What limo?" Tim says.

"The limo outside. We came in a limo."

"Oh, nice."

"The women are still out there."

"Anna?"

"Yes, and Svetlana and Chutney and Ms. Tiddybar."

"Who?" Tina says.

"Mrs. – nevermind," Lester says, going to the window again. "It looks like it's still swamped with reporters, so we should be able to make a break for it, if we keep our heads down."

"Then what?" Tim says.

"Then we make our getaway."

"But they've got us surrounded. With guns."

Lester strokes his chin again. "We'll discuss it in the car. Now, let's go."

"Uh, Mr. Ginn? I know this isn't exactly the best time, but—"

"An exclusive, primetime interview!" Lester says. "Just you and me."

"Really?"

"Really. As soon as all this is over with."

"In The Pyramid?"

"No. Somewhere else. A park bench or a restaurant or something. It's up to you."

"You mean, you're not going back to The Pyramid?"

"No."

"Why not?"

"Ti-na," Lester chirps in a sing-song voice. "Men outside. With guns."

"I'm sorry, go ahead. But please be careful."

"Careful is my middle name," Lester says. "Come on, son."

* * *

Svetlana looks at her watch and bites her lip. She's terribly worried – without even being aware of the men with guns. "He's been gone too long," she says. "This is crazy. I'm going out there." She reaches for the handle but it eludes her grasp, as someone has pulled the door open from the other side. She screams, as do Chutney and Anna, before realizing that it's Lester. He piles inside, followed by Tim.

"Tim! Thank God you're okay!" Anna gushes, pouncing on top of him.

Tim holds her in his arms and whispers in her ear, "I missed you."

"I missed you too."

"I missed *you*, Svety," Lester says.

"Whatever," she says, slapping him lightly on the chest. "Let's get out of here. Hey, where are we going, anyway?"

"Well, I'm not sure we're going anywhere quite yet," Lester says with a certain degree of sheepishness.

"Men with guns," Tim says.

"What?" Anna says.

"They're here already?" Chutney says.

Lester nods and strokes his chin.

* * *

"Start closing it down!" Bossy yells into the radio before turning to Jipt. "We'll squeeze 'em out of there like toothpaste."

At mention of the word toothpaste, Jipt rubs his tongue over the outsides of his teeth. *They could use a good brushing,* he thinks, and he wishes he could transport himself home, to the bathroom, where everything is familiar and compartmentalized.

On Bossy's command the black circle tightens, and many of the cameramen and reporters flee outside the lines. As if a vacuum were created within the circumference of lethal force, an eerie calm suddenly prevails – silent and tranquil, but evanescent. The air becomes fluid again with the peal and drone of faraway sirens.

"Shit!" Jipt says to himself. "We're fucked."

And indeed they are. Within a minute, another perimeter has formed, this one more than 100 strong with flashing police cruisers, vans and trucks, which dispense men with guns. Hundreds of them in tan uniforms emblazoned with the shield of P.M.P. – PyraVegas Municipal Police. They disperse in tactical fashion, using their vehicles and each other for cover, and their commanding officers rant and rave like cops are wont to do, instructing the perpetrators to drop their weapons, lie face-down on the ground, etcetera, etcetera. And the soldiers of fortune comply with the readiness of dogs pining for kibbled biscuits.

Jipt feels woozy and short of breath. He closes his eyes and leans forward, resting his head on the back of the jeep's driver's seat. A disturbing sense of *deja-vu* accompanies the words, "Seth Jipt. You're under arrest …"

* * *

Lester's face is pressed against the tinted window, but he can't see a damned thing. He jumps back at the sound of someone rapping lightly on the glass.

"Mr. Ginn? Lester? It's Sylvia. Everything's under control, so you can come on out now if you want."

After exchanging both relieved and jubilant glances, Lester, and Svetlana, and Anna, and Tim and Chutney all pile out of the limo, while Ms. Tiddybar remains dutifully at the wheel.

"So the cavalry arrived, eh?" Lester says, engaging Sylvia in a gracious, two-handed handshake.

"We have Mr. Hawkins to thank for that," Sylvia says, gesturing to the tall, distinguished-looking man at her flank, whom Lester doesn't recognize.

"Tommy Hawkins, pleasure to finally meet you, Mr. Ginn." Hawkins eye is temporarily caught by Chutney, who blushes and looks away.

"You're in law enforcement, then?" Lester says.

"No," Hawkins says. "I used to work for – Mr. Jipt before … well, he went astray."

"Oh, I see."

Apparently having eschewed her fit of bashfulness, Chutney is next to Lester now, extending her hand.

"Madeline Chutney."

"Tommy Hawkins, nice to meet you."

"Likewise. I suppose we owe you and Sylvia a debt of gratitude for dispatching the bad guys."

"No gratitude necessary Ms. Chutney. We just did what had to be done. And please, call me Tommy."

"Very well, Tommy. Most people call me Chutney, but you may call me whatever you'd like. Except Chuttles, I don't like that."

"All right, enough is enough! Pardon me, dear," Lester says. "Mr. Hawkins, I implore you to renounce the pleasantries and ask this fine lady out on a date." He lowers his voice to an exaggerated whisper and cups his hand around the side of his mouth. "For dinner perhaps – she fancies Italian."

Lester leaves them and goes over to where Tim, Anna, Svetlana and Sylvia are gathered, a few paces away. Lester places his hand on Sylvia's shoulder in a collegial manner. "Thank you, Sylvia."

"You're welcome. Fine looking family you have here."

"They are, aren't they?"

"So what now?"

"Oh, I'd reckon we could all use a good long holiday."

Sylvia glances to The Pyramid, then back at Lester. "What about …"

"For the time being, the keys to the castle are yours, Sylvia. Of course, there aren't really any keys, per se. Just some access codes and whatnot."

"I appreciate it, Lester, but I'm not sure where I'd even begin."

"Not to fear," Lester says. "You'll receive all the help you need from two of my most trusted associates, Mr. Squeakins and Ms. Tiddybar."

"Missus …"

"*Tiddy-bar*, yes. Unusual name, I know. If you want to know the truth, they're the ones who've been running the place all these years, not me." Lester moves aside and puts one arm around Tim and the other around Svetlana, pulling them close. "Well, that's enough fun for one day – and only it's just begun!"

"Let's talk about that vacation," Svetlana says.

"Yes, indeed! What do you think, my love? An exotic cruise, perhaps?"

She turns to Lester with a look of playful misgiving, one eyebrow raised, her lips forming a wry smile.

Chapter 75

"Did you really miss me?" Anna says over Tim's shoulder, her arms locked around his midsection.

"Did you really miss *me*?" He says, reaching back to pinch her thigh. With his other hand he grips the wheel.

"I'm sorry about how I acted, before you left. But I never wanted you to go."

"I should have listened."

"It's brilliant, isn't it?"

"Brilliant, yes," Tim says.

Like an un-caged bird *The Heinousmeistress* plies the azure tropical waters without deference to gravity, her sails fat with wind, her deck overflowing with music. The Visionaries, minus Lester, play a serpentine melody that is upbeat yet somehow evocative of bereavement. And indeed, Lester can't help but reminisce over all that's been lost, all that's been undone or otherwise squandered. He drifts back through the tributaries of his mind and the scenery looks quite different now, the varied events of his life hanging in space, inside-out, like wet laundry on a clothesline. He recognizes the individual pieces, yet he can't imagine having ever worn them together. It's all just so abstract and far away now. More so than even the zillions of stars hidden by the façade of a sunny day. A day just like this.

"Lester," Svetlana says. "What are you thinking about?"

"I don't really know," he says. "The stars?"

"The stars? What about them?"

"Well, like the fact that they're always up there. And you *know* they're always up there, but yet …"

"I'm sorry, Lester."

"What?"

"I'm sorry things didn't work out the way you hoped."

"Svety," he says, taking her hands in his. "Please don't be sorry. *I'm* not. I mean, the trouble with hope is … you don't always hope for the right things."

"I know. I just hope we can forget about all the bad things and remember the good ones."

"Or we can forget everything and just *live*," Lester says, looking up at the clear afternoon sky. "Live every moment like we're just happy to be alive."

"I *am*."

"What?"

"Happy to be alive."

"Me too," Lester says, and he twirls her around. Then the music grabs hold of them both like a divine puppeteer and yanks them apart, and twirls them around and pushes them back together again, and they hold on for dear life and they dance, and dance and dance.

AFTERWORD

From the editor's desk at *Skull & Bones Publishing*:

So ... what'd you think?

If you didn't like the book – and it took you 'til the very end to realize it – that really sucks. We'd give you your money back, but what wasn't spent on the actual fabrication of the book has likely already gone to a "good cause." That cause, of course, being the fight against Scurvy. So, hey, at least you can feel like you've made a contribution to society. Please accept our deepest apologies and well-wishes for the future – in particular, that you don't get Scurvy.

On the other hand, if you DID like the book, pass it on to someone who might also like it. Also, we'd highly suggest paying us a visit online at SkullandBonesPublishing.com – where you'll find:

- More published works by Steve Dupont and others
- Tips on how to be a grass roots supporter (our marketing budget is very limited due to the aforementioned "cause")
- Facts you probably don't know about Scurvy
- A tantalizing array of merchandise in our gift shop

Well, that's it. THE END.

Nevermind! I just realized Steve has a little memo he wanted to include. He's designed some T-shirts apparently ...

MEMORANDUM
From the Desk of Steve Dupont

TO: You

FROM: Me

RE: T-Shirts you might like

Dear Reader,

Just an FYI – the following T-shirts (and more) are currently available in the Steve Dupont Corporation Giftshop, located at stevedupont.com. You're quite welcome.

Have a day,

Steve

www.ingramcontent.com/pod-product-compliance
Lightning Source LLC
Chambersburg PA
CBHW030750030726
47497CB00001B/215